HEAR THE ECHO

About Rob Gittins's previous novels

Gimme Shelter

'A definite contender for my book of the year... a startling and original debut novel.' – *Crime Fiction Lover*

'A major new crime writer has given us the definitive interpretation of "page turnability"... This is a book that will haunt the reader long after the covers are closed.' – Katherine John

'This disturbing and exhilarating novel should quickly establish its author as a fiction writer of universal note.' – *Morning Star*

'Terrifying and suspenseful, non-stop jeopardy. Just be glad you're only reading it and not in it.' – Tony Garnett

Secret Shelter

'An unputdownable sequel to *Gimme Shelter*. In Ros Gilet, Rob Gittins has created a character so real she just steps off the page and into your mind. *Secret Shelter* is a brilliant thriller that keeps you awake and reading at night. This deserves every one of the five stars. I would have given it more if I could have.' – Reviewer on Amazon.com

The Poet and the Private Eye

'A remarkable parable of human frailty and brilliance, with the private eye bearing witness to the loneliness of the long-distance poet.' – Menna Elfyn

Investigating Mr Wakefield

'A superb, unsettling book, both culturally significant and beautifully written.' – Jeni Williams

'This has all the hallmarks in place to be a cult classic, and I couldn't recommend it highly enough.' – Jack Clothier, Gwales

HEAR THE ECHO

Two strong Welsh-Italian women...
separated by a lifetime, linked forever

ROB GITTINS

To the memory of
Norman, Grace, Dulcie and Beryl.

First impression: 2018
© Rob Gittins & Y Lolfa Cyf., 2018

Cover design: Matthew Tyson
Cover images: 'Chiara' – istockphoto/George Marks
'Frankie' – istockphoto/drbimages
café – Alamy/Neil Setchfield

Paperback ISBN: 978 1 78461 523 9
Hardback ISBN: 978 1 78461 634 2

The publishers wish to acknowledge the support of
Cyngor Llyfrau Cymru

Published and printed in Wales
on paper from well-maintained forests by
Y Lolfa Cyf., Talybont, Ceredigion SY24 5HE
e-mail ylolfa@ylolfa.com
website www.ylolfa.com
tel 01970 832 304
fax 832 782

Prologue

*I*N THE EARLY *decades of the twentieth century, an Italian girl travelled from Italy to Wales in search of a better life.*

Almost one hundred years later, a Welsh woman visited Italy, seeking the same.

Both women kept journals recording their life and experiences. For their own reasons, both women hid these journals from their families, from friends and from everyone they were close to at the time. They addressed their journals to each other instead.

Neither woman could be sure of the other's existence. Neither really knew why they'd fixed on the other in the way they had. They just seemed to find it easier to talk to a person, albeit one conjured from their own imagination, rather than pouring out their thoughts, feelings and hopes, as well as their deepest and darkest secrets, onto a blank page.

Each seemed to be a necessary fiction for the other. A ghost that kept silent step with them.

Then something happened.

'Hear the echo, very quiet,
It returns again from far away'

'Senti L'Eco', Trio Lescano (1939)

PART ONE

'Offerings at the Feast of Tabernacles'

(Numbers 29)

Frankie

I HOPE YOU'RE broad-minded. Like, really – really – broad-minded. I hope you're not one of those black-suited buzzards you see in all those old Italian films, sitting in hard-backed chairs, arms folded, eyes staring out at you in some sort of silent judgement.

Not that you'd have seen too many of the films I've seen, I suppose. That's going to be one of the problems here, isn't it? I'll be going on about *The Godfather* and you'll be thinking, what the hell's she talking about?

Doesn't matter, I'll just tell you about it all anyway and you'll just have to skip the bits that don't make sense.

Right now, I'm down in the docks – well, one of the few parts that still is the actual docks, most of it's called something else now. I'm sitting in this pub by a door that keeps opening and closing as people go in and out. There's a light from a street lamp outside flashing on and off. That's not deliberate by the way: it's not Christmas and they haven't put up the illuminations. The bulb's on its way out, that's all.

There's an old pool table in the middle of the pub floor, covered with ripped green baize. The snooker table's not seeing much action and that street lamp really isn't doing the place or anyone inside it too many favours either. Everything – and everyone – really would look a whole lot better right now with the lights turned way down low.

There's a group of older women sitting behind us at a

table next door to the toilets and whatever good – or more probably bad – intentions they came in with are being well and truly pissed to the wind by now. They won't be getting up to much tonight. But there's a couple of younger women dotted around the place who still look ready for some action this evening. Right now, one of them's passing our table, hardly giving us a glance, her eyes only on the door and whatever dubious delights await the poor cow outside.

It sounds ridiculous, I know – and you're not going to know who she is or even begin to understand why this sounds quite so crazy – but she's got the look of the young Julia Roberts about her. Which is a bit like me going on about *The Godfather* – you're never going to have heard of *Pretty Woman* either, but she's got that same long, dark, hair and fine cheekbones. But if someone had told me I'd see a Julia Roberts lookalike in this backstreet Cardiff boozer, I wouldn't have believed them either, so feel free to tell me I'm losing it.

Then again, I must have lost something to be in here in the first place, down among the drunks fallen by the bar, the taxi drivers stomping inside every couple of minutes to try and find punters too far gone to even know who they are right now, let alone that at some dim and distant point in the last few hours they'd ordered a cab to go somewhere else, if only they could remember where.

In the corner a jukebox is playing an old song.

Salt 'n' Pepa.

'Let's Talk About Sex, Baby'.

What else, eh?

Psaila looks up from her drink. We live in the same town, about twenty miles away up in the Valleys. We've both lived there for years. She's got three kids to my two. One up to her, I used to think when they were little and times were different, but now the boot's very much on the other foot. These days I thank heaven for small mercies.

Right now, Psaila and myself are dressed in the same sort of outfits too. We did think, briefly, about skirts, but one blast of that cold night air as we stepped off the train and we went straight into the station toilets and opted for jeans instead. Tight though. And heels. High. I'm not used to them and they're going to be a bastard to walk in, but as Psaila pointed out, walking's not exactly going to be high on the list of priorities for either of us for the next few hours with luck.

Or not.

Depending how you look at it.

It's my first time down here – my first time anywhere doing this sort of thing – but Psaila's done it before. She won't say how many times, but something in the way all the other girls, young and old, greeted her when we first walked in tonight told me she's not exactly a novice.

'Come on, Frankie.'

Through the door, now opening and closing again, I see the Julia Roberts lookalike. She's just climbed into a car that's idling outside, exhaust gases pumping up into the air, thin wisps circling the yellow street bulb that's still blinking on and off. I can't see her punter, only the back of his head. Psaila tells me the faces don't register after a while anyway, they just tend to merge. Anyway, eye contact isn't exactly the point either.

The car drives away. It's a saloon, four door. Most of them are, from what I've seen. There's not too many small little sports jobs cruising round these streets right now, for maybe obvious reasons.

'Just one more.'

I drain my glass, glancing over towards the bar. I'm ready to negotiate the fallen drunks, not to mention the pool table and its ripped green baize, to fetch myself a refill, but Psaila's having none of it.

'You've had three already.'

'It'll relax me.'

'Knock you out, more like.'

I look back at her, not needing to reply, the expression on my face saying it for me anyway.

So what's so bad about that?

But Psaila just takes my glass, picking up hers at the same time, reaches behind her and puts both down on another stained and chipped small table close by. As she does so, a sudden commotion sounds across the room as the gaggle of older women kick off. An old man has just thrown up on his way to the toilets and a thin splatter of vomit has just splashed on one of the girl's shoes – a dom dyke, if how she's dressed is anything to go by – and she really doesn't look as if she appreciates this latest addition to her choice of footwear. And from the way she's eyeing the swaying and still-spluttering culprit, I'd lay odds someone's just about to have their face rubbed in it, too.

Psaila hunches closer, blocking my view, which may be no bad thing right now.

'It's not how it works, Frankie. These blokes may be nothing special but you've still got to make them feel as if they are, and falling asleep on them halfway through isn't exactly going to do that, is it?'

Across the room, there's a strange, gurgling, retching noise. Sure enough, the old boy's now getting up close and personal with the dom dyke's vomit-spattered shoe, but Psaila doesn't take any notice.

Psaila knows the signs. She probably sat in this same

boozer herself on her first night making all the same excuses, telling herself all the same sad, stupid, little lies.

Just one more drink.

Then maybe another.

Just to warm me up.

Calm me down.

Then I'll be fine.

Another blast of cold air buffets us as the door opens again, that same yellow illumination flashing as the dodgy street light once more blinks its way inside. I look towards it – anything's better than looking at Psaila right now – to see another of the younger girls exiting, another passing car stopping the moment she does so, brake lights flaring in the neon-lit darkness.

Then I look back at Psaila.

Business seems to be good tonight.

Chiara

As I open the steel manhole cover, two eyes stare up at me.

White. Unblinking. The sudden sunlight bleaching that underground chamber must have been blinding, but those white eyes don't flinch, not once.

I drop the steel cover back, quickly, and stand for a moment or two, listening to the blood which is roaring now in my ears.

Then I turn and call out to my two younger brothers, who are playing on the scrubland nearby.

Then we all go home for lunch.

The next morning, after a night's lost sleep, I go back. This time I'm alone. I stand by that steel manhole for what seems like hours, but it's probably only minutes, daring myself to open it again. On the street, no more than a few metres away from this abandoned stretch of land where all the town's children play, where they've always played, men and women pass, most making their daily trek to the local market. No-one takes any notice of a young girl standing by an empty well, or what should be an empty well.

Then footsteps sound behind me, and I turn to see Papà approaching. He pauses, puzzled. For a moment he just stands there, looking at me. Then he looks at the steel manhole cover I seem to be guarding for some reason. He puts his hand on my shoulder and gently steers me back towards my mother, who I can now see standing behind him. With the two of us out of harm's way, he returns to that steel manhole cover and lifts it up.

The call's put through from the Mayor's office ten minutes later. The magistrate on duty in the Public Prosecutor's office at the time is a former policeman in his forties, Damiano Ruggeri. Signor Ruggeri, so everyone had been told when he'd first arrived, had formerly battled against the Cosa Nostra in Sicily. He'd come back to the region of his birth hoping for a quieter life – a hope destined to be crushed, that day at least, by that one phone call.

It's a forty-five minute journey from the Prosecutor's office, a journey that takes him up through a narrow valley via a series of hairpin bends. As Signor Ruggeri comes closer he can hear the sound of waterfalls as water runs down from the hills. He passes tiny white houses and a local war memorial outside a small church where names of the fallen from the Great War, most of them from just three local families, are carved in stone.

Then he approaches the three of us, still standing a few metres away from a steel manhole cover on a tired-looking patch of land. Signor Ruggeri moves past and opens the manhole cover for himself.

Two years later and I'm pacing my room, a window open in front of me.

The river winding down in the valley below is sparkling in the sunlight, and that sunlight's now picking out not alabaster faces with white and unblinking eyes, but those same tiny white houses dotted in amongst all those green hills.

Strips of land run down from those houses to potholed

lanes. Here and there an ox pulls, or tries to pull, a plough down the hillside, tilling the *granoturco* or Turkish Corn. Downhill is all the poor creature can manage. To even attempt to cut an upward furrow in this unforgiving soil is impossible. Here and there are orchards, but they're struggling to stay alive too. All over the hillsides, small patches of shrivelled vines also labour to produce their fruit.

Some in the town below pick mushrooms and chestnuts, some craft baskets, pots, barrels or cribs to sell at local fairs. But they're selling to people like themselves. People with no money to buy. Some, like my father, journey to Liguria to buy olive oil and then travel up into the mountains hoping to sell their wares on again, but it's the same story there too.

Now and again, rumours circulate of different trades. One of those different trades led to that putrid, supposedly-empty well that day. But details like that are usually kept from the town's children, as if we don't have eyes to see or ears to hear what's going on all around us. We see and hear everything everyone else does, even if no-one wants us to.

Other news can't be kept from anyone. A volcano erupted just a matter of months earlier in the south, and buried a whole town near Naples. Another volcano followed and a tidal wave then swept through the strait between Sicily and the mainland killing, so they say, hundreds of people in the city of Messina alone.

All that's a long way from here. It would take days of travelling to reach those places even if you wanted to go there, which none do, but it seems prophetic somehow. As if storm clouds are gathering over the whole of the country, clouds that are rumbling along in their wake the same message, repeated over and over again.

Go.

Get out.

Get out now.

'Chiara –'

Suddenly, the door opens behind me and she's standing in the doorway. They say we look alike, myself and Mamma, but I can't see it. All I see are the dark circles under her eyes and the lines that criss-cross her face. I don't see the young and beautiful girl my father first fell in love with, although he tells us he still sees that same girl every single day.

For a moment she catches her breath and that's nothing to do with the steep climb to my room. She knows how important today might be – and not just for me, her only daughter, but for Luigi and for Peppo, her two younger sons, as well.

There's something else too, something in her face, something behind her eyes that I don't recognise or understand for now, but how could I? What did I understand of such things back then?

'He's here.'

Briefly I turn back to the window again, not knowing what to say.

'He's with your father now.'

I keep my face turned to the light, looking down at the river below and at the ox that's now taking what it clearly believes is a well-deserved rest at the foot of its recently ploughed single furrow.

'I'm scared.'

I am, but of what exactly I don't know. It's something nameless, unfocused, but real nonetheless. All of a sudden I feel like I'm on the very edge of a precipice, maybe on the very roof of the castle that towers over our home town, giddy and dizzying, terrifying and intoxicating, all at the same time.

'There's no need.'

She joins me at the window, sitting close to me in the small wooden seat that was handcrafted years before by my father to fit into the curve of the wall.

I looked at her, doubting her all of a sudden, doubting everything now.

'What if it's like last time?'

'It won't be.'

'So now you're a fortune teller?'

'Chiara –'

I pause as she stares at me. It had come out sharp, sharper than I'd intended. It always does, especially at times like these when I'm feeling like this, but I'm beyond caring at the moment.

'What if he says no? He did last year. He didn't even come to see us.'

Now she just looks at me, and again if I'd had the eyes to see it, I'd have realised just why she now takes my hand in the way she does.

'You were a child last year.'

She pauses again.

'You're fifteen now. You're becoming a woman.'

I look down, instinctively, at the slight swell underneath my blouse, a change in my body that's crept up on me over the last year or so, almost without my realising. Then Mamma smiles at me again, almost sadly this time.

'It will make a difference.'

She hesitates, then smiles once more.

'Believe me.'

Frankie

Y OUR COUNTRY'S WARM, right? At least it's always been warm when I've been there, on trips and that. And, OK, that was in the summer, in the school holidays usually, so it was always going to be, I suppose, but looking out on all those whitewashed villages under all that blue sky, I could never imagine it ever getting really cold.

Not like tonight.

In this dirty, shitty, city.

In this dirtiest, shittiest part of this dirty, shitty, city.

There's a place to stand right outside the pub door, but that's a prime spot and not just because it's the first place the drivers see when they swing in off the main road, but also because whichever lucky cow has bagged it gets a welcome waft of warm air every few seconds as the door to the bar opens and closes behind her.

According to Psaila, there's been fist fights in the past over that particular piece of prime local pavement and by the look on the current squatter's face as we come out into the darkness – an older woman this time – there's going to be another one if we even try to lay any sort of claim to it.

So Psaila steers me on, past the alleyway that leads down to what looks like a builder's yard, past a barbed wire fence and on towards another pub at the far corner of the street. It's nowhere near as good a spot, but beggars can't be choosers and, as Psaila pointed out on more than one occasion on the train ride down here, neither of us may actually be beggars right now but that's what we could be – and pretty quickly too – if one or both of us don't get our acts together.

'OK, stand here.'

Psaila stops a few metres from the second of the pubs and a short distance away from another small gaggle of girls on the corner, all huddling together for warmth, and it's easy enough to understand why.

'It's freezing.'

'It'll be warm enough in the cars.'

From the mainline railway station a few hundred metres away, a train's sounding its whistle as it pulls away. It sounds like the final note in a requiem mass I heard in a funeral once.

'I don't know about this.'

But Psaila cuts across, impatient, trotting out – for the umpteenth time – the pep talk, the mantra.

'It's two hundred quid a night, Frankie. And that's minimum looking like you, two hundred in your hand, no questions asked, no tax, no national insurance, no PAYE and yeah, it's cold, and yeah I'd rather be tucked up at home pigging out on pizza and watching the telly, but tell me, where else are you ever, in your life, going to lay your hands on easy money like that?'

But I'm not listening. A car's slowing now as it passes. I'm sure I saw it when we first came out of the pub, the driver looking sideways at us, past the lady of a certain age currently hogging that prime local pavement, taking in the new girl on the block, the fresh meat on offer.

Psaila hesitates, spotting him too, and now she nods at him, slow and deliberate, heavy on the invitation, unambiguous in the intent. But the driver hardly seems to see her. He's looking at me all the time, and the look he's giving me is pretty unambiguous, too.

He likes what he's seeing.

And he wants to see more.

A lot more.

'Oh, Jesus.'

That's me, by the way. But Psaila's not listening, Psaila's talking in my ear again, giving me all the last minute reminders, everything we'd discussed, all we'd rehearsed coming down on that small train in the company of a few other women in the same compartment, all with similar intentions in mind that night, judging by the way most of them were dressed.

'You know what to do. You know how much to ask for and that's upfront – don't be a fucking amateur and expect them to pay afterwards because none of them ever do. And don't say exactly what it's for, that way if they want something a bit out of the ordinary, you can say it's not included, meaning it's extra.'

The car's idling by the pavement now, the driver looking up, momentarily, towards the second pub on the corner where a girl has just detached herself from the rest of the small gaggle and is looking back down the street towards him, cool and appraising, the silent nod she's giving him also all too eloquent.

What are you doing down there?

With her?

Look what I've got to offer instead.

You won't regret it.

'No hotels or houses.'

Psaila's voice keeps sounding in my ear as all the while she shepherds me towards the car. She's also seen the competition and she obviously doesn't intend to let this all too interested

21

punter slip off the hook, not for the sake of a pushy scrubber from some overspill estate out Newport way.

'And nothing – and that is nothing – without a rubber and you make them use one of yours, don't let them say they'll use their own, God knows how long they've had them or even what they've done to them.'

Then Psaila pauses.

'Don't think Frankie, don't feel, don't talk. Just take the money, then go, OK?'

And out it comes again.

'Oh, Jesus.'

Which is my sole contribution to this particular exchange, but I can't think of too much else to say and anyway that seems to just about sum it all up.

Psaila eyes the occupant of the nearby idling motor for a moment, then nods back at me again.

'He looks quite cuddly.'

Finally I find the rest of my voice.

'So did Fred West.'

Then, as the girl on the corner begins to make her way down the street towards us, and none too slowly either, I open the passenger door and climb inside.

Chiara

Now I'm downstairs, walking along the narrow passageway that leads to our front room.

We don't call it what you call it, a parlour; although perhaps you don't any more. It was a bit of an old-fashioned phrase even then. But it's where, if really important visitors call (or any ancient relatives) they're always taken. Or if anyone in the family dies, that's where they're laid out before the funeral. In all the time I've lived there, few really important guests have ever called and no-one in the family has died, thank God, so no-one's ever been laid out there either, but still it remains untouched, inviolate somehow: the one room in the house where we're never allowed to play.

Not that we'd ever want to play in there anyway. It seems to be in perpetual darkness, and that's not just because no-one's ever allowed to pull back the curtains in case the sun bleaches the furniture that's always being kept for best.

But best for what? I could never understand it. Whenever we did go in there, everyone seemed to speak in hushed tones as if the very walls were watching. A room that laid a dead hand on the rest of the house.

Did you ever read Lewis Caroll? Is he even in print any more? It was already an old book when I first read about his young heroine Alice and her adventures. One phrase from the story always stuck in my head; *curiouser and curiouser*. And that just about summed up that front room in my old home, where everything always seemed to be held in a sort of suspension. A strange little room where only curious things happened.

But today the door is open. Today the curtains are pulled back and today, miracle of miracles, I actually hear laughter as we approach. Laughter from my father and from my brothers, who are now joining in too. I can hear another man's laughter as well, deeper than my brothers', though not as deep as my father's.

But we don't immediately head inside so we can share the joke. Mamma holds me back at the door, apparently to straighten a lock of hair that's dared stray out of place, but for another reason too.

'Chiara.'

Then she hesitates again.

Inside the room, our best room, I can hear my father talking to our guest about my brothers, his soft voice easy, familiar.

'Peppo left school this year. He's been travelling with me for most of the summer to the fairs, getting to know people, the ones who can help.'

Even though he's on the other side of the door, I can almost see him bending closer, his voice dipping now, conspiratorial.

'You know the way it works.'

Outside, Mamma bends closer to me too.

'Listen to me.'

From the other side of the door, I hear my father's voice once more.

'Luigi left the year before. He's been helping the Riccis, across the valley.'

Instinctively, I can't help it, my nose recoils. The Riccis are charcoal burners, much of the charcoal they produce being sent across the mountains to fire smelters to be used, so we were told in school, in gold and silver mines. I'd pick up the smell from Luigi when he came back from his occasional work, just as sometimes I'd catch that same smell as it floated across the river and snaked its way in through our open windows, and I'd always hated it.

My mother was still looking at me.

'Your tongue, Chiara; the way it runs away with you sometimes –'

I'm still just listening to Papà's voice as it floats from the other side of that door again.

'They're good boys, both of them, boys who'll become fine men one day.'

I look back at Mamma.

'I thought this was my turn.'

She looks at me.

'It is.'

'So why's Papà talking about Peppo and Luigi all the time?'

Her eyes crease in irritation.

'Chiara –'

I'm looking back towards the open door, not registering anything now: her irritated eyes, the warning note in her voice. I'm hearing one thing and one thing only at this moment, the sound of some silent door closing somewhere.

'Has he changed his mind? Is one of them going instead?'

Before she can reply, the sun that always streams down that narrow passageway at that time of the day is eclipsed as the door in front of us suddenly opens more fully and a large form blocks out the light for a moment.

'I thought I heard voices.'

Papà smiles down at me. Behind him, at the far end of the room, standing next to my brothers, who are dressed today in clothes that Mamma also always describes as best, is Enrico.

I'd only the vaguest memories of him before he left for England. He was eight years ahead of me in the local school, a lifetime at that age, but I remember he was one of the first to stay on till fourteen, almost unheard of at a time when most pupils left at twelve. Now he's looking across at me and smiling but I don't smile back. I just stare at him instead.

This man is the reason I might be leaving my home. This is the man I might be travelling to live with in a strange land I'd barely heard of across a sea I'd never seen. A man who might be feeding and clothing me from now on in place of my parents. I can't help it, I just want to look at him, to study him I suppose, because even then I knew to trust my instincts, maybe because even then I knew that first impressions were rarely wrong.

Even then I knew to trust the moment you looked at someone, uncluttered by anything they might say or do, look into their eyes and if you're lucky (and if you have the eyes to see it) it's like looking into their soul.

'Enrico, this is Chiara.'

Now my father's making introductions, although they're not exactly necessary. Who did he think I was, this young girl who's just been brought in to meet him, the Mother Superior?

The slight nod Papà now gives me tells me to smile back, but I don't. Papà's smile grows more fixed as he realises what I'm doing. By his side, the expression on Enrico's face tells me he knows what I'm doing too, is only too aware I'm trying to work him out. While all the other smiles in that room are faltering now (Mamma and Papà's, the nervous smiles on the faces of my two younger brothers), Enrico's does not. His smile stays bright.

So what were my first impressions? Standing there in that room, our best room, looking across at him? What did I think?

'You've grown, Chiara.'

Out it comes, like it always does. No second thought, the first thing that comes into my head barrelling into my mouth as I glance (I can't help it) at his belly.

'So have you, Enrico.'

All I can think is, what the hell's happened? He was a slim young man the last time I saw him. What have they been feeding him on his new home, in that land I'd never heard of across that sea I'd never seen?

He can see it. He can see what I'm thinking and everyone else can see it too, and everyone's looking at each other, even more nervous now and with good cause. This is the man who might become my employer, my protector indeed, and within a few seconds of meeting him again, I've as good as called him fat.

Then there's a great bellow of laughter as Enrico clasps his hands around his now ample waist.

Frankie

S o now I'm in the punter's car. A Vauxhall, I think, maybe an Astra – although why I'm giving you chapter and verse on the model I don't know, it's not exactly going to mean that much to you either, is it?

Maybe I'm just doing what I always do. Talking rubbish because I'm nervous. My old mum, God bless, always said I had a tongue that ran about a hundred miles an hour ahead of my head and my old gran, God bless her too, always said I had a mouth like a parish oven, not that I know what one of those is anyway.

Doing it again, aren't I?

'Left.'

'What?'

'Take the next left.'

Which is me trying to sound like I'm in control, making out I know what I'm doing.

'There isn't one.'

'What?'

The punter's gesturing at the road ahead.

'There isn't a left. Look, it's all warehouses on that side.'

'Right. I meant, right.'

The punter hesitates, but then nods. Then he swings the car off the road – the road that led down to the actual docks in the old days when there were ships and sailors and bananas and stuff, but which now leads down to Legoland. Identikit apartments all bolted together, most of them empty, most of them looking empty even when they weren't. It was that kind of place and that kind of neighbourhood. In other words, no sort of neighbourhood at all.

We pull into a small car park with closed and boarded-up offices on either side. Psaila brought me down here on a recce last week. Welcome to my Executive Residence she said, as we pulled in. It sounded funny at the time. I even thought I might use the line myself, maybe break the ice a bit because let's face it, you need to do something don't you? You don't even know someone's name but within thirty seconds you're supposed to be doing things you wouldn't let your old man do, not till he'd actually become your old man anyway.

The punter shuts off his engine, which probably constituted some kind of mercy killing because it really was not sounding all that healthy. Then he looks at me again.

'So what's your name?'

I hesitate. What was the form? Psaila hadn't covered this one. Do I make up a name or use my real one? I hesitate for another millisecond before realising it probably doesn't matter anyway.

'Frankie.'

Silence falls again. I've still made no move, haven't even checked in my bag for a rubber.

The punter nods, slowly as if it's the most extraordinary name he's ever heard, or maybe he's just nervous too. It'd be just my luck to have bagged myself a newbie. I was relying on someone at least halfway experienced to show me some of the ropes.

On second thoughts, forget ropes. Nothing kinky, not on a first night and not ever.

The punter steals another look at me.

'So what's it short for?'

Back it comes, quick as a flash.

'Nebuchadnezzar.'

His face tenses immediately.

Me and my big gob again.

'Funny.'

Something tells me he's not exactly telling the truth. But it does seem to have acted as some sort of signal at least, because now he starts shifting around in his seat, begins unclipping his seat belt.

'Let's get on, shall we?'

I nod back, trying to sound casual.

'Sure.'

And the sounds are coming out of my mouth OK, and I'm making sense, the problem being that all I'm saying isn't being accompanied by too much in the way of what you might call purposeful action. I'm still just sitting there, looking at a boarded up office that used to sell, according to the sign on the door, wholesale pet food.

But now he's pausing too. For a moment relief washes over me. Maybe he's changed his mind. Maybe he just wants to go home. Maybe I can too.

'Do you do any extras?'

I look back at him.

'Like what?'

'Anything?'

'For example?'

'Don't you have a list?'

Now I stare at him, not saying anything, not needing to.

A *what*?

'I was down here a month or so ago and one of the girls had a list, laminated and everything it was, stuff on one side, prices on the other. She handed it to me, and I picked out what I wanted.'

'Like a Chinese?'

'She wasn't Chinese.'

'As in takeaway?'

'Oh. Yeah.'

I take a deep breath, dredge the details of Psaila's pep talk from the mush in my head currently masquerading as memory.

'Anything out of the ordinary, meaning anything apart from straight is extra, but there's things I don't do, lots of them actually, and no, I haven't got a price list.'

I shake my head, still can't get my brain round that one.

'And if I had, I definitely wouldn't have the front to go into some poxy photocopy shop and have it laminated! Just imagine standing there while some kid behind the counter reads what you do and don't do.'

'There was nothing she didn't do.'

'Struck lucky then, didn't you? You should have gone for her instead.'

'I was going to. Then I saw her mate.'

Psaila?

For God's sake.

And now the punter's shifting in his seat again, beginning to get ever more restless.

'Look – Frankie – Nebu –'

He stumbles, doesn't even attempt to finish that one, gestures down at the now-darkened dashboard in front of him instead.

'Whatever your name is, the engine's off and I don't know if you've noticed but it's starting to get cold. A night like this, it's going to get even colder the longer we sit here and I do not want to get frostbite – that's not exactly going to be too easy to explain, is it – so are you going to get in the back and are we going to get down to this, or what?'

Briefly, a pair of headlights illuminate the inside of the car. Another car has swung into the small car park and is parking up opposite, the headlights switching off, another light coming on as a woman emerges from the passenger side – the one who, a few moments earlier, had bagged the prime-time pavement. She opens the rear door and climbs into the back, the driver following a moment later, already unbuttoning his flies.

Class.

I look back at the punter who's now holding out two twenties.

'Let's start with this shall we, see how far we get?'

I take the money and open my bag. Rule Number Two or Three, I couldn't quite remember, the one after always get the money first: always put it somewhere safe.

Then, just as I make to stash the notes in a zipped compartment inside, I suddenly throw them back at the punter, opening the passenger door at the same time.

He stares at me.

'What are you doing?'

A moment later what I'm doing is only too obvious as I walk past the only other occupants of that car park, their car already rocking backwards and forwards on its springs.

Emboldened by frustration, my punter lowers his window and yells after me.

'I'm talking to you!'

But I keep walking, just catching his parting shot as I turn the corner back onto the main road.

'Bitch.'

Chiara

THE REST OF the afternoon passes in a blur, most of it spent listening to Enrico as he tells us all about his new life in his new country.

My new life, perhaps, in my new country.

As long as I keep my mouth shut and don't call him fat again, or point out how his hair is already beginning to thin, or all the other things I'm thinking as I keep looking at him but know, from the warning glances that keep flashing my way from my now very much not-so-amused Mamma and Papà, I daren't say.

I make Enrico sound like an old man, but he wasn't. It was just that he'd lived, I suppose. And yes, OK, he looked as if he had too. He'd travelled to distant places, seen things I'd never seen, met interesting new people from other cultures. Far away from places like this, where oxen travel downhill but can't make it back up again. Where boys are conscripted into the Sons of the She Wolf at four, into the *Balilla* at eight and into the *Avanguardista* at fourteen. Where those same boys are taught that war, to them, is as natural as childbearing to girls, that history began in 1922 with a march on Rome and that troublemakers (meaning anyone who dares to express a contrary opinion to the only man who can lead our country back to greatness, or so he says) is held down by that man's bullyboys and has a litre of oil forced down their throat before being made to eat a live toad.

All right, I don't actually know if all of that was true. I'd only ever seen a live toad once and I'd run from it, screaming, but tales still come back to us and even if they gain in the travelling, what lies behind those tales still feels only too real. A country that has always felt warm, like home, is starting to feel alien and cold.

Briefly now an image flashes in front of my eyes, as if I'm standing outside my own body, seeing myself from above, standing by that steel manhole cover concealing an old, disused well.

Across the room, Enrico continues.

'There are four shops selling Italian provisions on just the one street.'

'There aren't four in this whole town.'

That's Peppo, my youngest brother, breaking in, eyes wide with growing wonder.

'The Valvonas –'

'The Valvonas from Ronchi?'

My father now cuts in, nodding at Mamma, who's also staring at Enrico with much the same expression on her face as her youngest child.

'Have you seen their old cottage?'

Papà shakes his head, sadly. He passed it on his way to Brembate di Sopra last week.

'The roof fell in last month.'

Our visitor, it seems, has little time for tales from his former home and his past. Enrico is brimming with pride and quite clearly has one thing and one thing only on his mind: the present and the future. Like a conjurer producing rabbits out of a hat, he opens a small bag he's brought with him, and starts handing round photographs.

'Then there's the Antonellis, and the Lannis, and the Granellis, all open within a few doors of each other.'

We all stare at the pictures: whole families from small children to elderly grandparents standing together proudly in front of different shops, most of the shops double-fronted, their window displays packed with chocolates and cigarettes and sweets. They aren't the first such pictures we've seen. Almost everyone who goes away comes back with similar photographs, sometimes numbering in their hundreds. It's almost as if the further they travel, the more pictures they seem to need to bring back to the place they once called home.

'And they're all doing a roaring trade.'

I look up at him. Now and again he does that. Slips in those strange-sounding English phrases.

Roaring?

What? Why?

'And that doesn't include the factories that have opened in the last few months too: Colaluca and Rocca at Mill Street, they're making wafers, as well as Robino in Rodney Street.'

Mill Street.

Rodney Street.

Again, it's ridiculous I know, but why do those names sound so impossibly exotic to me?

All the time an ever more animated Enrico gallops on, tapping a couple more of the photographs.

'Domenico – he came originally from across the mountain I think – he owns an organ factory and Marco, he's just opened a wine merchants. He's taken over one of the local pubs as well, not that he's there all that much, and not that he spends too much time looking after his wine business either. All his time is taken up with the Bersaglieri.'

Papà shakes his head, fondly, his own memories of former friends and companions flooding back now too.

'Domenico and his music.'

35

A smiling Enrico nods back once more.

'You should see him, always right at the head of the Whitsun procession. And his son. He can't be much more than fourteen, but he's already following in his father's footsteps. When he's not playing his music then every weekday he's down at the local market, selling – guess what, Chiara?'

All of a sudden, and for the first time in over an hour, he's looking directly at me, his kindly eyes glowing.

'I don't know.'

Enrico smiles, shaking his head.

'And you'll never guess, not in a month of Sundays.'

There he goes again. And now he's almost purring, obviously proud of all the phrases he's collected in these last couple of years and equally obviously intent on showing off each and every one.

'Chestnuts. And black peas.'

All I can do is blink at that again.

Then all of a sudden I start to wonder. Perhaps he's not just enjoying an extended tease here. Perhaps he's saying all this for a very different reason. Perhaps he already knows it won't be long before I see all this for myself.

'Three tailors have opened up in a warehouse behind my shop. And a terrazzo business was opening when I left too.'

Enrico pauses, finally, to take breath.

'Sometimes I think I travelled all that way to leave my home behind only for it to follow me, every step of the way.'

Then suddenly he pauses again and looks at me once more.

'So how does it sound, Chiara?'

I can almost hear Mamma holding her breath behind me as if she's already wondering what I'm going to say next, but I say the only thing I can say, the only thing I'm thinking.

'Black *what*?'

There it is again. That same full-bodied, full-bellied laugh echoing around the room: a sound that tells me more than anything he could actually say that Enrico is a good man and that while he might enjoy showing off his new phrases just that little bit too eagerly, there is little harm in a man who can laugh like that.

'Would you like to find out for yourself?'

It's the first time the question has been asked: the question that's hovered in the air for days, for weeks even; the question that's brought Enrico all the way from his new home to his old, the question that hardly even needs an answer. It's an answer that comes back nevertheless, from brain to mouth, with no second thoughts, nothing in between.

'Yes.'

Now Enrico looks at me for a long, long moment and then Papà steps in, nodding at Mamma as he does so, including Luigi and Peppo in his next, gentle, instruction.

'Perhaps Enrico and I could be left alone for a few moments?'

Papà hesitates.

'To discuss a few things.'

I stare back at them, not moving for a moment. What does that mean? I've no idea. Does it mean I'm going to England? Am I about to start living my new life among the people Enrico's just described?

They all stay silent. Why? Why isn't anyone telling me what's happening here? Why have we spent the last hour talking about anything and everything apart from the one thing I want to know?

Am I about to start my own adventure? Am I about to start living too?

Perhaps I'm already beginning to learn a lesson or two because, for once, I keep my mouth shut.

Frankie

IT'S NINE O'CLOCK at night and the local cemetery's probably seeing more action right now, but Uncle Tony's still open.

Uncle Tony's café is always open. Not through choice – he's not a workaholic, nothing like that. It's just tradition, I suppose. His coffee shop is open from early morning to late into the evening, seven days a week and always has been, right from your time and maybe even longer than that.

But that's the other problem here, isn't it? I don't really know when your time was. Or even if you were actually here at all. But if you ever were then believe me nothing's changed, not even the pies. Most of them taste like they've been around a fair few decades as well.

I've seen pictures of Tony's café in the old days. Then, you could hardly see inside for all the punters, which is one thing that's definitely changed. There's still lots milling about, but now they're congregating across the road outside a Chinese next to a newly opened Bargain Booze shop. There's an Indian on the other side of the road and that does good business too. By the time midnight rolls round, it's all you can smell. Chicken Vindaloo, Beef Chop Suey and cheap cider.

I head into the café only to stop as I head through the door. Then I look up, puzzled. The bell's not ringing. I can't honestly say I'd ever really noticed it before, but I definitely notice it now it's gone, if that makes any sort of sense. I close the door and open it again. Still no ring. So I look over at Tony in his usual place, sitting on a high stool behind the counter, music – one of his old Italian songs – playing on the music system behind him, and he just shrugs back at me.

'It got shot.'

And now I'm staring at him like I'm hearing things.

I mean, 'it got shot'?

WTF?!

Actually, you won't get that either, will you? Don't suppose you had abbreviations in your day, just like you won't know any of the films I go on about. Maybe you'd better just skip over those bits too.

Tony nods back at me. I'm still staring and I'm still thinking, *WTF*?!

'It got what?'

'Serious. A couple of kids were messing about with an air rifle.'

'And they shot your bell?'

'They were aiming at a cat. Only the cat did a runner. Came dashing in here, it did, and the little bastards let off a volley after it. If the cat had known what crap shots they were, it could have saved itself the effort – they missed by about three miles, hit my bell instead.'

All the time he's talking, Tony's filling a cup with espresso before pushing it across the counter.

'You look frozen.'

'Ta.'

I smile and quickly take a gulp – too quick, the liquid already beginning to burn the back of my throat.

'Didn't walk, did you? It's miles.'

'Got the train.'

'And what are you doing back anyway? I thought you were having a night out with Psaila and the girls?'

I keep sipping my coffee, trying not to make it obvious I'm already beginning to squirm.

'It was just me and Psaila in the end, no-one else could make it.'

'You still normally have a good time when you go out with her.'

'Well, this time I didn't.'

'Night didn't quite catch fire, then?'

'Something like that.'

While he's talking, Tony's walking round the counter and now he joins me, the two of us sitting at one of the dark oak tables that have been there as long as I can remember too.

'I can never understand it, you know.'

'What?'

I look back at the empty cavity above the shop doorway that used to house the now-broken bell, and for a moment my mind drifts as I wonder what Tyler's doing. Tyler's my eldest, although he's not that old – he's only just turned twelve but he's already been in trouble at school. I'm hoping to God that husband of mine has made sure he's come in at a reasonable time and hasn't let him just wander the streets with his so-called mates.

'The women round here.'

By my side, Tony's talking on all the while.

'They have a night out in Cardiff and it's like some sort of miracle, back they come with more money than they went out with. They come in here sometimes, just before I'm closing up, compare what's in their purses – how they do it, I've no idea.'

All the time he's looking anywhere but at me.

He knows exactly how they do it.

And he knows I know too.

'Different story with the fellers – look at your Steve. How

40

often does he go out these days – one night a week, maybe two, max? He comes in here sometimes too, end of the night, usually bladdered, but when he turns out his pockets to pay for his Americano, more often than not I've got to sub him because he's got sod all left to even pay for a bullseye.'

I cut across, don't want to hear any more.

'OK, Uncle Tony.'

But that doesn't stop him, because he's going to finish what he wants to say anyway, and he does. He always does.

Tony leans close, his voice gentle enough, but there's steel there too. There always is.

'It's not the way, Frankie.'

Chiara

I<small>T'S LATER THAT</small> same afternoon. A lot later. Whatever Enrico and Papà have been talking about, it's taken forever.

Outside, Luigi and Peppo are playing with the pig. We fatten and kill one every year. The fattening is never very exciting but the killing's always something of an event as it's dragged to a table in the yard before its throat is cut, quickly, by Papà before Mamma catches the blood in a collection of buckets, all ready for making the *sanguinaccio*, or black pudding.

I can hear my brothers' shouts and yells as I sit in my wooden seat carved into the wall. On another day I might have gone down and joined them. From the sounds drifting in from outside, they're playing *Lupo Mangia-Frutta* (the Fruit-Eating Wolf) and I've always made a great wolf. But not today. Today I sit and wait.

From across the valley, something else wafts its way inside my room, borne in on the breeze, along with the laughter of my brothers. Charcoal again. The burners are hard at work once more and the smell is beginning to hang over the whole of the valley.

From outside, Luigi shouts again, Peppo shouting back at him, the pig scampering between them, snorting all the while. Luigi and Peppo don't play on the scrub ground any more. No-one does. It's not closed off or anything. No-one seems to want to, that's all.

Those white, staring, unblinking eyes that looked back up at me from inside that well that day belonged to a young girl. Her name was Yara Bonicelli and she was twelve years old. She wasn't from our town, which was the first mystery. Yara was from Chignolo d'Isola, a few kilometres south of Bergamo.

No-one we knew had ever been to her home town, although I had learnt about the area in school. Just a few kilometres to the north was another small settlement called Pontida, where, centuries before, the Lombard League (an alliance of northern Italian cities) joined together to resist the German Emperor, Frederick I. We'd learnt that in our history class, delivered by our small, dark, intense schoolteacher, Professoressa Quadrelli. In Geography, also taught by the Professoressa, we learnt that area around the town was split in two. The lower slopes were fertile, their inhabitants wealthy. The upper part of the region was remote, more traditional.

Yara came from a rich family whose house was on those fertile plains and she'd been seen talking to a man from the mountains just before she disappeared. After her body was discovered, an autopsy found traces of lime in her throat and the presence of jute on her clothing. Lime and jute were staples of the building industry and the main industry in the mountainous part of Yara's home region, aside from hill agriculture, was construction.

Suspicion soon fell on a local man, Mario Guerinoni. Not only was he a builder and would therefore have been in daily contact with those kinds of materials, but his brother, Giuseppe, had left their home some time before and was now living in one of the small, white cottages I could see from my window. The coincidence seemed too great, and so it proved. Giuseppe's house was raided and while no evidence that Yara had ever been there was found, the police did find a draft of a ransom note.

Giuseppe Guerinoni was questioned and he soon confessed, leading his brother Mario to confess in turn. Yara had been snatched for money. The two men had intended to hide her away until her family paid for her release.

Unfortunately the kidnap was rushed and Yara struggled. In that struggle the small and slight Yara had died. The men panicked and dumped her body in an empty local well, where she might have remained undiscovered forever had it not been for one single inquisitive child playing nearby some weeks later.

Murders had happened before. All sorts of crimes had taken place in our town and beyond, but this seemed to mark something of a change for many, perhaps because crimes against children were still mercifully rare. All over the town and all over the surrounding towns, for months afterwards parents huddled together and hushed inquests took place. Then, one by one, their children began to leave for other towns and countries further away.

Suddenly the door opens behind me again and Mamma looks at me once more from the open doorway.

I stare back at her.

'What did he say?'

'Enrico and your father are still talking.'

I almost explode with frustration.

'They've been talking for hours.'

From outside, the charcoal's smelling stronger now. I reach up and slam the window shut even though the sun's high in the sky.

Mamma cuts across.

'What did I say?'

Standing by the now-closed window, I look back at her.

'What did I tell you, the last thing I said to you before you went in to meet him, my very last words?'

Her eyes flash.

'Your tongue, Chiara. Always your tongue. Why, for once in your life, don't you think before you open your mouth?'

I'm not listening to her, because another shadow has now fallen across the room. Mamma turns, and she stops too as she sees my father standing behind her.

He's not doing anything, and he's not saying anything either. He's just standing there.

Looking at me.

Frankie

IT'S ALL RIGHT for him isn't it? For Uncle Tony and his family business.

For him and his, *It's not the way, Frankie*.

So what is the way? I used to know, we all used to know, when things were simple: when factories stayed open for longer than the time it took the owners to pocket the start-up grants, when shops survived beyond the first week's non-existent trade. Then everything was simple. Even Steve managed to make a living back then and believe me, that man of mine is not exactly a natural hard worker. When the going gets tough, Steve gets going all right, but usually only to the nearest pub.

As for savings, don't make me laugh. We tried when we first got married – no, correction, I tried. Put a little bit away for a rainy day – we even tried getting together a deposit for one of those new-builds they were putting up on the other side of the old rec. And OK, it did all look a bit like Toy Town and the developers pulled some sneaky tricks, like putting three-quarter size furniture in the show house so the whole place looked a hell of a lot bigger than it actually was, but at least it would have been ours. Maybe not ours as in outright, but it would still have been better than paying rent to some of the landlords round here.

I'm ranting, I know, just like I'm ranting to Tony, and he's sitting here and he's letting me. First because he's nice and second because he's family – sort of, anyway – and he knows what this is all about, that it's just my way of letting off steam, getting it all out there, all the fears and all the frustrations, just to see if – maybe – I can make any sense of it all.

Maybe that's why I'm doing this too. Maybe that's why I'm telling you all this, talking to you. For the times that Uncle Tony isn't around. Or for the things I really can't come out with to him.

'We're way behind with the rent.'

'So are most people round here. So what are they going to do, throw you all out on the street?'

Still sitting across that dark oak table from me, Tony shrugs.

'What's the point? Even if they do, no-one else can afford to move in anyway.'

'Tyler's just started big school, he needs things.'

'All his mates have just started big school too, none of their families can get them things either.'

'And Vicky's starting next year.'

'By next year maybe things'll be better.'

'Said that about the war, didn't they? Over by Christmas?'

'They didn't say which one.'

I look out of the window at a gang of kids, not much older than Tyler, running out of the Chinese, one of them with a plastic salt cellar in his hand, being chased by one of the waiters. I think of my son, my daughter, growing up in a town where a kid would even dream of stealing a plastic salt cellar and where a waiter can actually be arsed chasing after him to get it back.

All the time, Tony's looking at me.

'You need a holiday.'

I nod.

I do.

'From life.'

Tony picks up my espresso, stands to get me a refill. The layer of *crema* on the top has long gone and it offends the barista in him, I can tell. But I shake my head, tell him not to bother. Now I just want to go home.

Tony looks at me, hesitating, sudden doubt creeping in.

'You're still coming though, yeah? The trip?'

And I nod, because even though things are bad and times are desperate, things will be even worse and times will be even more desperate if we don't all get on that bus in a few weeks' time just like we always do each and every year, and just like we always will if I've got anything to do with it.

'It's the only thing that's keeping me going.'

I look out of the window again and now I'm not seeing kids with plastic salt cellars or air rifles, or irate Chinese waiters.

'Just the thought of it.'

Now I'm seeing vines and smelling figs and feeling myself bathed in sunshine.

'Italy.'

Chiara

HE'S STILL JUST standing there, still just looking at me and I can see it in his eyes. I've ruined everything. By my side, my mother's shoulders sag as if she can read the silent signals too.

It wouldn't be so bad if it was just me, but it's not. That's not the way it works. It's Luigi and Peppo too, Once someone from one family is taken then it opens the doors for the rest. Enrico hadn't said he'd take them too, of course, and we wouldn't have expected him to, but without the first recruit there's never a second or third.

'You called him fat.'

Mamma closes her eyes as Papà keeps staring at me and out it comes again, before my tongue has time to bite it back; brain to mouth, nothing in between.

'Well, he's not thin.'

When am I going to learn? Answer, never. Are you the same? I'll never know (how can I?), but I hope not. The trouble it causes.

Papà nods.

'Fortunately, he also has a sense of humour.'

Now both Mamma and myself are looking at him. What does he mean? And why is there now a small smile playing across his face?

'I asked for one hundred and twenty lire a month. And all your food. And your own room, of course.'

I stare at him.

'You asked? You mean, there's a chance?'

'Of course there's a chance. Why do you think he came here in the first place? There was very definitely a chance.'

Now my shoulders are drooping again, my brain picking out only one word in all of that.

Was?

I expect it, but it still hits me like a hammer blow. The charcoal, the hated charcoal burning again from across the river, seems to fill the room despite the closed window behind me. By my side, Mamma now begins to weep, silently – but it's strange, she's crying but her eyes are dancing, like I saw them dance when my brothers were little and they did something that made her laugh so much that she cried at the same time.

I see that Papà's smiling too.

'Now there's a yes.'

He comes up to me and kisses me, soft and light, on the top of my head.

'He said yes to everything I asked for. Yes to the one hundred and twenty lire a month, yes to all your food and yes to your own room.'

Mamma's sobbing now, properly sobbing, but all the time my father's just looking at me.

'You're going to England.'

PART TWO

'The Cities of the Priests'

(Chronicles 6)

Frankie

WELCOME TO PARADISE. That was actually the first thing I said into this machine. Can you believe that? Those actual, exact words. I had to stop for the next half hour, I was pissing myself so much. Although maybe that was more down to the bottle of red wine I was drinking at the time.

Well, bottles to be strictly accurate. Might as well get it all out in the open from the start, I suppose. I do like my *vino rosso*.

Actually, that's not strictly true. Yes, I drink a fair bit of the stuff. But do I like it that much? To tell you the truth, I've forgotten. It's just part of what passes for life these days.

Steve gave me this. It was a present. Actually, that's not quite right either – may as well get all that out in the open too. He acquired it. By not totally legitimate means. Knocked if off, in other words. He's not a thief as such, even though a hell of a lot of stolen stuff seems to be finding its way into our house these days.

Steve used to run his own business and no, I'm not apologising for calling it that. OK, he did have just the one employee – himself – and he did only have just the one mobile tuning van, but a couple of years ago things were going well. He even branched out into mobile tyres, which, when he first told me about them, brought on a mega-fit of the giggles. I mean, have you ever heard of tyres that weren't?

Steve laughed at that too. He laughed a lot in those days. Now he doesn't laugh so much, but no-one seems to right now. Maybe because there really isn't too much to laugh about.

What they called the crash killed Steve's business. You had them too, didn't you? I'm sure I read about a couple from way back when. I don't even know what kind of crash it was or who caused it. Some clever arse we met in a pub once explained it was all to do with crooks and mortgages and banks going mad lending all sorts of money to all sorts of people, but none of that seemed to find its way back down to us. And anyway it isn't what caused it that really matters but what it's done – to people like us: me and Steve. People who wouldn't know what a mortgage looked like if it came up from behind and bit us both on the jacksy.

Most people round here don't have cars any more, and those that have managed to cling onto their little mechanical pride and joy are having to do their own maintenance on them. The days when you got someone in to do work for you, any kind of work, are long gone. So it's not just Steve who's down to scratching around for whatever he can lay his hands on. All the local chippies – that's a carpenter, by the way – the sparks – that's an electrician – and all the builders – small and big – are doing the same, because they've nothing else to do either.

Like Uncle Tony always says, it'll probably be all over by Christmas – even if he's not exactly sure which one. Right, and maybe I'll look out of this window tonight and see a pig flying over the moon.

Actually, forget pigs, flying or otherwise. The amount of cheap wine I'm putting away these days, I don't really want to tempt fate.

This machine's a sort of recorder. Not the kind my kids

play – usually badly – in school concerts, but the kind you speak into. The kind of thing you might use if you're some business type and want to remind yourself about some important meeting you've got coming up, or if you're some kind of writer and want to get down some really neat idea you've had before you forget it. Or if you just fancy doing some stupid rambling like I'm doing right now.

Steve had tried to flog it around the local pubs and clubs, along with all kinds of other stuff including toys and a side of mutton he'd knocked off at the same time, but there weren't too many takers – multi-national executives and dreamy scribes being a bit thin on the ground in this neck of the woods. So I got it instead.

'Frankie?'

I switch the machine off, quick, as I hear the man himself approaching along the corridor. It's weird: it's not as if I'm doing anything wrong, but I still feel a bit of a knob sitting here all by myself and talking into this thing. I just have time to slide an old magazine over the top of it to hide it from view as Steve pokes his head round the door.

'Tyler's pissed the bed.'

I stare back at him.

Did I mention Tyler's my eldest and he's twelve? Now you see why I'm just staring.

'You know you couldn't find all them towels?'

Steve looks at me, momentarily injured, pained almost.

'You even accused me of flogging them – for Christ's sake, Frankie, I knocked them off in the first place. They've still got the name of the hotel in the corner, so who's going to buy knock-off towels when they can just go out and knock them off themselves?'

I cut across, getting back to the actual matter of the moment here.

'Tyler's done what?'

That's Steve all over. Drop a bombshell, then go off on a total tangent. My old mum always said he was a grasshopper. Never settling. Always hopping from one thing to the next. At the time, I thought she found it amusing. Now I think she was warning me, although about what exactly I still haven't quite worked out.

'He hasn't pissed the bed since he was a toddler, for Christ's sake!'

Steve nods.

'Must have done it last night. He's gone out. Don't think he'll be back for a bit, either. I reckon he's a bit embarrassed.'

Steve turns back towards the door.

'Vicky's out too.'

Vicky's my other kid. She's nine. And Steve had done the impossible: all I could think about ten seconds ago was a twelve year old who still pisses beds, now all I can think about is a nine year old girl who, apparently, is –

'Out?'

I repeat it while staring at him all the time.

'Out where?'

Steve shrugs.

'I don't know.'

'Didn't you ask her?'

But now Steve's looking round the room, curious.

'What are you doing in here all by yourself anyway?'

Now, instinctively, I'm glancing down towards the portable recorder I've just covered with that old magazine. Steve's still looking round the whitewashed walls of our box room, a room he'd earmarked once as a den but which now seems to have become some kind of confessional.

'Steve, it's ten o'clock at night!'

'I know. Last orders in half an hour.'

56

I keep staring at him but Steve's already heading for the door. He used to head down the pub most nights, now he rations it to one night a week. Or two, max, as Uncle Tony has already pointed out. And then only for the last half hour. But wild horses wouldn't keep him away, let alone such obviously trifling considerations as two kids out on the streets somewhere when at least one of them really should be tucked up in bed.

'Do something about them sheets, eh, Frankie?'

'Steve –'

'It honks in there.'

And then he's gone.

I turn back to the portable recorder, sliding the magazine away and looking down at it again.

If truth be told, Tyler and Vicky aren't in any sort of danger. Loads of kids roam round the streets of this estate for hours at night, especially these warm summer nights when there's no school the next day. Most of the time they're just doing what all kids do, I suppose – what all kids *should* be doing, probably, if truth be told. Just having fun.

We were kids once too, Steve and myself, and once – a long time ago – we used to have fun too.

And then suddenly, from all those years ago, sitting in front of that little portable tape recorder in that whitewashed room, out of absolutely nowhere, comes a memory.

And out of nowhere again, I suddenly start to smile.

'Take off your knickers.'

Relax, OK, I'm not about to invite you into our bedroom. This diary/letter/journal/whatever you want to call it (and someone else had better decide on that because I still haven't got a clue) – this *thing,* whatever it is – isn't about to become X-rated.

Believe it or not, we're in one of the most public places you can imagine and I'm staring at a grinning Steve as if he's suddenly gone totally cuckoo.

I hiss back at him.

'We're in church.'

Steve, wide-eyed, takes in the pews, the old man in front of us standing in a pulpit in a cassock, the bent heads of the assorted worshippers dotted all around. Then he nods back at me, still wide-eyed.

'No shit, Sherlock.'

It's not that either of us have ever been what you might call religious. We wanted a church wedding but that was more for the pictures. The nearest one was a C of E church where Steve used to go as a kid, but it didn't matter which one you went to, back in those days they had to read out your banns. To be honest, I never quite understood it myself and looking back I'm sure compulsory attendance when some vicar reads out the list of upcoming services for the next few weeks isn't laid down anywhere in any holy book. Let's face it, it definitely isn't one of the Ten Commandments, is it? But when it's you and your intended who are having the details of your wedding read out, then you really had better be there because it would be one hell of a big black mark against you if you weren't.

So for three weeks, every Sunday, regular as clockwork, we shuffle into that gloomy old church. Which is where – two weeks in and with one week to go – Steve says it.

'Take off your knickers.'

And now I'm staring at him like he really has gone cuckoo. There's not that many people in the congregation right now: an old boy behind us who rings the bells at the start and the end of the service as well as handing out the Bibles and hymn books as you walk in, some old ladies down the front who spend most of their time on their knees, from what I can see, the vicar himself, a well-fed sort of gent who looks like he's doing missionary work or something, and me and Steve. And OK, it's not much of an audience, but it's still way too many for me. I've always been a strictly-behind-closed-doors kind of girl when it comes to that kind of thing.

'Go on, Frankie.'

'Here?'

He's lost it.

He must have.

'Yeah.'

'Right here? Right now?'

'Why not?'

And I don't know where to start, I really don't. All I can do is repeat it again, hoping by some miracle – and let's face it we're in the right place for one of those – he might just get the message.

'We're in a church.'

'I know.'

And then I splutter suddenly – can't help it – because this is so ridiculous, and one of the old ladies at the front turns and looks at me like people look at you in the pictures sometimes when there's a really emotional bit and you're being a bit too noisy with the popcorn.

'Go on.'

And now I feel myself starting to splutter some more, and I try to choke it off because I really don't want that old bloke behind us to hit us with his bell or something.

'What's the point?'

Now I'm hissing back at him in turn and the Vicar's faltering as he rambles on with his sermon, and I'm starting to feel like some naughty schoolkid which, I have to admit, is actually becoming a bit of a turn-on.

'We can't do anything.'

'I don't want to do anything.'

I stare at him, blank, and now Steve's looking back at me, his large eyes ever wider.

'So what do you want to do?'

'I want to blow my nose.'

And I don't care who's looking at us now, and I don't care that a second old crone has turned round, and I don't care that the old bell ringer behind us has started shifting about on his seat as well. I'm just staring at this man who, in a few weeks' time, I'm going to promise to spend the rest of my life with, forsaking all others and all that – which makes it even more important, so far as I'm concerned, that I have heard what I think he's just said.

So I take it slowly, whispering all the while.

'You want to blow your nose in my knickers while the vicar's reading out our banns?'

Steve nods.

'Yeah.'

And I swear to God – my God, your God, whoever's God might be listening – that now I really can't help it, now I feel myself starting to giggle and Steve – bastard – although I don't suppose you should even think something like that in a church, should you? – he knows he's got me and the bastard – oops, did it again – starts pushing me.

'I forgot my hanky. And I can't use my sleeve, can I? Or your dress, that's your Sunday best, that is – how's that going to look, a great big trail of snot running down the arm?'

'Shut up.'

Now I'm trying to turn the splutters into coughs like I'm clearing my throat or something, only I don't think it's fooling the bell ringer or the old crones and it's definitely not pulling the wool over the vicar's eyes either. He probably knows his sermon's lacking a little something in the attention-grabbing stakes and is probably used to the odd cough and snuffle, but I'd have been prepared to bet whatever we had back then – which wasn't much, but I'd have bet it anyway – that he's never had something like this punctuating his weekly ramblings.

Then Steve sniffs, a revolting big sniff and now, and more to shut him up than anything else, I reach down under my dress – although I do admit the old Devil has got into me a bit by now, which I'm guessing is another thing you really shouldn't admit to in a place of worship – and I do it. As subtly as I can, but it probably wasn't all that subtle, in truth.

I was pretty sure the vicar couldn't actually see me rolling my knickers down my legs and over my shoes – black patent, very smart and shiny – before handing them over to Steve. But he hears Steve all right. They could probably hear him up among the angels and archangels, he milks it that much. This was one blowing of a nose that was going to be savoured, which is just what he did.

Long and loud.

Pronounced and prolonged.

So much so that the Vicar actually dries up for a moment and looks across at us.

Steve looks back at him, my knickers still held up to his nose and he nods up at him, clear as the bell that old bloke was ringing behind us just a little while earlier.

'Sorry.'

Only I don't hear any more because now I've started laughing and I don't stop till we're miles away from that church, just me and Steve, my knickers still in his hand, running like naughty schoolkids all the way home.

Chiara

I STARTED WRITING this a few weeks before I left home. But from the moment I started, I hid it from everyone.

I didn't really know why at the time. Perhaps at the start I didn't want anyone too close to me to read it. Now? Reading back over all these entries, journeying with a younger version of myself I sometimes hardly recognise, I still don't know. I don't even know what this is, in truth. It's not a simple diary, I know that. And I've addressed it to you even though I don't know who you are.

So who was I imagining might one day read these words, might journey with me as I began what seemed to me then (and still seems to me now, sometimes) this great adventure? All right, compared to some of the pioneers we used to read about in school, I wasn't exactly an intrepid explorer. But my journey still seemed extraordinary enough to me.

Which still doesn't answer the question. Who exactly was I, am I, talking to?

At first I imagined that one day, long into the future, a daughter or a granddaughter might read this. But as time went on I decided to address it to someone more distant still. For reasons you'll understand only too well if you reach the end of this tale, I really don't want to be alive when these words are read.

So I invented you. But the strange thing is that from the moment I did, I saw you, almost as clearly as I can still see

Luigi and Peppo playing outside our old house in Bardi, and my mother packing my trunk for the journey I'm about to take, and my father trying to hide the dampness in his eyes.

It's all Mamma's done for the last few nights: worry whether there are enough warm clothes in my case, which is to be secured with straps for the five-day journey, how many changes of clothes I should take in another smaller bag, where I'm going to keep the money I'm to take. The same questions over and over, even though she's already heard the answers a hundred times before.

I lie awake, listening, and all I can think is that the next time I open that case secured with straps, I won't be in this small hillside house in the shadow of a castle, the only home I've actually ever known. The next time I see those clothes she's packing away for me, I'll be in a different house in a different country and a different world.

It starts then. That strangest of feelings creeping over me, because I'm going by choice, and out of no choice. I'm going because I want to, but also because I have to, and it's all getting mixed up and now I can't separate it out any more.

Partly it's that day by the well. What happened to a young girl called Yara Bonicelli. Partly that's the reason I know I have to go, but there's another reason too.

Back in those days, there was a law. When someone died, their estate had to be split between all surviving members of their family. It sounded fair, but in practice it was a disaster. On the death of my grandfather, his farm had to be split between eight children and four of his brothers and sisters. Twelve people taking a share of a farm that could barely support one! Each of the so-called beneficiaries took a tiny strip of land and tried to make it pay. It couldn't, of course.

When my father dies, his tiny strip of land will have to be split between myself, Luigi and Peppo, and Papà's remaining relatives as well. So then life will become even more impossible. So now one of us has to start building a new life, make a fresh start in some other country, a country that hopefully won't seem as cursed as this.

As the oldest, and despite being a girl, it's my job to make that happen.

The next morning, it's time. My bags (both large and small) and the clothes I'll next see in that different country, that different world, have been sitting in the hall since last night. We share a simple meal and for once Luigi and Peppo don't go out to play. No-one talks about the journey I'm about to take or the life I'm about to embrace. We talk about anything and everything else instead. When we run out of things to say, we sit in a silence so loud it threatens to deafen us all.

Then everyone comes with me to the main Square. Already there are people milling around everywhere. Some I'll be travelling with: some will be stopping off in France (musicians and artisans mainly), some journeying on, as I will, to England.

There's only one girl in amongst the travellers and that's myself. The rest are male, but there's no time to ponder that or be alarmed by it either. The engine of the bus clatters into life and it's time to get into our seats for the journey down to the plain and the onward journey by train.

I look at my father and there's the same dampness in his eyes, and I look at my mother and she's not even trying to hold back her tears. I look across at Luigi and he scowls at me like he always does when he's upset and doesn't want to show it, and then he hits Peppo, who's scowling too and who hits him back, and Papà barks at them in relief at having something to do apart from look at me and blink back tears.

Suddenly I smile, because I know that if I don't then I'll

give way and then I might say what I've thought every night for the last few nights as this day approached, this day I'd wanted above all others and have now come to dread: that maybe the wrong child's going, that maybe we should wait a couple of years until he's older and then Luigi can go instead.

If I said that then I know Mamma and Papà would probably unload my few possessions and we'd all go home and no-one would ever say another word about it.

So I keep smiling because I know I can't give even the smallest sign of how I'm feeling, that I have to keep it from them, not just for their sakes but for mine as well. I have to give them that sunshine smile to take back with them to a house I'm already missing more in the last few seconds than I'd ever thought possible. That smile becomes my foundation stone. It's everything my life is built on at this moment, and if it wavers even for a single second, I know I'll be lost.

So I look up at the castle that towers over our small town instead, an ancient building visible from all around, and force myself to concentrate on all we were taught about it in school by Professoressa Quadrelli. It was mentioned as far back as 898 ad, so we were told, although back then it was just a rock fort built to resist invasion, a fortress for the Bishop of Piacenza. It became a fortified castle a couple of hundred years later before becoming a stronghold for the Bourbons and temporary home to the later wife of Napoleon, no less. Now it's everything: Town Hall, Jail and Court. And as I keep looking up at it, trying to let half-remembered facts fill a growing ache inside, for a moment, unbidden and out of nowhere, a memory returns.

I'm small, little more than a child, and my father's taken me to the very top of the ramparts, to a place I believed must be the very top of the world because the whole world is what we now seem to see, spread out far below us. At the time it seemed as if I was looking down on heaven.

Then the bus rolls out of the Square and Papà and Mamma and Luigi and Peppo wave me off until the bus turns a corner ahead and they disappear from view.

I make two friends on that journey across to my new country, my new home.

One is a boy, Florio Virilli. Florio's about the same age as myself, but if I've developed sudden fears at leaving all I've ever known, Florio has none because before he left (as he tells everyone who'll listen), he'd wooed the Goddess of Good Fortune and wooed her boldly. She might not have smiled on him too kindly up to then (and she really hadn't, there was no doubt about that), but in his new home and working for his new employer, whoever that might be, Florio just knows that everything's going to change.

Florio certainly travels light. He carries a cheap cardboard valise inside which is just a pair of broken-down old shoes. And he carries a smell around with him as well. Don't get me wrong, he isn't dirty and his teeth, when he smiles, flash white. I can't place exactly what it is, but one of the inspectors who boards the train at one of the different stops along the way knows exactly what that smell is, and where it's coming from too.

The inspector opens Florio's valise and from inside one of the old and broken down shoes he brings out a creased and crumpled hunk of Bologna sausage. The other shoe is stuffed with a soft and sticky mass of cheese. From such humble beginnings, Florio had intended to build his fortune, but he's going to have to start doing that in an even humbler fashion as his precious delicacies are immediately confiscated before the smell overpowers us all.

My other companion, Pietro Vincenzo, is much older, almost Papà's age. Pietro is grey-haired and round-shouldered. But he too is travelling to make his fortune and is also determinedly hopeful, like Florio. His valise is canvas and lined with paper. Inside, as he demonstrates to us with pride, are two striped cotton shirts, one neckerchief of yellow silk with blue flowers, a black hat (a bit worn, in truth), one waistcoat, a pint of olive oil, half a pack of *taralli* and a quart of Vesuvian wine with a distinctive and rich purple hue that I'd seen in the markets I'd been taken to as a child.

But halfway into the journey disaster strikes when Pietro drops his valise as he carelessly tries to return it to an overhead rack after another of the now-regular inspections. His quart of wine smashes and while he manages to keep it away from his clothes, he's less fortunate with his biscuits. And, with little choice but to share them before they spoil completely, we all have something of a feast.

But neither Florio nor Pietro are destined to reach journey's end; or at least having reached it, they are returned home before spending even a single night there.

The days when a penniless immigrant could enter your country are long gone. Now you need the influence of a *padrone*, a word I can't quite translate properly. I suppose you'd call him a Master: a *padrone* was always male. Most recruit from the area they themselves call home, the reason I suppose that so many Italians arriving in Britain in the last few years have come from my own home town of Bardi.

Most are fine and respectable employers. Partly because they recruit from their former homes, they've actually recreated that home overseas in a way. Whole districts packed so full of émigrés from the same few streets it's as if they're still living beneath the bell tower in their old home square. *Campanilismo*, it's called, although some countries have a different name for it. Little Italy's just one of the ones I've heard.

But some are different. Some are the harshest of overseers. I've seen them in a few of the markets back home, scouring the young boys on offer, picking the strongest and poorest out from the rest. Once a few *lire* have secured their services and, by way of an introduction to the life they're about to endure, they're forced to walk from their old home to their new, from town to town, from village to village until they reach a port from which they cross by boat to England.

These *padroni* are cruel and pitiless and treat their charges like slaves. If those charges don't bring home a sufficient sum each day through their labour, whatever form that might take, they're beaten as well as being kept without food and sent to bed.

Technically, Enrico was a *padrone* too, but he was far from that type of man. There truly didn't seem an ounce of harm in him. But perhaps, and as you'll see, there was too much good in Enrico.

We travel for four whole days, first picking up the train at Piacenza to Milan, then taking another train through France. From there it's a short ferry ride before docking in what must be England, in a slipway next to a large building. A gangplank is put down and a man at the bottom starts shouting, telling the men to go one way and the few (very few) women and children to go another. Then we all walk up one of two large staircases that leads to a Registry room with more men watching us closely all the way, and then we all take what I learn later is called the 'six-second exam'.

In those six seconds, we are scanned for any obvious medical or health problems. In those same six seconds our new inquisitors take in the same number of details about us: our scalps, faces, hands, neck and gait, as well as our general condition. If anything is noted or strikes any of our new inquisitors as amiss, we're stopped and a closer examination is carried out.

A woman behind me, one who joined us on the boat in France, is stopped immediately as she seems to have a problem focusing on the stairs in front of her and has already stumbled on them more than once. A strange instrument is produced: something called a buttonhook, a metal instrument more usually used to fix buttons onto gloves. Her eyelid is pulled back and an instant (and potentially devastating) diagnosis is made. She has a trachoma, an eye disease or infection, it seems, and immediately she's sent on to another room for a more detailed examination to take place.

On the other staircase, I can see men being marked with chalk on their coats: 'H' for heart problems, although how they spot that with the naked eye, I'll never understand; 'L' for lameness. Again they're sent on to other rooms for their own more detailed investigations.

At the same time come the questions. These are questions that have already been asked by the shipping company, but they're asked again anyway to check that the answers match. These last no more than two to three minutes, but for some reason it feels like forever.

What's your name?
How old are you?
What is your calling or occupation?
Are you able to read and write?
Did you pay for your passage over and if not, who did?
Are you going to join a relative?
What relative, and what's his name and address?
Do you have any money with you?
Have you ever been in prison, in a poorhouse or supported by charity?

69

Dimly, on the other side of a door at the very end of the hall, I very briefly see the anxiously waiting Enrico, picking out his kindly face in the sea of all the other waiting faces.

However, that hall is as far as Florio and Pietro will travel. They pass the cursory medical but are already stumbling under the verbal assault to which we're all next subjected. Because they've no name to vouch for them, or address of any relative or sponsor to offer, and no money in their pockets to support themselves either. The decisions reached by our interrogators are swift and final and my two companions are refused entry by an unsmiling guard, deaf to their ever more desperate entreaties as there's no *padrone*, cruel or otherwise, to champion their cause.

When I leave them, sitting on the floor to join the return boat back across the Channel, I feel a pang of separation as acute as anything I felt at leaving my actual home. Perhaps even more so, in a sense, because I know I'll never see either of them again.

Perhaps also because I already fear for them. They've both fallen so low already, but how much further can they now fall? I don't know the answer, but as I'm led towards the main door at the end of the entry hall, their sad eyes watching me every step of the way, all I know is that even the question chills me to the bone.

Then I'm outside. Immediately my ears are assaulted by a blank wall of noise. It seems impossible to separate anything out: the shouting of men, the banging of machinery, the echoing drum of wheels on cobbles, the blasting sirens of docking ships.

But then I see him again. As we emerge from the hall, we're brought out one by one on a raised platform so those who've sponsored our entry into our new country can see us in turn and can identify us to one of the attending officers.

Enrico raises his hand as a signal to an officer that I should be brought down from the platform. As he does so I smile across at him, shyly for some reason, which is curious. I've not felt shy around him before but now, in this strange place and among all these other strangers, maybe it's suddenly being brought home to me just how much from this moment on I'm going to depend on a man I barely know.

And Enrico smiles back at me, but I can see straight away that something is wrong.

All those names Enrico told me about, and all those photographs he showed me and Mamma and Papà and Luigi and Peppo, those pictures of the Antonellis and the Lannis and the Granellis, all with their own shops, all opening up within a few doors of each other. And all those factories he'd told us about that had opened up too: Colaluca and Rocca in Mill Street who were making wafers, as well as Robino in Rodney Street.

And Domenico, who came originally from across the mountain from my own home town but who now owns an organ factory, and Marco, who'd just opened a wine merchants and who'd also taken over one of the local pubs, although he wasn't there all that much and didn't spend too much time looking after his wine business either because all his time was taken up with the Bersaglieri.

I actually saw all that and all of them, and not only in the pictures Enrico had produced from his small bag. I replayed all those pictures inside my head as I was waiting to see them for real. I felt as if I already knew that life, but it was not a life I was ever to know. I was to know a quite different life instead.

A different life to the one Enrico had promised me.

A different life to the one Enrico had promised himself.

Within hours of first seeing Enrico outside that crowded hall, all I'm seeing is grey. I didn't think there could be a world without colour, but there is and this is it.

Everywhere I look, I see grey houses packed tightly together and none of those grey houses have any sort of gardens. If there are any trees standing outside on the streets their leaves are grey too, and while I can see some berries every now and again on the branches, the berries are black, not red.

Then there's the rain. It's just pouring from the skies without stopping, even though this is the height of the summer; or at least that's what I've been told.

It's all feeling as if some gigantic trick is being played on me, for reasons I can't even begin to understand; but it's not a trick, it's real. All too real, as Enrico tries, and largely fails, at least at the start, to explain.

It had happened a couple of weeks before, before Mamma had packed that large case for me to head away from home and long before I'd boarded the ship that would take me across to England. While Florio and Pietro were still dreaming of fresh starts and brand new lives, before we shared those wine-drenched biscuits and listened to Pietro's heartfelt thanks to his own Goddess of Good Fortune that the wine hadn't ruined his only shirts, proclaiming loudly that it must be the same sign from above that had blessed Florio too. Before all of that happened, something happened with Enrico too.

Enrico had made a genuine success of his business in London. He'd built it from nothing to the sort of enterprise that could justify taking on extra staff, including a young girl who was soon to join him. He'd been rewarded with a short holiday by his grateful employer and he'd travelled to the north of the country to walk in the hills of a district criss-crossed with lakes.

On his return he found that the shop, the business he'd built up from virtually nothing, had been taken from him and given to the youngest son of the owner, who'd arrived from Naples in Enrico's absence. Enrico had been given another business to establish and then build up in another town a short distance away instead; a business that could hardly support him at that stage, let alone a new arrival.

Exactly the same thing had happened to him two years before. Enrico had built up a business in another shop too, only to have that also taken from him after he'd made a success of it and given to another member of the owner's family, recently arrived from the old family home.

Enrico had reluctantly accepted the first decision, but he didn't accept the second. Not long before my ship docked, there'd been a huge argument and Enrico had been told to leave. He'd decided to start his own business instead. At least that way he wouldn't ever go away on holiday again only to find on his return that all he'd worked for had been given to someone completely undeserving.

Enrico had managed to save a little out of his wages, and with that he'd scoured all the shops in the immediate area, but the rents demanded were way above anything he could afford. Over the next few days he'd scoured all the shops further afield and then further afield again, until a chance remark had sent him on a long train journey to a different country altogether where the people talked in a strange accent and occasionally a different language, but where property was cheap and competition was thin on the ground. It was a country whose name sounded like some giant fish, which was perhaps why it was always so wet there.

Which is where I am now: in a land called Wales. Not

a land called England which I'd heard of; not a city called London which I'd heard of too, but a town whose name I can't pronounce in a country I didn't even know existed.

'Are you Chiara?'

A bright-eyed, bubbly girl who looks a year or so older than me meets me at the door of a grey-fronted café. What other colour would it be?

I nod back.

'So I've pronounced it right?'

She hasn't, but I nod again anyway. Anything even resembling speech is beyond me at the moment. In fact, standing in the doorway of that small, café with Enrico's name (or at least his surname: *Carini's*) in between the misted-up front windows, I don't think I'll ever be able to speak again.

'Well, I'm Grace, which might be my name, but which definitely ain't my nature.'

The same bubbly young girl nods behind her at what looks like a whole sea of faces, some seated, some standing, around a wooden counter.

'Least that's what this lot always say, cheeky lot of bastards.'

A voice cuts across from inside a whirling mass of smoke.

'Are you serving or what?'

She grins back at me again, not even looking at the man who's just addressed her.

'Be such a nice place without the customers.'

I look into the gloom, my eyes beginning to pick out small details of the interior. There's a strange-looking door inlaid with dark glass at the far end of the room. A counter, a wooden counter around which most of the waiting men are grouped (and they all seem to be men: I can't see any women) runs the whole length of one side. And in the middle I can see a giant, pot-bellied stove with what looks like a kettle, burnished red so it must be copper, steaming away on top.

Grace cuts across again.

'You're from the same place as him, yeah?'

I look back at her. I still haven't spoken.

Grace grins wider, nodding over at Enrico, now talking to some of the men at the counter. I just feel like crying, out loud.

'Enrico.'

I nod back.

At last. A word, or at least a name, that speaks of home, of somewhere I know; not this place: a place I'll never know, never want to know.

The heat from that pot-bellied stove is overpowering. I look behind the counter and now I can see glasses and bottles, all in different colours, along with rows of china cups. Below the shelves are boxes stuffed full of what looks like multi-coloured sweets, and alongside them packet after packet of cigarettes, which explains the swirling smoke.

'I've been working here for two years – I used to work for the old owners and Enrico agreed to keep me on when he took over last week. I'm going to show you the ropes.'

Instinctively, I look behind her. Now I see a glass case containing cakes, some iced, some filled with cream and, at the far end of the counter as far away as possible from the overheated stove, an ice cream container, a coloured cabinet with a lid like a sailor's cap.

I look back at Grace, still no more enlightened.

'The ropes?'

Grace looks at the blank expression on my face and she

keeps looking at me as I stare round the café once more, still failing to spot them. Then she gives the biggest, deepest belly laugh I have ever heard in my life, deeper even than Enrico's. Wiping away her sudden tears,she leans close.

'OK, here's the introduction. I'll leave the detail till later. Call it a quick dash through the day, or at least the start of the day, but it should give you the flavour.'

Grace leans forward, her voice getting faster and faster, words tumbling out of her mouth, her eyes shining ever brighter all the time. Something's already telling me that I'm going to like her, even if I only understand roughly one word in every five she's saying right now.

'Six o'clock: rise. Shine too if you can, not that I ever do at that time in the morning, I leave my shining to my night off.'

And there it is again, the biggest, deepest (and dirtiest) laugh in the world.

'Quarter-past: clean. Half-past: prepare the machines for the day. Quarter-to: make the ice cream. Don't worry about the how, I'll show you later on. It looks like something you'll never get the hang of at first but after a bit it's simple enough. Seven o'clock: boil the milk and make the custard. Then breakfast, as in your breakfast; never mind filling the bellies of these gannets.'

A roar of protest sounds around the café as a grinning Grace nods at the customers again, all listening, all still packed tightly together around that wooden counter.

'And now you've been up for an hour, which already feels like three and you've still got another eleven to go, maybe even more, and you're starting to think that even a dog shouldn't have to work like this...'

On and on she talks. All those words tumbling out ever faster as the steam from the kettle swirls and the door opens

76

and closes. And as more laughter sounds and more shouts echo, all of a sudden it's as if I'm standing outside my own body again and then, suddenly, I'm what seems to be a million kilometres away, in another world, or at least what feels like another and totally different world at this moment.

I'm back in my small room, looking up at the castle. I'm back in my home square, feeling the sunshine on my face, seeing my mother's tears and seeing my father and my brothers trying to hide their own.

Then mine come. Tears I've banished for the whole of that long journey from my old home to this; tears I don't even know are inside me, but they are and now they fall.

Enrico is so kind and he tries to make me feel better, he really does. He takes me into a small whitewashed room at the back of the café, sits me down and takes my hand and out they pour. All those honeyed words, and in my own language; a warm language, not the strange language I've been listening to for the last few hours.

'I know it's not what you expected. But it's not just here, it's not just this place. It would have been the same in London, I promise you, Chiara; everything would have felt just as strange at first.'

I look at him, willing him to make it different; willing him to take all the sights and sounds I've carried with me for the last few weeks and make them all appear before me as if by magic.

'I felt just the same when I first came here. I saw the rain and the dirt and I thought, what's happened to all those stories I've been told, about a land where dreams come true?'

Enrico leans closer still and for a moment it's like being home again, back in my small bed at the top of the house with Mamma fussing over me and Papà bringing me food.

'But this is the promised land. It may not look like it at

77

the moment, but you need to see below the surface. You just need to search for it, that's all.'

Finally, I find my voice as I look into his eyes.

'And that's a promise, Enrico?'

Those kindly eyes glow again and he nods.

'It's a promise.'

It doesn't make any difference. Still those same tears flow. For the next few hours, as Grace keeps running in, bringing with her all sorts of strange lotions and potions and drinks that taste more like food, and as Enrico keeps talking to me and fussing over me, I don't think they're ever going to stop.

Frankie

IT'S EARLY MORNING and I've been here since eight. Uncle Tony opened two hours before that. He's always opened early. He reckons that way he'll catch some trade as everyone goes off to work – takeaway coffees – bacon rolls – even just a packet of cigs. Now no-one's going off to work because there isn't any, not to speak of anyway, but Tony still opens up. Old habits die hard, I suppose.

'I remember one of my old regulars telling me about this young couple once.'

Tony joins me at the counter. It must have looked pretty impressive when it was new, all that polished wood stretching one whole side of the café. Now it's like everything else. Worn and pock-marked and way past its sell-by. I told him that once, but as he pointed out, what difference does that make when no-one'd buy it anyway?

'They'd come in for three hours each and every evening. Six o'clock on the dot they'd be here, sitting themselves down smack bang in front of the stove.'

Tony nods towards the centre of the room. He calls it a stove but to me it looked more like a pot-bellied saucepan with a kettle on top.

Tony shakes his head, half-amused, half-sad.

'Every night they always ordered the same thing too. Just the one pork pie with two plates and two sets of knives and forks. Then they'd settle down for the evening.'

Tony keeps looking round the empty café and now I can see the effort it's taking him to keep pasting on that smile.

'Half a pork pie each. Sometimes I think I'd settle for that.'

I nod back at him.

'Makes you wonder why you keep me on.'

'I still need help, Frankie.'

'Or you reckon I do.'

'This isn't a charity. How can it be? I don't pay you enough.'

'Shouldn't be paying me anything, amount of work I do these days.'

'Yeah, well, it's better than –'

And now Tony's hesitating and I can see what he's thinking. He really doesn't need to say it, so I say it for him.

'Nights out with the girls?'

'I was going to say, nothing.'

No, he wasn't. I know it and he knows it, and he knows I know it, but neither of us push it. Tony just looks out of the window at the Chinese across the street instead, and shakes his head.

'What have they got, Frankie? Saturday nights, it's packed to the rafters. Half an hour – an hour sometimes – most of them have to wait, but they don't mind. I watch them, standing out in the rain they are sometimes, and all for a soggy spring roll and a mouthful of bean sprouts.'

Then, miracle of miracles, the café door opens, the bell – restored – ringing again as a customer – an actual customer – comes in. Another miracle. I unpeel myself from the counter as a woman approaches, nodding back at Tony as I do so.

'There's your answer, Tone. Start knocking out prawn crackers with the espresso.'

Tony, grinning now, nods back.

'Skinny Cappucino with a shot of vindaloo.'

I manage a more or less welcoming smile at the woman as she comes up to the counter. She's from our estate, lives a few streets away. I can't remember her name for now, but one of her kids, Michael I think, hangs around with Tyler.

I pick up a dog-eared pad and get ready to take her order. The next thing I know, I'm crashing back against the rows of bottles and jars behind me as the crazy cow smashes me in the face.

'What the – ?'

'You tell your Tyler –'

For a moment I can't do a thing, let alone tell anyone anything. I just lie on the floor, staring up at her as she stands over me, spit flecking her lips, her cheeks all red and mottled.

''Cos if you don't, that's just for starters.'

'What are you doing?'

That's Uncle Tony which, even in the state I'm in right now, strikes me as a pretty stupid question. It's obvious what she's doing. She's right in the middle of inflicting a particularly nasty bit of not-so-casual GBH. What she's doing isn't exactly the issue – why the fuck she's doing it, that's what I want to know.

'And it won't be me next time, it'll be my husband. You just thank your lucky stars I haven't told him about this yet 'cos if I had, bits of that feller of yours'd be spread out all over the rec.'

'What the hell's wrong with you, you stupid bitch?'

My teeth feel like they're rattling around inside my mouth. And now I'm using my tongue to explore a bit more closely, I can feel one tooth actually rattling around my mouth. Then I finally manage to get my brain – which also feels like it's rattling round inside my throbbing head right now – into some kind of gear.

'What's wrong with me?'

Elaine: that's her name – I've finally placed her. Elaine from a few streets away, has a husband called Dean who everyone calls Pit Bull for reasons which, right now, I really don't want to think about. Elaine's obviously pretty handy herself with the old left jab but from the little I've glimpsed of the Missing Link that passes as her other half, I've absolutely no doubt that she's a total amateur compared to him.

'Ask your Tyler.'

'What's Tyler done?'

'Ask him.'

More spit sprays from her mouth, spattering the counter, the bottles behind the counter and my face.

Meanwhile Uncle Tony, God bless him, makes another attempt to sort things out.

'Look – can we please all just calm down here –'

'And don't you start interfering neither, you Iti bastard.'

And that's typical, that is. Born and bred in this town, has only ever gone back to the land of his distant ancestors on his annual holidays, but he's still a man apart and always will be.

Spit's now flecking Tony's face too, and he's blinking under the onslaught as he also receives the full force of what Elaine clearly feels to be her justifiable fury.

'Or you'll get what for an' all.'

Then, mercifully, she stops. Not that she has much choice. Because I've never been one of life's natural victims and I don't care if she does have a mean left hook or a husband called Pit Bull, a girl can only take so much.

'Frankie!'

That's Uncle Tony. Whether he's telling me to calm down

too or whether he's telling me to put down his much-prized heirloom, I can't quite decide, but I don't care too much either. The next thing Elaine knows she's sparked out on the floor, smashed over the head by the old copper kettle that sits on that saucepan Tony calls a stove.

Not that it stops the gobby mare. She just looks up at me, woozy now, but with very definitely the same old fire burning in those crazed eyes of hers.

'You ask him. You just fucking ask him.'

I stand over her, Uncle Tony's copper kettle in hand – which now has an Elaine-shaped dent in it – and decide that maybe I will.

One hour later. Tyler's sitting in front of me and Steve's sitting next to us both, although he's about as much use as a chocolate fireguard when it comes to this kind of thing. He always has been when it comes to anything to do with the kids. He reckons I'm best at handling them, which is another way of saying he doesn't really want to know.

Maybe I'm being unfair. Maybe, as they've got older, he's just started to feel more and more out of his depth. Or maybe he's just getting to be more and more of a knob. But right now it's not Steve who's on my mind, but a sulky twelve year old who won't look me in the eye.

'Why did you do it, Tyler?'

'Dunno.'

'Dunno!'

I almost explode and for a minute I think Steve's actually going to say something, is finally going to back me up for once, but then he looks down at the floor instead.

'You've got to know why – Michael's your mate, or at least he's supposed to be.'

'So?'

Which is an advance on Tyler's first response, I suppose, but not too much of one.

'So mates don't usually go round beating holy hell out of each other for no good reason.'

Now Tyler's glancing at Steve like he's asking him to help him out or something, and I look at him too.

'Do you know anything about this?'

'No.'

Then Steve hesitates.

'Not really.'

'What does that mean?'

Then Tyler cuts across.

'He's a flash git.'

'What?'

'Should see the way he ponces about all over the place.'

I stare at him like I'm staring at some visitor from outer space, which is exactly how I'm feeling right now. But I swallow, try and stay calm, try counting to ten before I say another single, solitary, word – because I know that if I'm right on the ragged edge right now then so is Tyler, and I'm not going to get anywhere by just screaming at him.

'So let me get this straight.'

I actually only manage up to eight but who's counting? Tyler certainly isn't. And now Tyler's getting up because he's not only right on the ragged edge right now, he's gone way over it.

'I'm going to my room.'

'You sit down.'

But he doesn't. He just keeps making for the door instead. Steve – still doing his chocolate fireguard impersonation – watches him all the way and, I swear to God, looks like he's on his side in all this, too.

I yell after my retreating son.

'You beat up one of your best mates because you don't like the way he walks?'

The door slams behind Tyler.

My only reply.

Half an hour later again and Steve's making some sort of attempt to defend the indefensible – or at least to try and make me understand just what's behind our son turning into some kind of psycho, and right at this moment in time he really isn't making too much sense.

'It's how he's decked out, isn't it?'

'What are you talking about?'

'Have you looked at him lately?'

'Have I been going round getting up close and personal with twelve-year-old friends of my son, you mean? 'Course I haven't, Steve – I'd get arrested.'

'You don't need to get too up close and personal, not with that one, talk about in your face.'

I'm still staring at him, no more enlightened than I was a few moments before.

'Look at them trainers of his.'

'His what?'

'Looks like he's stepped out of some boy band or something.'

I keep staring at him. As explanation goes I suppose it's something, although that's just about all you can say for it. Because it's still making absolutely no sense to me.

'And that's why Tyler hit him? Because he's got a nice pair of trainers that some kid wears in some boy band somewhere?'

'I didn't say they did wear them, I just said they were the kind of thing they might wear.'

Steve hesitates.

'Expensive. Cost a few bob. Not like them things Tyler runs around in or tries to run around in – have you seen the soles on them? It's only the dirt holding them together.'

'I still don't see –'

But now Steve's shaking his head and going off on a tangent again like he always does, only this is one tangent I really don't want him pursuing, memories of a certain night out in the big city lately still well and truly on my mind.

'Don't know how that Mam of his does it.'

Steve nods at me.

'Or that mate of yours.'

'What mate?'

'Psaila.'

And now I really do want to choke this one off.

'What are we talking about Psaila for, this is your own flesh and blood. Cute little Tyler, that's what everyone always says about him – only he isn't so cute now, is he, and I want to know why.'

But Steve sticks to it.

'She's out all the time too, just like Michael's mum. Buying stuff – spending. And her feller – I see him out too, pubbing it just about every night of the week, clubbing it too when he gets chance. How do they all do it? That's what I don't get.'

I cut across, trying to get his mind back to the main matter of the moment, at least so far as I'm concerned.

'Tyler?'

'They're both in that factory aren't they? Down in Cardiff?'

And I can't help it, I know I should keep my big gob shut but out it comes, just like it always does, mouth like a parish oven again.

'Is that what they say?'

Steve looks at me, puzzled.

'Meaning?'

'For Christ's sake, Steve!'

I try to get back to Tyler but he's looking at me, strangely now. Steve may not be the sharpest tool in the box, but he's not exactly thick either. And I've always been terrible at hiding things.

'Can't you get taken on down there?'

I try again.

'Tyler.'

'Wouldn't need to be for long, just till things pick up again.'

'I've got a job, if you hadn't noticed.'

'In your Uncle Tony's café?'

'Hallelujah. You have.'

'Call that a job?'

'What would you call it?'

'Wouldn't even call it a café. And how much longer is it going to stay open anyway? There's never anyone in there.'

And now I'm really losing patience with this and I yell at the top of my voice towards the upstairs and Tyler's bedroom, although to be absolutely honest it's as much to stop Steve going on about Uncle Tony and dying cafés and factories down in Cardiff that don't exist.

'Tyler! Down here!'

Steve shrugs.

'Don't know why you're the touchy one all of a sudden.'

I shout again.

'Now!'

Steve shrugs again.

'I've heard you telling Tony yourself. There's more life in a morgue.'

Another hour on and I still haven't talked to Tyler. But he

did say he'd talk to his dad, which was better than nothing, so I said yes. Didn't stop me listening at the door though, and it would probably have been better if I hadn't. If I'd felt frustrated talking to Tyler, that was nothing compared to listening to Steve talking to him in my place.

Or – typically, in his case – not really talking to him at all.

'It's just not fair.'

All the time the same silent questions are screaming inside my head from the other side of the door.

What's not fair?

What's he talking about?

And why, for fuck's sake, isn't Steve asking him?

'He gets everything he wants.'

I stare at the closed door in front of me again. So do the kids of bankers, head teachers and prime ministers. What the hell's Tyler going to do, march round to their houses and lay them out too?

'And he's in your face with it all the time as well, telling you what he's got, what he's going to get.'

Still there's silence from Steve. Still he's still not saying a word. What the hell's happening in there, has he fallen asleep or something?

'I didn't even want them trainers.'

What?

That's me, by the way. On the other side of that closed bedroom door, Steve's still doing his Trappist monk bit.

'They don't fit. I knew they wouldn't – Michael's got feet like an elephant.'

'So why did you do it?'

At last – at long, long last – a question from Steve, only it isn't really a question at all. It's difficult to explain, but there's something in Steve's voice that sounds like sympathy, some kind of fellow feeling, as if he understands everything his son is stumbling towards saying to him, as if he doesn't really need any kind of answer at all.

But he got one. It might have been stumbling again and it might have been hesitant and it might not really have made too much sense, but he did get an answer. And maybe it does make sense to Steve – maybe the only person it doesn't make sense to is his stupid mum on the other side of the door, trying to understand something that was already completely inexplicable and was now rapidly becoming totally incomprehensible.

'I just wanted – I don't know –'

And now Tyler's pausing. And Steve doesn't push him, just lets the silence stretch and stretch until I don't think Tyler's going to say another word, but then he does.

'– something.'

And now there's a grunt from Steve.

And not a grunt that's saying, what the flying fuck does that mean? Steve's grunt is different. It's almost like telling Tyler it's OK, that he understands and I can't help it, I truly can't, the next thing I know I've pushed the door open and I'm staring in at them both, huddled together like two naughty schoolkids just let out of class.

'Well?'

Steve looks up at me and there's something in his eyes, and there's the same something in Tyler's eyes now, too – defiance almost, the two of them against the world – which in the case of the here and now means an all too familiar story.

Dad and son against Mum.

'Have you even begun to sort this?'

And now a look's exchanged between them, an exchange of glances that's almost conspiratorial, and now they're looking even more like moody schoolboys.

I try again.

'Steve?'

He nods.

'Yeah.'

'And?'

Which is going to turn into yet another question from me neatly sidestepped, if not completely and utterly ignored by him. Steve stands instead, nodding at Tyler as he does so.

'Come on.'

And Tyler stands and follows him straight away, which is more than he ever does when I tell him to do something like help with the washing up, or tidy his room, or walk his sister to the shops – even though she hates being in his company even more than he hates being in hers. Then his feet drag like he's got some sort of sleeping sickness. But now he's springing up as if he's got the best quality, top of the range trainers underneath him.

'Where are you going?'

'We're going to start sorting this.'

'What does that mean?'

'You'll see.'

'Steve?'

I catch him by the door and grab him by the arm and he looks back at me, but there isn't just defiance in the way he looks at me now, there's something almost approaching pity. Maybe because, deep down and at some level I really don't understand and probably never will, Steve and Tyler have connected. And it's a connection that right at this moment in time I don't feel I'm ever going to understand.

There's this other expression my old mum used to trot out. Whenever she'd see one of the local likely lads strolling past in some new outfit or driving past in some pimped-up hot hatch, music pounding from oversized speakers in the boot, she'd say it.

Cock of the walk.

Four hours later, Steve and Tyler are walking round as if the expression's just been invented and they're the ones that inspired it.

So how's this transformation come about? What's happened in the last few hours to turn Tyler from a mumbling shambles of a kid into a bright-eyed, fired-up you-know-what? Simple. Good old-fashioned villainy. Although there was nothing old-fashioned about the stroke Steve had pulled. Even I had to admit there was the whiff of genius about it.

Which made the fact he'd involved our son in it all – our twelve-year old son, for Christ's sake! – even worse.

Three hours earlier – and one hour after leaving our small terraced house clinging to the side of a hill – Steve and Tyler are outside a supermarket.

This isn't a supermarket in our home town. This is a supermarket a long way away, on the road heading for the border where the fields are greener and the pickings are a lot, lot, richer.

As Steve and Tyler are just about to prove.

When they first came back, Steve stinking of booze, Tyler dressed head to toe in labels I'd never even imagined buying, I thought my husband's finally done it. He's finally sunk to the lowest of the low. Not only has he gone thieving, he's taken our son out on his first bit of serious stealing too. At least I assumed it was his first. For all I knew, maybe he was already a seasoned campaigner in the have-it-on-your-toes stakes.

Steve sways in the doorway as I fire the accusation at him, and just looks back at me for a moment, injured innocence once again in his eyes. What did I take him for, he wants to know? A common or garden tea-leaf? Give him credit, he pleads. And then out it comes, the whole story, some supplied by Steve, some supplied by Tyler, who obviously thinks this is just about the neatest trick he's ever heard in his short life.

Not that it stops me being every bit as appalled as I would have been if they'd told me they'd heaved a house brick through the window of the Bargain Booze shop across the road from Tony's café and had it away with a few cases of Jameson's finest.

For this scam to work you need a really nice class of clientele, which explains them heading for that upmarket supermarket in the middle of all those green fields. Once they got there, Tyler and Steve had stood outside, buckets in hand, which Steve had decorated with a home-made slogan: Rugby Trip to Canada. At least I think it was Canada. And I think it was rugby. It didn't really matter. For the next hour they were, apparently, collecting on behalf of some local team that wanted to send its young players off on some overseas tour somewhere.

They might have collected a few coins if that had been the limit of their fairly paltry ambition, but Steve had much bigger fish to fry than that. And he wasn't interested in charity hand-outs either. As he made clear to anyone and everyone who emerged from the inside of that air-conditioned supermarket, him and his boy were there to work.

And they did. They escorted the shoppers – almost exclusively ladies who drove equally exclusive cars – back to their upmarket motors. The ladies stood by them as Tyler unpacked their trolley and secured their purchases neatly in the boots of their Chelsea tractors. All the time Steve kept an eagle eye out for what he was really interested in, the all-important till receipt, and most times he found it too, usually thrown carelessly in some bag somewhere.

Then Steve palmed the receipt as he stood with Tyler to wave the grateful shopper away.

Most were useless so far as they were concerned. It took them a few such trips and a few such encounters to bag the main prize. But when it came it was worth the wait.

They'd nearly used a receipt they'd come across a few moments before. There were a few items on there they really didn't want – a single goose egg for one thing, costing over a fiver? – but then Steve spotted a much more promising target.

The lady in question was stocking up for a birthday party. But she didn't want her husband – in whose honour the party was being thrown – to know anything about it, so all her purchases were paid for in cash. It was a special birthday too – he was just about to hit the big five-zero – and she was pulling out all the stops.

That much Steve gleaned from her as they helped load the cartons of booze – ultra-carefully – into the boot of her gleaming Beemer. Steve responded in turn with a few details regarding the rugby trip his son was about to embark on with his mates in the team as he casually palmed her till receipt too which she'd probably have just chucked away anyway. Tyler even played his part with a description of some of the choicer victories his team had enjoyed lately. As Steve told me later, chest puffing with pride, the boy was a natural.

Then it was back into the store with that till receipt in hand and they matched it all, item for single item. Then they simply wheeled the trolley, with matching receipt, back outside again.

There was a checkout time printed at the bottom of the receipt, of course, which could have provided a difficult moment if they'd been challenged by any of the security guards, but Steve even had a story all ready and waiting for that eventuality too. While they were stacking the boxes in their car – which wasn't actually our car at all but Uncle Tony's, borrowed for the evening – they'd found that one of the bottles they'd bought had a chip in it. So they'd come back into the store to change it and decided to check out the new TVs on offer in the electrical department while they were there.

As it happened, they weren't challenged. They simply walked away with all their purchases, the duplicates of which had already been paid for by a grateful lady who didn't want her husband to know she was throwing him a surprise. Then they took what they'd managed to filch around all the local clubs and pubs – local to us, that is, not to the lady who was about to party – pocketing a tidy little sum for their efforts along the way.

And then, best of all – and this was the bit Tyler enjoyed more than anything – they'd gone to visit his former mate, Michael. Steve had insisted, promising Tyler this would be just about the sweetest bit of the whole day, and it quite clearly was the absolute icing on the cake if the expression on Tyler's face as he told me all about it was anything to go by.

After visiting a local clothes shop and decking Tyler out in the latest trainers and a few others items besides, Steve steered him towards Michael's house. Outside, he'd told him to play it absolutely straight just like he had done for the past few hours, and as those past few hours had obviously been one of the very best experiences of our son's life up to that moment in time, Tyler had absolutely no hesitation in doing exactly what his now quite clearly adored father was telling him to do.

Steve composed his face. Tyler shuffled his expensively clad feet. As the door opened, Steve told Michael's mum that his son had come to make an apology. In person. To Michael and to herself for all the grief he'd caused. And Steve had come along to make sure that apology was delivered and in the right spirit too. There were to be no half-mumbled expressions of regret. Tyler had to be taught a lesson here and Steve was there to make sure that lesson was well and truly learnt.

Tyler was led into the small kitchen at the rear. He stood in front of Michael and his mum and recited the handsome apology he'd rehearsed – giggling all the while – with his dad a few moments before. Steve tried to keep from giggling himself as he registered the expressions of blank incredulity on the faces of Michael and his mum as they took in the ultra-expensive trainers Tyler seemed to have acquired from somewhere – a definite cut above Michael's offerings – not to mention the brand new Jack Wills top and the equally new O'Neill T-shirt.

Steve didn't think Michael heard a single solitary syllable of Tyler's apology. He might as well have been reciting the phone book for all that was sinking in inside that small kitchen at the rear of that tiny terraced house.

And then Steve and Tyler had left. And, to give them credit, they'd managed to hold their uncontrollable laughter until they'd turned the corner at the end of the street but it had, apparently, been one fuck of a close-run thing.

Chiara

EVERYTHING'S STILL A blur. Literally. A fog of steam, smoke, laughter, yells, catcalls and cheers. Sometimes that laughter and those catcalls seem to be directed at me. Usually if they are, it's because of some misunderstanding on my part: an incorrect expression, an inappropriate response to the expressions of others. It's the same sport the world over, I suppose: revelling in the limited vocabulary of the long-distance traveller.

I learn something else too, in those early days in Carini's, and it's Grace who teaches me.

'What are you doing?'

'Making the ice cream.'

Grace looks at me.

I am, and I'm not – and Grace knows it too.

The ice cream produced in Enrico's café is made on the premises in a small back room. It's produced by a hand-operated machine which consists of nothing grander than a large wooden tub with a central cylinder inside. This is the freezer compartment. Around it is packed a mixture of ice and salt. Place the ingredients inside the cylinder – but keep them secret, as Enrico always warns me (and I do: even now I can't bring myself to write them down in case someone might see them) – and then stir, and stir again with a handle until the ice cream forms. Then scoop it out and take it through to the customers in the café.

The first time I did it, I stood in that small whitewashed room, suddenly rooted as if out of the ether I heard Papà's voice telling me all about Marco Polo first bringing ice cream back to Italy from his one of his expeditions to China. And for that moment I simply stared across at the door, not seeing anything from the world I was now living in, because all I was seeing all of a sudden was the world I'd left behind.

But then Grace came in, and I told her the latest batch was ready. She did what she always does: took it through, to the accompaniment of another bout of cheers and catcalls and stamping of feet as it appeared, as if some visitation from the gods had suddenly manifested itself. A blast of sunshine from a foreign shore.

And maybe it is. Enrico's ice cream – in all its different incarnations and with all its different flavours, not to mention its oh-so-secret recipe – brings a welcome echo of the exotic to a world where, at the end of their shift, all the men look exactly the same in their soot-stained overalls and with their faces caked in black dust.

Not that I heard the catcalls and the cheers and the stamping of feet. By then I was too busy making the next batch of ice cream, locked away in my cocoon, that brief interior glimpse of home still with me.

By the door, Grace is still just eyeing me.

'No you're not, you're skulking away.'

Skulking?

She was doing it again. They all did; not just Grace, but everyone in the café: throw in all those phrases I couldn't possibly understand. Was it deliberate? Back in my much-missed home, did they seriously imagine Professoressa Quadrelli would take down an English dictionary from that rickety wooden shelf above her desk and tell her bewildered pupils that today we were all going to learn the meaning of that famous old English word, *skulking*?

I'm doing it again, aren't I? Talking for the sake of it. Using words as some kind of shield. I know exactly what Grace means; and she knows I do from the way my face is colouring and the way I'm growing hot all over, as I always do when someone catches me out. And as she keeps on looking at me, I grow hotter still, even though I'm standing just inches away from a freezer lined with yet another batch of ice cream.

I nod to the ice cream: one last stab at staving off what I now strongly suspect is going to be the inevitable.

'Take it through. It'll spoil if you don't.'

Grace is still staring at me. At first I think I'm in for another lecture. I've had a few of them in the last couple of days and could practically repeat word for word everything she'd say.

They don't mean anything, it's just their way. They're not laughing at you, not really. They laugh at everyone. It's how things are round here: there's precious little else to laugh about, so everyone makes their own amusement.

Right. Mainly at the expense of a young Italian girl with a vocabulary that seems to provoke helpless mirth every time she opens her mouth.

Grace nods at the ice cream herself.

'You take it through.'

I just turn back to the machine. At the door Grace hesitates a moment longer, her stare challenging me all the while. Then, just when she's about to insist (I can actually see it in her eyes), the door opens behind her and Enrico pops in with a letter for me before hurrying back to the counter again.

There have been letters from home before. News from the town, reports about Luigi and Peppo and all they'd been getting up to. But this one's different. Not because of what's in it; not because there's any particularly memorable or earth-shattering news to impart, but because of the smell.

I know Mamma has taken to going into my old room at the top of the house to write to me, sitting on the same seat hand-carved into the wall that I used to sit on. On this occasion, quite obviously the charcoal burners were at work while she was doing so.

The moment I pick up the envelope, I can smell it. Suddenly, as that all too familiar smell assaults my nostrils again, I'm back there: in my small room, in my home, with Mamma, with all of them. The next moment, without my realising it's happening, the writing on the front of the envelope begins to dissolve as my tears once again begin to fall.

It's ridiculous and I know it. I keep telling myself that, but it makes no difference. Every other time I've smelt those acrid fumes, they've felt like they were burning the inside of my throat. Even on the hottest days I've jumped up and closed the windows, trying to shut them out. Today I sink down on to a stool and bring the envelope, already sodden, up to my nose and breathe it in and I feel those tears fall all the more freely. This is even more ridiculous and I know that too, but I do it all the same. It's a smell I've hated all my life. Now it seems I can't get enough of it.

I remain there like a statue for what seems like hours. Grace comes in to see me again to fetch the latest batch of ice cream, and just stands there looking at me, more and more alarmed. Then she calls Enrico because something awful must have happened: there must be some terrible news from home. Why else would I be sitting there in that small whitewashed room with a letter in my hands with tears rolling down my cheeks, refusing (unable, indeed) to speak?

Enrico knows why. He knows the moment he sees me. Perhaps he's had that same feeling wash over him too: the feeling I first sensed, albeit briefly, when I heard my father's voice inside my head telling me once again about Marco Polo. The feeling that totally overwhelmed me when I smelt the charcoal on Mamma's letter. The feeling of being no part of that world any more, at the same time as feeling no part of this one.

Enrico coaxes me, gently, to my feet. Then he opens the rear door and we go outside to walk, leaving a worried Grace to look after the customers.

Enrico doesn't speak to me at first, just keeps company with me all the way. All the time we keep on moving, I don't see the streets we're walking down or the people we pass. I see the castle towering high above my home and the struggling ox across the valley, and I smell the charcoal again now too. It's like a huge weight crushing down on my chest, an ache inside that feels more like a void. It's as if I've become nothing all of a sudden, as if I don't exist. As if I'm floating inside a world that isn't real, and I've never felt anything like it before.

All I can think about is home, but when I do finally speak, I don't talk about it. I talk about a small girl in my old school instead. I've not thought about her in years, but as I begin to tell Enrico all about her, I start to realise that maybe I've not actually stopped thinking about her for a single day.

She was my age, around eight years old, and in my class. For some reason she latched onto me in the way children do sometimes. She followed me everywhere.

For a time, I didn't do anything. I didn't talk to her, didn't really take too much notice. Then she became impossible to ignore any longer and I rounded on her, asked her what she wanted. She just stared at me, eyes wide, and didn't reply. I turned away, expecting her to slink away, rebuffed; but she didn't. She followed me again. Every time I stopped, she stopped. Every time I stared at her, she just stared back at me. I enlisted help from other children in the class, pointing her out, encouraging their taunts. All the time those wide eyes never left my face.

Enrico just listens. He doesn't pass any judgement, doesn't offer any comment or attempt any sort of explanation. It wouldn't have mattered anyway; I wouldn't have heard him if he had. I just start talking again, moving on from one injustice inflicted in the past to another currently being endured. Perhaps this is why she popped into my head in the first place. My mind is racing now, my words tumbling over each other as my tongue lashes out.

'Why do they call your café 'Bracchi's'?'

They did, I'd heard them. Even with Enrico's actual name on the door, it was all they said out on the street as they headed there before or after work: *See you at Bracchi's.*

'You're not a Bracchi. Can't they read, don't they know your name? And if they do, don't they care? Why do we even call it an Italian café anyway? What's Italian about it? All we serve is Oxo and Bovril and tea. If we offered anyone a coffee they'd look at us as if we'd sworn at them. The cigarettes are British: Will's Gold Flake and Players. The chocolates are all British: Fry's and Cadbury's and Rowntree. I don't understand.'

By now we're high up on one of the hills that looms above the town much as the castle towered over our home town. Finally, as my words slow and my mind begins to settle, Enrico starts speaking too, soft and warm, as always, responding not to what I was saying but to all that was underneath.

'It's a sickness, Chiara.'

I look back at him.

'It's a sickness and it's crept up on you without you even realising it. Only for this kind of sickness there's nothing you can take. No pills, no potions. You can't consult any doctor or a nurse, but that doesn't mean there isn't a cure.'

Enrico nods at me.

'There is and it's a simple one. It's called time.'

I look back at him, now only taking in one word in every two he's saying.

'I caught it before you. A lot of people I've talked to who've done what we've done, they caught it too. But eventually it leaves you and infects someone else, just like it's doing right now with you.'

Enrico leans ever closer to me.

'You're homesick, Chiara. It's as simple as that. Only it's not simple at all, not really. Sometimes it happens straight away, the moment you get off the boat. Sometimes it doesn't happen for so long, it seems it's not going to happen at all. But it's still lying there inside, waiting, and one day, something unexpectedly ambushes you. Sometimes it's something big like a birthday or an anniversary or Christmas; and the strange thing is, you've lived through them before, so why this particular one should hit you in that way is something you just don't understand. But it doesn't matter, because it has and from the moment it does, all you can think about is the home you've left. Every second of every day after that, all you can think about is going back. Only you can't and you know you can't, because there's nothing for you there. If there had been, you wouldn't have come here in the first place.'

I break in, repeating just the one single word in all he has just said that I'm clinging onto.

'Time.'

Enrico nods.

'Once it happens to you, it's the only thing that makes a difference.'

I keep looking at him.

'How much time?'

Enrico looks back at me, hesitating now.

'It's different for everyone.'

'How long was it for you?'

Enrico pauses again, looks out over the town we've both adopted stretching out below us, and doesn't reply.

The next morning I'm back in that whitewashed room making the ice cream again. Grace is coming in, fetching the latest batch, heading out to the packed café. The walls seem to be closing in more and more all the time.

I walk out halfway through the latest batch. It'll spoil, I know, but I can't help it. I walk back in three hours later and have no idea where I've been and no-one asks me. No-one mentions the spoiled ice cream either.

I wouldn't have heard them if they had. All I can see is my old room and my mother sitting on that seat hand-carved into the wall, writing to me. Sometimes she's writing the letter that started all this, this sickness that Enrico describes. Sometimes she's not writing anything at all, just sitting there, a pen in her hand, paper on her lap. It's like I can reach out and touch her, only I can't.

Sometimes I see behind her, out of the window itself, and I see that single ox ploughing yet another downward furrow before resting, exhausted. Another sight I'd seen every day for as long as I could remember. Another sight now denied anywhere except in my mind's eye.

Time passes, or at least I think it does. Sometimes, when I'm walking, I think a single day has gone by since that earlier walk with Enrico up on to that hill. Sometimes I think a week has passed. I don't know, and once again I don't care.

'He.'

Grace tries to help, in her own way. Enrico takes me out for walks; Grace gives me English lessons.

I repeat the single word back to her.

'He.'

Grace's lessons always follow a very particular pattern. A young man (usually a miner) comes into the café, takes his place at the counter and Grace beckons me over, her face solemn. Then she nods across at him, just out of earshot (or so I hope) and instructs me to repeat, word for word, the sentence she's about to teach me.

'Over there.'

I glance across at the young miner, who must by now sense the two pairs of eyes on him from across the café, but that doesn't deter Grace. She has a lesson to get through. It's her duty, and she is not going to fail in her task.

I nod back.

'Over there.'

'Has got.'

I falter a little, but only a little for now, repeating her words once more.

'Has got.'

Grace lowers her voice for the final segment of the lesson but I'm sure to this day, and from the way the young miner's ears now start to colour, that he hears each and every word.

'A beautiful bum.'

By now I'm giggling so much I can't do it. I can't parrot back to her the words she's just intoned in that so-solemn voice that sends me into fits of hysterics all by itself. However, Grace is a stern task master, I soon learnt that. There's a determination in her that will brook no obstacle, and I'm going to have to finish my lesson and I know it.

Gasping all the while, I try.

'A beautiful –'

Still I can't do it, and my hysterics only increase as Grace looks at me, almost sadly, cocking her head to one side in the way an aged tutor might look at a backward child, more in pity than in anger, before telling me that now I have to say the whole sentence, omitting no words, from start to finish.

I do. It takes another two minutes, by which time the whole café is staring at two girls in the grip of uncontrollable fits of giggles, not just the young miner, whose ears really are now tinged bright red. Finally I manage it, in between more great gasps and splutters.

By which time the owner of the beautiful bum has left his seat and is heading for the door. As we watch him go from behind the dark oak counter I can see that once again, as in most things, Grace is absolutely right.

Then, one second later or so it seems, as the door swings closed behind him, I smell that same charcoal smell again, borne in on the wind somehow, a smell from a country many hundreds of kilometres away, and my smile vanishes and that void is back, the brief distraction provided by Grace's latest lesson wiped, the all too brief interlude over.

Sometimes another distraction filled the void. I soon learnt that although the café was always packed, Enrico didn't actually make much money. At most times it seemed more a place of retreat than anything else. Most of his customers seemed to treat it as a meeting place and on different evenings, different groups would congregate.

Sometimes an earnest band of strange-looking brothers would sit down and debate the politics of the day. At other times a teacher would hold what looked like a small class for young adults keen to improve their minds. It seemed the supreme irony. I'd travelled what felt like a million kilometres to get to a place which all its inhabitants wanted to get away from in turn. Perhaps it is the same the whole world over. Perhaps everyone has dreams of leaving, whatever their circumstances and wherever they may be.

How could Enrico make any money, in truth? A packet of cigarettes sold for a penny, a quarter of sweets even less. Even the favourite of the absolute favourites (the Five Boys chocolate bars) changed hands for a pittance.

There was one couple who used to come in each night. They'd sit by the stove for at least three hours each evening, day in, day out. During the whole of those three hours they'd buy one pork pie, asking for two plates, two sets of cutlery and two cups of tea. They were saving for their wedding, they explained. I once tried to work out just how much they were spending per hour while they were in the café, but Enrico just smiled and told me to leave them alone, so we did.

However, Enrico was nothing if not enterprising. A cinema opened in another town nearby, and for a time Enrico worried that a lot of his customers would surely head there in the evening rather than making their nightly visit to us. If the customers wouldn't come to him, the solution was simple: we must go to the customers. So that night, Enrico and myself carried trays packed full of tiny tubs of ice cream along with sweets and all manner of sticky treats into the cinema itself. Enrico negotiated a share of the proceeds with the manager and we managed to sell out of all our stock halfway through the second reel. After that, Grace and I went every Friday and Saturday night with our wares.

All the time, Grace was my constant companion. Each and every day she was at my side, sometimes bullying me, sometimes chiding me, sometimes pushing me to do all I knew I should do, and all I wanted to do deep down. To talk to that person, to go to that place, to climb that hill, to visit that shop, to stay on after our stock had been sold and lose myself in the final reel of this wonderful world of film.

For a few moments, it would work. For those few moments, I stared up at the screen or walked up a hillside, that ache inside forgotten. Then something would happen: a shaft of light would illuminate a seat in front of me as the door to an exit opened, smoke from a newly-lit cigarette would snake my way, and that would be that.

That void again. That ache once more. Still there, just waiting for its moment to ambush me again.

I do try, I really do.

One morning, as Grace comes into that small, whitewashed room to collect the latest batch of ice cream, suddenly it happens. A voice I don't recognise calls her back. Then a person I don't recognise either takes the tub from her and walks on into the café instead. As I walk in, all conversation seems to cease and all eyes seem to swivel my way.

Then comes a voice, and this one isn't in my imagination. This time the voice of one of the men sitting around the pot-bellied stove sounds loud across the room, clearly scenting sport.

'So what flavour is it?'

Now all eyes are turning my way. Grace has now appeared behind me and I sense her, wary, keeping watch, ready to head off any of the more boisterous excesses that might be hurled my way from a misplaced word on my part, an odd-sounding phrase.

Then, from somewhere, comes another voice I once again

don't recognise, as I look the grinning man full in the face, hold out a spoon and say just one word.

'Guess.'

Enrico was a few kilometres away at the time. Every morning he left Grace in charge of the café. There was a market in one of the other towns over the hill which sold different wares on different days of the week: sometimes livestock, sometimes produce, sometimes crafts and other homemade goods. But it didn't matter what was being sold on the stalls. Markets of whatever description meant one thing and one thing only to the hard-working and perennially hard-pressed Enrico: people. People with bellies to fill and pockets to empty.

Not that they'd be handing over a fortune for a cornet of home-made ice cream churned to a secret recipe by an Italian girl in the rear of his café, but they emptied enough small change from those often-threadbare pockets to justify the effort.

Enrico lived by a strict and self-imposed rule. If he sold all the ice cream on his handcart, he treated himself to a train ride home out of the day's takings. If he was left with ice cream to sell, then he completed the return journey on foot selling, or attempting to sell, his remaining stock of ice cream (often at rapidly decreasing prices) along the way.

On this particular day he hadn't sold his last remaining cornet until he was turning the corner at the bottom of our street. He was exhausted, having just completed a ten-mile round trip pushing the handcart. He'd been working for eight hours already and had at least another six to go. It didn't look like they were destined to be trouble-free hours either.

Enrico looked towards his café, alarmed, because what sounded like a mini-riot seemed to be going on inside. He immediately abandoned his empty handcart, forgot all about his aching feet and fairly bolted for the door, pushing in past customer after customer. He stopped dead as he came up to the counter, to find a young girl he'd recently brought across from his home town in the middle of orchestrating some strange sort of mass game in which grown men, some actually wearing blindfolds, were being commanded to sample different flavours of ice cream. They were allowed to keep the small tub if they guessed its flavour correctly, but had to pay a forfeit (in the form of a single farthing) if they guessed wrong, the whole café ringing with laughter and cheers as they did so.

Laughter's so strange: I began to understand that then. It can sound so hostile, mocking; can make a strange world even stranger. Until you start laughing too. Laughing along with the laughter. All of a sudden, I'm starting to see that what Grace is saying is true.

No-one's laughing at me. Not really. Just as I'm not really laughing at the helpless grown men before me, their mouths smeared with all those different flavours of ice cream I've produced in my self-imposed exile in the back of that café. Across the café, his aching feet forgotten, all the tiredness of that day banished, Enrico is now laughing along with everyone else, his deep voice booming, those kindly eyes of his glowing ever brighter.

It's not the end of the excitement that day either. A large parcel is then delivered and, bursting with pride, Enrico tells Grace and me to open it, in front of the whole café. Inside is a fountain made of mock-marble with several taps each dispensing a different flavour of cordial, all courtesy of a supply of soda water using bottled gas. So it is that I first make my acquaintance with a strange-sounding, and even stranger-tasting, drink called sarsaparilla.

I'm the first to try it, my reward for my efforts that day.

I screw up my mouth, then relax, as it's nowhere near as bad as I expected. Again, laughter rings round the café as everyone watches, and I laugh with them – which is when, in the middle of everything that's good and innocent and fun, it hits me again, as if it's been waiting for just that moment, the moment my defences are totally down.

No-one else sees my smile start to fade, but Enrico does; and no-one else there would ever understand why apart from him.

Late on Sundays, because that's our busiest day of the week by far, Grace and I head off in the early evening high up into the hills above her home town (now my adopted town), far away from all those packed houses on all those grey streets.

This is when I see that the place really does possess its own kind of beauty after all and, in truth, it's a beauty that matches anything I remember in my own home. From up here I can see a valley sheltered by mountains that seem to stretch up and touch the sky, and there are trees and grass and ferns everywhere I look.

On those same early evenings there are people all over that mountain too. Groups of girls, dark-eyed and animated, saunter along arm in arm in search of adventure or mischief or both, and young men too, also in groups, well dressed for once, are on the lookout for the same.

This is the moment when Grace hisses in my ear.

'Talk to him.'

I hiss back.

'No.'

Grace nods at another potential quarry.

'OK, him then.'

'Grace!'

'You want to, it's written all over your face.'

'I'm just enjoying the view.'

Grace grins.

'So am I.'

There it is again: that deep, dark, wonderful and oh-so-dirty belly laugh. I can't help it, every time I hear it I collapse in giggles too.

Grace eyes me fondly as yet another group of young men passes by, another opportunity (in her eyes, at least) just slipped through our fingers.

'What is it, are you training to be a nun or something?'

It should be the beginning: the beginning of a transformation for me too. I should be starting to change from a frightened young child, should be starting to see something in this new life that I never experienced in my old one. I should be starting to feel excitement at what might be just around the corner, at what new adventures this new life might reveal to me.

But the moment I allow myself to feel that, the second I sense that excitement rising inside me, it happens again. Insinuating itself deep inside, sometimes faint, sometimes overpowering but always there: that sickness I was told would go, but isn't going. It's just lying dormant inside me, it seems; sometimes for hours, sometimes for longer. Sometimes for so long I think it has finally done what Enrico promised it would do, that it has gone; only it hasn't.

Then, suddenly, all that's driven from my thoughts because without any sort of warning, myself, Grace and Enrico have something else to think about instead.

Grace and I return from our latest Sunday walk to find Enrico hunched over the counter.

Behind Enrico, a figure rises. It's a man I've seen before around the town, a man who's called in on several occasions, in fact; a man who always seems kind and well-disposed to everyone despite the fact he's wearing a police officer's uniform.

Only he doesn't look kind or well-disposed now. He looks more confused than anything else, but that doesn't stop him nodding in silent confirmation as Enrico tells Grace and me that he's being arrested so we are going to have to look after the café for a while as he's being taken down to the police station.

Then Enrico tells us, in a voice that sounds broken, there's no other word for it, that when he returns the café will be closing for good and Grace will have to look for work elsewhere, and I will have to return home to Bardi.

PART THREE

'The Dedication of the Temple'

(Kings 8)

Frankie

FOR A COUPLE of days everything's OK. Actually, things are better than OK. And no, I do not approve of my old man introducing our twelve-year-old son to the dubious delights of supermarket scamming, but I have to admit Steve's nothing if not generous. Too generous, I suppose. If he's got money burning a hole in his pocket, he spends it as if it really is on fire. On me, on Vicky, on Tyler, whatever we want. All any of us have to do is ask.

Vicky's always wanted a pup. Nothing special, just a mongrel will do. I've always put my foot down – how could we look after a dog when we have enough trouble getting to the end of the week keeping anything like a roof over our own heads and food in our own bellies, let alone feeding and housing some four-legged mutt?

But Vicky comes down the morning after Steve's very own version of *Supermarket Sweep* to find a big parcel waiting for her in the middle of the kitchen floor. God knows how he'd done it – Steve told me later the pup was a quick learner, but my guess is he'd just dosed it up with something – but the little thing stayed silent all the time Vicky was unwrapping the box. Then out he comes, barking and licking her all over, and the look on her face – well, let's just say it made it easy to forget how the little darling had actually been paid for in the first place.

And it seems to have helped Tyler turn a corner too. He

actually starts to listen to his dad, and even to me too, so when we tell him to go to school, he doesn't make his usual fuss, he just picks up his bag and heads down the hill to catch the bus. Mind you, that might have been to show off his new trainers more than anything else, but still – it's something.

And, again, it makes it all too easy to forget that if our lives have taken a turn for the better, there's still something really not right in how all that's come about.

My mum always had this thing about karma. About how your deeds or misdeeds follow you round. How it might take months or years for them to catch up with you, but they will in the end. And my old gran used to say, 'Be sure your lies will find you out.' Same thing, I suppose.

In our case it doesn't take months or years. In our case it takes exactly one week. One week of Vicky showing off her new pup to all and sundry, of Tyler showing off his new designer gear, of Steve treating me to night out after night out and of me forgetting, for a short while anyway, that there was such a thing as a financial crash somewhere far away which was nothing to do with us but which we seemed to be paying for, and just losing myself in a life that had suddenly turned into some kind of holiday.

And then it arrives. What my old mum and my even older gran had always talked about.

Karma.

In the not-particularly-appealing shape of a local and dangerously unpleasant chancer called Eddie Thomas.

Eddie used to be a half-decent rugby player. At one time he'd had real prospects, or so a couple of the local coaches had reckoned. Until everyone worked out that it wasn't so much the game he liked as the excuse it gave him to spend eighty-odd minutes hitting people. Then those same local coaches changed their minds. Eddie wasn't a prospect,

Eddie was a psychopath who had no place on a rugby pitch. Meaning Eddie was banned from all the local leagues, which didn't bother him too much as he'd joined his uncle by then in his new and booming business of debt recovery. And there'd been one shed-load of debts to recover lately, with more coming in – so it seemed – by the day. Eddie and his uncle had made sure of it, by branching out into the loan business too.

It was a neat little circle. Lend people money they can't afford to repay, and then lean on them – softly at first, but then harder and harder as time went by – to pay it back in any way they could. For some of the women in this town that meant the train down to Cardiff. The Have-It-Away-Day special, as some local wag christened it. I'd managed to avoid that particular excursion so far, albeit only by the skin of my teeth. But now, crouching under our kitchen table, along with a terrified Vicky and an even more terrified pup – Tyler out with his mates, Steve just out, probably on the lash somewhere – listening to some maniac trying to turn my back door into firewood, I was beginning to wonder how much longer I'd be able to put that off.

It had been, like everything else, Steve's fault. And yeah, OK, my fault too in going along with it all. Tyler's new clothes had been noticed. Vicky's recently acquired pup had been noted. And Steve and myself suddenly turning into party animals had registered too.

And with all the wrong people.

In all the wrong sort of places.

It hadn't been that much of a loan. At least not at the start. Just a hundred quid or so to tide us over. But when we missed a payment and the extra interest was added on to the next repayment, it all began to mount up. And, yes, we should have done the sensible thing – we should have used Steve's windfall, if that's what you can call it, to pay off as much of it as we could. But for those few days after it all fell into our laps, it just felt like time off from all that. Time off from worry, from scrimping and saving, from everything our lives had become in the last couple of years.

Time off from ever more desperate solutions such as that train ride all those nights before.

We needed it, in a way. At least that's how I reasoned it all out if I actually tried to think about it, which if I'm honest I probably didn't – until reality came knocking in the shape of a psycho's fist hitting our back door.

'Are you in there, Mrs Morrissey?'

'Mum?'

A panicky Vicky's clinging to my arm with her one free hand, her other round her beloved pup. He always springs up the minute anyone comes to the door, all ready with the kisses and the licks, but now he's cowering away with the pair of us. Who ever said animals were dumb?

'Ssh, Vicky.'

'I need a pee.'

I stare at her in disbelief.

'What?'

From outside the door, the banging's increasing in volume and the voice that's accompanying it is now beginning to positively drip with menace.

'Mrs Morrissey!'

'I've got to go.'

'Well you can't, not yet.'

From the door the same voice is rising in volume – not to mention menace – all the while.

'You're three weeks behind, there's no point hiding away like this.'

Actually, it was only just over two but I didn't point that out. It would have sort of sabotaged the whole point of hiding under that kitchen table in the first place.

'I'm going to do it in my knickers.'

'For God's sake!'

And all right, I'm being a bit unfair, I know. If we were going off on a trip somewhere and Vicky announced she wanted to pee within thirty seconds of setting off – as she has done on more than one occasion in the not-so-distant past – then I might be entitled to feel a bit annoyed. The fact of the matter is, I have absolutely no right to be angry at all given the fact the poor kid has just been catapulted off her chair and practically bent double under the kitchen table as I spot a human gorilla coming up the garden path, arms brushing the ground. That kind of thing is bound to have an effect – in fact I know it is, because it's having precisely the same effect on me. Which is probably why I want Vicky to stop going on about her bladder. Right at this moment in time, I'm in serious danger of some heavy-duty leakage myself.

The door bends inwards as a fist hits it again.

'Mrs Morrissey!'

And that doesn't help either. Not one little bit. That voice from outside that's sounding more and more manic by the moment, and those bangs on the door that are beginning to sound more and more like the chimes of doom.

So now I'm clinging onto Vicky about as tightly as she's hanging onto her pup, hissing at her all the while.

'Just hold on a couple more minutes. Even Bonehead out there's going to get the message that we're out by then. Then he'll give up and come back some other time.'

I hurry on, registering Vicky's ever more panicked expression, correcting – or trying to correct – my mistake immediately. The last thing Vicky wants to think about right now are return visits.

'By which time we'll have paid what we owe.'

And now Vicky's blinking at that.

'So why would he come back then?'

'What?'

'If we've paid what we owe?'

Yet more evidence if any were needed that, first, my daughter very definitely has a brain and, second, that I'm not very good at thinking on my feet. But it doesn't matter. In a few minutes surely even Eddie's going to have to give this up as a bad job.

The crash roughly ten seconds later, which I discover is our kitchen door being smashed in, tells me I'm wrong.

'What the – ?'

I stand up, forgetting for a moment that I can't actually stand at all, given I'm bent double under a kitchen table. The table somersaults over, exposing Vicky and her pup at the same time, but not for long. The pup does not like the look of Eddie and bolts for the hall, Vicky following a moment later. If I could, I'd follow too, but that's a non-starter right from the word go. There's something in Eddie's stare, not to mention his deep and angry breathing right now, that's telling me his patience is well and truly exhausted and any further attempt to dodge what he sees as a necessary confrontation is not going to be tolerated.

But it's still a diabolical liberty, the damage he's inflicted to our back door.

'So what's this, hide and seek?'

'What have you done?'

'Really are playing games, aren't you?'

'You can't just smash down our back door like that.'

'You can't hide away when you owe someone money.'

'This is breaking and entering.'

'Call that breaking?'

Eddie regards the smashed pieces of what now looks like plywood behind him with a look of what can only be described as total contempt.

'That don't even come close.'

And right at that moment I believe him, I really do.

Vicky appears again in the doorway. Bless her, she could have just run out into the street, but there's a stroppy streak in her and she's not about to abandon her mum just like that. Which means that maybe she isn't all that blessed in the grey-matter department after all, because if she had any sense, she'd have already hightailed it out of there pronto.

'Go away, Vicky.'

'No.'

Eddie doesn't even look at her, he's still looking at me.

'I'm sick of this.'

But – and maybe emboldened now by Vicky – I turn to face him.

'You listen to me.'

'No, you listen to me, you cheating, lying, slag.'

Which is the moment everything begins to change. It might have sounded more than a little threatening up to now – the two of us cowering under a kitchen table listening to the sound of our back door being kicked in – but something's beginning to tell me all that was nothing, and that's as in absolutely nothing, compared to what's about to come next. As more than one of our acquaintances and neighbours has already pointed out, there was more than a touch of the sadist in Eddie, and the sight of a young kid and a helpless woman is very definitely speaking to something evil and twisted in him right now.

The same something that seems to be telling him there

isn't just going to be business conducted that afternoon, but some sport might be enjoyed here too.

In the doorway, Vicky begins to whimper.

'Mum.'

Because it's not just the language, it's the tone. A tone that's turning darker by the second.

'Think I do this for my health, do you?'

Eddie gestures towards the smashed door again.

'Think I stand out there in all weathers because I enjoy it?'

'Mum, please –'

Vicky's telling me to get him to stop, but he's not going to stop because he's only just started, and already I'm beginning to have real fears as to how this is all going to end.

Eddie swings his face her way.

'Shut it.'

'And you can't talk to her like that neither.'

'I said, shut it!'

And now the pup starts whimpering too and there's a weird light that's shining ever brighter in Eddie's eyes as he swings them back in my direction.

'I can talk to you any way I want, Mrs Morrissey. And you know why?'

Eddie leans closer and I swear the scent of raw meat blasts my nostrils. I'm hoping that's down to the steak he probably ate last night while the rest of the town was making do with Pot Noodles, although knowing Eddie it might have been the carcasses of past defaulters.

'Because you've got my fucking money.'

In the doorway, Vicky's whimpering louder and I turn to her, trying to ignore Eddie, whose face is now even closer to mine.

'It's OK, Vicky.'

Eddie cuts across, clearly enjoying this more and more. It's like I'm his stooge all of a sudden, feeding him his lines.

'No, it's not OK, Vicky.'

Eddie strangles his vowels, making a passable effort at mimicking my own voice, pitched – as even I could hear – a good octave or so higher than usual.

'It's not OK at all. When are you going to pay me what you fucking well owe?'

'We can let you have some by the end of the week.'

'What?'

Eddie cups a hand to his ear in an exaggerated gesture of sudden deafness.

'I didn't catch that.'

Meaning it obviously doesn't sound like all that good an offer and now I do some quick mental calculations. Steve's just bought me a couple of presents – a new dress and a bit of costume jewellery. None of it's been worn and I still have the receipts.

'Maybe tomorrow.'

And once again, I've done it. Once more I've fed him just the line he wants, because he pounces on the only word he seems to find interesting right now.

'Maybe?'

He stares at me.

'That's the best you can do, is it? You take my money off me and all you give me back is a "maybe"?'

Eddie shakes his head, changing tack suddenly. Now he's not roaring like a bull on heat. Now he sounds almost saddened. Sorry for himself and for a world in which a man who tries to do the right thing always ends up on the losing side. In other words playing us like the vicious, twisted, bastard he really is.

'How would you feel, Mrs Morrissey? I come to you, I take

your money, I agree to pay you back and when you come to me and say, please can I have what you owe me, what you promised me –'

Neat touch, the "please", isn't it? I don't actually remember anyone saying that.

Eddie spreads his arms, wide.

'All you get back is a "maybe".'

'I don't know what else I can do.'

'You don't know?'

And all of a sudden his tone hardens again, all of a sudden it's like another switch has just been pressed, Mr Nice turning back into Mr Nasty.

At the same time Eddie stares at me, his eyes flickering down my body from my head down to my feet, and for a moment, for one horrible moment, I think the unthinkable.

Surely not – not here, in my own home – not in front of my nine-year-old daughter, for fuck's sake?

But the thought – unbidden and awful as it is – is banished almost as quickly as Eddie turns and starts looking round the kitchen, taking in the drawers overflowing with drawings, school stuff, the occasional letter from the gas and electricity board. The normal family stuff you'd find in any kitchen in any house in this terrace or in this town or any other; and it's normal family stuff that's very much on his weasel brain right now.

'You get child benefit, don't you?'

I just stare at him, not replying.

'Two kids, both well under sixteen. Tyler, he's the eldest, isn't he – what is he now: twelve, thirteen?'

'Twelve.'

That's Vicky, who's now quite clearly falling into my habit of feeding Eddie all the lines he needs.

He nods back.

'And you are how old now, sweetheart?'

'None of your fucking business.'

Good girl.

Not that I approved of the language.

But still, good girl.

Not that Eddie seems even remotely fazed at being sworn at by a nine year old.

'Doesn't matter – never ask a lady her age, I understand that. But you don't look a lot older than eight or nine to me.'

Then Eddie turns back to me.

'So I'll ask you again, Mrs Morrissey. You still get child benefit, don't you?'

The silence stretches and then stretches some more. Because I've seen this before. It happens to more families than I care to think about. Sometimes it's the husband or partner who takes the money. Sometimes it's chancers like Eddie. But whoever takes it, it doesn't really matter – the point is that's just about the only independent money any mum in these parts can count on. It's not a lot, but week in, week out, it's there. A few quid for school dinners, for clothes, for books maybe. It's intended for lots of things. It's very definitely not intended for the likes of Eddie.

'What's the matter, Mrs Morrissey? Cat got your tongue?'

'I need that money.'

Straight back, quick as a flash it comes.

'I need my money too.'

'It's the only thing keeping us going.'

'And what am I supposed to live on, fresh air?'

Eddie stops, hits his brow, reminding himself.

'Oh no, I forgot. I'm supposed to live on "maybes".'

'Please?'

Now I'm starting to unravel.

'Just give us a couple of days.'

'What for?'

Eddie gestures at the kitchen table, still upturned, the remains of our kitchen door still swaying on its broken hinges.

'So you can find somewhere else to hide?'

I take a deep breath, try and sound reasonable which, in the circumstances, really isn't easy.

'Look – I know we've been a bit stupid, and I know we should have come to see you before, but we'll get back on track, back on an even keel and then we can start paying again.'

I might as well have saved my breath. For some reason I have the impression he doesn't find my assurances all that convincing. Which is when I say it again.

'Please?'

And that definitely doesn't help either.

Eddie nods round the kitchen once more, looks out past Vicky towards the hall, where the pup has taken up residence by the door, wanting to be anywhere but here right now but unwilling to leave his young protector, even if he's obviously beginning to wonder if Vicky's actually any sort of protector at all.

'Do you want me to start taking things? Some of the furniture maybe? The TV? Go into your kids' bedrooms and start taking some of their stuff too? Because if that's the way you want to play it, then I will, and I'll be back for whatever you still owe me too.'

'It's the only regular money we've got coming in.'

'It'd still be coming in.'

Eddie gestures across at Vicky.

'Only difference is, it'll be going to pay off your debts not buy fucking ponies for your little girl.'

'We haven't been buying any ponies.'

'Whatever.'

And now there's something else here too. Something else in his tone. And now I'm starting to understand just why this has become such a big deal. It happens every time someone lifts their heads above what some people call the parapet, when they forget – in a phrase I've heard Uncle Tony use time and again – their place.

Briefly, we'd forgotten ours. For a few moments, with money in our pockets, we'd done things. Not just bought things, we'd lived for a change. Lived a life we weren't supposed to be living.

Maybe that's what all those strikes round here all those years ago were about too. It couldn't have been about money after a time, could it? How much would the Coal Board have lost as all that went on for Christ's sake, for all those weeks and months? It couldn't have mattered how much in the way of wages they might have saved, there was no way they could ever make that back. But maybe I was missing the point. Maybe we all were. Maybe, for a short time, people who shouldn't have done poked their heads above another parapet, maybe people who really should know their place had forgotten it and maybe that's why the reaction, backlash, call it what you will, was so strong and devastated so many in the end.

Everyone says it's all about economics. The harsh realities of life. But maybe deep down it's like Eddie and his debts. We're supposed to be his. Bought and paid for. And what Eddie really can't forgive right now is that for a few brief moments we forgot that, and that's what this visit of his is really all about. It's not just a chance to collect a pathetic little bit of money, no matter how important that might be to us right now. It's a chance to remind us who we are. And to remind us who he is too.

Psaila went to some of the bigger loan companies down in Cardiff before she started on the game. In two months, thanks to the interest they charged, she owed twelve hundred quid to some outfit called Pounds In Your Pocket, just over a grand to another lot of chancers called Sameday Money, just under a grand to another great name for a bunch of sharks, Quick N' Easy, and four hundred and fifty quid to Express Cash. At the end of each month she'd pay back the first, then borrow from someone else to pay the second, then borrow from someone else again to pay back the third, and so it went. On and on. No end in sight.

Maybe, compared to some, I still had it easy right now – but it didn't feel all that easy, especially not with the way Eddie was still looking at me from across the other side of that upturned table.

'And what are we going to live on in the meantime?'

'You'll get by.'

'Steve's out of work, almost the whole of this town's out of work if you hadn't noticed.'

'Out of work?'

Eddie grimaces another contemptuous smile.

'Out of his head more like.'

I look back at him.

What the hell does that mean?

But Eddie's moving on because Eddie's always moving on. And he's moving on to the real object of this visit, so far as he's concerned. And now, all of a sudden, there it is again. That same mood switch. That same change in tone.

How many times has he played this scene over these last few months? Put on the good guy/bad guy act? The bad guy's just reminded us of our responsibilities, pointed out our failings, made crystal clear exactly where we've fallen down in our duty.

But now the good guy's here to make everything right again. To lead us out from the darkness. To set us on the one true path, as those crazy nuns of mine used to say back in my old Sunday school.

Lead us into even more shit, more like.

'I'll front you.'

I'm about to ask Mr Neanderthal if he's serious, but I can see it in his eyes. He's deadly serious. And he's deadly serious because it all makes a glorious sort of sense, probably because it restores the natural balance of the universe, at least in his eyes.

Eddie spreads his arms wide.

'All you've got to do is take out another loan to cover this month's interest. I'll roll it up into a new loan along with the rest of the money you owe, then you start paying back next month. Things'll probably have picked up by then. Or maybe that feller of yours will have done a couple more of his scams – only this time, if he does, remind him where his priorities lie in the spending stakes, yeah?'

Eddie spreads his arms wider.

'A month. Just think. Four whole weeks. Twenty-eight days. Things change in a second, isn't that what they say? Just think how much can change in one whole month.'

'We can't pay what we owe you now.'

'You can if you borrow a bit more. Call it an investment. In your future.'

'In your fucking bank balance, more like.'

Eddie shrugs.

'It's a free country, call it whatever you want. So long as I walk out of here with some of my money, or your child benefit book, I really don't care.'

'And if things don't change in a second, or four weeks or twenty-eight days or a month, what happens then?'

And now Eddie smiles, a smile that never even remotely flecks his hooded eyes.

'You'll do it, Mrs Morrissey. You'll pay me back. Everyone always does.'

He nods at me again, deadly intent in his stare.

'In the end.'

Two hours later and Vicky's up in her bedroom cuddling her pup. Tyler still hasn't come in from football. I'm sitting in a chair, a large bottle of red in front of me, but not destined to be in front of me for much longer, not if I have to keep listening to the caged animal that Steve has turned into right now.

The contents of that bottle and any other bottle I can find are going to be inside me and pronto.

'I'll kill him.'

Briefly, I permit the ghost of a smile to play across my face. I can't help it. It's just the thought of it. The man-mountain that's Eddie and my Steve, together in a head to head.

Don't get me wrong, he's a plucky little bleeder. If anyone has a pop at me when we're out, if any drunk comes onto me when he shouldn't, it doesn't matter how big he might be, Steve's in there. But he'd very definitely be punching above his weight with the likes of that one.

Steve catches the look and decodes it pretty easily too.

'You're my wife, for Christ's sake.'

'Leave it, Steve.'

'He can't come in here and knock you about like that.'

'He didn't actually knock me about.'

'OK, he can't come in here at all. Have you seen Vicky? Have you seen that pup of hers? It's pissed itself three times already 'cos it won't go outside for its walk.'

I don't reply. What's to say? Steve's just letting off steam.

I reach out for another glass of *vino* from the last of the bottles Steve and Tyler scammed from the supermarket. And all of a sudden there it is. The same weird change in tone I'd heard from Eddie. Only Eddie was playing games. Steve isn't.

'Frankie – look, I know things have been a bit –'

He hesitates.

'– difficult, these last few months.'

I nod. And some.

'For you, me and the rest of the world.'

'It's only me and you I'm interested in. Well, me, you and the kids.'

'And things haven't been difficult, Steve, they've been fucking impossible.'

Usually he'd hit back straight away with some crack or other. But now he's just looking at me instead, and out it comes, from nowhere.

'I do love you, you know.'

That's Steve all over. One minute he's a raging bull, the next minute he's this soppy sod.

I crack back anyway.

'Spin on it, Steve.'

He knows the rules. We don't do big, meaningful exchanges. It doesn't mean we don't feel things, course we do. We just don't wear our hearts on our sleeves like some couples, snogging each other's faces off in public, walking round hand in hand, sitting in bars or Uncle Tony's café wearing matching anoraks. Me and Steve have always pissed ourselves at all that.

And now, there it is again, another mood swing, another change of tone. Now he's back to raging headcase again, only this time it's not the absent Eddie that's the object of his anger, now it's yours truly who's getting it in the neck.

'I'm just trying to do my best you know. For you, for the kids, for all of us.'

And he is and I know it. Even if, in his book, that meant introducing our twelve-year-old son to the delights of supermarket shopping twenty-first century-style. And then, as suddenly as it blows in, it's like all his sudden rage vanishes again and he's back to being some little lost boy.

'It'll be fine, Frankie. We'll be fine.'

I look at him, mentally replaying that last bit inside my head.

It'll be fine.

We'll be fine.

Two statements.

Two lies.

Chiara

I DON'T BELIEVE it at first. I can't even begin to understand it. Maybe you'd find it easier, but somehow I doubt it. If you do find it difficult to believe and impossible to understand, just think how much harder it must have been for a young girl who came here from a small Italian hill village decades before you were even born.

It began years before with something called the Temperance Movement. Temperance. Even the word sounded strange to my ears. It seemed almost sinister. When I found out it was a name that had been given to a whole movement, it sounded even more so. Up to then I'd associated movements with rivers or the wind. Movements were something that swept all before them, but perhaps that was fitting: this movement was also about to sweep away Enrico's home, his business and his living, and with it Grace's living and my living and my new home too.

Men in Britain like beer. Men in Italy like wine. Different drinks, but they have the same effect; although men in Britain, and some women too, definitely drank more and for far longer at a time than any of the men and the women I knew back in Bardi. It never offended me, but it certainly seemed to have offended others. And they demanded that those who drink must stop, that they must sign what they called a pledge and that they must join a body of people who'd formed that movement, that Temperance Movement.

As a first step, because there always has to be a first step somewhere along the way, they had demanded all those years ago that the Government ban the sale of alcohol on a Sunday, describing it as a desecration of the Lord's Day.

The Government had agreed, but it didn't end there: the strictest of the Sabbatarians then demanded that all businesses close on the Lord's Day. The Reverend Rhidian Keller was among the most zealous of those Sabbatarians, and the most vocal in calling for all businesses to observe the new trading laws.

So it was unfortunate from Enrico's point of view that the Reverend Keller had just been appointed Deacon of the largest chapel in our valley. It was doubly unfortunate that his walk from his manse to that same chapel should have taken the gimlet-eyed cleric past Enrico's café, twice each weekday and four times on a Sunday.

Enrico had affixed the sign in one of the front windows a short time before. Our establishment, it proudly proclaimed, was a Temperance Bar. It wasn't that Enrico held particularly strong views about intoxicating liquor – as with everything else, the gentle Enrico was no zealot. He just wanted to create a relaxed atmosphere, a safe haven where parents could let their children roam free, secure in the knowledge they wouldn't come into contact with drunks, and so had decided from the start not to apply for a licence.

There were still plenty of places where you could drink. All over our town and in surrounding towns too, so-called private clubs had sprung up, and because they were composed of what were also called private members they could flout the laws regarding the sale of strong drink. In that sense, businesses like Enrico's should have been congratulated for offering local people a different place to congregate, a place where the most intoxicating drinks on offer were lime cordial or the locally famed sarsaparilla, but that wasn't how the Reverend Keller saw it. Reverend Keller watched young men and women head in and out of Enrico's café when, as far as he was concerned, they should have been streaming into his nearby chapel. He watched younger children come out clutching bags of sweets when, in his opinion, they should have had their faces buried in Bibles.

'What can I do?'

The policeman with the kindly face and the well-disposed manner looks genuinely troubled, and he is.

'It's no good saying everyone does it – I have – and it's no good saying all the other cafés are doing it – I've done that too – because technically he's right: there is a law, you're breaking it and I'm the poor sod who's supposed to be enforcing it.'

'But you come in here on a Sunday yourself.'

Grace, as is her wont, cuts right to the heart of the matter and Sergeant James (he of the kindly face and the well-disposed manner) is now looking even more troubled.

'Do me a favour, Grace. You know that and I know that, but for God's sake don't tell that flaming minister.'

'But I don't understand. We're not breaking any law: we even have a refreshment licence, look.'

Enrico disappears into his office at the back of the café and reappears a few moments later brandishing the licence. It doesn't allow him to serve alcohol, of course, but he's never tried to do so. It does, however, mean he can provide food and drink for those who don't want to frequent the bogus clubs or who couldn't afford the prices in the few hotels that are still allowed to offer drink to travellers, who were often little more than masquerading locals.

Now I chip in myself.

'Please show Reverend Keller our licence. Tell him this

isn't like a normal café; that we are allowed to open on a Sunday because it says so here.'

Sergeant James just sinks lower in his seat, looking more and more like a despondent bloodhound.

'He's got an answer for that too. Got an answer for everything, that one.'

The policeman winces as if he can hear the Reverend Keller's voice grating in his ear; as it had obviously grated in the ear of his equally long-suffering Chief Constable who, it seems, had then instructed his hapless Sergeant to act.

'If you look here, down at the bottom in the small print, then, yes: it says you can offer refreshment on a Sunday, but it says that any that you do offer has to be consumed immediately and on the premises, or –'

Sergeant James hesitates.

'Or what?'

Now Grace is looking at him, fearful.

'Well, that you can be fined.'

'How much?'

'Five shillings.'

I look at Grace, who looks back at me, the same thought in both our minds. Five shillings isn't a trifle to be discounted lightly, but we take several pounds on a Sunday: it's our busiest day of the week. So maybe this isn't so disastrous after all. If the price of opening on the busiest day of the week is, in effect, a five shilling fine, then maybe we should pay it and just keep on.

'For each offence.'

Now we all just stare at him.

Sergeant James grimaces.

'Reverend Keller's got the Council to introduce a new bye-law.'

Sergeant James nods back at us as the full enormity of this begins to sink in.

'And that's for every child that walks out of here with a bag of sweets in their hand, every young man who walks out with a packet of cigarettes. If anyone has a mind to report them, that's a new offence each time. And for each and every new offence –'

Enrico finishes it for him.

'A five shilling fine.'

Sergeant James doesn't reply. He doesn't need to. I look back at Enrico again and now I realise just why he was looking so defeated when we first came in, and why everything he said then might just be true, and why this might well spell the end of a business he's only begun because he suffered such a cruel reverse in another.

Then the door opens. Looming in the doorway now is the Reverend Keller himself. He doesn't advance any further inside than the door itself. He just stands there looking round, taking in the young couples drinking cordial and the older people drinking tea, while others queue for cigarettes and sweets to take out with them on their travels. He doesn't speak either, but again he doesn't need to. It's obvious what he wants.

He wants to find customers flouting the law, and he has done. Now he has found them, he's going to demand that the local constabulary act, which he now does.

The next Sunday, we're all crammed into the local chapel, just a short distance along the main street from the café. Carini's is still open, but it's been left in the hands of a couple of volunteers who've agreed to look after it while Enrico, Grace and myself join the rest of the Reverend Keller's generally unhappy-looking congregation.

All right, it's a blatant attempt to curry favour, a transparent peace offering. This is Enrico's way of trying to demonstrate to the fiery cleric that we can all get along together if we're so disposed, that we can take our place in his congregation as he can take his place in ours.

Reverend Keller's brand of religion isn't Enrico's and it definitely isn't mine. As for Grace, I'm not altogether sure she has any religion as such. She told us she used to be taken along to a Sunday school when she was small, but she's pretty sure that was only to give her hard-pressed mother some sort of respite from the demands of her and her four other sisters for a precious few hours.

However, Grace plays her part as we play ours. We stand when the Reverend stands, along with the rest of the always-large congregation, intone the responses when he declaims the prayers, and sing the unfamiliar verses to the accompaniment of a reedy organ that's in desperate need of a tune. All the time Enrico tries to look enthusiastic and he nods at us, urging us to do the same.

Then comes the sermon.

I call it a sermon, but it's more of a sustained diatribe, an extended burst of vitriol at those who dare defy the Lord by defiling the one day of the week set aside for His worship. He doesn't name Enrico as such, but he doesn't need to. He describes our café and numerous others just like it in other towns. He describes the temptations they place in the way of souls who would otherwise be directing their thoughts and hearts and minds to the glory of God.

Fat chance, Grace murmurs at this point; a muttered aside that strangles into a yelp as Enrico kicks her shin.

The Reverend Keller rides on regardless. This is clearly his moment and he will not be denied it. Next he brings a newspaper out of his pocket and reads out all the prosecutions that have taken place in just this one town in the course of the previous week, prosecutions he himself has instigated, prosecutions that will continue so long as there are those sacrilegious souls out there who continue to flout the word of their Saviour.

And there's something else here too, behind the thinly-veiled references to those from cultures not native to these shores. There's something uncharitable and very definitely unchristian here, something that looks out on all that's different and distrusts it immediately and wants it banished. I can't help wondering if that's what's really behind all this, every bit as much as a desire to worship a Lord who I'm pretty sure really doesn't care what day of the week a soul's thoughts turn to him.

However, that's of no consequence. All that matters as we file out behind a chastened Enrico, at the end of a sermon that has come more and more to resemble a personal and extended attack, is that war seems to have been declared.

The next Sunday dawns, and with it one of the most amazing sights I've ever seen.

There has always been a constant crush of people passing outside from early morning to late at night. That fabled monkey parade, as a couple of the older residents of the town still call it, indulgent eyes smiling as they remember their own participation in the age-old ritual of boy attracting girl, as girl pretends not to be attracted by any boy at all.

After a week of often backbreaking work in the local mine, in some shop or in service, it's just so good to dress up and parade along the main street looking and feeling for one day at least as if the whole world is at your feet.

The café Enrico's taken over has always been a favourite

staging post on that journey: a place to call in and claim refreshment, a place to meet and talk and begin relationships. Relationships that sometimes led to marriage in the chapel whose newly-appointed minister was seeking to destroy the very place where those relationships had been created in the first place.

Only word has got round. Privately I suspect Sergeant James has more than a hand in it all. He patrols the town from morning to night, talking to everyone from prince (not that there are too many of those) to pauper, of whom there were definitely a fair few. It wouldn't have taken much. A slight shake of the head here, a veiled reference to poor old Enrico there; a sketchy résumé of the campaign that had been initiated against him; a heartfelt expression of sympathy that the man who'd done so much to establish such a loved local landmark was now on the brink of losing it completely, as were they all.

From such small beginnings, movements begin. Movements like the one that was born in the week following our first attendance in Reverend Keller's chapel. The movement to save the local *Bracchi*.

I'd already told Enrico that I'd no idea why everyone always calls it that. There isn't a Bracchi working there, and never had been. Bracchi isn't the name emblazoned on the front, but that doesn't matter because the earliest café owners, the ones who first arrived in the country, were Bracchis from Bardi (where else?) and so everyone who came in their wake had to be Bracchis too. *'See you at Bracchi's'* is the cry you hear the length and breadth of the main street of that town a hundred times every day. The news that perhaps there soon won't be a Bracchi's at all has spread like wildfire and produced the remarkable sight that greets our stunned eyes as we open up that Sunday morning.

People, packed the whole length of the street, all waiting for us to open, all ready to come in and spend their few coppers and defy whatever lunatic law has been invoked to close the one place they can congregate on a Sunday free from the attentions of alcohol-fuelled drunks, where their children can deliberate for hours over their choice of sweets, where sons and daughters can meet other sons and other daughters, where unions can be formed and dynasties created; and all thanks to a place called *Bracchi's*.

No-one makes even a passing reference to Reverend Keller and his campaign. I see the gentleman in question as he passes on his way to his chapel, stopping in amazement (and not a little anger) as he takes in the sea of faces inside our small café, some of whom turn to him and lift a glass of cordial in an ironic salute. But I don't pay him too much attention. I can't. None of us can. We're all so frantically busy we can do nothing but serve ice cream and tea and dispense sweets and cigarettes, and all the time the till keeps ringing and the total keeps climbing until by the end of that one Sunday, we've taken more in a single day than we've taken in the whole of the previous week.

That night an exhausted but very happy Enrico finally permits himself a small moment of hope. His younger brother, Michele, has been trying to make his own living in France but has experienced little success. Enrico cautiously starts to wonder if he could take his brother and set him on the road to perhaps opening his own shop someday too.

After Michele perhaps there might be two more familiar faces following him as well, because my own brothers, Luigi and Peppo, will both be reaching the age when they too will start to look for a life beyond our home town.

Everything had changed, it seemed. The town had voted with its feet as well as with all the spare change it could summon from its pockets. One clerical gentleman might not like it, but as far as the rest of his congregation are concerned, that didn't matter. They would quite clearly countenance no threat to their local *Bracchi*, and surely even a man of God could not go against the clear will of the overwhelming majority.

But in that, as in so much else, we were about to be severely disillusioned.

The list of names is hand-delivered to our door the very next morning. Moments later, a copy of the same list is hand-delivered to a yawning Sergeant James as he opens up the small police station just a few doors further along the main street from the chapel itself.

I don't recognize many of the names immediately but Sergeant James does, and so does Grace. They're an almost complete roll-call of just about everyone who called into the café and made a purchase the previous day: the Sunday, the Lord's Day, the day of rest.

The Reverend Keller, it seems, has widened his attack. Now it isn't just local businesses – principally Enrico's local business – he is denouncing from his pulpit and reporting to the authorities. Now he is following the strict letter of the law in naming those people who frequent those businesses too. Now he is handing the hapless Sergeant James a lengthy list of law-breakers and demanding their prosecution, and just in case Sergeant James is tempted to turn a blind eye to what he may regard as a fairly minor transgression, the Reverend Keller has sent that same list to his Chief Constable and also to the editor of the local paper.

The chapel is a powerful force. Many of the main local movers and shakers (the colliery owners, the factory overseers) are staunch supporters, not to mention all the different businesses who advertise in that same paper. The battle, always unequal, now seems hopelessly one-sided.

The next Sunday brings the inevitable result. From a packed café the previous week, we have virtually no custom at all. Enrico still attends the service in the chapel, as do Grace and myself. He's not going to be completely defeated by the Reverend Keller, but it's a desperate and a doomed gesture. I'm seated one side of Enrico, Grace on the other. For the vast majority of his latest sermon, we and the rest of the squirming congregation have to listen to another diatribe by the Reverend Keller on the evils of turning one's face away from the one true path, peppered with names read out from that day's paper, a list of those against whom charges have been brought during the last week.

Each name sounds like a death knell to Enrico. You can see it in his face. He clearly feels like he's not only failed in his business, but that he's failed his loyal customers, who are now being hung out to dry in a court that is uncompromising and unforgiving.

We return to an empty café. It remains empty all afternoon and evening. Enrico is determined to remain open just in case any hardy soul does decide to defy those forces working against us and step inside, but no-one does. The support was total last week. Now, it seems, a dose of cold reality has set in. The café is still as much loved by our customers as it was last Sunday, but not as loved as those customers' livelihoods and jobs.

Enrico closes the café and we all retire to the small, whitewashed room at the back, our sanctuary. The heat from the large stove warms it, courtesy of the pipes that lead down into the kitchen in the basement. Then Enrico, with now-shaking hands, fills in that day's ledger.

It makes grim reading that night, but for once I'm not

paying attention. Usually it's a time-honoured ritual. A good day or a good week might mean the day we think of bringing over my beloved brothers is drawing closer. Tonight I'm thinking instead. As Enrico finishes completing his ledger, a task that takes a significantly shorter time to accomplish that time than most other evenings, I tell him I want to talk to him and to Grace.

I talk to them for the next half hour and they listen for the main part and then, stunned, they argue for the rest. And then, with Enrico and Grace staring after me, both still in a clear state of what looks like dumb stupefaction, I let myself out of the café, walk the few steps down the street to the local police station and knock on the door.

As it opens I look at Sergeant James, who stands there in his regulation blue trousers and his non-regulation white vest, before demanding that our local representative of law and order go along to the nearby chapel and arrest the Reverend Keller.

'You can't.'

That wasn't Sergeant James. That was Enrico a few minutes earlier. Five minutes after I'd first told him and Grace what I intended to do.

Grace hadn't said a word. The absolutely impossible had happened, even more impossible than a whole army of people appearing one week only to vanish the next. I'd finally robbed Grace of the power of speech.

'Why not?'

'Chiara!'

But that's all Enrico says. He lapses into a stunned silence. Then he just stares at me again.

One hour later I'm following Sergeant James along the main street towards the Reverend Keller's chapel.

He hasn't told me I can't do this. He just listened to me, thought for a long moment, then turned and donned his regulation blue shirt and jacket. He is, after all, on official business now.

Ahead of us, lights still gleam in the chapel itself. The services have concluded for the day, but the Reverend Keller quite clearly still has some duties left to perform.

Collecting the Bibles.

Sweeping the pews.

Compiling the next list of names to publicise and persecute.

The Reverend greets Sergeant James warmly as we appear. In his eyes he's quite clearly an ally. He expresses his gratitude for the good Sergeant's efforts in applying the letter of the law and applauds the all too visible results we've witnessed that day. Then he stops and stares as Sergeant James tells him exactly why he's called on him that evening, and then he speaks two words. The same two words that Enrico spoke just an hour or so earlier, and with much the same expression on his face as he says them too.

'You can't.'

Then he looks beyond the police officer, which is when, and as if for the first time, he sees me. He sees something in my expression too, a silent message that really doesn't need any words.

I say those words anyway.

'Oh yes, he can.'

'This is today's paper, Reverend Keller. Your copy.'

There's little point in denying it, even were the Reverend so inclined. Almost every page is annotated with the Reverend's scribblings, underlining this and that name, adding quotes from the scriptures alongside.

The Reverend Keller stares at the paper, which seems to have suddenly turned into some kind of smoking gun.

'And you purchased this paper today?'

Sergeant James rolls on, no answer really necessary.

'Well, you had to, of course: you read out a list of names from it this morning, I remember. I was here, along with most of this town.'

Reverend Keller looks beyond Sergeant James towards me once again. Once again I hold his stare as the Sergeant continues.

'Now it could be that you were given this paper by a friend or a companion, in which case I will need their name or names, Reverend, as I'm sure you understand.'

Sergeant James nods at the list of heavily-annotated names in the paper before him.

'We can have no fear or favour in this regard.'

Sergeant James hunches closer to the now stunned and still staring cleric.

'But if you bought this paper yourself from the shop by the station, which is where I think you usually buy your daily paper, then that means you entered a place of commerce and conducted a commercial transaction with the proprietor on a day exempted from any such transaction or trade by the Sunday trading laws. As such, Reverend Keller, I'm going to have to ask you to report to the station in the morning, but please be aware you may be there for some time.'

Sergeant James looks back at the heavily annotated list of names in the paper again.

'I do have a lot of people to interview and charge as well as yourself.'

'But it's a paper.'

Finally, the Reverend finds his voice.

Sergeant James views the object in question for a moment, then nods back in solemn agreement.

'It is.'

'A single newspaper.'

Sergeant James nods again.

'But, in principle, no different from a boiled sweet or a packet of cigarettes. Not when the offending article in question is purchased on a Sunday.'

And now I nod too.

'The Lord's Day.'

Sergeant James nods, solemnly again, by my side.

'The Day of Rest.'

Before us, the Reverend Keller's mouth opens and closes much in the manner of a fish on a slab.

For once no words come out.

Once again, it doesn't take much, and once again it's Sergeant James who's the instigator.

All that's needed from him is a veiled reference to common sense seeming to have prevailed: a coded expression of support for the man who's done so much to establish such a loved local amenity and who seemed to be on the brink of losing it. Then the good Sergeant smiles, and mentions how pleased he is that the Reverend Keller has decided to draw on that inexhaustible well of Christian sympathy for which his chapel is so renowned, and agree with the police that no public interest would be served by pressing charges.

And, perhaps by way of a reward for all that, the Reverend Keller is now being transferred away from the town to a new posting some hundreds of kilometres away. Sergeant James is a little hazy as to geography but he understands it to be in a rather remote community in the Highlands of Scotland where there are just a few solitary crofters and a lot of sheep.

The following Sunday we all attend the local chapel again and listen to a pleasant sermon by the replacement minister, who's taken the theme of community as his subject; specifically, the importance of including all in that community and excluding none. Then he joins us in Enrico's café and enjoys an equally pleasant and restorative cup of tea.

That night, Enrico completes his ledger again. It hasn't scaled the dizzying heights of the Sunday of the famous protest, but it's a long way away from the date with disaster promised by the subsequent Sunday when the Reverend Keller fulminated from the pulpit, brandished his incendiary newspaper (incendiary in more ways than one, as it turned out) and denounced everyone on his list.

Enrico, Grace and I gather in that small back room that night. Wild horses wouldn't have dragged Grace home with a celebration in store. Enrico, always a stickler for what's right, waits until the very stroke of midnight and then opens a bottle of Barolo he's brought with him from home and which he's been keeping for a special occasion. It has been maturing for ten years and could have remained in the bottle for another five. But tonight it's to be drunk and the first toast of the night, despite my protests, is in my honour.

Enrico makes the toast and we all sip the wine, although Grace rather gulps at hers and has to be slapped on the back to get over her subsequent coughing fit. Then we keep on drinking that mellow Barolo for another hour or so and I remember two things above all others about that equally mellow night.

First, as I sip my wine, I realise something. I can't smell it any more. And I haven't smelt it for the last few days either.

I can't smell the charcoal. It's gone.

Second, I remember Enrico looking towards the closed door and the café behind it, his closed café which would be open and bustling again in just a few short hours, and making a prediction.

'Everything's going to be all right.'

Then he looks back at me and smiles.

'You're a good girl, Chiara.'

Two statements.

Two lies.

PART FOUR

'The Sun and Moon Stand Still'

(Joshua 10)

Frankie

THE HOUSE IS in chaos. It has been since first thing. Normally raising those two kids of mine from their beds is like trying to wake the dead, but not this morning. This morning Tyler's been up since the crack of dawn and as for Vicky, Steve's nearly done himself an injury waiting for her to come out of the bathroom.

When I was nine I had Barbie – that's a doll, by the way – and ponies – as in My Little, not the genuine article – on my mind. Judging by the slap plastered all over her face today, my daughter's thoughts are on something totally different right now. Thank God this fair only happens once a year, is all I can say.

According to all Uncle Tony's told me – Tony being the custodian of all things to do with the history of the Welsh-Italians in our town – this fair probably started round about your time or just before. Of course, he can't be sure. Not about the fair. It's more you that's the puzzle.

Tony traced the history of all the people who'd worked before him in the café. It was almost like a family tree. He's on it, so am I – even Vicky and Tyler are on it, as they've helped out there from time to time. He came over to the house one night to show it off and Vicky spent ages staring at all the names of all those people who'd been there before her, while Tyler just picked his nose. Then Vicky spotted the gap. The gap that's you – or at least we think is you.

The fact is, you're Tony's one big failure so far. He knows bits about you, so he's pretty sure you existed. He's pretty sure you came here too. But everyone he spoke to from those days didn't seem to know too much else. It's like some conspiracy of silence seems to have descended so far as you were concerned, and there's no-one around now who can fill in the missing bits. Meaning you're here and you're not here. You're part of the extended family of sorts that's the old and new Carini's – we think – and you're its biggest mystery, all at the same time.

Maybe that's why I latched onto you when I first started talking into this machine. Why I conjured you up, started telling you about all this. The truth was I didn't know what the hell I was doing or why I was doing it. Still don't, really. And seeing as how no-one seemed to know who the hell you were or why no-one can find out anything about you either, it just seemed fitting in a way.

But if you are something of a closed book, this fair we're all going to today definitely isn't. Tony could do Mastermind on it. He sent us all to sleep one night telling us how the whole thing started, something to do with some Master Baker or other, which sent Steve into fits of giggles when he first said it, him being the big kid he is.

Years later – last year, in fact – when we were all heading off to the latest fair, Tyler suddenly came out with it too. Master Baker. And then he broke down in fits of giggles too, with Steve joining in as well. Which didn't do an awful lot to reassure me as to either of their emotional maturities, but it did give me a clue as to Tyler's changing interests, if you get my drift.

Tyler at twelve and now Vicky. OK, she hasn't got the same taste in juvenile jokes, but she has got the same interest in bodies now – hers in the first instance and very definitely some of the older boys in school coming a not very distant second. And I know it's natural and I know we've all been through it, and I know I'd worry more if she wasn't interested, but she still keeps me awake at night in a way Tyler's never managed to.

Maybe I'm just old fashioned. Or maybe I can see into the future or something. All I know is, I pray it's the first and not the second. If you ever had kids – and it's difficult to know, along with everything else about you – but if you ever did have your own little bundle of scary joy then you'll know exactly what I'm talking about.

One hour later, Vicky's finally chosen a top to go with her jeans. And her heels – for God's sake, heels at nine! But Steve tells me to stop fussing. That could have been him talking sterling common sense or it could have been the call of the beer tent, which is due to open in less than an hour. I'm hoping it's the first but would bet the mortgage, if we'd ever been able to scrape together enough of a deposit to be given one, on it probably being the second.

Tony wants to get off too. He's come to collect us, but that isn't down to the lure of the beer tent. This year it's his turn.

Every year there's one. God knows when or how – or even why – it all started. But for as long as anyone can remember there's been a magician on the gate greeting everyone as they arrive. I wondered at one time if it was some kind of contest – let's find the most useless magic act in the world and put it on full view. It couldn't be coincidence that each and every year the shittest card tricks were paraded before a whole sea of disbelieving eyes by some bloke in a totally crap disguise. But it didn't matter. As Uncle Tony always said, it was just part of the fun – and the weird thing was, he was right. If there'd been some ace act on that gate, it would have spoilt it somehow.

As we arrive, Tony – this year's shit card merchant – nods at me.

'Pick a card.'

'Piss off.'

'Come on Frankie, this is practice.'

I stare at him witheringly.

'Which is obviously going to make such a difference.'

We'd got there early. Steve had gone to help set up the beer tent. Surprise, surprise. And nab himself a few freebies along the way. Vicky had gone to check out the nearest full-length mirror. Which left Tyler with me, and he's about as interested in Tony's currently fumbling fingers as I am right now.

'Just the one.'

And with that the whole pack falls onto the grass.

Tyler nods at him, sounding as caustic as only a twelve year old can.

'Wicked.'

Tyler wanders off to join a couple of his mates, who are hovering around the music tent. There's a Ratpack tribute act kicking off a bit later on, according to one of the posters, and they think it might have something to do with heavy metal. I haven't disillusioned him. Let him and the rest of his mates find out for themselves. By that time they'll hopefully be trapped in the first few rows having to endure at least another half hour's crooning from a Dean Martin wannabe who really should be prosecuted under the Trades Descriptions Act if he'd sold himself as a lookalike. And who should have the book thrown at him if he tried claiming he was even remotely a soundalike.

I'm about to join him. Or maybe check out the beer tent and that husband of mine. Or maybe just the beer tent. Which is when a voice cuts in, with an accent as warm as sunshine.

'He really has been practising.'

A pair of blue-green eyes look at me. I don't take in the rest of the face at first. Those blue-green eyes are all I can see for the first few moments. And I'm not talking thunderbolts and lightning here, and I'm not talking about suddenly going weak at the knees either. It's just something about those eyes.

Uncle Tony smiles at the new arrival.

'Meet my tutor.'

Then Tony nods back at me.

'Francesca – although if you call her that, she'll probably kill you.'

I nod in response.

I would.

So I introduce myself properly.

'Frankie.'

'Francesca's a nice name.'

I eye him, holding those blue-green eyes steady, more than a hint of a warning in my stare and he gets the hint.

'But Frankie's nicer.'

A grinning Tony completes the introduction.

'Zeno.'

I nod at him again.

'And your real name?'

By now, the new arrival's grinning too.

'So you don't like my name and you don't believe in magic?'

'I didn't say I didn't like your name, I've just never heard it before. And as for magic...'

I eye Uncle Tony, still shuffling cards, spilling at least a good half dozen more onto the grass as he does so.

'Let's say the jury's still out on that one.'

I'm about to move on to find Steve – or, more importantly,

the beer tent – but the man with the blue-green eyes cuts across again.

'Do you believe in the stigmata?'

I stop at that, staring at him.

'You're Catholic, yes? Must be.'

I keep staring. I'm like Tony. And like most of the people I grew up with, too. I might have been at one time, but I'm in serious need of some practice to remind me what it's all about.

Zeno, or whatever his name is, smiles again as he decodes my stare.

'But you do know what the stigmata is?'

And I do, of course I do, that sort of stuff having been drummed into us by all those nuns back in Sunday school. I hadn't thought about it for more years than I cared to remember and definitely more than I was ever going to admit to, but all of a sudden as he said it, I was back there, among those shrivelled-up old women and their warnings of eternal damnation if we didn't come back next week with our patent shoes all buffed and shined.

Which was when Uncle Tony cut in.

'The sign of Christ's suffering on the cross.'

I stare at him. That's typical, isn't it? The one chance I get to prove all those lessons in that Sunday school weren't totally wasted, and in he comes, stealing my thunder.

I nod back, flat.

'Ten out of ten, Tone.'

'Can I?'

Zeno nods at my cigarette. I don't actually remember lighting one, but I must have done unless Tony has been putting in some seriously impressive practice in the optical illusion stakes and I'm not actually holding a lighted ciggy at all.

'Just for a minute or so.'

'What is this?'

'One minute, that's all.'

Tony's looking puzzled now too, but I'm thinking 'what the hell', so I hand it over.

'It's not just our Saviour who can bear the imprint of the stigmata, right? Every one of us can, that's what the Good Book says. All we need to do is believe, have a little faith. Trust in what some people might call magic.'

All the time he's been talking, the ash on my cig in his hand is getting longer and longer and now Zeno tips it into his palm. Then he reaches out – soft, gentle – and takes my right hand.

Then he looks up at me, those same blue-green eyes suddenly clouding, growing serious now as if this crazy loon actually means all this.

'Now I'm going to rub this ash into the back of your hand. Then we're going to wait a moment or two and then we're going to turn your hand over. And then we're going to see the ash, which will have passed through your hand and will have appeared – like the stigmata – in the very centre of your palm on the other side.'

And it sounds crazy, I know, really crazy, but for a moment I actually believe him. He's so serious that for a moment all there is on that field is myself, a stranger called Zeno and a pile of ash that's being rubbed in a semi-circle into my skin.

Then Zeno smiles, releases my hand and nods at me.

'Now turn your hand over.'

By now, Tony's at my side. Even though it's obviously all total bollocks, he seems to have been taken in by all this now too. And I think he's as disappointed as – privately – I am now when I turn my hand over, slowly, to reveal absolutely nothing.

'Ah.'

Zeno's blue-green eyes crease in puzzlement as I salute his efforts with an ironic cheer and a nod.

'Can I have my cig back now?'

Zeno smiles ruefully and holds it out. I make to take it, but at the last minute he holds it back, looking at my now-outstretched hand as he does so.

'Are you left-handed?'

'What?'

He nods at my outstretched hand again.

'I didn't notice before, you smoke with your left hand.'

I nod across at Tony.

'Quick on the uptake, isn't he?'

But Zeno's not listening. Zeno's now reaching for my left hand, still outstretched for my now fast-dwindling ciggy. Then he turns it over and displays my palm.

And there, right in the middle, is a small smearing of cigarette ash in the unmistakeable shape of a cross.

Steve's looking serious. As in really serious. In fact he's wearing the sort of expression I'd have expected to see if he'd turned up to the beer tent to find out it had been requisitioned by the Mormons.

Tyler's not looking serious. Tyler's looking tragic. As if his whole world has suddenly collapsed in on him – which, in his book, it has. And Steve's serious demeanour, I'm about to discover, is his way of sharing his son's pain.

Vicky doesn't look serious and she doesn't look tragic either. Vicky – to Tyler and Steve's clear and obvious annoyance – is pissing herself. And it doesn't exactly help matters that her small crew of female friends, all kitted out like mini-Victoria Beckhams – not that you're going to know who Little Miss Pouty Gob is either – are also pissing themselves at what seems to be Tyler's expense as well.

I can't work it out at first. What the hell's happened? Steve's too busy trying to shush Vicky and her cackling mates and Tyler's too upset to tell me at first, and to be absolutely honest I really don't want to stand too close to him either, because there's a very strange smell coming from somewhere and it doesn't seem to be a million miles away from Tyler.

'Spaghetti.'

'What?'

That's about all that Vicky's managed to say so far. The rest's been choked off in another extended bout of giggling, fuelled by her friends.

'Spaghetti?'

Which only sends them off again.

I look at Steve, but he's staring after Tyler, who's now turned and is heading for the exit, making a very strange squelching sound as he does so. Which only provokes yet another bout of hysterics from Vicky and her supporting chorus of apprentice witches.

'He went in for the competition, didn't he?'

Spaghetti eating. Did they have that in your day? Tony reckons they did, but after his ongoing disasters with those card tricks, I'm not setting too much store by anything he says.

Zeno's a different matter, though. How he did that with the ash, I don't know – but it was cute, I have to admit. But then I swat all thoughts of Italian émigrés with blue-green eyes from my mind, bringing it back to my son, who looks as if the world has just ended.

'And?'

'And he won.'

'Good old Tyler.'

I nod, approving. That should save us a few quid on the various snack stalls that are just beginning to open up.

'Then he was sick.'

Then again, maybe not.

Steve hesitates.

'Over his trainers.'

I stare at him.

'His new trainers?'

Behind Steve, Vicky is now almost on the floor in fits of giggles. Roughly five seconds later I've joined her.

I shouldn't, I know that, but be fair.

Wouldn't you?

The rest of the day passes in a bit of a blur. The Dean Martin crooner can't croon and looks more like Jerry Lewis, but by that time I've unscrewed the top of the bottle of cheap red wine I bought from Bargain Booze last night, so I really don't care all that much.

Vicky has got over her fit of giggles and is now stepping it out with her mates in the dance tent. Steve has taken up more or less permanent residence in the beer tent. Tyler has decided to clean up his soiled trainers by taking part in the Grape Stomp contest and is doing pretty well, too, although maybe that's more down to the other contestants giving him a wide berth than anything else. The sun's shining, the field's packed and I've forgotten all about tricks with cigarettes and Italians with blue-green eyes.

Until a long-forgotten nugget of some barely-remembered school lesson swims into my head.

A gift from the gods.

That's what it means.

His name – Zeno.

I look around to suddenly see the man himself passing, no

more than a few metres away. Instinctively I glance down at my palm, but there's nothing there. Even the original faint smear of ash on the back of my hand has completely gone, almost as if it was never there in the first place.

Then I look back at him, which is when Zeno himself looks back at me, as if he knew I was just thinking about him.

And smiles.

Which is when it does happen. When there is a definite whiff of thunderbolt and a distant, but definite, flash of lightning and when my knees do seem, all of a sudden, to go more than a little weak.

Later, I tell myself it was just the sunshine and the singing and the laughter and all that red wine.

But it wasn't.

Was it?

Chiara

HUGE EXCITEMENT. TODAY the café closes for half a day. Believe me, that's astonishing enough all by itself. In the last few months, Enrico has been staying open later and later, mainly due to the local bus company changing its timetable. Now the first bus starts running at 5.30 in the morning and the last one doesn't pull in until 10.30 at night, so Enrico makes sure he's open then too.

Enrico calls it a service. Some of those early-morning and late-night passengers might be hungry or thirsty, and he sees it as his duty to be open, just in case. Grace just calls him a money-grabber. I may not have heard the expression before, but I know exactly what she means and from the rueful look on Enrico's face it seems he does too.

However, today the café is closing for a whole half day, because today is the day of the annual fair.

It's all Grace has been talking about for weeks. She's been to it three times before, while working for Enrico's predecessors. Across the country, émigrés from all over Italy gather – from Bardi, from Liguria, from Marche, from the south, even some from Sicily. For one afternoon a local park becomes a small part of a country we might all have left, but will never forget. Gatherings like this will make sure of it.

Gatherings like this don't mean quite the same thing to the currently flushed Grace, though. They mean one thing and one thing only to my now-constant companion.

'What about this one?'

'What was wrong with the other one?'

'Does this one look better?'

'The other one looked fine.'

'Chiara!'

Grace parades before me in that whitewashed rear room in the second of three dresses she's brought with her.

'It's nice.'

Now she's staring at me.

'Nice?!'

Grace keeps staring at me.

'That's what that couple say, the ones who come in for the pork pie and the two plates, every time I serve them their tea, they take a sip and they nod at each other and they say it, every time, "That's –"'

Grace explodes.

'Nice isn't enough, Chiara – nice isn't anywhere near enough! I don't want nice, I want –'

I get the point as Grace tails off. I'd have to be deaf, blind and stupid not to.

'Are boys going to fall at my feet?'

I start grinning.

'Are they going to be following me round all afternoon, tongues hanging out like a pack of hungry wolves?'

I'm grinning even more widely. I can't help it. Grace always has this effect on me.

'Are they going to fall down the minute I walk into that park?'

'What do you want them to do, fall down or follow you round?'

'I want them to foam at the mouth.'

I start giggling again.

'With their tongues hanging out?'

Grace nods.

'Wail at the stars. Beat their breasts. Howl at the moon.'

By now we're both helpless. In both our heads now is the same picture, every boy the length and breadth of this town prostrate at Grace's feet, Grace herself stepping daintily over the prone bodies of men afflicted by the worst sort of fever – helpless, hopeless, undisguised, unendurable, and unrequited adoration.

Grace pauses again.

'But a simple look'll do.'

Then Grace falters and we both look towards the door, because from inside the café we're now both hearing a terrible commotion.

He'd been in once or twice before. Some said he was an ex-miner, invalided out of the pit by an accident. Others said he wasn't really a miner at all; that he'd only taken the job to recruit his fellow-workers into a union he was attempting to establish at the time.

Whatever the truth behind his past or present circumstances, one thing was clear. Robin Thomas was a wild-eyed hothead of a man, fired by the political texts he always carried around in his pocket and fuelled by what he saw as injustice on all sides.

Looking back now, I have to admit he had a point. There was injustice, great injustice in fact, and there was unnecessary suffering; and perhaps it was all down, as Robin continually told Enrico, Grace and myself, and anyone else who'd care to listen, to the abandoning of a simple principle which should rule all lives no matter how high or low born: that no man should profit by another man's labour.

The problem was that most men and women in that town at that time had rather more pressing matters in mind, such as putting food on the family table or, as in Grace's case, the choice of a dress for the annual fair.

Grace follows me back into the café as the voices get louder. The dispute, whatever it's about, is quite obviously escalating all the while. As we come inside, we can see Robin on one side of the urn that heats the hot water, a hapless Enrico on the other, and a red-faced Sergeant James (clearly not enjoying his close proximity to the water heater at the moment) standing next to Robin, trying to calm him down.

'Enrico?'

Grace cuts across the heated exchange, three pairs of eyes now swivelling her way as she does so.

I cut in too.

'What are you arguing about?'

The same three pairs of eyes swivel my way, then Enrico turns his confused face back towards the fiery Robin. It's quite clear already that he doesn't really know what this argument is all about. Robin has a fine brain and constructs many an elegant thesis, but his passion often sabotages his ability to communicate any sort of thesis, fine or otherwise.

That's what it's doing now. For now he's just staring past the hot water urn at a book on a shelf above Enrico's head. I've never taken any notice of it before, but Robin's taking notice of it and now he's drawing everyone else's attention to it too.

'Look! There – there – !'

Sergeant James lifts the book down from the shelf, and begins leafing through it, growing ever more bewildered as he does so.

'It's just a list of businesses.'

'*Guida Generale degli Italiani in Gran Bretagna.*'

All eyes now swivel towards Enrico, three of those pairs of eyes totally uncomprehending, but not mine.

'A Directory of Italian businesses in Britain.'

Enrico nods.

'It came out two years ago. We're on page 63.'

Sergeant James stares back at Robin, who now looks if he's about to catch fire.

'What's your beef with Italian businesses, Robin?

Robin almost combusts.

'There, look – on the front cover – and on the back! Look.'

Sergeant James turns the book over, no more enlightened than he was a few moments before, but Enrico knows what's so incensing Robin and now I see it too. It's the symbol, stamped on the cover and on the back, depicting a bundle of rods and an axe.

I know that symbol. Each and every one of my countrymen and women knows that symbol as well. It's the symbol of chastisement before a high magistrate. The man who created the symbol was born not far from my home town, so I perhaps know more about him than most. Some of my old teachers (although not Professoressa Quadrelli) actually taught him, and remembered a wilful and quarrelsome child with a record of expulsions and suspensions; perfect training perhaps for a man who would, in just a few years, become leader of a whole country.

Mussolini. *Il Duce*.

To some he's a saviour; to others, and there are many my father has talked to in Bardi who feel this way, he's a clown who's fast turning out to be not such a clown after all.

It's politics, so it doesn't mean a lot to myself or to Grace, but that symbol on that innocent-looking book quite obviously means a lot to our customer, who's now, finally, beginning to find something resembling a coherent voice.

'This is a proud town. A democratic town.'

Robin nods at us, eyes burning ever fiercer now.

'A town where a working man can express his opinion every few years at the ballot box. It doesn't matter that most of them are too stupid and pig-headed to see things as they are, too broken by a system that enslaves them to see how simple it would be to just break free.'

'Robin –'

Sergeant James breaks in. He's listened to speeches like this before. He knows that once Robin starts on his hobby horse, he can ride it for hours; and the now-perspiring policeman obviously does not want to spend those next few hours in a hot café by an even hotter water urn on a hot summer's day. Besides, he has no idea what that symbol means or about its links to a man named Benito Amilcare Andrea Mussolini.

Perhaps he'd never even heard of him, but he would. Everyone would.

'What, exactly, don't you like about this book then?'

Robin now does explode in the same way Grace exploded a few moments before, about her dress for the fair.

'It's a blackshirt book! A Fascist book!'

We all stare at the offending book.

Then, suddenly, out of the blue:

'I like it no better than you.'

I stare at Enrico in amazement. I've never heard him express anything remotely resembling an opinion about any political issue in the whole time I've been working for him. He's one of Nature's listeners, or at least appeared to be. He just nods, sagely, as one customer or another raves about this or that current issue, always careful never to actually ally himself with one side or another. In that respect he's more like some sort of unofficial Father Confessor, although that's probably driven more by necessity than principle. Customers are precious commodities in our line of work and it doesn't do to upset any of them.

Enrico inclines his head towards the fiery Robin, his tone warm now, supportive.

'Back home I have two friends. I haven't seen them for three years but I hear news of them every month. Right now, they're in prison. Their crime?'

Enrico's voice now takes on the timbre of a conspiratorial whisper.

'To argue with a blackshirt in the market square in Ronchi about some pronouncement made by their beloved Benito. Their punishment?'

Enrico shakes his head, growing visibly upset now.

'Arrest on an invented charge. Some nonsense about stealing from a party stall. Do you know what their sentence was?'

Enrico shakes his head again, his face now a mixture of sorrow and real anger.

'Three months in prison. Three months when they can't work, three months when their families must go without food.'

Robin is still staring at him.

'So why not get rid of it?'

'The book?'

Enrico looks at it heavily.

'Every time I look at it, I want to do just that. Every time I look at it, all I see are my two friends and their two families, who will probably now lose their homes.'

'So why don't you?'

Enrico beckons Robin closer to the offending book on the counter and the two men hunch over it as, across the café, Sergeant James, Grace and myself keep watch.

'I first met the man who gave me this in the Casa del Littorio in London. The old Italian Clubhouse on the Charing Cross Road. It was a place of wonder when I first arrived here. In every room something was happening: music, dance classes, language classes – day trips to the seaside every weekend. It was like stumbling on a tiny piece of paradise.'

Enrico paused.

'I didn't suspect anything more was going on for weeks. Not even when I saw the Balilla for the boys and the Piccole Italiane for the girls – I just thought it was like your Boy Scouts and Girl Guides.'

Enrico nodded at the now-staring Robin.

'I swear that ninety per cent of the people who went there – ninety per cent at least – were like me. We had no idea what was really behind it. By the time I realised it was all a front for the *fascio*, it was too late.'

'How? Why too late?' I now cut in, becoming as caught up in all this as Robin.

Enrico pauses, the struggle of all this clear on his face.

'One of the language tutors arranged a loan for me. With that money I bought this business. The committee who granted the loan gave me the deeds in one hand – '

Enrico nodded at the counter.

'– and that book in the other. As soon as I looked at it, I realised it had that symbol on the cover. I looked round the clubhouse and for the first time I saw the same symbol on a wall here, a door there.'

Enrico struggled a bit more.

'That book's not a gift. It's a reminder, and that's not just my imagination. It was said to me as those deeds were handed over: "Remember who paid for all this."'

Enrico pauses again.

'The man who arranged my loan calls in once a month to collect the payments. The first thing he does is look on that shelf to see if I'm still displaying the book.'

Enrico looks at Robin, but a light's now shining in Robin's

eyes as he looks back at him. There's something new in there too, the look of fraternity, of companionship.

'So not only do you not like this dog, Mussolini, you're also in the grip of a moneylender?'

Enrico considers the notion carefully, but he doesn't need to answer because all of a sudden Robin crosses to him and folds the startled Enrico in a close and intense embrace. Robin isn't a large man and only comes up to Enrico's shoulders, but he still manages to squeeze every ounce of breath from his lungs as he welcomes him into what – from that point on – would obviously be some sort of eternal inner circle.

'You know what you are, don't you Enrico?'

Enrico gasps.

'What am I?'

'You're one of us.'

Enrico gasps again.

'I am?'

Robin's comradely embrace enfolds him ever tighter, which only intensify Enrico's gasps.

'I'll tell everyone that too. If anyone ever wants to say anything about you, about that book on the shelf above your counter, about that Fascist symbol on its cover, then I'll tell them.'

Robin leans back slightly, nods at him, solemn.

'Enrico has no choice.'

Robin keeps looking Enrico fully in the eyes.

'But when you've paid off this oppressor, when you've freed yourself from his grasp, we'll take that book outside and we'll build a big bonfire. We'll put the book right on the top and then we'll burn it, in full view of this whole town.'

Robin nods at Enrico, eagerly.

'What do you say?'

Enrico nods back at him, a solemn promise in his eyes.

'Yes. That's exactly what we'll do.'

Half an hour later Grace is still choosing a hair ribbon to go with her dress. I'm with Enrico, who's going to finish off some tasks in the café before joining us later.

'I didn't know about your friends.'

For a moment Enrico doesn't respond, then he just smiles back at me; doesn't say a word, moves on. As I watch him go, I look at him, realising almost for the first time that there's a lot I don't know about him; this protector, this man who's chosen me to come and help him in his new life, offering me a new life along the way. For the first time perhaps I begin to see him as more than just that kindly protector, more than just the provider of a new life far away from a home that could provide a life no more.

Then something else happens too. I didn't have the vocabulary to explain it at the time, either in my adopted tongue or my own, or even to understand it properly. All I know is, for the first time since I arrived, I actually discover I want to find out more about this man who's come into and changed my life: this man called Enrico.

But first –

'Chiara!'

Grace bounds into the café, her ribbon for the day finally (thankfully!) chosen.

'Come on!'

There's a fair to go to.

Even a few years previously, the thought of celebrating his Italian heritage was just a dream for Luigi Cefalu. A native of Porticello, he'd made his mark on another town near ours by opening a bakery and selling the kind of breads and pastries he'd first sampled at his mother's knee.

But overseeing a booming business wasn't enough for Luigi. Having introduced one custom and tradition from his home country to his new, he was keen to introduce more. And the catalyst for translating that desire into concrete action was the railway.

When I first arrived at Enrico's, there were four families from Luigi's home region working in the area. Each week they'd travel the few kilometres across the valley and down to Cardiff, the nearest large city, where Our Lady Of The Rosary Church provided a place of peace and refuge and allowed the community to continue some home traditions. But the ever-expanding railway destroyed that as new lines knocked down houses in their wake, including the homes of three of the families who'd journey with Luigi each week. They were forced to move across the border to England to seek work. The small church in the city struggled to stay open for a few more months but the depleted congregation made it impossible. When it closed, Luigi felt as if the last link to his old home country had gone.

Some would have simply accepted it as fate, the inevitable march of what others might call progress; but not Luigi.

Luigi applied to a local magistrate for permission to close a couple of streets near to his business on a Sunday (the second, as it turned out) in June. The rest of the residents watched, bewildered, as a small stage was erected and a band began playing. Luigi himself had been working all night to fill a stall with the best of his breads and pastries and the families that had been exiled returned with cooked pasta dishes and the freshest vegetables. A band played all day and dancing continued well into the night; dancing in which almost every single one of Luigi's fellow-townsfolk took part along with the returning Italians; and a tradition was born as Luigi recreated his home country in his adopted land.

It's grown a lot since that first festival on those two streets with a single stage. Now it takes over a whole park, people from all of the surrounding towns come along, and the entertainment begins the moment you walk up to the festival gates.

There, we're greeted by a magician who delights the children in particular. Card tricks, fire eating, you name it, he does it; and when you've finally manoeuvred your way past the unofficial guard attending the entrance to the *Festa*, there's the opening ceremony to savour, with an opera singer performing arias while a military band strikes out melodies in the breaks.

Next, it's down to the lake for the first of the gondola races before heading back to the main tent for the spaghetti-eating contest, which is (and always has been) less about applauding appetites than a chance for girls to take a first, usually appreciative, look at the competing boys.

We linger in this tent more than most; Grace makes sure of it. The boy who's the winner in her eyes might not have the largest appetite, but he definitely has the most beautiful bum.

Next, there's dancing and a grape-stomp contest (open to boys and girls) providing the first opportunity to actually meet up in what approximates to a kind of mass wrestling match. Grace's hat falls off and gets trampled in the melee but it's clearly worth it as it's trampled on by a boy, as she tells me later, breathlessly, with an even more beautiful bum.

Now the pace lessens, a touch at least, as it's time for the *Bambini*'s Italian Dance (for the children), before another band takes to the stage for more adult dancing that lasts well into the evening until it's time for the gates of the park to close.

It isn't until those gates are actually closing behind myself and a now-dreamy Grace that I realise I haven't seen Enrico for the whole of the afternoon. I try asking Grace if she's seen him, but it's a little difficult getting any sort of conversation out of her at the moment. The new boy she discovered in the *Bambini*'s Dance, a boy who'd accompanied his little sister into the tent and who possessed an even more beautiful bum than the previous two, has his lips pressed to hers almost permanently by then, and I don't think she even hears me.

I do find Sergeant James, who's come along ostensibly in his official capacity to make sure there's no trouble, but who's actually there like everyone else, because he loves it. He hasn't seen Enrico all day either, though.

All of a sudden I'm growing concerned. Has something happened? While we were away enjoying ourselves at the fair, and not giving Enrico and the café even a second thought, in truth, has there been some problem?

As I hurry back to the café I can see all the lights blazing inside even though the door's closed, and a hundred thoughts suddenly assail me.

Did Robin return to hurl some fresh invective at the hapless Enrico when we were all away? Or has Enrico fallen foul of some thief looking to take advantage of the town being practically deserted today? There had been burglaries on similar days before.

I reach into my bag, fingers fumbling for the key to the front door. There are just three: one retained by Enrico, one in the charge of the long-serving Grace and one presented to me in the aftermath of what Enrico still refers to as our 'famous victory' over Reverend Keller. Clearly I passed some kind of test that day.

At this moment I don't care about any sort of victory or

test, all I want to do is get inside that café and find out why Enrico hasn't turned up and why all the lights are blazing away inside, and why music (as I can now hear) is playing. It's a favourite of his from a year or so before, I think, but I don't even register that right now. All I can hear are the sounds of voices, raised voices, cascading out onto the street, even though the closed sign is on the front door and Enrico is clearly not open for business.

I open that front door as quickly as I can. Now I can hear laughter in amongst the raised voices, Enrico's laughter and someone else's, which reassures me a little, though it still doesn't solve the puzzle as to why Enrico hasn't followed us to a fair he was looking forward to just as eagerly as anyone and where there are always old friends to meet up with.

I cross the empty café, past the counter and the book (now back on the shelf) that just a few hours before so enraged Robin, and head on into the small whitewashed rear room, where the voices and laughter are loudest. I swing open the door and then stop in some confusion as a stranger stares up at me. Then Enrico appears, smiling his usual kindly welcome.

'This is Chiara.'

The stranger looks at me, a boy of about my age.

'This is the girl I was telling you about, the girl who made all this possible.'

The young man keeps looking back at me. He's tall, taller than Enrico, and slim, very slim. He wears his black hair a lot longer too.

'Without Chiara, if we'd had to close one day a week –'

Enrico shrugs, but then smiles, disaster averted.

'I could never have sent for you.'

Now the young man smiles at me too. A smile that's not like Enrico's, which has always reminded me of the smile of some kindly uncle, forever indulgent towards a young charge's foibles and faults. This smile is different.

'Michele – Chiara.'

Enrico, finally, makes the formal introductions.

'Chiara – my younger brother, Michele.'

Then Enrico nods at me, his smile growing wider all the while.

'Michele's come to join us. From now on you'll be working together.'

When I was five, I was helping my father out on the land at the back of our house. We had a goat then, just a single goat: in truth, more of a pet than a working animal. I'd run around with him most of the day, given half a chance. But one day, as I was running behind him, something must have scared him and he suddenly kicked back at me, catching me in the stomach.

Michele breaks in, speaking for the first time as he extends his hand towards me.

'It's good to meet you, Chiara.'

For those few moments, lying on the ground, looking up at the cloudless blue sky, the goat now still and shocked beside me, the sun blazing down, listening to the sound of Papà's footsteps as he dashed across to check I was all right, it was as if all the life had been knocked out of me.

Working as if on some sort of automatic reflex, I take Michele's hand in mine and mouth my response.

'It's good to meet you too, Michele.'

Enrico beams back at us both.

I'd forgotten about that day till then; that kick from the goat, my papà's anxious face, the way all the breath seemed to suddenly have been sucked out of my body. Now, all of a sudden, it's here again: that exact same feeling.

No-one's kicked me; I'm not lying helpless on the ground

looking up at the sky; I'm not seeing my father's face as he leans over me, making sure that I'm just winded, that I haven't broken any bones.

All that's happened is I've looked at a boy recently arrived from my home country, and for the second time in my life, I feel as if all the breath has just been kicked out of me.

Frankie

Today I ran a man over. Literally. In a car. Not my car, Uncle Tony's – although that doesn't really matter. All that matters is that one minute a man was standing up minding his own business and the next he'd been mown down, and it was all my fault.

I didn't mean it to happen. Not that it was much consolation to the man in question, not when he's lying on the pavement staring up at the underside of half a ton of motor that's just rolled on top of him.

Steve had finally managed to coax Tone's trusty – well, not so trusty – ancient Mini into life again. OK, I know you don't know what a Mini is, but I'm guessing you get an idea from the name? It isn't exactly a car for a growing family but whenever we can borrow it, we do. I love it and the kids love it, and they don't care that as they get older they're having to compete for an ever-decreasing supply of space in the back. When we all go out in it, that car's simply the dog's.

There's just one problem. Cars need petrol. Otherwise they don't tend to go very far. And as we haven't been able to afford to put petrol into it lately, that Mini hasn't gone anywhere at all lately either, one supermarket scam trip excepted. But then Steve did a bit of work for some mate of his who couldn't pay in cash, but who could pay in jerry cans filled with fuel. I've no idea where he got hold of it and Steve doesn't ask. He just sloshes the petrol in through the filler cap and puts the key in the ignition. Then, praying for a miracle, he whirs the starter.

It catches the very first time. Sitting outside our house, I swear it isn't running, it's purring. Next minute, the kids have piled in the back and Steve crams himself into the passenger seat alongside me. I find out where my little pride and joy is hiding first gear that day – because I love driving, I really do, so Steve can butt out of this one – and off we go up onto the mountain just like we used to do in the old days, windows down, radio on, everyone singing at the top of their voices.

Everyone we pass, we wave at, like we're royalty or something. Psaila gets a massive great honk on the horn as well. Uncle Tony nearly gets a bit more, as I lunge across the road towards him when I see him walking along, although I do shoot back across to the right side of the road pretty sharpish when I see he's with Zeno. I don't know why – maybe it was that stunt with the magic trick – but he definitely makes me uneasy.

Or maybe it's something else.

Something I really don't want to think about.

Something that makes me even more uneasy.

An hour later and Steve reckons we're close to running out of fuel. There's another jerry can at home, but that's for the next excursion. But no problem, it's downhill all the way from our new vantage point high above the town, so I just turn off the engine as we start our descent and we should be able to roll pretty well all the way home.

And we do. It may not be as much fun as going up, and at times – on the occasional level stretch of road – we do slow to pretty much a crawl before the next downhill slope takes us back to something like respectable speed again. And I am pressing the brakes a bit more than normal too, given that I can't use the gears to slow us down. By the time we've parked back outside the house, there's the definite whiff of something resembling burning coming from those front and rear wheels, but we don't care. We've just been on an adventure. We've had fun. And that's been in too-short supply lately. Who cares about the occasional whiff of brake dust?

Answer: the Mini does. I still don't know exactly what I did. Overcooked something, boiled something – I had no idea and Steve didn't have much more of a clue either. It didn't matter – all that did matter was that I'd put the handbrake on but it had problems engaging or whatever handbrakes do, probably because something somewhere was still overheating. And as we exit out of the two front doors and I slam the driver's door behind me, that Mini must have decided it was some sort of signal or something. Untethered by its now obviously redundant handbrake, it decides to set off on a little solo adventure of its own. Which, in this case, meant slipping down the hill towards the junction at the bottom.

Or, more accurately, towards two figures that have suddenly appeared at that junction at the bottom.

And have just turned up our street, heads bent in conversation, unaware that a stray Mini is now heading straight for them.

'You want two hundred quid?'

I look back at him, a man I'd last seen towering over me in my own kitchen, a flimsy wooden door smashed to the floor behind him. A man who'd turned Vicky's pup into a quivering wreck and who hadn't exactly done too much for my emotional well-being either. A man I never wanted to see again – and yet here I am, sitting opposite him in a smoke-filled portakabin, the wall behind him covered with pictures of naked women torn from the pages of various magazines, looking into his bewildered and – it has to be said – increasingly suspicious eyes.

I nod.

'Yeah.'

Eddie looks at me for a moment longer, then looks down and studies a ledger on his desk.

'And that's on top of what you already owe?'

I nod again.

'Yeah.'

'Which you're already behind on?'

'Still got my child benefit, haven't you?'

'I'm just saying.'

'So what's the problem? Vicky's just coming up to ten – there's going to be another eight years at least before that stops paying out on her, and there's Tyler too.'

Eddie pushes the ledger to one side and eyes me, ever more puzzled, ever more suspicious.

'Just can't work this out, that's all.'

'What's to work out? I want some money, you've got it. Seems simple enough to me.'

I hold his stare. Even for a Neanderthal throwback like you, I was going to say.

But I don't. I just keep looking at him instead.

'And you want this money for what exactly?'

'What the fuck has that got to do with you?'

'Only asking.'

'Ask away.'

He keeps staring at me.

'But you aren't going to say?'

I struggle for a moment. There is some brief attraction in stringing him along, but what's the point? He's going to find out soon enough anyway. And if I make some big deal out of all this, he really is going to have me down for some sort of local loon.

All the time, Eddie keeps eyeing me, his curiousity getting well and truly piqued. Which is another reason not to keep this going too much longer. Eddie being curious means Eddie taking an interest. That means another home visit, in all probability – just in case this two hundred quid was about to finance some money-making scam he can take an even bigger interest in.

And, as if by way of confirmation, he nods across his desk at me, a desk pockmarked by cigarette burns, coffee stains and the failed pleas of a thousand and one desperate souls.

'There must be some really special reason you want this money.'

I hesitate, one last time, then nod.

'There is.'

A day later and Steve, Tyler and Vicky are all blindfolded. That isn't anything to do with Eddie. This isn't some sort of heavyweight torture inflicted on the whole family this time. My business with Eddie had been concluded pretty speedily once he found out just why I wanted that cash.

'What's going on?'

Steve's asked the same question roughly every thirty seconds for the last five minutes. I blindfolded him first and he'd then had to wait while I fixed Tyler's and Vicky's in place.

'You'll see.'

'How can we? You've blindfolded us.'

That's Vicky. Unshakeable logic as ever.

'All right, you'll see when I take your blindfolds off. How's that?'

'So it's a surprise?'

That's Tyler, bless him. When it came to handing out the brains, he was definitely a little further down the line.

'You've flipped.'

I shake my head. No, I haven't.

'All will be revealed.'

'When?'

'Any minute now.'

'I've got an itch.'

'What?'

I stare at Tyler.

'On my nose.'

'Well scratch it then.'

'It's under the blindfold.'

Now Steve chips in.

'So have I.'

Vicky chips in too.

'And I hate the dark.'

'For God's sake!'

And the message must have got through because they all stop moaning, for a minute or two at least. I nod towards it. Not that they can see me do it, but I do anyway.

'Now walk to the door.'

'How?'

'One foot in front of the other?'

Steve cuts in again, as if he's some schoolteacher talking to a kid with special needs.

'We can't see where we're going.'

'You don't need to. Just start walking and I'll tell you if you start going wrong.'

They set off, Vicky leading, complaining all the while.

'This feels really weird.'

'I'll tell you if you're going to hit anything.'

I just get it out before there's a great crash. I've been

looking at Vicky and Tyler so I haven't been taking too much notice of Steve. In my book he's big enough and ugly enough to look after himself, which – and as with so many things when it comes to my husband – proves something of a fond hope as he now smashes into the side of the sofa and goes arse over tit onto the floor.

OK, that doesn't do too much for the general morale among the troops. And it doesn't help that for the next couple of minutes no-one can get any sense out of me, seeing as how I'm almost doubled up in fits of giggles.

'Cow.'

That's the now-sulky Steve's only contribution to the proceedings, which doesn't exactly help my attack of the giggles. In fact it only makes them worse, and I think Steve realises that because he repeats it.

'Cow.'

Which only sends me off on more fits of giggles, and they must be infectious because first Vicky joins in and then – more reluctantly, male solidarity and all that – so does Tyler. None of which does anything for the main man's mood.

'Look, if this is Let's-all-have-a-laugh-at-Steve Day, tell me – maybe I can start enjoying the joke too.'

I gasp.

'It's not Have-a-laugh-at-Steve Day.'

'Could have fooled me.'

'And it'll be worth it, I promise.'

'It'd better be.'

I shepherd them all to the door, making sure to avoid any more stray obstacles like Vicky's pup along the way. Something's telling me patience is already at a premium right now and I really don't want to stretch it beyond breaking point.

I open the door, pause for a moment, then nod at them.

'OK, you can all take your blindfolds off now.'

And they do. All three of them. And they stand there blinking in the sudden sunlight for a moment as their eyes grow accustomed to the view, which, in this case, comprises something pretty special – at least so far as I'm concerned.

'What's that?'

That's Steve, and he doesn't sound too impressed. I stare back at him.

'An elephant, what's it look like?'

Tyler sounds more enthusiastic.

'A caravan?'

So does Vicky.

'Wow.'

Steve surveys it some more.

'Is it ours?'

'No, I knocked it off from that new supermarket down the road.'

Steve just eyes me, sour.

'Yes, it's ours. Bought and paid for.'

Sort of, anyway. Steve turns his eyes away from me and back onto the new addition to the family.

'And you've bought and paid for it because...?'

'Why do you think?'

'What are we going to do with it?'

'What does anyone do with a caravan, for God's sake?'

I turn back to it. The new acquisition's been newly washed by myself and Uncle Tony, and now seems to be positively sparkling in the sunlight.

'We're going on holiday.'

Oh yeah, that bloke. The one I ran over. The one who was walking along minding his own business one minute, only to find himself underneath a Mini the next.

That was Zeno.

For a minute or two it all looks more than a bit serious. Well, I know it's always going to look more than a bit serious to Zeno anyway, but for a few moments I really think we've killed him. Actually, more accurately, I think I've killed him, given that I was the one who seems not to have secured the handbrake – as a near-hysterical Vicky, followed closely by a similarly-hysterical Tyler, and Steve (who is in very much the same sort of state) keep telling me. Luckily Tony is of more practical use, his efforts being directed less at targeting the culprit and more at helping the victim, which in this case means removing a Mini from on top of one prone Italian.

It doesn't take too long, thank God. Zeno regains the full power of speech almost immediately, a tirade of abuse erupting from his muffled mouth.

Later, he apologises. That was down to the shock, he explains, and it was pretty understandable in the circumstances too, as we all agree. Over a drink. In fact, over more than one drink. Which is the least we can do, take him out for a good few drinks, after the damage – actual and potential – we've inflicted.

Or – correction again – I've inflicted.

I've kept away from him up to this point. Don't need to tell you why, do I? He hasn't come on heavy to me. Nothing untoward has passed between us and all that. But you just know it sometimes, don't you? You can almost feel it in the air. Something dancing between you as some bloke walks by, says hello, passes the time of day, asks after the kids, whatever.

It doesn't matter what they say. It doesn't matter what you talk about. All that matters is that you can't remember afterwards what it was that you actually talked about, and that's when the alarm bells really should start ringing loud and clear.

Only now I'm not keeping away from him. Now I'm in a pub high up on the mountain with him. There isn't just me and him, of course – there's Steve and Uncle Tony and Tyler and Vicky as well, so this isn't some sort of illicit date. We're just having a family night out – well, extended family anyway, as Uncle Tony seems to have all but adopted Zeno at the moment too. There's nothing more to it than that, as I keep telling myself. And for most of the night there isn't.

Sometimes I wonder. Maybe all this isn't some kind of diary. Maybe I'm putting all this down for a different reason. Maybe by telling you about all that stuff down in the docks – and all that with Steve and Tyler and the trainers and that supermarket – and all that with Eddie and the money – maybe I'm trying to make everything feel OK.

I thought I was trying to make sense of it, but maybe that's not it at all. Maybe I'm just putting all this down so someone else can look at it sometime, can take a long, hard look at my life right now and can say: yeah Frankie, go on, why not? You deserve a bit of time off for good behaviour now and again, and anyway, who's going to know?

I've gone out for a ciggy. I'm standing outside that pub looking at all the lights in the town twinkling down below me. On nights like this it actually looks quite lovely. Until the sun rises and you can see all the shit again.

But tonight I can't see the shit. Tonight all I can see are those lights. And all I can smell is the heather, which seems to have a special sort of tang tonight too, until I realise it's not the heather at all but the scent of someone standing behind me wearing some special sort of aftershave or something. Or maybe that's just his natural smell, in which case I really am in trouble.

Zeno doesn't do anything, to be fair to him. He just stands next to me. I hold out the fag packet and he takes one and lights it and then just stands by my side, also looking out over those twinkling lights. And he doesn't speak for the next few minutes.

We just stand together in the kind of silence that settles between you when you're with someone you've known all your life, and there's no need for words.

One day later, after we set off in the new caravan, we pull up outside a church. And if the kids were bewildered when I'd frogmarched them out of bed and started handing out blindfolds, they're even more so now.

Steve's a little less bewildered, but then again he does have a bit of a head start on them. He's been here before, hasn't he?

'I don't get this.'

'Tyler, just shush will you.'

I'm glaring at him. OK, the vicar – not the same vicar, thank his boss – hasn't actually started the service yet, he's still leafing through what looks like notes for a depressingly long sermon while some old woman hands out Bibles and hymn books.

Behind us, some even older bloke is pulling on the same big rope, and he's definitely not the same old bloke as before when we turned up to hear our banns, but a close relation, by the grizzled look of him. As he pulls and lets go, pulls and lets go, a bell is ringing again high up in the tower above. I suppose it's some sort of signal, summoning everyone from far and wide to come and join the service, but if it is, it's not working. Apart from the old lady with the Bibles and the hymn books and the bloke ringing the bell and the Vicar with what looks like those notes for that depressingly long sermon, it's a pretty sparse congregation. Just a few other people dotted here and there and, this morning, the ragtag and bobtail Morrisseys.

'I don't get it either.'

I hiss at her now too.

'Vicky!'

'We're supposed to be going on holiday.'

Gobby little cow. You can usually silence Tyler with a glower but that daughter of mine always has been made of sterner stuff.

'So?'

'So Tyler's right, this don't make sense.'

'Holidays are for doing things you want to do, right?'

That's Steve, bless him. Trying to step in, support me. Not that it's convincing the kids too much. Not that he sounds all that convinced himself.

'So?'

That's Vicky again. Sometimes she's like a broken record.

'So this is what your mum wants to do.'

'Go to a church?'

'Yeah.'

'But we never go to church. We never even go to church when we're home.'

Tyler nods in heartfelt agreement.

'So what are we doing here now?'

'Just shut up, will you?'

That collects me a glare from the old woman who's handing out the Bibles. Truth be told, she's been looking at us suspiciously ever since we arrived – maybe she thinks we're some sort of advance party, looking to have it away with the lead from the roof or something.

Vicky doesn't. Shut up, that is.

'It's not like you're religious or nothing. Not even at

Christmas when Uncle Tony calls round and tries to get us to go to Midnight Mass – you always go down the pub with Dad instead.'

And the old woman hears that too, nosy old crone. And now she's moving back towards the vicar, probably to warn him that if one of us slips away during his sermon he'd better check his roof tiles.

'It's for old times' sake.'

'I still don't get it.'

I look at Steve.

'Are you sniffing?'

Steve begins grinning. He's been stifling the odd giggle ever since we walked in – actually ever since he woke up and I told him exactly what was on my mind – and that grin of his now just keeps on spreading.

He nods back.

'Think I've got a bit of a cold coming on.'

And now I'm grinning too and the kids are looking at each other like they really have woken up on the Planet Zog. Sorry, you won't know what that is either – the possibility of space travel's probably something that never even crossed your mind when you were growing up – but just imagine two kids looking at you as if you'd landed from some other world completely and that sort of sums up how my kids are looking at their two parents right now.

All the time I've been doing this sort of gentle shimmy, hoping to be discreet and really hoping I'm succeeding.

'Here.'

I reach out a hand, my fingers now closed tight, and hand the result of that gentle shimmy over to him. Steve nods.

'Cheers.'

And there it is again, just like I remember it: one great nose blow, sounding out all over that church, causing the bell ringer to pause, the old crone with the Bible to turn round, even the vicar to look up from what I thought were notes for his depressingly long sermon but which now looks to be his shopping list.

Steve clears his throat as the echo fades around the ancient, draughty old building.

'Sorry.'

By Steve's side, Tyler and Vicky just shake their heads. They've given up. They haven't got a clue what's going on.

For the next few days it was all pretty much as you'd expect. Well, pretty much as I assume you'd expect – I don't really know what holidays were like in your day. I don't even know if you had holidays, but then again you must have, because Uncle Tony's shown me pictures of outings you probably went on to Tredegar Park and Jersey Marine. Hundreds of you, there were, in all those black and white snaps – all crowded onto buses and into trains, so you must have had some sort of time off.

And if you did, then you'd probably have done everything we do. Beaches and candy floss and sandcastles and fun fairs. Actually, we didn't really do the sandcastles bit – that was just me, strictly speaking. My two kids are way too cool to be doing things like that these days, and Steve might have gone along with that stunt in the church, but no way was he about to get jiggy with a bucket and spade.

Something that does float his boat a bit more is the two of us going back to the caravan in the afternoon while Tyler and Vicky hit some arcade or other.

And now I'm thinking maybe I've got this wrong. This whole thing I'm doing right now – speaking into this machine, putting it all down like this, maybe it's not some attempt to justify things so if I do something bad – something involving,

193

say, Zeno for the sake of argument – then I'd be able to look back and say, who could blame me?

Because I'm not just recording the crap things, am I? Like Tyler and Steve and the supermarket, and Eddie and his close encounter with our kitchen door, or Psaila and our excursion down to the docks and a meeting with a man who met a woman called Nebuchadnezzar.

Now I'm recording the good things too: family things, like walks on a beach and late night barbecues, handkerchiefs and churches, shagging Steve senseless in the caravan after bribing our only too willing kids to leave their parents alone for a few hours.

Maybe I'm looking for a pattern here. Maybe that's what this is all about. Maybe I'm putting all this down so I can look back on it in months to come and take some sort of comfort from it all. So if anything else bad happens – like Tyler and the supermarket, or Eddie and the kitchen door, or Psaila and her excursions – I can see that for every bad time there's a good one too. Maybe this isn't about me talking to you at all, a woman I've never met and a woman no-one seems to know anything about. Maybe I'm talking to myself, and maybe I'm telling myself that if I just hang on, then everything'll be OK. And all I've got to do is go back over everything I've put down, and I'll see that.

And I believe that, I really do.

For the rest of that whole caravan trip and for the whole of the journey home, too.

Until we actually get home, that is.

And then everything changes again.

Chiara

G RACE IS TALKING. Actually, Grace hasn't stopped talking since the fair. Non-stop, on and on.

The same subject all the time.

'Doesn't he?'

'Grace!'

'He must do.'

'Pass me the kettle.'

She stares at me.

'How can you think about kettles? How can you think about anything?'

'We're working.'

'Especially work!'

Now Grace is eyeing me in something approaching total bewilderment. Not for the first time, she's obviously wondering if we even live in the same world.

'I mean, all right: I know you're little Miss Virtue.'

I blink.

'Little Miss what?'

'Keeping yourself for Mr Right.'

This time I don't answer.

'Whoever he is.'

I really am keeping silent now.

'Wherever he might be.'

However, my voice is sounding, ever louder, inside my head: please Grace, just stop.

Perhaps fortunately (or she really would have pressed me, I know), Grace isn't even looking at me now. Instead she has the same dreamy expression on her face she's had since the day of the fair. Or, more accurately, since she came back from the fair, lips still burning, only to forget all about boys with beautiful bums the moment she walked back inside the café and saw Michele.

'You won't even talk to any of the local boys.'

'I do talk to them, I talk to them all the time. I serve them drinks and sweets and –'

Grace cuts across again. I'm talking too much, I know. Babbling, she calls it; but this time Grace is barely listening. She's locked in a dream world of her own and in that world right now, three is very definitely a crowd.

'But be fair, Chiara: just looking at him, doesn't he make you want to –'

That's when the door opens, a customer comes in and Grace, reluctantly, tears herself away to serve him. She doesn't finish what she was saying, but she doesn't need to.

I don't answer, but I don't need to either.

Yes. He does.

One hour later and Grace's mind is still running on the same track. Michele himself is out. Enrico has put him on the ice cream run and he's been away from the café since first thing this morning. Fair-minded Enrico has offered him the same deal he was offered himself in his first job, the same self-imposed deal Enrico has strictly observed these last couple of years.

Sell all the ice cream, and Michele can catch the train back. Don't sell it all, and he'll have to push the handcart back all the way from the seaside, trying to sell the remainder en route.

It's unseasonably cold outside. There's little chance of any ice cream sales that day. Grace has all but resigned herself to not seeing Michele until nearly closing time, and it's hurting.

'You've put soap in the teapot.'

I stare at her as one of our regular customers on the other side of the counter gasps and splutters, his tea, untouched aside from one now much-regretted sip, abandoned in front of him.

'Those eyes.'

Once again the dreamy Grace hardly hears me.

I hiss at her.

'You've poisoned Mr Bevan.'

A pair of accusing eyes swing my way, and they don't belong to the still-gasping Mr Bevan.

'You were watching when he set off this morning too, I saw you.'

'Grace!'

'Well, weren't you?'

Once again and as always under her challenging stare, I can't help it. I feel the beginning of an unwilling grin spreading across my face, signalling, as it always does, that Chiara's been caught out.

'Well?'

Across the café, sounding ever louder now, all I can hear is another extended bout of coughing.

Reluctantly, I concede the inevitable admission.

'Perhaps.'

Grace practically snorts, tossing back those red curls of hers.

'Perhaps nothing. I saw you: your tongue was practically hanging out, so don't think – oh my God!'

I wheel round as Grace suddenly stares behind me.

Standing in the doorway is Michele.

Grace is the first to recover.

'Back already?'

Michele smiles, almost shyly. He seems quietly pleased with himself, but for now just contents himself with a simple acknowledgement and a question.

'But I've run out of –'

Michele hesitates.

'That drink.'

'What drink?'

'Someone just asked me for it while I was putting away the cart.'

Michele hesitates again.

'Ox-something.'

Grace steps in.

'O.'

'What?'

'Put them together.'

Under a now-grinning Grace's tutelage, Michele begins to do so.

'O.'

Michele repeats it.

'O.'

Grace nods.

'X.'

'X.'

Grace nods again.

'O.'

Michele nod backs, putting it all together just as Grace told him.

'OXO.'

All the time Grace is moving closer.

'Clever boy.'

Michele smile grows wider as Grace nods across the room.

'There's a pot up on the counter.'

Behind Grace, Mr Bevan has decided some fresh air is needed and is heading for the door, shooting her a savage look as he does so. It doesn't register. Nothing short of the heavens crashing in will register with Grace right now. Grace is still eyeing Michele and now a certain smile is playing on her lips, a smile I know only too well, a smile that means one thing and one thing only.

'Your English really isn't too good, is it, Michele?'

'Not too good, no.'

'You need lessons.'

'Yes.'

Grace looks up into Michele's eyes, practically drinking him in as she does so.

'Why don't you come out with me and Chiara? Sunday afternoon? We always get an hour or so off in the evening. We can go for a walk up on the mountain and we can teach you some English words. What do you say?'

What could Michele say?

He nods back.

'Thank you.'

Grace's smile widens.

'In fact, why don't we start right now?'

I tense. I've no idea what Grace has in mind but I can tell from the expression on her face that the last thing she's interested in right now is grammar.

'Grace?'

But Grace ignores me, her eyes fixed only on Michele.

'Repeat after me.'

Michele looks at her. Perhaps he's picking up on the expression on my face, but now he's beginning to look nervous.

'OK.'

'I.'

Michele hesitates.

'I.'

'Have got.'

Across the crowded café, I stare at her. She can't be serious. Then again, this is Grace.

Michele looks at me again, and can see that same something in my eyes as I hiss at her.

'Grace!'

Then he looks back at Grace, who's now eyeing him, mock-sternly; a teacher fixing a recalcitrant pupil with her stare.

Grace prompts him again.

'Have got –'

Michele continues.

'Have got.'

Grace smiles, her eyes softening as she does so.

'A beautiful –'

I close my eyes. I'd have closed my ears too if I could. I know exactly what's going to come next, and I know what's going to happen when it does. I'm going to collapse in giggles either because Michele has completed the sentence or because he hasn't. Either way, it doesn't matter; I'm not going to be able to help myself.

The unsuspecting Michele repeats her soft instruction.

'A beautiful –'

Grace hesitates for a tantalising moment. Dimly, I'm aware of a door opening behind us, but all I'm waiting for is Grace's next word and the expression on Michele's face.

'Name.'

I open my eyes, this time to find Grace grinning at me as Michele smiles, shyly again, and makes to repeat the final word of today's lesson. But Enrico cuts across from the doorway before he can do so.

'Michele.'

Michele turns, his smile fading, and no wonder. Enrico's face is like thunder. I look across at Grace. What's the matter? Has he been standing there, listening? Does he not approve or something? That wouldn't be like Enrico: he enjoys the constant conversation in the café, the exchanges between Grace and myself, the light teasing with the customers. There are café owners (we'd met some at the fair) who insist on their employees conducting themselves in near-silence while doing their duties, but Enrico has never been one of them.

Enrico nods outside.

'You've not sold the ice cream.'

Michele hesitates.

'No, Enrico.'

'But you came back on the train.'

Michele hesitates again.

'Yes.'

'Did you not understand your instructions?'

This time Michele doesn't hesitate at all.

'I understood them, Enrico.'

I look at Grace, hesitating now as Enrico's cheeks began to mottle. Is Michele openly defying his elder brother already?

'I couldn't sell all that ice cream, not today. It's too cold. I only sold what I did by asking a lower price.'

Enrico's cheeks mottle further.

'But you still came back on the train. You didn't even try selling it on the road.'

'I didn't come back on the train to avoid walking. I came back on the train to raise money, not to spend it.'

'What are you talking about?'

'I used the money I made from the ice cream I sold to buy chips.'

Enrico blinks.

'Chips?'

'From that shop down on the – what do they call it, the long street next to the beach –'

Grace, quite clearly his unofficial tutor now in all matters to do with language, steps in.

'The Strand.'

Michele nods.

'I checked the timetable. There was a train leaving in five minutes and that was the nearest chip shop to the station. Before they could cook more chips, the train would be gone.'

Michele leans his arms on the counter. A thin down covers his forearms that I'd not noticed before. Soft. Almost like fur.

'I bought all the chips in the shop. The train was busy. A lot of the passengers went to that shop after me, to buy something to eat on the train, but there was nothing. Then I walked up and down the train and called: "bags of chips, bags of chips." With the beautiful smell in the small train, everybody wanted some!'

Michele shook his head.

'It made me hungry too! After three stops, all the chips were sold for double the price. I counted the money and I have more than if I sold all the ice cream, and we still have some ice cream to sell in the café.'

There's a stunned silence as Michele finishes and Enrico sees the money in his brother's hand.

Then it starts. A trademark, massive, booming Enrico belly-laugh. A laugh of absolute delight, and we can't help it: I join in, Grace joins in and Michele joins in too. Across the café, customers join in as well. They don't know what they're laughing about, but they don't care.

Enrico eyes his brother, his eyes brimming with tears of pleasure and pride. Then he nods at him.

'You and a cart full of chips.'

Then he nods back at me.

'Chiara and the Reverend Keller.'

My smile begins to fade. I try to subdue the sudden stab of pleasure that has ambushed me as Enrico includes Michele and myself in the same approving glance, knowing that it's nothing to do with Enrico's approval.

'What a team.'

Grace chips in.

'And just wait till he has his lessons.'

'Lessons?'

Grace nods.

'Me and Chiara are giving him English lessons. Starting this Sunday, up on the *bryn*: an hour each week.'

But I cut across, quickly.

'Your English is much better than mine, Grace.'

Grace looks back at me.

'You give Michele his lessons. I'll look after the café.'

For a moment, I'm aware of something passing across Michele's face, but I keep my eyes fixed on Grace as I nod at her, a silent signal dispatched and, from the look on her face now, understood.

'I insist.'

Later that night it's just Enrico and myself clearing up the café before we close for the night. For one of the few times I can remember, we're alone.

It seems strange now, looking back, but it had almost never happened before. Back home, I was only ever with

Enrico in the company of others, my mother, my father and my brothers. In the café I was only ever with Enrico in the company of Grace and the customers who'd pack those small rooms all hours of the day as well as some of the night.

Tonight, as I'm clearing up and Enrico is checking the daily ledger, while Grace is showing Michele some of the sights of the town, it's just the two of us. All of a sudden, out of the blue, Enrico asks me a question.

'Has it gone now, Chiara? That sickness we talked about?'

I look back at him, my smile his answer. Enrico smiles back.

'It didn't leave me for months when I left Bardi. When I first walked along those strange streets, looked at all those strange sights, listened to people talking in a strange tongue, barely understanding any of the words I was hearing. For the whole of the first year, I just wanted to go home.'

Enrico looks out of the window. For once it isn't raining.

'I thought, how can I ever get used to this? How can I ever make any sort of sense of it?'

'But you did.'

Enrico looks round his café wryly.

'Some would wonder sometimes.'

Then he looks back at me.

'When I came to your house that day, the day we talked about your coming here, that wasn't the first time I'd visited.'

I nod. I know.

'The year before.'

'Not the year before.'

I stare back at him, puzzled.

'I'd been there a few days before. I'd asked to see your father. We'd talked in the market before that about the possibility of your coming over, and I felt I owed him an explanation.'

I keep staring at him, even more puzzled now.

'For what?'

'For why I'd changed my mind. Why I'd decided to give up my life over here.'

I'm still staring at him, all this a complete revelation to me.

Enrico shrugs.

'But he changed my mind.'

'How?'

'By not even trying.'

Enrico smiles again.

'We went for a walk instead. Up to the castle. And he talked about his early years, coming there from the south, not understanding the dialect or even most of the words, having that feeling that no matter how long he stayed, he'd never fit in there, that it was always going to be too strange for him, that he really didn't know how long he could take it, being a stranger in what felt like an alien land.'

It's like listening to someone talking about a complete stranger, but Enrico's talking about my father. One of the few constants in my life. A man who never had doubts about anything; at least none he'd ever expressed to me.

'But he didn't return. He stayed where he was, and you know why?'

I shake my head and now there's a faraway look in Enrico's eyes as if he's back there, that day, up on those castle ramparts with my beloved Papà.

'He realised it wasn't a land that makes a home, or your surroundings that make you happy. It wasn't where you were that mattered at all, not really. Like he said to me, you could be in the coldest place on the planet and still feel warm. You could be in some tropical jungle and still feel a deep chill in your bones. What mattered was something else.'

Enrico smiles again as I keep staring at him, rapt.

'He realised that when he met your mother. All of a sudden everything that hadn't made any sort of sense to him suddenly did. All of a sudden all those feelings he had of being a man apart – a man alone, I suppose – vanished. He felt like he'd come home, even though he was far away from the place he knew as home. And he hoped that one day, wherever I was in the world, I'd have that same feeling; the feeling that I'd come home, even if it wasn't where I'd originally thought of as home. Because that feeling, when it comes, can come upon you anywhere. You could be anywhere in the world, when all of a sudden you look round and everything feels –'

Enrico pauses now, searching for the word.

'Right.'

I keep looking at him.

'Is that how you feel now?'

'Yes.'

Enrico smiles at me.

'Listen to me. Listen how serious I sound. I don't mean to. I don't even know what I'm saying, not really.'

Enrico pauses.

'I suppose I'm trying to say that I owe your father a great deal. For his words, for that walk, for making me see something I couldn't see myself.'

Enrico nods at me and I smile back, and then a silence falls. A silence that lingers and feels warm and comfortable. A silence that used to fall on me in my old country.

A silence I always associate with home.

Do you ever look back on what seem like chances and accidents? Events that seem to come from nowhere and have no significance you can see at the time? Then, later, sometimes a lot later, you realise they're not just accidents at all? That in some way it's as if some sort of destiny is shaping it all, that fate is taking a hand.

Then, maybe years later, you see it for what it really is. You see that all those moments and incidents and events all fit together so neatly somehow, it's as if someone's welded them together. Perhaps it was you yourself who did it – you've willed them all together, somehow. For a reason you couldn't have understood at the time.

It's one day soon after my late-evening conversation with Enrico, and suddenly there's a huge commotion out in the street.

'Chiara!'

Grace dashes in and her face, usually so bubbly, so warm, is contorted in fear and panic. She's in such a state she can barely get out her words.

I stare at her. What's happened?

Then, behind her, the door opens again and Sergeant James comes in; but this isn't the usual kindly and gentle Sergeant James. He looks as grim as Grace is panicky. In a tone that brooks no refusal, he tells us to lock the doors and bar the windows, to call Enrico in from the rear room where he's doing the daily ledger, and to try and get a message to Michele, who's out with the ice-cream cart, to warn him not to come back to the café till nightfall.

Then the rest of his instruction is cut short, as are all my increasingly panicked questions, as a brick smashes through the plate glass window behind him. It shatters into tiny shards which cascade down over the counter, the hot water urn and the rows and rows of boiled sweets, sending the customers inside diving for cover.

I stare at Sergeant James as he turns and barricades the door, dragging benches from across the café to make some sort of temporary barrier against what sounds like the onset of Armaggedon outside.

It's money, of course. It was always about money back in those days. Perhaps it's still the same for you or perhaps you've moved beyond all that by now. Maybe the golden days the flame-haired Robin predicted have become reality, and maybe where there was discord and division there's now a fairer age when brother doesn't need to stand with brother against men who see themselves as providers, but whom others call oppressors.

I hope so, I truly do; but it always sounded too good to ever come true to me. Perhaps I just needed to have a little more faith.

Years before, times had been good. They'd been good because coal, mined in all the local collieries, was flowing like tap water. Nantgwyn, Clydach Vale, Ely, the Glamorgan and Naval: everywhere you looked, there was colliery after colliery, each one employing hundreds, sometimes thousands of men. Grace said that the café's former owners had told her that what sometimes seemed like hundreds if not thousands more would walk along the main street outside the café each morning, before splitting to enter what looked like a dozen different gates. They would re-emerge hours later, tired, caked in coal dust, hungry and thirsty; meaning good times for every shopkeeper as they returned back along that same main street. Many would even come in on their way into work for a cup of tea and a smoke, leaving their packets of cigarettes on a shelf behind the counter to be picked up at the end of their shift.

Their wages weren't fixed in the way mine and Grace's

wages were decided at the start of each year. Yes, we had those wages reviewed on an annual basis – and if we'd had a particularly good week then sometimes there'd be a little extra at the end of it – but by and large we knew what we'd be earning. Then again, the income of the café didn't vary all that much, Reverend Keller-type protests aside.

For the miners it was different. Their wages were linked to the selling price of the coal they produced. If the supply was good and the seam easily worked then everyone benefited as they had for years. Everyone thought it would last forever.

But then more and more companies opened up, all attracted by those seemingly never-ending times of plenty. More and more coal came onto the market, but the miners were still making a good living. There was still money flowing into the pits and from the pits into their pockets and so into ours.

There'd been rumblings for years, but as autumn began to pass into winter that year, the rumblings grew louder and louder. It was always a difficult time in the valley anyway: the cold had really begun to bite, as it always did, and Christmas was fast approaching; the time of year when everyone needed a little extra. More and more mines meant harder and harder seams were being accessed, producing smaller and smaller yields. It was just about the worst possible time for those thousands and thousands of miners to start taking home not just a little, but a lot, lot less.

Suddenly, all those workers started returning home not only exhausted and hungry, but frustrated and angry too. It probably had to happen sooner or later, looking back. The earth offers up its riches for only so long. Now it had decided to withhold them.

According to the basic economics that I'd just about managed to understand from Robin, a reduced supply should have meant the price rising, and so the wage any individual miner received should have stayed roughly the same. But that wasn't the way it worked, apparently, although when I asked him why, Robin became so incandescent with rage that he didn't actually manage to explain it at all.

It was of no consequence anyway. The effects were all too obvious. Less and less money went into the pockets of those ever more exhausted miners each week, and bitterness and anger grew. One attempt to negotiate a new agreement foundered, then another, and then another. And then the unthinkable happened.

Twelve thousand men, almost the whole of the workforce in the town, came out on strike. Pickets were posted at the entrances to all the collieries in case any stray miner felt like defying the union and heading into work, but not one miner, stray or otherwise, seemed so inclined. At first it all felt a little like the annual festa, especially when all the miners went on a protest march through the town, singing songs, chanting slogans and parading placards. While it was all policed at a local level by Sergeant James and his men, the whole thing was peaceful, if boisterous.

Then higher authorities than Sergeant James decided that extra policing was required. The problem was that there were no more officers available and so troops were drafted in. Whether it was the unexpected sight of the military uniforms or the fact that some of those troops were less than sensitive to the feelings of the local population (to put it mildly) was a matter that was going to be debated for months to come.

Miners from out of town came to join those in the town to protest. More troops came in to quell the growing disturbances. That provoked the arrival of yet more protestors, swelling the ranks of the miners from the town and the ones who'd come to join them. The whole area had been simmering for days. Today, it exploded, provoking Grace's panicky entrance back into the café just a few moments before, to the sound of windows smashing along the street.

There's been trouble like it before, of course. Other cultures, people from different nationalities, move into a community that isn't their own: it always causes tensions. A lead mine just a few kilometres away caused a lot of trouble when a change of owners led to a mass importation of labour from elsewhere. It was doubly unfortunate that their arrival coincided with an outbreak of a new sickness, miners' anaemia, and as usually happened, the incomers were blamed. It didn't matter that samples taken by a government inspector cleared the new migrants of any part in the outbreak. The damage had been done, and attitudes had hardened. The mine in question struggled on for a few more years, but no locals would work there and no more immigrants wanted to follow those who'd blazed their now dubious trail, and the mine closed.

And if there was trouble just a few kilometres away, that was nothing compared to the troubles scarring France at the time. Italians have always flocked to France: it's closer than Britain and there's no forbidding stretch of water to cross. All sorts go to ply their trades (shoe blacks, organ grinders, poodle clippers) but even more go to work in the factories, on the building sites, in the docks and in the mines.

The problem is that the owners of those building sites, docks and mines see one thing, and one thing only. Cheap labour. Or, at least, labour that can be employed considerably more cheaply than anything available at home. It isn't the new arrivals' fault. Most of them have no idea what the usual rate for any particular job might be in a strange country and among people who don't speak their native tongue, so they accept whatever's on offer. The French workers were incensed at being effectively priced out of their own jobs by those working for sometimes half their wages. Clashes occurred again, everything coming to a head when a whole series of riots broke out. Stories about some of the worst excesses filtered back to us here. Men roamed the streets with coshes, pickaxes, even firearms, in a battle that lasted two whole days. By the end of it all, at least fifty men had been killed and more than a hundred and fifty wounded.

And even when there's no open hostility, there can still be trouble. We heard tales back home of travellers who'd ventured further north to Scotland, a country even colder than this one (though it scarcely seemed possible to us at the time). The incomers were dispersed among the community, but that community wasn't mobile; didn't travel, by and large. They stayed in the same city in the same country for most of their lives. They understood people would come in from outside from time to time and they tolerated them, but that was all. Time and again, people would return home, not with tales of any outright hostility or opposition, just a general feeling that whatever happened they were simply never going to fit in.

Even here, in this largely tolerant town, there are those who are never going to fit in either. Up to now it hasn't been Italians who have been the object of dislike, but another set of incomers: Jews, though this is less about these people as a race than about their occupation. Many have opened pawnbroker's shops, which might offer a service, much-needed at times, but it's a trade always associated with the last refuge of the desperate and the damned. No-one will ever welcome a walk into those sort of establishments, and the owners manning them didn't receive any thanks for their endeavours either.

It's totally different for us, probably due to what we actually do. Most of the Italians working in our valley don't work in the mines or the factories: they work in cafés much like Enrico's. Our customers come in because they want to. Many stay for hours on end, talking, laughing, sharing stories, swapping tales. We've got to know them and they've come to know us. We've posed no threat and our services have been enjoyed and appreciated.

'What the – ?'

That's Enrico, who's just dashed down from upstairs and is now staring in shock at his smashed window, at the hands already reaching inside to take what they can from the display. These are strangers' hands, not the hands of our customers; but that hardly matters. The only thing that does is that we're under siege, and Enrico springs forward to stop the looters.

I spring forward too to try to stop him, but all he can see is our livelihood literally vanishing before our eyes. He heads outside to remonstrate with the miscreants just as Michele returns with his cart, right in the middle of the trouble, to see his brother being attacked.

Michele joins his brother, both himself and Enrico now facing the looters, standing shoulder to shoulder with each other. Then bricks started to rain down on the two brothers' heads, and before Enrico's disbelieving eyes Michele turns and runs inside. Even the smitten Grace looks momentarily stunned at what seems to be the hasty retreat. The next moment we both stare, even more stunned, as he dashes back outside again with the sarsaparilla fountaina soda siphon in hand, pausing only to hiss two single words at the two of us as he passes.

'Ice cream!'

Then he's back by Enrico's side again.

Grace stares at me, totally lost. A few feet in front of us, Michele steadies himself. Then, as another brick is about to be launched in their direction, Michele scores a direct hit on the perpetrator with soda from the siphon, the sudden jet of compressed liquid leaving the would-be assailant gasping.

Enrico dashes back inside for another soda siphon and he hisses the same two words at us too. Grace is still just staring at him bewildered but, realisation finally dawning, I turn and dash for the ice cream tub.

'What the hell are you doing?'

Between gasps, I get it out.

'It's a weapon.'

'You can't throw a tub at them!'

'We can throw the ice cream.'

By now we're manhandling the tub outside.

'Oh, that's really going to make them turn tail and run! They're chucking bricks at us and we throw back a couple of cornets!'

By now Enrico is spraying the looters with soda, Michele continuing to blast them with sarsaparilla. I dig inside the tub, fashion a large scoop of ice cream into a ball, hurl it at another of the looters who's managed to dodge the combined efforts of Enrico and Michele and is actually reaching inside the smashed window towards the fallen display of cigarettes. The makeshift snowball hits him full in the face, and, unbalanced, he falls to the ground. Spluttering, he opens his mouth to receive a direct hit from Enrico's soda siphon. He scrambles to his feet choking on the soda only to be blinded by a blast of sarsaparilla from Michele. Grace now gets in on the act by hurling a newly-fashioned ball of solid ice cream which hits him in the very middle of his fast-retreating back.

Across the street, Sergeant James is now playing no part in rebuffing the increasingly disorientated efforts of the looters. He can't. He's too busy holding his sides, weeping in helpless hysterics at the sight of an angry mob being driven back by a combination of sarsaparilla, soda and different flavours of Italian ice cream.

At the same time Robin arrives, summoned by the commotion, and decides to abandon his moral objections to the ownership of private property (for the rest of the evening at least) by dipping his own hands into the ice cream tub and firing off yet more makeshift snowballs – although he'll later claim he was really standing in solidarity with one of his fellow oppressed, as evidenced by the symbol of the Blackshirts on Enrico's now infamous book.

Within moments the street is quiet again, if now awash with sticky drink and melting ice cream. Peace begins to descend, broken only by Sergeant James's helpless and continuing fits of laughter. Enrico turns to Michele and embraces him. He indicates to Grace and myself to join them and she needs no second invitation. All four of us stand on the street in silent triumph for a moment, arm in arm, the café relatively intact behind us.

Then Enrico breaks free.

'Come on.'

I look at him.

'Where are we going?'

'We're opening the second bottle of Barolo.'

Grace stares at him.

'The one you're keeping for Christmas?'

A grinning Michele breaks in.

'Christmas has come early.'

It's infectious; it always is. Sergeant James' continuing huge snorts of laughter set off first Enrico, then Michele, then Grace, then myself. We turn to head back inside to celebrate this, our unlikeliest of victories.

That's when Michele slips on one of the melting makeshift snowballs. He crashes to the floor, smashing his head on the kerb as he does so. He moans for a second, then lies still. As we all stare at him, I see blood streaming from underneath his head. In that moment, I'm convinced he's dead.

Enrico rushes Michele back into the warm, whitewashed, rear room to treat his head wound. Grace runs between them and the kitchen with hot water and bandages; then I step in.

I've treated injuries before. Living off the land, or trying to live off the land, as we did back home, there were always minor cuts and scrapes and bruises to treat and my mother had taught me from an early age how to look after my brothers, and even my father on one occasion, when our sole goat decided he was due for a kick as well.

My fingers might have fumbled at first, but after a while I became quite proficient. Mamma even suggested I might want to take it up at one time, that I might travel to a larger town or city somewhere and become a nurse, but that wasn't what the fates had determined for me. I am here instead. Michele, thank God, is now coming round, albeit very, very slowly. But his wound (not deep, but quite wide) is still in urgent need of cleaning and dressing.

What did I do? Simple. I had two bottles of antiseptic on the shelf, or at least I thought I did. Actually one was antiseptic, and the other was a bottle of hard liquor which we used to feed a cake on which we all feasted each Easter. Enrico dripped a few drops into it each week. With my fingers fumbling ever more, I shake the bottle of liquor over the head wound rather than the gently cleansing antiseptic.

The effect's instantaneous. Michele springs up as if stung by a horde of crazed bees and, before I can stop him, charges past Grace, through the café and out into the street.

He howls like a madman. Those few rioters who are still out on the street and resisting Sergeant James' entreaties to go home immediately abandon their sport and vanish in the face of a clear lunatic's sudden arrival on the scene. Michele howls again as the liquor bites deeper into his head wound, cleaning it more efficiently (if rather more harshly) than any simple antiseptic could have managed. By now we're all outside with Michele and I've gasped out an explanation of the mistake I've made and the suffering I've accidentally inflicted. The treatment has been more than a little drastic, but Michele's wound is healing more quickly than would have been the case with the rather more humane antiseptic.

By now too the lacerating stings are beginning to wear off. Behind Michele, the street is now almost deserted. A neighbour, a draper, is now collecting rolls of cloth and buckets of buttons from the pavement where looters have dropped them. Robin and a few other volunteers are tacking some wood in place to make good, temporarily at least, the damage to the front of the café.

Michele looks at me and I look back at him. I start to stammer an apology, then stop as a smile begins to spread across his face; a smile that just keeps widening as my obvious confusion and distress continues.

Then, and just like Enrico (in an exact carbon copy of his brother, in fact), Michele starts to laugh, a great belly-laugh that seems to burst from the very pit of his stomach, and soon we're all doing the same.

It's everything: a release of tension, an expression of thanks that the night has passed with such little cost compared to what might have happened, as well as an acknowledgement of an honest mistake.

However, none of that explains why I made that honest mistake in the first place, or why my fingers start to fumble and my breath begins to catch in the back of my throat whenever Michele simply walks into a room.

PART FIVE

'Moral Virtues and their Contrary Vices'

(Proverbs 12–24)

Frankie

THE HOLIDAY WAS just what we wanted. Correction, it was just what we needed – even if the kids found bits of it totally baffling, if not completely wacko. Vicky definitely looked at me and Steve very strangely for days after that knickers-in-the-church moment.

It didn't help that the grizzled old bell ringer from the same church turned out to have a permanent caravan parked right next to the pitch we'd booked for the first of our two weeks away. God knows whether he thought I was sending out some sort of signal or something that day, but he got in the habit of popping in every so often just to make sure we were all right, that there was nothing I needed, nothing he couldn't help me with, if I got his drift. I got his drift all right and we cut short that bit of the holiday by three full nights and spent them camped out in a dead village by the sea instead. Well, what used to be a dead village by the sea.

Maybe you visited it yourself when it was full of people. I never quite understood the timescale of events but from the bits I read about the place, it would still have been a working village in your day. Ten years before our visit it was still derelict. All that was left were a couple of rows of old tinplate workers' houses marooned at the bottom of the steepest ravine you'd ever seen, accessed by the steepest road you'd probably ever dare travel. But when you got there, it was as if you'd suddenly arrived at the edge of the world. Nothing between you and the sea. No sounds, aside from the surf, absolutely no traffic, just the occasional screech of a gull. It was one of those pockets of peace you occasionally stumble across and never want to leave. Even the kids shut up for once as we walked down into it. Then they – and we – just sat on rocks and looked out over the water and dreamt of days gone by and better days to come.

In other words, we got back to what we're good at. What we're the best at, I've always believed deep down. Being a family. A family that spends time together, that talks to each other, that listens to each other and laughs. All the simple things we don't seem to find time for at home, even though in the case of Steve, time was the one thing he had in bucketfuls. Even if everything else was in pretty short supply.

Maybe sometimes it needs a change of scene like that to make you realise what you've already got. Listen to me – I sound like Dorothy from *The Wizard of Oz*, although maybe you've never have heard of that either. It's a film that takes a good couple of hours to play out, but what it's really about in the end can be summed up in five simple words: There's No Place Like Home.

Towing the caravan back along the main street, the first person we see is Uncle Tony outside his café, cleaning the windows. Maybe it was the same window you used to look out from if and when you were here. There'd been some riot decades before and the original window had been smashed, but Tony reckoned the replacement had been there ever since. I used to stand behind the counter sometimes and think of the thousands of pairs of eyes that must have looked out through that window in all those years since, and I found it comforting somehow. A reminder that time goes on but sometimes things don't really change. That people still do exactly the same things they always did. Spend time together, talk to each other, listen to each other and laugh.

Apart from buying the same amount of tea, coffee and snacks, as Uncle Tony pointed out. He still had some of the old ledgers kept by one of the old owners, the original Signor Carini from – where else? – Bardi. Adjusting for inflation, as them economic pundits on the TV always seem to say, his takings put Uncle Tony's present-day meagre pocketings well and truly in the shade.

Tony nods at us as I slow and wind down the window.

'Didn't fall to bits then?'

I nod back at our temporary and – now much-loved – home being towed along behind us.

'This thing's solid as a rock.'

Tony shot a half-glance across at the slumbering Steve by my side.

'Wasn't talking about the caravan.'

'Cheeky bastard.'

Tony just smiles that warm smile of his.

'And you had a good time?'

'No.'

I pause.

'We had a great time.'

In the back of the car, the sleepy Vicky and Tyler hear that and they nod, then suddenly stop in case any of their mates see them and they don't look cool.

But then I hesitate, making sure they – or Steve – can't hear this next bit.

'Tony.'

I hesitate again as he looks back at me.

'I've got a favour to ask.'

Ten minutes later the kids are unpacking the caravan. They wanted to know why it was just the two of them that had to do it when half that mess at least was mine and Steve's. I told them they had to do it because I said so and, that day's lesson in good parenting done and dusted, I took Uncle Tony out to the back garden.

On the way he tells me Zeno has left town. Him and the rest of his mates from the old country have gone to take part in some massive march that's taking place up in Scotland protesting about some cuts or something. He didn't know exactly which ones, but there were always cuts of some kind. After that Zeno didn't know his plans, but thought he'd probably return home.

I nod in all the right places and try to look none too interested, but I don't fool Tony and I don't fool myself either.

'I wondered if he had anything to do with you heading away so quick.'

I don't reply for a moment. Maybe because I don't really want to say anything. Up to now any demons that have prodded me have done so inside. I really don't want to give them a voice.

'Things do need to change, Tone. For me, for Steve, for the kids, but –'

I tail off but don't need to go on. Tony – wise old Tony – finishes it for me anyway.

'Not that much.'

'No.'

He smiles at me and I smile back. No need to say any more really.

'So. This favour?'

I dig into my pocket, hold up a small key.

'If I give this to you once I've finished getting things sorted, can you keep it for me?'

'What is it?'

'The key to the shed.'

Tony looks at me, puzzled, then looks down the crumbling path towards the bottom of the garden. Steve had put the shed up a few years before. Like all sheds, it didn't house anything much. Over the years it had become more of a dumping ground for all sorts of stuff – old bikes, broken toys, revolving washing lines that didn't revolve any more – all the usual sort of useless rubbish you always say you really should just chuck away but never do, for reasons you can't remember.

Tony looks back at me and I take a deep breath. Stage two in the grand new master plan. First, get me well away from temptation and get us all functioning as a proper family once again, doing proper family things like stripping off in churches, outraging old ladies and intriguing randy bell ringers.

Then, second, get me functioning as a human being again.

'I'm putting all the booze from the house in there.'

Tony just keeps looking at me.

'I could just bin it, but that's a waste isn't it? I'm not going to stop completely. Parties, special occasions, I'm going to enjoy myself as much as everyone else.'

I pause.

'But for the rest of the time –'

Tony finishes it for me again.

'You're laying off it.'

I nod.

'I'm going to do other things instead. Go to the park, take up keep-fit classes, help you out in the café a bit more, take Vicky shopping, get Tyler and Steve to teach me the offside rule.'

I look down the garden at the shed again.

'Not spend every evening getting smashed out of my skull.'

225

Then I look back at him.

'If I ask you for it, and you know there aren't any parties or any special occasions coming up – and you're going to know because if there are, you'll be invited –'

I nod at him again.

'You say no, OK?'

And there it is again, that same kind smile, that same understanding nod.

'Course.'

It's a strange thing about Uncle Tony. I make him sound like the head of the family or something, and in a way he is. He's certainly a world expert on anything to do with it. The odd thing being that he's not really family at all. Meaning he's not really my uncle, I've just always called him that. He's related, but in a much more distant way. His parents were killed in a car crash when he was little and my grandparents, who'd been friends with them, took him in and raised him as their own.

It was just the way things were done in those days. No-one went to any social worker or consulted any sort of court. The family just got together and decided what they had to do with this problem that had landed in its lap. My grandparents didn't have any children and had an extra room, so from that moment on that was that. And then when they did end up having some kids of their own, they were all brought up as brothers and sisters. There was never any mystery about it and Tony knew from his earliest days what had happened to the couple everyone always still called his real parents.

And that's when it had all started. Tony's passion for all things connected to his adopted family – and not just about the family either, anything to do with where we all originally came from. Our joint Italian heritage, if that's what you want to call it. He even took all of us down to Cardiff a few years ago for the unveiling of a memorial to some Italian internees who'd drowned on some old ship as it tried to make its way to Canada during the Second World War. Steve hadn't wanted to go, of course. Tyler was just a toddler and Vicky had only just been born and as Steve had pointed out, they weren't exactly going to get too much out of it, were they? But it was obviously important to Tony so down we went and the strange thing was how moving the whole thing was. I'd never heard of the ship before – the *Arandora Star* – and I'd certainly never heard of it sinking like that, but that cathedral down on Charles Street was packed with relatives of those that had been lost and even a few of the survivors too. And as the hymns started I actually started to cry. Why, I've still no idea. I didn't have any connection with the ship and didn't know anyone who'd been on it. Maybe it was because, like Tony, those passengers and those survivors were from my home community. Descendants of those pioneers who'd first travelled across land and sea for a life they'd hoped would be better hundreds of miles away from home. For some the hope was real and the dream came true. For others, like the poor souls on that ill-fated ship, things worked out different.

I watched Tony that day as he greeted people in that packed cathedral, listened to him as he even gave a short address, pointing out in his always gentle way that even though that sinking had prompted the government of the time to reverse its policy on transporting internees in such an inhumane way, successive governments had never actually officially apologised to the victims of that original disaster. His passion when he said it was genuine and even Steve stopped shifting about on his seat for a moment or two. My eyes never left his face throughout the whole thing, and I wasn't the only one. You could have heard a pin drop during his address that day.

When I was a kid, it always seemed strange to me that a man who only had a fairly distant connection to our family should have been so keen to find out as much about it as he could. But as I got older I began to understand it a little more. Maybe the rest of us took it for granted. And maybe having had one family snatched away from him made his new one even more important. He was certainly the one constant in my life. The one person who always was – and always would be – there for me.

One hour later and the caravan's cleared and cleaned as well as two kids of twelve and nine can clear and clean a caravan, which means not that well at all, but it'll just about pass muster so long as you don't investigate too deeply. I'm in the middle of retrieving half-drunk bottles of just about every variety of booze you can think of and some I can't even pronounce from all kinds of hiding places around the house. It makes for a fair old collection. I don't even like the taste of most of them, but that hasn't ever really been the point. My drinking – which has been spiralling out of control for months now, I know – has nothing to do with what I like and don't like. It's to do with needing it more than wanting it and it's that – along with the obvious temptation offered by Zeno – that's finally scared me into action. I don't actually want to need anything – be that exotic émigrés from a land far away or a bottle of some concoction that only makes me forget what I can't remember anyway.

Which means two things have been achieved this week. One demon has been dispatched without my really having to do that much about him. Zeno's gone and the chances of his

228

returning are pretty remote. He's an intelligent man as well as a dangerously attractive one. He'll have known he was being well and truly blanked.

And another demon's about to be locked away too, stacked neatly on a shelf at the back of our shed. From today on I'm going to look at that shed and it will be a daily reminder that if I want to do something – as in really want to do it – then I can, and those bottles aren't going to rule me any more. I'm going to control them.

It's as I'm putting the last of the bottles on the final shelf, getting ready to lock up and hand the key to Tony as promised, that I see it. Poking out from under some old plant pot I've had to move to get the last bottle stacked alongside the rest. I reach out, turn the plant pot over and don't understand what I'm looking at for a moment.

Then I realise exactly what I'm looking at.

And then I turn and let out a great big yell.

'Steve!'

Five minutes later and I'm back in our small kitchen. I'm pacing the floor and Steve's standing by the table, stammering like a guilty schoolboy.

'That's nothing to do with me.'

For a moment I just stare at him. He's looking at anything and anywhere apart from the one thing I've been staring at for the past five minutes. The small stash of white powder on the kitchen table. The small stash of powder I'd found underneath the plant pot in our shed. And it's not what Steve's saying and it's not the slightly higher pitch to his voice when he says it either – none of that's what's convincing me he's as guilty as sin.

What's doing that is the telltale flush that's starting at the base of his neck. As well as his eyes, which are swivelling round the room like they're on stalks right now, taking in anything and everything again, resolutely avoiding my eyes and what's on the table.

'I do booze, Frankie. You know that. Beer, lager, OK, the odd bottle of spirits when we're feeling a bit flush – birthdays, Christmas, all that.'

'Steve!'

I cut across, sharp. Now he's talking too much as well.

'But I don't do drugs.'

I pick the stash up and wave it in his face. Still he won't look at it.

'So what was this doing in our shed?'

'I don't know.'

'Tooth fairy left it, did she?'

'I don't know who left it. I don't know how it got there. All I know is it's not mine.'

I hit my head. Of course. How could I have been so stupid?

'Vicky's pup.'

Steve stares at me.

'Her pup's a junkie, why didn't I think of it before? That explains everything – it goes in there when we chuck it out to have a shit and shoots up.'

He should keep quiet. And he probably knows it too. But that's another thing about Steve. When he's lying, he can't help talking. When he should say nothing he just can't help himself – he elaborates all the while, throws out all sorts of rubbish. Although even I don't remotely expect what he comes up with next.

'Could be Tyler's.'

Which really does stop me in my tracks.

'What?'

I stare at him again, my eyes filling with ever-increasing

levels of disbelief. And that isn't at what he's saying, it's more that it had even entered his head.

'Why did he want them trainers?'

'What are you talking about, you know why he wanted them, because he was jealous of his mate.'

Steve shrugs, still looking at anything and everything apart from me and what's in my hand.

'Maybe that wasn't the real reason. Maybe he wanted to sell them.'

'He hasn't sold them.'

I stop. This is getting more and more ridiculous and I'm actually dignifying it by answering him too.

But Steve rolls on.

'Or maybe it's one of his other mates. They're always calling round – maybe one of them's been using our shed. He didn't want to take stuff like that home, so he used our place.'

'I don't believe this, Steve. Your own son? His mates?'

I shake my head, battling upset now as well as anger.

'You'll blame your own son or his mates rather than face up to this yourself?'

Then I stop again. Because I can feel myself giving way, can feel myself really starting to lose it and I do not want to lose it, I do not want to give him the satisfaction of seeing me burst into tears while he just stands there by the kitchen table affecting injured innocence.

'I'm just trying to work out what's going on here, Frankie, same as you.'

'You're pathetic.'

And now Steve begins to still.

'A pathetic little worm.'

'Just shut it, Frankie.'

'How long, Steve?'

'I said, shut it.'

'How long has our money been going on shit like this?'

'I'm warning you.'

But now I'm in his face, waving the stash just an inch or so from him.

'The money we haven't got, the money we've had to borrow from the likes of Eddie, the money that got our back door smashed and me and Vicky nearly beaten up, how long have you been pissing it all away like this?'

Then I stop again. Not because I've given way, not because I've finally given in to the tears I can feel welling behind my eyes.

I stop because Steve suddenly lashes out with his fist, smashing it into my cheek as I stand there, inches from him. Sending me crashing to the floor, knocking over the kitchen table and a couple of chairs along the way, the stash of white powder flying out of my hand, hitting the floor at the same time I do, the bag bursting, sending a thin scattering of coke all over the lino.

Chiara

DAYS MERGE INTO weeks, weeks into months. The café buzzes with speculation of a possible war, speculation that builds as the weeks go on. But such matters seem far away from a small Italian café in a remote Valleys town. And each Sunday we still join the parade, that seemingly never-ending line of young men and women walking in a loop from the main street of the town up onto the mountain before finally winding their way back again.

Grace always spends the hours before those walks in an agony of impatience, her whole week focused on one thing and one thing only. Those few, all-too-short, hours when Enrico would take pity on her, on us all, and tell us to go.

Grace didn't need a second invitation. She'd be in that whitewashed rear room I'd come to love so much, out of her work clothes and out of that front door in an instant, barking at Michele and myself to come on, hurry up!

Enrico was a strange combination. He wasn't actually a great deal older than the three of us, but to me he was always much more my parents' generation than mine, even though he was at least ten to fifteen years younger than them.

I suppose he was caught between two worlds in a way, as well as between two generations. He was our employer and our protector, which made him almost a father figure, but he was still a young man. A lonely young man too. Perhaps if I'd looked back as we all flew out of that door on those Sunday evenings, I'd have seen that more clearly. But on those days, at that time, there was only one thing on my mind. It was the same thing that was on Grace's mind and probably Michele's mind too, and that was escape.

The evenings followed much the same pattern. We walked out as a threesome, Grace passing loud and none-too-subtle comments on all the people we passed on the way, puncturing pretensions, proffering caustic asides on this overdressed young girl, that preening boy – meaning we were all usually in fits of giggles before we'd even set foot on the mountain path that led from the town's main street.

I came to see something else on those walks too. Grace always came across as so confident, so totally in control, so capable, but deep down she was anything but. Deep down she was shy and insecure. She was nervous too, deeply nervous, which was why she went on the attack like that from the moment we set foot outside the café. One of the reasons for that shyness, that insecurity, those attacks of nerves was walking alongside us all the time. At least most of the time.

'I'll go ahead. Open the gate.'

Grace nods at me, trying to look and sound casual, not even remotely succeeding.

'You talk to Michele.'

We've rehearsed what is to happen next. We went over it time and again in that whitewashed rear room while Enrico was behind the counter talking to one or other of our regular customers, arbitrating on some discussion or other on the matter of the moment or putting on one of his beloved records, some of which he'd managed to bring with him from home, some of which he'd found in the second-hand shops he'd visit down in Cardiff on his rare days off.

We've decided that I'll begin by talking about some news from home. Another letter from my mother perhaps, or I'll talk about his home and his family and ask if he's heard from them lately. Then I am to steer the conversation round as quickly as I can to the girl who's now lingering over the gate ahead and casting glances back our way, trying to decode from our body language just what we're saying; or more accurately what I'm saying and how Michele is responding to it all.

He makes it so easy for me. All the rehearsals, all the ways we've agreed to manoeuvre the conversation around to Grace: none of that's needed.

'She's fun.'

He just comes straight out with it. No preamble, no talk of family, nothing. He just looks across at Grace instead and says it.

I nod back, enthusiastically, in total agreement. Grace is nothing if not fun.

'Back in the café, when we're working, she makes me laugh all the time.'

Michele keeps his eyes fixed firmly on Grace, who seems to be attempting to set some sort of world record for the longest time ever taken to open a gate.

I nod towards her again.

'Not just fun, she's kind too. When I first came here –'

I shrug, helpless.

'I don't know how I'd have managed without her.'

I pause. Grace is fast running out of reasons to stay by that now-open gate. It's now or never.

'Do you like Grace, Michele?'

Michele turns and looks at me for a moment. Then he smiles, a smile I can't really decipher. Perhaps I don't want to decipher it.

'Has Grace asked you to ask me that?'

This isn't what we planned. This isn't one of the responses we even remotely batted backwards and forwards in that small back room as we attempted to second-guess all the potential twists and turns in this conversation. Neither is my response.

'Yes.'

Then I stop, flushing madly, feeling like I've betrayed her in some way. But Michele's smile just widens even more as he turns back to look at Grace, now approaching and attempting to set another world record. The longest time taken by a living soul to travel the short distance from a mountain gate back to a waiting couple on a nearby path.

Just before Grace comes back into earshot, he says it.

'Yes. I like her.'

Three hours later we're back in that small whitewashed room. Michele and Enrico are still in the café, checking the ledger for the day, getting ready to close. If Grace was in an agony of impatience before, she's even more agitated now. We didn't have a single moment alone together for the whole of the rest of that walk. Either Michele was with us or some of the regulars from the café fell in step with us (even Sergeant James kept us company part of the way), so there's been no opportunity for her to broach the burning issue of today and every other day for weeks past.

'Well?'

A breathless Grace eyes me, the door into the café finally and firmly closed behind her.

'Did you ask him?'

I nod.

'I asked him.'

'And what did he say?'

I instruct my mouth to smile, to ignore the uneasy voice sounding inside my head.

'He said he likes you.'

Out it comes, exultant.

'Yes!'

It comes out so loud and so exultant that Enrico scuttles in from the café to find out what's wrong, but as Grace has now collapsed into yet more fits of excited giggles, he doesn't find out.

Why didn't I tell her what Michele said next? Was I already starting to fool myself that he didn't mean it, or was I just trying to pretend that I hadn't really heard it at all?

But I had heard it. Those other few simple words spoken almost in a whisper by Michele as Grace approached down that mountain path.

Back in the café, Enrico has returned to the counter, shaking his head at the impossibility of ever understanding a certain giggly young girl. Grace is pacing the floor, already making plans for the next Sunday, and the next, and every one after that.

'So is he going to ask me to walk out with him?'

'I don't know.'

'Didn't you ask?'

'Of course not!'

Grace looks at me and for the first time she pauses.

'So what were you talking about? I left you alone for ages.'

I don't reply. I'm back on that mountain again, listening to Michele's next, low, whisper.

It's an hour or so later into our walk. Grace is talking to another of the café regulars a short distance along the track. All the time, Michele's looking at me with that same, steady, unsettling stare.

'Did you hear what I said?'

I hesitate. I had heard; all too clearly. I've just no idea how to respond.

'Chiara?'

'Yes.'

Michele leans forward and for a moment I'm not here, up on this mountain; I'm back in the square in my home town, about to set off for a new life, about to leave my old behind, excited beyond measure, fearful beyond belief all at the same time. All of a sudden I start talking, jabbering almost, speaking mostly nonsense; anything to fill the suddenly dangerous silence.

'How do you feel about this place now? Are you settling in any better? We work so hard, we hardly get chance to talk.'

I take a deep breath, press on.

'I know it wasn't easy for you at the start. It wasn't for me, and it can't have been for your brother either, but is it better now? Are you liking it more?'

All the time there's just that same, steady, unsettling stare. He answers, but when he does, things turn even more dangerous.

'If I answer that, will you answer a question too?'

I know what his question is. I know exactly what he's going to say, but I can't stop myself. I just nod, perhaps because deep down I want to hear him say it.

Just along the path, Grace is finishing her conversation with the customer from the café, her eyes darting continually from him to the two of us some short distance away.

'Yes, I'm more settled now. Yes, I'm enjoying myself more. I didn't think I would; I really didn't think it would happen, but these last few weeks...'

Michele tails off. He knows he doesn't need to expand or explain further.

238

'So. My question?'

Michele half-turns now so his back is to Grace, making doubly sure anything he now says to me is out of her earshot.

I nod, growing desperate now, towards the watching Grace, her laughter trickling down the mountain.

'Grace is coming back.'

'It's just a simple question, Chiara.'

Michele pauses and I don't think he's going to say it, but he does.

The next Sunday we walk out again. Grace has suggested it and the way Michele instantly agrees gives her even more hope that something might soon develop between them. Once again she stages a diversion so I can talk to him, and once again a conversation that should have been about Grace turns into a conversation about someone else altogether.

Then Grace rejoins us and we all go further up the mountain. Grace maintains the same constant running commentary on the people we encounter as we climb higher and higher and Michele and myself laugh and respond, but all the time it's there between us as heavy as a veil: that question I'm still refusing to answer.

I know the impossibility of answering it. I know where the answer might lead. Now I'm back again in the square in my home town on the day I'm to leave, listening again to a conversation I barely registered at the time; a conversation that's played more and more on my mind ever since.

'Enrico's a good man, Chiara.'

It was one of the last conversations we had. Luigi and Peppo were looking at the engine of the bus that was to take me down to the station. The driver was stacking the last of the bags into the luggage space at the rear. For a short time it was just the three of us saying our farewells, but something else was being said at the same time.

Mamma nods in agreement.

'Kind.'

I nod back, puzzled. I know that. Why they feel the sudden need to say this, I don't understand.

'A man of his word.'

Now Papà hesitates.

'That's important in a man.'

Then they both fall silent. For once I don't break the silence, perhaps because I'm already starting to learn to listen to what's behind the words rather than just the words themselves.

'It's something to hold onto, Chiara, something to believe in. Not just now, but in the future too.'

Then Papà smiles at me, and I can see now that he was saying goodbye in more than one way that day. He was saying goodbye to a young girl who was travelling hundreds of kilometres away to begin a new life overseas. But he was also saying goodbye to a child who was becoming a woman.

'He's taken with you. He likes you. And, in time, it's his hope that you might like him too.'

It didn't sink in at the time. The driver returned and Luigi and Peppo tore themselves away from their detailed inspection of that dirty old engine and everyone in the square began to say their final farewells. I climbed on the bus and waved along with everyone else and then forgot about everything that had been said to me.

It came back later. It started to resurface as we journeyed through different countries and across that small stretch of sea. My father's words and, more than those words, the expression on his face, kept returning to me all the while.

It would return again at odd times too: when Enrico was showing me how to operate some new machine; when I read letters to him with news from home; when I'd catch him looking at me across the counter as I talked to customers or served them food or drink.

There's never been any sort of contract. I'm not enslaved in any way: I'm a young woman who can do as she wishes, but I understood what my father was saying that day and I understand the hopes of the man who'd made my new life possible too.

Enrico wasn't just bringing a new employee from his old country to his new one. Enrico was also bringing someone who might, in the fullness of time, become his wife.

'He's asked me again.'

Grace bolts into the small whitewashed rear room, breathless with excitement.

'Michele?'

Grace nods.

'This evening. He asked if I'd like to go to the pictures.'

I struggle back a smile.

'And he asked if you'd come too.'

I look at her, pausing at that.

'He thinks it'd be best.'

Grace nods at me.

'Make it respectable.'

At the local cinema that night, in between the different reels, it starts all over again. Half of me keeps telling myself this is just because I seem unavailable and Grace seems anything but; that it's just a game: the thrill of the chase. The other half of me really fears it's not.

'It's complicated.'

'Complicated? How?'

I take refuge in silence again. In truth, I don't totally understand it myself. I know what was said to me before I left home. I know my family's hopes of settling Luigi and Peppo in some way depend on it. On the other hand, I also know that if things change, if I meet someone else, then Enrico will never hold that against me. This isn't the Dark Ages and he isn't some primeval tyrant. He's sweet and kind and understanding, which is perhaps the problem. Had he been that tyrant, that throwback to those Dark Ages, maybe all of this would have been easier to deal with.

Then, all of a sudden, Michele shakes his head, seeming genuinely lost now.

'All right. I'll stop, yes? I'll stop walking out with you? I'll do my work, we'll smile and nod at each other when we meet, we'll talk when we need to and that will be that. Nothing more, not now, not ever. You don't answer my question, you don't tell me you like me like I like you, I never ask it again?'

I say it. Not because I mean it, but because all of a sudden it makes everything so simple.

'Yes.'

Michele stares at me.

'That's exactly what we do.'

Michele keeps staring at me.

'You don't mean that.'

It's exactly the wrong thing to say, because in that moment I really and truly do.

'I mean it, Michele.'

The next Sunday, I ask Enrico if he can come out for a walk with me. It's the first time I've ever done that and I can see the surprise on his face.

Grace steps in quickly, and urges us to go. That means Michele and herself will have to look after the café, which suits her perfectly; and, to give him credit, Michele makes no objection. For the whole of that week it's been as he'd reluctantly said it would be. We've been pleasant around each other; we've behaved as work colleagues might be expected to behave; nothing more and nothing less.

I'm aware of him watching me as I move towards the door with a shyly smiling Enrico, but I don't look back for even a single moment. The moment I step outside, it's like a weight has been lifted from my shoulders, although I can't really explain how or why.

Perhaps that's what that walk up onto the mountain with Enrico was all about that day. Perhaps it was all part of my trying to find out.

'It's the highest spot in the whole area, Chiara. Look: everything spread out before us, as far as you can see.'

I nod, as entranced by the view as he is.

'It's like looking down from the castle at home.'

For a moment, that's where I am: back on top of those ramparts, people passing below as small as ants, my father at my side, his strong arm encircling my waist just in case I stray too close to the edge in my eagerness to see every last detail of the constantly changing picture before us.

Enrico doesn't have his arm round my waist but he is looking at me, and not how Papà used to look at me, indulgently amused at the awe all too obvious in my eyes. Enrico looks concerned instead.

'Do you miss it?'

I look back at him, quizzical.

'The castle?'

'Home?'

I consider for a moment. I've thought about it a lot. I still think about Papà and Mamma and Luigi and Peppo at different times every day, wondering what they're doing. At mealtimes I pause sometimes and imagine them all sitting around that large table outside in our small courtyard, the smell of Mamma's cooking percolating into every corner, the sound of one of Papà's scratchy old records playing in the background (much like Enrico's records play in the background of my new life now too) and, of course, the smell of the charcoal drifting across the valley.

I do miss it, of course. I missed it cruelly in those weeks after I first arrived and could only think of going back. But, now, do I actually want to leave this new home I've found and return, permanently, to the old?

'It's just these last few weeks.'

Enrico stumbles, then stops. I look at him and his expression looks troubled now.

'Since Michele arrived.'

I keep looking at him, not saying a word.

'You've been so quiet.'

I stay silent, willing my face not to betray me.

Enrico hesitates, and looks back at me.

'I wondered if he'd turned your mind back to all you'd left? If you'd become homesick again?'

I answer, rather more quickly than I intended, relieved to divert any attention away from the subject of Michele and back onto something else.

'I'm not homesick, Enrico.'

'So you're happy here?'

I look out over the town again: so different from my home town, so different from anything I'd ever known. It's the strangest thing. I've never actually thought about it before. I've never actually sat down and tried to work out how I feel about this new and sometimes strange place in which I now find myself. For the first time, prompted by Enrico's gentle questioning, I'm now trying to do that: trying to work it out, to understand my feelings. In truth, they're not difficult to work out or understand at all.

I could have asked myself that same question over and over and not arrived at any sort of answer, but the simple fact of someone else asking it has suddenly made it all crystal clear. I nod, hesitating now, but not because I'm unsure. I'm hesitating because I'm surprising myself.

'I'm happy here.'

I am. Standing on the top of that mountain, looking down on a town that would never be as beautiful as the one I'd left but was still beautiful in its own way, standing with a man who could never take the place of those I'd left behind but who might occupy a different place instead, I can put my hand on my heart and swear that all I'm saying is true. I'm actually happy.

Enrico hesitates again.

'With your new life, your work? You're happy with – ?'

I look at him as he tails off. The sun's behind him now and I can't really see his face. I can hear the doubt and hesitation in his voice and I can hear something else too, something that sounds like fear: fear at asking the question; fear at the answer he might receive. Now he sounds not like the grown man he actually is but someone a lot younger, like an unsure schoolboy. I think my heart's going to break. Perhaps that's why it happens.

I smile back at him, the sun still in my eyes.

'I'm happy. Here in my new life, with my new work.'

Then I nod at him, answering the question he's never actually put into words but has still asked anyway. We both know what it is, and we both know what's behind it too.

'I'm happy here with you.'

And then I lean forward and kiss him, lightly, on the lips. It's the first time: the first time I've ever kissed a man that way.

We walk back down the mountain in silence, but it's an easy silence. Life is simple again. Everything is back in order; everything is once more in place.

Michele is in his room when we arrive home, which makes things even simpler. Just Grace and a troubled-looking Sergeant James. We can't really work out what he's saying at first and (shades of Reverend Keller) he doesn't seem to want to say what he's come to say.

In the end he does say it, because he has to. He's come on official business. To arrest Enrico. Immediately. A stunned Enrico is told he has to leave his café, leave his employees and accompany Sergeant James back to the police station, from which he'll be transported to a destination as yet unknown.

An equally stunned Grace and myself stare back at Enrico. All of a sudden life isn't simple any more.

Frankie

H E'S DONE THAT once before. Hit me like that. And it wasn't the blow I remembered so much, although that did stick in my mind. Steve might not be built like a heavyweight boxer, but his fist could still feel like it belonged to one when he really put some effort behind it. It was what happened afterwards, the very next day.

I can't even remember what the row was about. It was probably about something and nothing, the kind of thing you might scream and shout about one minute then forget about the next.

If it hadn't been for the single, savage, blow that ended it.

The next morning I was sitting in our kitchen – a different kitchen at the time. This was really early on in our marriage, the kids hadn't come along and we were living in some tiny little flat on the other side of town. The door opens and Steve comes in and he just nods at me, for all the world as if it's just a totally normal day, like any other day, not a day where the whole world's suddenly standing on its head.

And then he says it.

'Any tea in that pot?'

I hesitate for a moment, but then I nod back, I actually nod back and I say:

'Just made some.'

And Steve smiles, easy, casual, natural.

'Cheers.'

Then he reaches for a mug. By now he's standing just inches away from me, inches away from my face, from the large red mark that's come up overnight on my cheek, a mark I've made no attempt to disguise.

Steve takes a big, long glug of his tea, puts the mug down on the table, then looks round for the paper. Then, as he picks it up – and making sure he's looking anywhere but at me – he says:

'That's a nasty bruise you've got on your cheek there, Frankie.'

I stare at him.

'You want to be more careful, that rug's lethal. Trip over that again, you could do yourself a real injury.'

I keep looking at him for another long, long moment, and then I nod. And that was it. We never talked about it again, although I couldn't decide for months afterwards exactly why or what that was all about.

Was it cowardice? Did I just look the other way? Or was it the kind of thing that takes place in any relationship, some kind of unspoken agreement that what had happened shouldn't have and that it was best to forget it ever had?

After months of trying to work it out, I did what so many couples do, I suppose. I gave up trying. I shoved it to the back of my mind, decided it was something that was in the past, forgotten.

But it wasn't totally forgotten, because I made one promise to myself. Before I filed it away as one of life's more regrettable experiences, I vowed it would never happen again. And that was never as in ever. And if it ever did happen again, I made a second vow. Which is why, later that same night, I'm sitting in Psaila's house with the kids sleeping upstairs.

They hadn't said too much when I'd told them we were all going to their Aunty Psaila's for a few days. They hadn't needed to. One look at the bruise spreading across my face told them all they needed to know. They just packed the few clothes I told them they'd need and Vicky picked up her pup. Then they followed me out of the door, leaving the house to Steve when he came back from the pub.

'Bastard.'

The kids may not have said anything, but Psaila was saying plenty. She took one look at my bruised face on her doorstep, looked at the two cowed kids either side of me, both keeping their heads down, and then she delivered her one-word verdict.

For all the lippy in Vicky's case and for all the new trainers and supermarket scams in Tyler's, they were still little kids at heart and right now they were both feeling well and truly out of their depth. So they hightailed it upstairs to join Psaila's kids the moment she opened her front door and nodded at us all to come inside, accompanied again by just that one-word verdict on everything that had all too obviously happened in her friend's household that evening.

She delivers that same one word verdict again and again over the course of the long and dark night that follows too.

'You don't mind, do you? Us landing on you like this?'

'Course I don't.'

'It's just till I get my head together.'

'Stay as long as you like, you know that.'

'Work out what I'm going to do next.'

Psaila doesn't reply, just looks at me, seeming to be struggling with something now. And I soon find out what it is. I might have had two shocks already that night, but that was nothing compared to the one that was coming next.

'So what are you going to tell the kids?'

'The truth.'

I gesture at my cheek.

'Not much point saying anything else, is there? Not with me looking like this.'

Psaila looks at me, still struggling. I can see it in her eyes. Should she say something? Would it just make things worse? Or is she about to do me the biggest favour any friend could do, open a poor sod's eyes to what's really going on in her life?

Psaila hunches closer over the kitchen table, every word now a clear struggle.

'He told me it was to feed the kids.'

I look back at her, puzzled. What does that mean?

Psaila pauses again, really struggling now. But she's already said way too much to stop.

'You all needed extra cash, he said – you were desperate – there was nothing coming in and all that money was still going out, he didn't know where you were all going to end up and he said –'

Psaila pauses again, then it all comes out in a great big rush.

'He said you'd never even think of doing something like that, not on your own.'

I keep staring at her, a cold feeling starting in the pit of my stomach, beginning to spread.

'What are you talking about?'

But Psaila just keeps looking at me. She doesn't need to say any more, not really. I'm already way ahead of her, but she says it anyway.

'Last month. That night. Fred West.'

That cold feeling?

Now it's like ice.

'Haven't you worked it out yet?'

Psaila hesitates again.

'It was all Steve's idea.'

I nod, as if it's the most natural thing in the world. A husband pimping out his wife via her best friend. Happens in all the best sorts of circles.

Psaila shakes her head.

'He swore me to secrecy. Said it was for your sake, that you'd never be able to face him, not if you knew he knew.'

I close my eyes. I'm not hearing this.

But I am.

Every single, solitary word.

Psaila shakes her head again, growing ever more savage now.

'Ten out of ten in the acting stakes, Frankie, I'll give him that. He really took me in, I swallowed it all – hook, line and sinker.'

Instinctively, I touch my cheek, the only part of my body that isn't ice cold right now.

Psaila looks at me again, her eyes every bit as cold.

'Feeding your kids, that's one thing. I can understand that. Why do you think I do what I do? Why do you think lots of us round here do it?'

Psaila shakes her head again.

'But feeding a habit? That's different.'

All the time those same cold eyes stay fixed on me.

'Get rid of him, Frankie.'

Chiara

OUTSIDE THE CAFÉ a black van with a little grille at the back pulls up. I'd never seen a van like it before but later I'd learn it was called a Black Maria. Inside, and through that same grille, we can see three other people, men I recognised immediately.

Giovanni Bertoia, a man in his sixties who works in a building firm in a town further up the valley. Beppe Moruzzi has been helping out in his father's shop a few streets away from ours while his father himself recovers from a bout of TB. Aurelio Cavalli is sitting next to Beppe, but Aurelio isn't even working yet. He's about to start in a new holiday camp that's opening up this summer forty or so miles away in Porthcawl. Now all three have been arrested and are about to be transported down to the local prison, and Enrico's just about to join them.

'He's just made the announcement.'

I look at Enrico, bewildered. I have no idea what Sergeant James is talking about. From the expressions on their faces I can see that Grace and Michele have no idea either, but Enrico does. It's him again, isn't it? That clown, as so many from my home town saw him. That clown who is turning into anything but.

'Mussolini announced it from Rome, from Palazzo Venezia. It was on the radio. Italy's joined the German side in the war.'

I blink at Enrico stupidly, still not taking it in. Enrico doesn't say anything else, but Sergeant James does.

'He's declared war on Britain.'

I didn't know much about history; not then, anyway. However, I did know that my country had been on the same side as yours in the First World War: that we were allies, had been comrades in arms against a common threat. Perhaps this was one of the reasons Italians had been welcomed so warmly in the country ever since. One look at that Black Maria told me all I now needed to know. All that had changed.

Grace steps in, her eyes wide with disbelief.

'That's nothing to do with Enrico.'

Then she steals a quick, sideways, almost involuntary glance across at Michele, who's just joined us.

'It's nothing to do with any of us.'

All eyes have been on Enrico up to now. With a sickening lurch in my stomach, I realise that Sergeant James hasn't mentioned Michele yet.

'It's my duty under the Aliens Restriction Amendment Act of 1919 –'

Then Sergeant James pauses for a moment, and can't go on. He's found it hard enough arresting the other three men that evening. He's obviously finding this latest arrest impossible.

'Look, Enrico. You haven't heard me say this –'

Sergeant James lowers his voice, inclines his head including not only Enrico but Michele, Grace and myself now in the same conspiratorial nod.

'None of you have.'

Sergeant James struggles.

'But I can't arrest you if I can't find you.'

The police officer nods at him, urgent, almost pleading.

'Slip out of the back, take your chances. It's only Italian men this applies to. I won't stop you.'

I look at Enrico, as do Grace and Michele, brief hope flaring; but Enrico, perhaps the only soul in that room thinking even half-clearly right now, doesn't even look back at us.

'And where would I go? How would I live? Where would I live?'

And now the world really does seem to have stood on its head as Enrico moves forward and embraces the wracked Sergeant, the captive comforting his captor, letting him know he isn't to blame.

Michele steps in.

'Grace is right. How can you take Enrico away if he hasn't done anything?'

Just for a moment, raw emotion sears the room as Sergeant James nods back in total agreement, frustration erupting from inside him.

'No arrest without a charge. Innocent till proved guilty. That was drummed into us all through our basic training; that's what separates us from every other police force the world over because that's justice. Simple, basic justice.'

Then Sergeant James stops, ever more tortured, and glances at the waiting Enrico again, the expression on his face saying it all.

Enrico breaks in.

'It's been coming for some time.'

Now Michele stares at his brother.

'You knew?'

'I didn't think it would affect us. They'd drawn up a list, but there were three categories – it was only Category A we had to worry about: those who were expected to help Germany or hinder the war effort.'

Enrico falters, and looks at Sergeant James.

'But all that's now changed too, yes?'

Sergeant James nods back.

'Churchill's already ordered the bombing of Milan. There's munitions factories there apparently. And he's ordered the security services and the police to do this too.'

From out of nowhere, a memory flashes across my brain, the latest letter from home, Mamma telling me about a camp Luigi had been sent to near Rome. Before, they'd been little more than holiday camps but this time everything had been different. Large billboards had been displayed at every entrance and exit and on every wall were slogans:

'*Guerra: una parola che non ci fa paura*' – War: a word that does not frighten us.

'*Abbiamo dei conti veccchi e nuovi da regolare*' – We have some old and new accounts to settle.

'*Credere. Obbedire. Combattere.*' – Believe. Obey. Fight.

Luigi's whole time there had been spent in a makeshift uniform, being forced to march up and down hills. I'd just written it off as the latest excess perpetrated by the excitable *Duce*. How could I have been so stupid?

Across the room Sergeant James pauses, struggling again.

'I'm sorry, Enrico. I'm really so sorry.'

He is. You can see it in his eyes: he's almost in tears.

'But if you are coming with me, I need you to bring a few things with you.'

An increasingly unhappy Sergeant James waves a list he's been given, absurdity piling on top of the already grotesque.

'Your radio.'

'My what?'

'And any binoculars you might possess.'

Sergeant James, as helpless and disbelieving as the rest of us, studies the list in his hand.

'Anything that can be used against the country, that's what it says here.'

Enrico looks towards the door and the Black Maria, the faces of what are obviously now his three fellow-prisoners looking out at him from behind the grille.

Then Grace breaks in.

'But who's going to look after the business?'

Before I know what I'm saying, I step in.

'We'll look after it. Myself, Grace –'

I hesitate.

'– and Michele.'

I look at Sergeant James. For a moment he just looks back at me, then across at Michele, who's as pale as the rest of us. He's just been standing there, waiting for the unexpected and devastating axe to fall on his head too. How can it not? He hasn't been in the country anywhere near as long as Enrico, but everyone in the town knows where Michele comes from. Everyone knows he's every bit as much an Italian as Enrico and therefore, according to the document the unhappy Sergeant James is holding right now, one of the new enemy too. By rights (or at least by the same twisted rights that seem to have come into operation overnight), Michele should now be following his elder brother out of that door in the charge of his reluctant guard.

'It is a strange name for a Londoner, mind you.'

For a moment we all look at Sergeant James, unsure we've heard him correctly.

'We get more and more of them these days. Fewer and fewer of the old British names, more and more of what you'd call the exotic.'

Sergeant James nods at a now staring Michele.

'I suppose it's mixing so much with Italians like Enrico and Chiara. Working with them, living with them like you do. Some people might actually take you for one.'

Now it's Sergeant James's turn to hesitate.

'Even though you're not.'

Grace is looking from myself to Michele, totally puzzled by all of this. For once in her life, mercifully she keeps her mouth shut.

Then Sergeant James nods at Enrico.

'It's a stroke of luck in one way, I suppose. Having a family friend visiting you like this.'

Sergeant James hesitates again.

'Hopefully you won't be away too long, but while you are, at least he can lend a hand.'

Enrico nods back, slowly.

That night the three of us gather in the small back room. News of Enrico's internment has spread across the town and people have been calling in all evening with messages of support for him and condemnation of the heavy-handed actions of the authorities in removing him from his business and his home.

A blanket of silence seems to have descended around Michele. No-one even refers to him lest the fragile subterfuge which is guaranteeing his freedom right now should collapse.

I tell myself my intervention with Sergeant James was for the café, for the survival of Carini's; that there's nothing else behind it. That it's for the well-being of our business, our livelihood; an admittedly desperate measure designed to keep everything going until Enrico comes back.

And I keep telling myself that, too.

PART SIX

**'Sundry Prayers, Praises
and Professions of Obedience'**

(Psalms 119)

Frankie

I HAVEN'T DONE this for a bit. Recorded anything into Steve's machine. Not that you'd know if I have or haven't, so I don't really know why I'm telling you anyway.

Maybe it's what I said before. Maybe this isn't for you at all. Maybe you never even existed anyway. Or maybe you were just some unimportant employee Tony thought should be there in our old café family tree, but couldn't find anything out about for some reason.

I've already worked out that that's probably the real attraction too by the way. Talking to someone who can't answer back.

Rambling, aren't I? That's probably the booze. And yeah, before you ask, I'm back on it again. All those good resolutions well and truly pissed to the wind. I'm still at Psaila's too, and so are the kids. All of us living in limbo. Trying to decide what to do next. What to do for the best.

We can't go back to our old life – or at least we could, but what would happen to that promise I made to myself after the first time Steve lashed out at me like that? It'd be like all those other promises I've made to myself over the last few years. Not worth the paper none of them are written on.

So I go down to the café instead one morning. I haven't been there for a while either. I'd like to say Tony will have missed me, that he'll have been rushed off his feet, but of course he hasn't. Some things might have changed in my world, but not too much has in his.

It's weird how I always seem to end up there in the end. It's like some sort of invisible pull, which is double-weird seeing as all I get in there is more pressure to sort things out, principally the mess that's my life and marriage. But still, back I go. Maybe I'm just some kind of masochist. Or maybe it's something else. Or maybe that's just the booze talking again and I really am just spouting rubbish right now.

'Hello stranger.'

I hesitate in the doorway. Tony eyes me from behind the counter, a paper open in front of him, just the odd couple of customers dotted around the café sitting on the single frayed sofa and the chairs, his old Italian music from the 1930s or 40s playing soft in the background. I look round. Things aren't exactly down to one pork pie, two plates and two forks yet, but they don't look too far off.

I shuffle, uncomfortable, as Tony keeps looking at me.

'Yeah, I know I haven't been around for a bit.'

I hesitate again. How much does he know? I've been keeping a fairly low profile and the kids haven't been in to see him either, I'm pretty sure of that.

'Steve has.'

Typical Tony. Putting me out of my misery straight away.

I nod.

'So you know?'

A steaming macchiato appears in front of me as if by magic. A chair's pulled out and I sit down. Professional to the last, a small *cantuccino* biscuit is slipped onto the oversize saucer. I pick it up and dunk it.

'I'm sorry, Frankie.'

Tony looks at me, sympathetically.

'If there's anything I can do, you know that.'

I look back at him. Because there is one thing. It's the reason I've come in. That and the free coffee and the comfy chair and the biscuit that has now dissolved into the bottom of the cup and is going to taste so good when I finally get down to it.

'Are you still going? The trip?'

It's a stupid question. Of course he's going. He goes every year. Every year hundreds of descendants of the original émigrés return as well – and not just from Wales either. From America, Ireland – almost every country you could name and some I still can't. It wasn't just down to the pull of the old country, although there was that. With more bars in Bardi per square inch than Ibiza, one hell of a party was guaranteed. I still hadn't forgotten the hangovers, even if I could never quite remember what had caused them.

But it's not the bars – or the streets that always seem to be singing to the sound of a thousand different accents but whose owners all still count themselves part of the same extended family. That's not the real attraction right now. What's on my mind is so much simpler than that.

Escape.

'Course.'

'So when does the bus leave?'

Every year that happens too. A bus sets off from the main square in our town, carrying dozens of families. Sometimes they have to lay on a couple of extra buses to cope with the demand, because even in these straitened times there's still a fair few travellers wanting to make that time-honoured trip.

Maybe it's even more important in these straitened times. A reminder of a life that used to be better. As well as a hope that it's going to be so again.

'At the weekend.'

'Can we still get on it? Me and the kids?'

Tony nods back, eager, all this obviously music to his ears. I've always been the closest he ever had to a daughter and Tyler and Vicky are the closest he's ever going to get to grandkids unless some miracle happens and he meets some nubile twenty-something who has a thing for seventy year olds with failing businesses.

'So how much is it going to cost?'

Now Tony hesitates.

'Couple of hundred quid.'

And now I hesitate too, because now I'm hearing a different voice that's not Tony's.

It's two hundred quid a night, Frankie. And that's minimum looking like you, two hundred in your hand, no questions asked.

I smile a smile that isn't any sort of smile at all.

Two hundred.

Just had to be, didn't it?

Tony looks at me as if he can read my thoughts, which maybe he can, but even if he can't, he can see the problem because it's written all over my face. I'm just hoping he isn't even beginning to guess what I'm wondering might be the solution.

'Do you want me to front you?'

I look round the café. One customer's fallen asleep over his coffee. Another's on the fourth of the day's papers that Tony still manages to get delivered free to the café each morning, and won't be leaving till he's finished the sixth and final one, on account of having nowhere else to go and nothing else to do and no money to do it anyway even if he had.

How the hell is he going to front me two hundred quid?

He's still looking at me.

'I know that holiday must have cleaned you out.'

I squirm, uncomfortable again, because it did – and for

264

what? My big gesture to save everything we had, all gone up in a cloud of smoke. Or, more accurately, all gone up Steve's nose.

Tony catches my quick glance round the café, decoding the look just as quickly.

'I'll find it, Frankie, don't worry.'

I shake my head.

'So will I.'

Which is when I hear it again. Psaila's voice. Only this is no blast from the not-so-recent past suddenly playing inside my head, cajoling, persuasive. This is very much from the here and now because suddenly there she is, in the café, behind me.

And Psaila isn't cajoling or persuasive right now.

She's near hysterical.

Psaila's chain-smoking.

So am I.

She needs to.

So do I.

'I'm sorry, Frankie.'

'It's not your fault.'

'You know what he's like.'

I thought I did. I thought I knew that husband of mine inside out. But I didn't have a clue, did I?

'I tried standing up to him, I really did.'

Psaila shakes her head.

'All he said was that if I got in his way, I'd get what you got.'

'Bastard.'

Which was obviously becoming the word of the moment.

I pause, looking at her, something really starting to niggle away at me now.

'Didn't they say anything? Tyler and Vicky?'

Now Psaila hesitates.

'I mean, they're not exactly babes in arms, are they?'

I shake my head.

'Trying to get them to do anything they don't want to do at home's practically impossible. Asking Tyler to tidy his room is like asking him to fly to the moon. And some of the moods Vicky gets in these days, all I've got to do is look at her and we're into a screaming match.'

I look at a now silent Psaila, growing ever more uneasy because now this really isn't making any sort of sense.

'And Steve just walks in, tells them to get their things and they say OK?'

Now Psaila hesitates again.

'I suppose that's sort of the point, isn't it?'

'What is?'

'What you said. Getting them to do something they don't want to do. Just about impossible.'

I stare at her, not able to believe what she seems to be saying to me.

'You mean they wanted to go with him?'

Psaila hesitates once again, clearly choosing her next words ultra-carefully now.

'They didn't not want to.'

'What does that mean, for fuck's sake?'

Psaila spreads her hands, wide, appealing to me.

'Look at it from their point of view, Frankie. They're living in a place that isn't their home. They're living with a mum whose only long-term plan seems to be getting them on some bus to travel miles away to a country they don't really know, to stay God knows how long and do God knows what while they're there.'

Psaila shrugs.

'No, they didn't go quietly. No, they didn't run into Steve's arms. But I've got to be honest, I had the impression they weren't all that reluctant either.'

Psaila looks at me.

'He was taking them home, Frankie. Back to the only home those two kids have ever known. Where are you taking them?'

I don't reply. And I don't reply for a very good reason. Because I don't have an answer, do I?

Across the table, Psaila takes a deep breath. Despite the fact she's my mate and not his – and despite the fact she hates Steve right now for what he's done to me and for what he's still doing to me – I can tell there's some small part of her that can understand him marching round there and taking his kids away from a life they don't want in a place they don't want to be. Maybe some small part of me can understand that too, and maybe that's why I'm keeping silent right now as well.

'He said if you want to see them again, go home. Simple as that.'

Psaila hesitates one last time. She doesn't want to say the next bit but knows she has to.

'You don't go home, he said he'll go and see some brief. I think he meant it, Frankie, I really do. He said he'll go and see some brief, dig up all the dirt he can and any he can't he'll just make up to make sure you kiss goodbye to them for good.'

Chiara

S ERGEANT JAMES TRAVELLED with Enrico and his three other prisoners down to the main police station in Cardiff. There, and in the company of his three new companions, Enrico was strip-searched and then made to take a cold bath, in case he'd become infected with some disease or other on the short drive down there, I suppose. Then Enrico and the other men were locked together in a single cell for the following twenty-three hours. After that, they were allowed out for an hour to walk around a small exercise yard. Then they were locked up for another twenty-three hours in that same small cell.

After two further days staring at the same walls and a large iron door, Enrico was taken to what was called an alien collecting station over fifty miles away in Pembrokeshire. Though it had been a holiday destination before the war, now it was anything but. Enrico was herded with another two hundred or so men into a camp now surrounded by barbed wire, with armed guards patrolling the perimeters. Straw had been thrown down on a dirt floor inside a couple of makeshift barns, which was where the men all slept for the next few nights. The food was basic – just a couple of spoons each day of some sort of stew.

The food must have been something of a shock for at least three of Enrico's new friends. Enrico could cook well enough and he'd certainly produced many a hearty meal for hungry diners but now he found himself in the company of, among others, Cesare Bianchi, head chef at the Café Royal in London; Ettore Zavattoni, banqueting manager at the Savoy, also in London; and Luigi Vergano, chef at Quaglino's. Enrico also found himself to be the youngest in the camp by far. His new and illustrious companions from the world of fine dining were all men in their middle age.

However, it was another of his new companions who endured the strangest experience of all. Those like Enrico who were first-generation immigrants to Britain were classed as enemy aliens, but any children of those men born and bred in Britain weren't categorised as aliens but as native Britons, and were subject to call-up. All of which led to the totally unreal situation of Dino Albertelli, a prisoner in his fifties, waking on his straw inside one of those barns one morning to find his own son amongst those guarding him.

Sergeant James, having just escorted a couple more prisoners from the Valleys to the camp, tells Michele, Grace and me what happened next.

'He just stared at him for a minute, couldn't believe his eyes. His own son, just feet away from him across that barn. He started to head across to him, crying out his name, but another soldier stepped in between them, pointing his gun.'

Sergeant James shakes his head, still quite clearly finding it difficult, if not impossible, to understand any of this.

'"My father just wants to come and see me," the son said. "You can't see your father," the soldier said. "Your father is the enemy."'

I stare at him rapt, as do Michele and Grace.

'"How can my son be my enemy?" the old man said. "Because he was born in England and you were born in Italy," the soldier said back.'

I break in.

'This is madness.'

Sergeant James nods.

'That's exactly what I said to him. I said – and pardon the language, ladies – "That's just fucking stupid."'

'And what did he say?' presses Grace.

'He just nodded back. Then he said, "Yes."'

Sergeant James looks towards the back of the café at Enrico's old gramophone, his small collection of records neatly stacked on the top.

'It fucking is, isn't it?'

Life settles into a strange sort of pattern for the next few months. The odd stray hostile comment aside, usually from visitors, everyone in the town supports us. They know Enrico isn't the enemy; far from it. Even the fiery Robin, implacably an enemy of all that Messrs Mussolini and Hitler are doing, comes in each morning and every evening just to show the rest of the community that someone opposed in every way to the man who claims to be his leader is not, and should not be regarded as, any sort of foe.

I don't see very much of Michele. With Enrico away, he takes on more and more of his brother's duties as well as his own. Back then it was expected. A man would always be in charge of ordering from the suppliers and keeping the records. Michele struggled with it all, in truth, as it was so unfamiliar, but he still had to do it.

There is also the complication of rationing to deal with. Ice cream is banned, with sugar being in such short supply. Cheese and meat are hard to come by too. We need to source different kinds of food from different suppliers, all of which means Michele needs extra language lessons to cope with his new responsibilities. I leave that to Grace. It seems safer, somehow.

It seems Michele has accepted the situation between us, even though I would deny to my dying breath that any sort of situation exists. With his elder brother taken away like that, Michele keeps away from me. I feel that perhaps what has happened to Enrico has brought him to his senses, and so I start to relax.

We all know how dangerous that can be, don't we?

A crash that sounds like the sky falling in echoes round the small whitewashed rear room where I'm struggling to keep the ice cream machine in some kind of working order, all ready for the day when the war will end, when sugar will start flowing again and the world will stop spinning out of control.

It's another month later again, four months since Enrico was taken away, and Grace stands in the doorway, her eyes wild. She's so excited she can barely get the words out, and for a second or two she just nods down at a piece of paper in her hand instead. Then, finally, she manages it.

'Letter from Enrico.'

It doesn't take long to read it. It can't have taken long to write it. It comprises just three words, but one look at the card makes it only too obvious why Arrigio has rationed himself to just that one short sentence. The card is tiny, barely enough for the three words that stare back at Grace, myself and Michele as we stare down at it in turn.

I am well.

That's it. Nothing else. We pore over those three words for the next half hour, showing the card to every customer who comes into the café, almost willing those simple words to suddenly reveal more behind them.

The message itself was typical Enrico, of course; not

wanting us to worry. Unfortunately, we did worry. Small nuggets of gossip kept reaching us, telling of deteriorating conditions in all the internment camps. In some there were less than forty water taps for more than five thousand prisoners. The toilets quickly became choked and unusable. The floors, where there were proper floors, were caked in grease.

Then came the newspaper article; the one that Grace, Sergeant James and even Robin tried to hide from myself and Michele, but which we saw anyway. The article that told us, more than anything else had done, more even than the arrest and internment of Enrico, that we, the whole Italian immigrant population, were fast turning into the enemy within.

I can still see it now as if it's there, before my eyes. I can still recite each and every word. Each and every one of those words felt like a hammer blow striking deep into my soul.

The British Italian is an indigestible unit of population.

Indigestible. That was the first word that leapt out at me. As if we weren't people any more, as if all of a sudden we were something to be swallowed and then spat out.

All kinds of brown-eyed Francescas and Marias, beetle-browed Ginos, Titos and Marios are unloaded here, turning every Italian colony in Great Britain into a seething cauldron of smoking Italian politics.

'Chiara, stop it.'

That's Grace, trying to intervene, trying to physically take the newspaper away from me; the paper that one of our customers had brought in with him without realising what was tucked away inside. I stop her. I don't know why, but I want to read on, want to read what is being said even if I

272

hate what I'm seeing. Once again a few key words are what leaps out at me as I continue to read.

unloaded – colony – cauldron

No-one in the town feels that way and I know that, but looking up from the newspaper around the now uncharacteristically quiet café, it is suddenly as if everyone is looking back at Michele and myself with those same hate-filled eyes.

Every peaceful, law-abiding proprietor of the back-street coffee shop bounces into a fine patriotic frenzy at the sound of Mussolini's name.

What?!

I can't even begin to comprehend that at first, just staring at the blatant lie, my eyes blinking stupidly, any sort of coherent response frozen on my tongue. By my side, Michele just curses quietly, almost under his breath. I can't even manage that. I'm just staring at the next passage, the passage that describes the café in which I'm standing and all other shops like it, which are apparently breeding grounds of *Black Fascism. Hot as Hell.*

My cheeks are similarly burning as I read on towards the end of the article and the conclusion reached by the writer (whose name I still don't know and never want to); his verdict on the total folly of granting people such as Michele and myself a welcome and a home.

We are now honeycombed with little cells of potential betrayal and a storm is brewing, a storm that we, in our droning, silly tolerance, are helping to gather force.

Later that day, Michele has to go into Cardiff. One of our regular suppliers has been in touch to tell us he's managed to make something that MIGHT taste like ice cream, without any of the ingredients that actually make it ice cream. Just another example of a world that seems to have suddenly stood on its head. Michele was supposed to go on his own, but after the morning's assault courtesy of that article, Grace suggests I go as well.

'Michele's English, it's still not that good. Not as good as yours. It might be for the best.'

She's looking anywhere but at me as she says it. She always does whenever she isn't telling the complete truth. She knows I need to get away today: away from everything and from everyone, even though no-one in that small café, no-one in the town has had anything to do with making me feel as I'm feeling right now. I don't object, though. My head is in a whirl. Perhaps some space, some distance will help.

Michele has arranged assistance for Grace though, from the most unexpected of quarters. He's become friendly with the couple who come in for their one pork pie with two forks, and he's done a deal with them. For a free pork pie on a Sunday, they'll look after the café for a couple of hours while one or other of us has a break. It was an offer they jumped at, probably as a way of making some sort of embarrassed amends; which wasn't necessary, as Michele told them. No-one should be embarrassed about having no money. What did they think he was doing in this town, many hundreds of kilometres away from his home? What did they think any of us were doing there?

We catch the train down to the city. We talk about anything and everything apart from that newspaper article: the café, the customers, the plans to extend the opening hours with the summer coming up, despite the restrictions placed on us by rationing. Anything to fill the silence. Perhaps we both knew what demons would infest it otherwise.

Then Michele suggests we go into one of the cafés on the High Street in the capital to see how they compare to

Carini's, and I tell him that's a good idea. Once inside, and on a sudden impulse, he orders a single pork pie and two forks. The waitress gives us a very strange look as she gives us our food. Suddenly giggling now, which is an unexpected relief after all that has happened today, we agree that our customer service is far superior and, that point made, we eat, pay and leave.

It seems to set the tone for the rest of the day, somehow. We spend the next two hours in a fun fair that has set up on the dockside. We eat fake candy floss and take pot shots at toy bears in ornamental cages. Then we walk around a local park. All the while, time's marching on and still we haven't visited our supplier. By the time we remember the actual reason for our trip today, it's almost too late and his premises are on the point of closing.

We make it just in time. The supplier proudly unveils his ice cream substitute and invites us to try it. Michele's uncertain, I can tell, but what happens a moment or so later puts everything else out of my mind anyway, as the supplier nods past Michele and across at me.

'Let your wife try it.'

I freeze at the same time as Michele tenses. The supplier's scraping a sample from the inside of a metal drum and doesn't notice. He just scoops a spoonful onto a small wafer and holds it out.

It's the moment for one of us to step in to correct him. It's just an innocent mistake. How could he know we were just work colleagues and nothing more? But I don't say anything, and neither does Michele. Not for a few moments anyway. Then he nods at me.

'Try it, Chiara.'

I stare at him, my heart pounding. It's ridiculous: nothing has happened, nothing significant has been said by either of us to the other, but now it's as if we're suddenly co-conspirators in some sort of subterfuge. We hardly know this supplier and it doesn't matter what he thinks or what he says, but for some reason the idea of passing ourselves off as a young married couple to this virtual stranger is intoxicating.

I nod back at Michele and he holds out the wafer to me. I could just take it, but I don't. I lean forward instead and taste the ice cream outstretched on the wafer cradled in Michele's slim fingers.

Then I look at Michele, his steady stare holding mine.

The supplier breaks in, smiling.

'So what do you think?'

I keep looking at Michele for a moment and then, without taking my eyes off him, nod back.

The supplier's smile widens and he nods at Michele, whose eyes have still not left mine.

'What did I tell you? Little lady always knows best.'

Michele still doesn't respond and neither do I. I just take the wafer from his hands and proffer it back to him. In an exact copy of my own gesture from just moments before, Michele leans forward and takes a bite from the wafer, which is now cradled in my fingers.

We arrive home to find the café thronged with people and Sergeant James urging everyone to form an orderly queue. On the counter is a large piece of paper with what at first glance looks like a thousand signatures, but as we get closer I can see that's already beginning to look like a serious underestimate.

'It's a petition.'

Grace bounds up to us, her eyes shining with passionate resolve.

'Everyone in the town's going to sign it. Robin thought of it. We're all taking one page each.'

Grace hands Michele a blank page, thrusting another into my hands.

'Knock on doors, as many as you can – doesn't matter if anyone's been there before, get them to sign again.'

Then Grace pauses.

'They can't keep Enrico locked up then, can they? Not if everyone in the town's telling them he's not what they say he is?'

Then Grace turns and disappears back into the crush of men and women, all equally desperate to add their names to that ever-lengthening list. She hasn't even asked anything about our trip away today.

Within an hour we've collected dozens more names. It should feel like some sort of triumph, some sort of atonement for all the hate and bile that spilled out from the pages of that paper earlier today. Perhaps it is. A timely reminder that there is good as well as bad all around.

However, perhaps because of that, each of those names now reads like a kind of accusation or reproach for something else: for our day away, our trip down to the city, that innocent subterfuge with the ice cream supplier which was really anything but innocent.

This has to end and end now, I tell myself. In truth again, nothing has actually begun, not really; but it still has to stop, whatever it might be. As we are walking away from the houses in the latest street that have signed, without exception, our petition, I act on that in the only way I can think of, by telling Michele all about the agreement with Enrico (albeit unspoken) that has brought me from my home to this town, and my determination to honour it.

Michele listens in complete silence. I can't tell if this is all a surprise to him or if he's suspected it all along. It's all so strange saying it out loud for the first time. Even back home, in the town square, saying goodbye to Papà and Mamma, no-one actually made all of this clear. It was something hidden, almost, but understood all the same. Now, just the act of saying it makes it all real, somehow. Perhaps Michele feels that way too, because he doesn't say a single word the whole time I'm talking. In fact he only speaks once, and that's after I tell him about my walk with Enrico that day and the simple, single kiss we exchanged.

In my mind, there's nothing he really can say or do. He could perhaps point out, as Enrico would do himself, that this is hardly any sort of binding commitment and that Enrico would never expect me to honour it if I don't wish to do so; but he doesn't say any of that.

'Was it like this?'

That's all he says. Then he does it. Michele leans forward and kisses me, and not lightly like Enrico. He kisses me, full-bodied, on my lips; a kiss that might only have lasted a second or so but seems to me to last a lifetime.

Then he looks back at me and he doesn't need any sort of answer, because he knows. He can see it in my staring eyes.

No, Enrico's kiss wasn't anything like that. It wasn't anything like that at all.

We return to the café in silence, our pieces of paper all scrawled with signatures in hand. We haven't spoken since that kiss. Perhaps we both know that what we have, whatever is it, is simply too fragile to talk about. Perhaps it's something else; but as I approach the café, I feel I have to say something or I might burst inside.

'Michele –'

He cuts across.

'Tomorrow.'

It's as if he knows what I'm going to say almost before I know it myself.

'Why can't we talk now?'

'Because I don't want to spoil it.'

He looks at me steadily, but all of a sudden I'm not listening. I'm not looking at him either. All of a sudden I'm looking behind him, and Michele now turns too and stops as he also now sees Grace standing outside the café looking as if she's been waiting for a long time for us, which we soon find out she has.

For a moment the same thought's in both of our minds. She knows. Somehow she's found out about that kiss we just shared and what really happened on our day out today, which should have been a work trip but wasn't, not really. She's found out about that innocent mistake by the man trying to sell us our new ice cream that wasn't actually any sort of ice cream at all. Somehow she's seen us, or someone has told her. However, that isn't why she's waiting there outside the café.

What she says makes no sense at first so I make her repeat it, more slowly this time, and she does.

Enrico is missing.

Presumed dead.

Frankie

IT'S LIKE *HIGH NOON*, without the Sheriff or the guns or the train. Not that you'd know what that is either. With or without the Sheriff or the guns or the train. But you probably get the picture, right? It's like some massive face-off is taking place, which I suppose it is.

The face-off's between me and Steve. We're in Uncle Tony's café in a small room at the back with whitewashed walls. I wanted somewhere quiet for this and couldn't think of anywhere better. Apart from maybe the café itself on a normal working day.

This back room was once some sort of den for the people who used to work here, friends or family or just staff the owners brought across from Italy, according to Old Man Tone. Maybe you were one of them, we still don't know.

'I want you back, Frankie.'

I stare at him. I'd expected all sorts. I even half-expected a no-show. Steve and confrontations don't exactly go together. He huffs and puffs a lot – just like he did in the aftermath of the Eddie visit – but when it comes to actually fronting up to anything that involves something even remotely emotional, Steve's usually found skulking in the back somewhere.

But he's made this one.

And now he repeats it.

'We all do. Me and the kids.'

'Where are they?'

Steve hesitates, his brain now working overtime. It's obvious enough what he's thinking. What am I doing, planning some kind of snatch myself? Is that what this is really all about, distract him while the cavalry in the unlikely shape of Psaila rides to the rescue a couple of miles down the road?

'Away.'

'Away?'

I stare at him.

'Like, on the other side of the world?'

Steve doesn't reply for a moment.

'The moon?'

Steve struggles.

'Just – away.'

'This is stupid, Steve.'

'I mean it, Frankie. We all really – really – want you back.'

'And you're going to do it by kidnapping my kids?'

'They're my kids too.'

Steve looks at me, steady, really looking like he means it, every word. Maybe because he does.

'You're my wife.'

I shake my head.

'Don't tell me.'

I put on my best Steve voice, that whining, cajoling, voice he always uses when he wants something, usually money to go to the pub or sex to distract him when we don't have any.

'I still love you.'

Steve just nods.

'Yes.'

'Spin on it, Steve.'

But he just keeps looking at me, that same expression on his face.

'Please.'

Chiara

AFTER A SLEEPLESS night, the morning paper confirms everything that a pale Sergeant James told us.

Arandora Star sunk by U-boat.

Just underneath the headline, picked out in thick, black type, is an even more devastating statement.

Hundreds of Italian internees feared dead.

We run around all morning, frantically trying to get news. Little by little, how Enrico came to be on that ship in the first place comes to light and it's Robin, apparently using his trade union contacts, who manages to supply the main details. They make for the grimmest of listening.

Having arrested so many men, it seems the government then had to decide what to do with them. The internment camps that had been opened to deal with the new prisoners were already full. There were a few new camps about to be set up (one in Liverpool, one on the outskirts of Manchester, and we'd heard rumours that another was being prepared on the Isle of Man), but in the meantime the authorities still had a short-term problem. Private houses were requisitioned along with some schools, but the system was still in imminent danger of collapse. Worse, there was an element of self-fulfilling prophecy about the new policy as many normally mild-mannered internees were in serious danger of becoming full-blown rioters due to the conditions in which they were being held.

Then, suddenly, salvation was at hand. Canada, under considerable pressure from the British government, agreed to take a few thousand of the so-called prisoners of war. Among that number was Enrico. Two ships were sent to meet them and one, the *Duchess of York*, sailed almost immediately. The rest waited for the next ship to arrive, the *Arandora Star*.

By that time the prisoners waiting to board had swollen from five hundred to nearly two thousand, but there was no question of any surplus returning to their camps. However many were on that dockside, they would all be packed on that next ship; a ship that would normally host no more than three to four hundred passengers.

Just a few short years before, a trip on the *Arandora Star* would have been something of a treat. A modern and luxurious ship owned by the Blue Star Line, the vessel boasted elegant staterooms and spacious cabins for passengers cruising in pursuit of the sun. This is a different world and time. The Ministry of Shipping requisitioned the ship and it first took part in the evacuation of British troops from Narvik in Norway, as well as of troops and refugees from the Atlantic coast of France.

Then came its new incarnation and its new role. The funnels were painted grey and armaments added. The portholes were covered to stop light from inside giving away the ship's position. As the cargo now comprised enemy aliens, barbed wire was placed on the decks and around all the lifeboats to prevent any attempt at escape. Most importantly in this case, despite the fact that for this voyage she was at four times her normal capacity, no additional lifeboats were added to the ship's complement.

On 27 June she steamed into Liverpool to embark on her

latest trip, transporting hundreds of bewildered internees across the sea to a land that did not actually want them, and was not destined, in any event, to receive them.

We can't find out anything else in the town, so Michele and I leave Grace in charge of the café and speed as fast as the local bus will take us down to Cardiff. We can find out nothing of any use there either so we board a train to London, hoping the Italian Embassy might be able to help us instead. We finally find it later that same afternoon only for a sign outside to inform us that because of the war the Embassy is closed. It directs us to either the Brazilian or the Swiss Embassy, with a hand-drawn map showing their locations.

The Brazilian Embassy is closer and we dash there, praying that hasn't been closed too. Is Brazil at war with Britain as well? Is Switzerland? We have no idea. All we do know is that Enrico isn't at war with anyone. Not that it seems to make much difference.

We turn a corner to find an enormous queue ahead of us; mainly women, but a few men dotted here and there. We join the back of the queue to learn that we're to be shown into an office inside, that we're to give the name of the man we're seeking and that we will then be told his fate. Some in the queue have already been there four hours. It's another three before we are finally shown into a small room and a man with a handwritten ledger looks up at us from behind a desk.

In truth, he must be as shell-shocked as everyone in that queue by now. From the other side of that door as we waited outside, we've heard other relatives as he dispensed to them the news they absolutely did not want to hear, screaming at him even though, as a Brazilian, he has done no wrong.

'What have you done to him?'

'You've killed him, is that what you're telling me?'

Then it is our turn. We have agreed that I will speak, not Michele. We still don't want to draw any undue attention to him, even here. I give the man Enrico's full name and the number he was assigned on his arrest, rushed to us by Sergeant James just before we boarded the bus.

There is just the smallest of pauses as he traces the name on the list before us, then he intones the same three words we first heard last night. That is still less than a day ago but it already feels like a different lifetime.

'Missing, presumed dead.'

How didn't we see all this coming? Why didn't I find out more when there might still have been time to do something about it, even if I had no real idea what that might be?

We return to the café and (with Robin's help again) I plunge into every newspaper I can lay my hands on, local and national, trying to find out all I can about this war that has engulfed us and which might have cost Enrico his life. The worst thing, looking back, was that everyone could see the danger but no-one had done anything about it.

Everyone knew Mussolini had already rigged elections the length and breadth of my home country to consolidate his position as leader of the party. Actually, let me rephrase that: make that simple 'Dictator' instead. The usual and time-honoured methods were used, according to the letters I'd been receiving from home but hadn't taken, to my shame, too much notice of: violence, intimidation, then more violence and even more intimidation just in case the first lot hadn't worked. Then there were the so-called holiday camps that soon turned into something more sinister, as Luigi had already discovered.

At the same time, the press had been recruited to his cause and any journalists who defied him were hounded out of the country and their employers driven out of business. Looking back, it seems extraordinary that so many could be taken in by so few, but the madman did offer one thing that struck a chord with so many at that time.

Mussolini was offering an unstable country some degree of stability. He was telling people who'd lost their way that there was hope. They might feel as if there was no way forward, that economically and socially their country was doomed, but he insisted it was not. And if all those people just listened to him and followed his path, then the road to peace and riches would open up before them.

It wasn't just at home that his influence was being felt. At the same time, the self-styled *Duce* dispatched members of his new party to far-flung countries to win support among émigrés too. He didn't do that through tub-thumping speeches or through political campaigns: his new party sponsored days out instead, gathering great hordes of his countrymen and women together in what was supposed to be an excuse for us all to indulge in simple reunions but which, in retrospect, were much more than that.

They were rallying calls, not that any of those attending realised it at the time. They'd be dimly aware that the Italian Consulate was behind it, but anything even remotely sinister about that simply passed everyone by. It was recreation, nothing more: where was the harm in that?

We were to find out, weren't we? All too quickly, because the next thing we knew (almost overnight it seemed), we were at war with a different country, one most of us had never heard of, and with whom we had no argument. That didn't bother Mussolini. He decided that Italy should invade Ethiopia anyway. Sitting in the back room of the café, I pored over back copies of newspapers, reading Mussolini's claims that twenty-seven million people had lined up in towns and squares the length and breadth of the country to cheer the announcement of the invasion. It didn't matter that no-one ever seemed to be able to find even one of those twenty-seven million souls who said they were there. It was like anything else so far as Mussolini was concerned: a simple lie.

The mass condemnation of Italy's actions (it was always 'Italy's' actions, even if in truth it was being directed by just one man) did lead some to lend their support to him, as you do when a member of your family or your country is under attack. Some women were persuaded to donate their wedding rings to be smelted into gold to pay for part of the new war effort, but it was an isolated and pitifully small expression of support. The vast majority of his countrymen and women, both at home and abroad, simply got on with their day to day lives and looked forward to the time when the wheel would turn again and some other leader would rise instead.

I kept on reading as if I was possessed. Perhaps I was. Mussolini's military ambitions widened, and he started sending troops (although he called them 'volunteers') to Spain to fight alongside the Germans for Franco in the civil war. They lost badly at Guadalajara, where they were fighting mainly against their own countrymen, Italian anti-fascists, although Mussolini claimed no such people existed. With his trademark habit of twisting the truth inside out, Mussolini hailed the defeat as a famous victory, forging ever- deeper links with the new German Chancellor, a man many had come to hate in his own country as much as many in Italy were coming to fear and distrust our own leader.

The next thing anyone knew, the two dictators had signed a military pact as well. Although Mussolini didn't officially support Hitler in his invasion of Poland, it was only a matter of time, as was now only too obvious, before one despot threw in his hand with the other.

Then, as we'd all discovered too late and to our now devastating cost, Mussolini pulled Italy into the developing conflict on the side of the Germans, with Britain on the other. The world changed overnight, and not just for the soldiers who'd now have to fight against those they'd formerly believed to be friends. It had also changed for all those other Italians all over the world in countries that had fed and housed and supported them, but against whom they'd now appeared to turn.

That was how, overnight, we all became enemy aliens.

One year passes. Then another. Then, suddenly, the door to the rear room bursts open one night. Michele stands there, and behind him is an elderly man I recognise, but he seems an impossible sight at first. I blink, hardly able to take in the evidence of my eyes, because it's Giovanni Bertoia. One of the men who had been with Enrico in that police van, the Black Maria that had taken them on the first step of the journey that would lead them from an internment camp to a death ship.

I look behind him, wildly. Is Enrico back too? One look at Michele's face tells me that he isn't.

It's that same expression on Michele's face which tells me I really now have to hear what Giovanni has to say. We go back into the café so that a pale Grace can listen too.

'We had no idea where we were going. Some said the Isle of Man: there was a new camp there, or so some of the guards told us. They didn't seem to know either. They just herded us on board. Enrico and I went with the rest of the Italians onto Decks A and B, the German sailors went down to Deck

D and the rest, mainly Austrians, went wherever space could be found.'

Giovanni pauses, involuntary images obviously crowding his mind's eye.

'We passed the lifeboats as we came on board. Enrico took one look at them, took one look at all the men being loaded on in front of and behind us, and he just shook his head. He didn't have to say anything, I knew what he meant. If anything happened, we'd have no chance. I shook my head back and he knew what I meant too. With all that barbed wire guarding the way, we'd have no chance of launching those boats anyway.'

Giovanni pauses again as the café door opens behind him and Sergeant James now comes in to join us. He doesn't say anything, just sits down to listen to all of this too.

'When we set off, it was obvious quite quickly that we weren't making the hop across to the Isle of Man. Within a few hours we were out in open sea. We could feel the ship zigzagging from side to side: standard procedure, so some of the guards told us, to avoid U-boats. Then there was some trouble with some of the German sailors. They started putting up swastikas and singing Nazi songs and their quarters were right next to the bridge so the guards decided they had to be moved. It took a whole day to do it and while it was going on we were taken into what must have been the old ballroom because there was glass and mirrors everywhere.'

Giovanni pauses once more.

'That was when we all felt it, before we heard it. A massive crash deep down in the hull.'

By now Sergeant James has been joined by Robin and other regulars. Outside, word is spreading all round the town that a survivor of the *Arandora Star* has, miraculously, made it home and everyone wants to hear his story even if later many, like us, would wish they had not.

'One of the guards said it was probably engine trouble. Then there was another loud bang. The next thing we knew, all the glass from the ceiling and all the mirrors around the walls came crashing down.'

Giovanni shudders as more involuntary horrors claim him.

'The blood, the screaming –'

He shudders again.

'It was terrible.'

Grace reaches out, instinctively, and takes my hand. I look across at Michele. His eyes haven't left Giovanni's face.

'Then the ship began to list and it was obvious it had been torpedoed. The alarms began to ring and everyone – everyone who could move anyway – just started to dash for the decks. But when we got there, everything we'd suspected was correct. We couldn't even get near to the lifeboats at first because of that barbed wire. The guards were using their rifles and bayonets to try and clear a path, and some of the prisoners even started tearing at the wire with their bare hands. They did, finally, manage to get one launched but there was no chance of getting into it, there were so many in there already.'

Then Giovanni stares at the far wall, his memory replaying pictures he really never wants to see again.

'Thank God we didn't, that's all I can say. As it was being lowered, a big piece of ironwork fell from the deck straight onto it, smashing it down into the water. We just saw a pile of crushed bodies underneath it, and then it went under.'

Giovanni looks round the hushed room, which is packed to capacity now, more and more of our regular customers arriving by the minute.

'I was just going to jump but Enrico stopped me. He said it would be suicide and he was right. Jumping from that deck would have been like jumping from a four-storey building, and what if you didn't hit the sea, what if you hit some of the debris? Somehow, from somewhere he found a rope. We tied one end to the deck and started to make our way down it. The ship was listing even more now, it was obvious it was taking in more water all the time, so we knew we had to get as far away as possible or it would drag us all down with it when it finally sank.'

Giovanni pauses, takes a sip of the water Michele has provided for him. You could hear a pin drop in the silence that now fills the room.

'Once we were in the water we found some wooden debris floating and hung onto it. Enrico kept telling me to push, push. Neither of us could swim, but we kicked our legs and the wood began to take us away – and just in time. One of the guns on board tore itself from its mooring and crashed down into the water just feet behind us. It dislodged a huge line of barbed wire which hooked itself round the poor souls still left on the deck, dragging them all down with it into the sea as well.'

Giovanni shakes his head again.

'It had been less than half an hour since that torpedo had struck, but we knew, somehow we knew, that the moment was now upon that ship, that it was going to finally sink. We turned and watched it list further, then disappear beneath the waves. Then everything went quiet, so quiet.'

Giovanni reaches out, takes another sip of water.

'A lifeboat floated past and Enrico shouted up at the men on board. They couldn't take two more but they could manage one. I was nearest so Enrico told me to take that place and he'd go to another lifeboat we could see a short distance away, and off he went, clinging onto that same piece of wood all the time.'

Then Giovanni pauses, as if he can't go on for a moment.

Michele breaks in.

'And?'

Giovanni looks back at him.

'As I was being hauled into the first boat, I heard a man on board the second yell down at him that they couldn't take any Italians. They were only taking British survivors. I called out to Enrico to come back, that we'd find room for him with us – we had to.'

Giovanni falters.

'But by that time the lifeboat was being taken away by the waves and if he replied – if he even heard me – I don't know, because then I lost him.'

Frankie

It's a bright summer day. Everyone's in shirtsleeves and short skirts. Well, the men are in shirtsleeves and the women are in short skirts. The world hasn't turned that far upside down in the last couple of weeks. Even if it's felt like it has done at times.

I'm standing on the pavement outside the local bus station. People are everywhere, carrying bags and cases, shouting at kids. It's the day of the annual pilgrimage back to your home town, which we still think of as our home town. Two weeks of sun, two weeks of seeing old faces and visiting old friends. Tony hasn't missed one of these trips for over forty years. We've been going with him – that's we as in the whole family – for the last few. But we're not going on this trip. Because right now there isn't a family, or at least not a complete one.

I'm still at Psaila's. And Steve and the kids are still camped out in a house which is more and more resembling a bombsite, from the little I've seen of it whenever I've called to see my increasingly withdrawn and monosyllabic children. Who don't seem to be the slightest bit interested in leaving it no matter what it looks like, and coming back with me to their Aunty Psaila's.

It's not exactly helped that Psaila's been busted. One of her trips down to the city turned nasty a few nights ago when a punter tried demanding some stuff that even Psaila didn't do, and wouldn't take no for an answer. A fight broke out, which the punter didn't win but neither did Psaila. The police broke it up, charged the punter with assault and Psaila with soliciting. Her face was all over our local paper the next day and, as Tyler pointed out – no doubt prompted by Steve, in a totally staggering display of hypocrisy – no way was he going to live with a tom.

Uncle Tony's standing by the bus, his case already packed in the large luggage hold underneath the seats, and he's looking at me with the usual sympathetic twinkle in his eye.

'Do you want me to stay?'

'Not much point in that, is there?'

'Bit of moral support.'

'I'll be fine.'

'That mean you've decided?'

I hesitate. It's why I'm staying behind. To answer Steve's question, to decide what I feel and what I'm going to do.

Do I go back to him and – now – the kids? Or do I stick it out at Psaila's? Turn this split into something more permanent?

Which is when this really weird thing happens. When I hear it, and yet I don't – not an actual voice. If I had, I really would have started checking the alcohol ratings on all those red wine bottles I've been getting through lately. But something – outside? – inside? – I don't know where it came from – was telling me to get on that bus.

Tony looks at me, curious.

'What?'

I shake my head.

Now I really am losing it.

'Frankie?'

But suddenly, there it is again. Although why I'm telling you this I've no idea, because if it was you, then you know this already, don't you?

Tony repeats his question.

294

'You're really sure you don't want me to stay?'

I look at Tony, look at his battered old case visible in the still-open hold, look at the men in shirtsleeves and the women in short skirts yelling at their kids, and then I do it.

I do what you tell me to do.

If it was you.

I walk past a staring Tony and get on the bus.

Chiara

MORE TIME PASSES. Another year passes into another. There's still no news of Enrico. Many Italian internees were released in the wake of the sinking of the *Arandora Star* as the British government saw sense over their internment policy, or rather as the British public forced them to see sense. Giovanni, however, seems to be one of the few, the very few, lucky *Arandora Star* survivors.

We also discover that he's been lucky in more ways than that, because not all the survivors have actually been allowed home. Most of the others, after being picked up by one or other of the rescue boats, were then packed onto another ship to endure another ten-day voyage zigzagging the Atlantic in an attempt to dodge the attentions of any more U-boats.

On disembarking in Quebec they were met by a platoon of heavily armed guards who'd been warned to expect a shipload of dangerous characters. Not wanting to keep such people in Canada, the authorities packed them onto another ship, the *Dunera*. At first the internees imagined they were being sent back to Britain, but the fates had a rather more extreme journey in mind than that. As they set sail again, they learnt they were being dispatched to Australia. Partly to prevent revolt and partly so the crew could forget about their inconvenient cargo, the prisoners were placed in the hold with the hatches battened for most of the voyage, during which the boat was attacked by another U-boat and very nearly suffered the same fate as the *Arandora Star*. Finally, after two months, the exhausted and demoralised survivors arrived in Australia, where they were incarcerated in a camp of corrugated iron huts.

Was Enrico among them, or had he drowned in that pitiless Irish Sea? We keep haunting the police station, bombarding the War Office for news of Enrico, but to no avail.

We do what everyone else is doing through all the terrible wartime destruction and tragedy; what everyone has always done, I suppose. We keep on doing what we've always done. We open Carini's in the morning and close it at night. Clinging to the old routine. Embracing, or attempting to embrace, some semblance of normality. We observe another of the old rituals in also going to the annual fair, which is still being held despite everything. In fact, and because of everything, it is probably even more important that it is still being held and that we and everyone else should go.

The fair is where, months after Giovanni first stumbled back into the café, and with a crowd numbering in the several hundreds watching, Michele took a large scythe, arced it through the air above his head, then brought it down in a single stroke, ripping it through my body and severing my torso from my legs.

I don't realise until I arrive that day that Michele has been press-ganged into official service. I don't know when it was arranged or even whether it wasn't arranged at all, just sprung on him a few moments before, but as we walk up to the gates we are met by Michele in his new incarnation as the official magician.

Every fair has them: it is one of the oldest traditions. For the first half hour or so, it is the usual sort of thing: card tricks and conjuring tricks to greet all the new arrivals. I didn't even know Michele could do card tricks, but I soon find out that they aren't all he can do. It isn't long before he takes both myself and Grace to one side and asks for our help.

Michele saw the trick as a small boy in one of the fairs at home. The first time he saw it he watched, as open-mouthed as the rest of the audience, as a woman was apparently sliced in half and then put back together again, to stand totally unhurt and intact to stunned cheers and applause from the appreciative spectators. The second time he sneaked to the rear of the stage to see how it was done

Ten minutes later, Grace and I are behind a screen, two boxes resting on a stand before us. I crouch into the first box, my legs tucked out of sight underneath me, my head and upper body visible on the top. Grace lies in the second box, her head and upper body concealed, only her legs visible. When Michele puts the two boxes together, it looks like just one person is lying inside.

The curtain comes up, and the apparently single box is the first thing the hundreds of people assembled on that field now see. Shouts ring out as some of the regulars from the café recognise me. Then a hush descends as a drum roll sounds and Michele brings a huge scythe up above his head. A tiny gap has been left between the two boxes, although no-one in the audience is close enough to notice it. Then, in the only really tricky part of the whole illusion, Michele brings the scythe down in one smooth movement. It apparently slices straight through the box, although in reality it passes through the thin air of the gap between the two boxes.

I'm watching the audience all the time. Most of them actually close their eyes in horror as the blade slices down, making Michele's illusion even easier to achieve.

All over the field, everyone hushes. Then Michele separates

the two boxes, pulling them just a few inches apart. My head and my body detach themselves from the second box where, apparently, my legs remain. Then Michele puts the boxes together again.

He hisses a single word.

'Now.'

Then he opens the sides of the boxes facing away from the audience towards the back of the stage. With the sides of the boxes hiding her from view, Grace rolls away, scuttling out of sight behind some curtains at the rear of the stage. I roll out of the front box at the same time. Then I stand and Michele takes my hand. Then he escorts me to the front of the stage, where we bask in roars of approval and applause from the field for the miracle they all seem to have witnessed.

Michele turns to me and kisses my hand, a simple gesture of thanks from the magician to his assistant. Then he looks up into my eyes.

The rest of the day passes in a haze. Grace is treated to the same kiss on the hand by way of grateful thanks from Michele, which sends her into raptures. Small boys pester him all the while, trying to get him to explain how he did his trick. The fair then follows the time-honoured pattern with all the traditional shows and sideshows, but I don't see any of it. All I see are the pair of eyes that had held mine in a silent stare and the lips that had swooped down and kissed my hand and turned my skin molten.

Still, nothing happens. The next day, Michele and I take a walk up into the mountains. We maintain the fiction, to Grace and to ourselves, that it's all totally innocent, that we're just seeking peace and quiet to talk about work matters; which we do. We talk about ice cream that isn't really ice cream at all, and stock, and customers, and nothing else. Of course we're talking about anything but all of this.

Then, a week later, we go back to the see the supplier we saw before, to order again the substitute he'd offered. Once again he mistakes us for husband and wife. Once again we don't enlighten him. Still nothing happens. Still I can tell myself that we're just friends, colleagues; that there's no betrayal involved.

We arrive home to find a breathless and perspiring Sergeant James, just arrived at the café. Barely able to get out the words, he tells us that a party of survivors from the *Arandora Star*, all of whom were subsequently packed off to Australia, is to dock at Liverpool the following day. That's all he knows: he has no list of names, meaning he has no idea if Enrico is among them.

Michele and I leave early the following morning. Grace insists she can cope, and she can because there's no shortage of helpers right now. Everyone in the town has been calling in almost every minute to find out if there's news. Feelings are still running high. Even those newspapers which formerly attacked us have begun raging against the heavy-handed treatment of those who had come to these shores in peace, seeking only a better life for themselves and their families.

Many of those same newspapers, and many others besides, are also pointing out this is actually the principle the whole country is fighting for right now. It seems extraordinary it should then abandon that very principle in the treatment of those who mean and have committed no harm.

Perhaps things are different now. Perhaps refugees in search of a better life are able to travel to your country, and beyond, freely and without fear. Perhaps they're met with kindness and warmth now. I hope so.

The journey to Liverpool will take the best part of eight hours. Several other émigrés have also joined us, all equally anxious to spot their own relatives in among the hundred or so we're told will soon be disembarking. Even if hopes are to be dashed, there's always the possibility of news about our loved ones from those who are returning.

For the first part of the journey we hardly speak. We both seem locked in our own private worlds. But then, after an hour or so, I turn to Michele and, for the first time since it happened, I ask a question that's been on my mind ever since I saw Grace's tear-stained face outside the café that night, the night we heard of the sinking of Enrico's ship.

'Is this our fault?'

He stares back at me, puzzled.

'What happened to Enrico: is it some sort of punishment?'

Michele's brow creases in disbelief.

'Did we send that U-boat? Did we fire that torpedo? Is that really what you're asking?'

He knows exactly what I'm saying. The way he pounces on my words tells me he's been thinking those exact same thoughts, that he's feeling every bit as guilty about all that happened as I am.

'You know what I'm saying.'

Michele struggles.

'Enrico isn't your husband. You're not even walking out with him, not really.'

I look out of the window at the countryside speeding past the windows.

'If Enrico is on that boat, if he's been returned to us... I'll make it up to him, I swear.'

I nod at Michele, not really talking to him any more, just giving voice instead to some private contract I've now agreed with myself.

'You're not making any sense.'

I am and I know it, and Michele knows it too. I'm looking to the skies and making a silent appeal. Perhaps you will one day too. Please, I'm saying, just make everything all right. Do that and I promise I'll never doubt You and I'll never do anything I shouldn't do again. From this moment until the end of time, I'll honour our bargain; just make our world whole once again, keep him safe.

A few hours later we're standing on a quayside. Dozens of other similarly tense souls mill around us, eyes trained on a ship approaching across the water, distant figures already glimpsed on the deck.

I look across at Michele, who hasn't said a word since my outburst on the train. I haven't spoken either and the silence is becoming deafening. He knows exactly the way my mind is working, which is quite unnerving. No-one should be able to read your thoughts so easily. No-one has ever been able to before: not Papà, not Mamma, not Luigi and definitely not little Peppo.

Occasionally, back in our village school, Professoressa Quadrelli would decode a sudden silence on my part, giving whatever was troubling me a wry voice; but Michele seems to be able to look at me and answer questions I haven't even asked, put into words thoughts that are still only half-formed inside my head. What that says, I really don't want to think about, especially not here and now, waiting on this quayside.

'Enrico's my brother.'

I keep looking at him as he pauses. If Michele really does

have the happy knack of reading my mind, I don't seem to have the same. I have no idea what he's thinking or feeling at this moment, or what he's going to say next.

'More than anything in the world, I want him to step off that ship. More than anything, I want him home. You know that.'

I nod. I do. No doubts.

Then Michele pauses again.

'But if this has been taken out of our hands...'

I look at him again.

'What does that mean?'

'You know what that means.'

Michele keeps looking at me.

'If you're free.'

Michele doesn't finish; he doesn't need to. Perhaps I do have some kind of second sight after all, because now I know exactly what he's saying, or at least trying to say. I just don't have any sort of answer.

By now the ship is docking. We can see now that most of the figures on board are soldiers returning home. The internees or prisoners are below. Briefly, it's like I'm standing outside myself. For that moment, it's as if all normal life is suspended. I'm not a young girl waiting on a quayside for a man who's already changed my life and to whom I owe everything. I'm some sort of celestial chess player, debating moves, deliberating over options, wondering what would happen in the event of this circumstance, what in the event of that.

Even more than that, I'm wondering something else. If the Lord has taken Enrico, will that be some sort of sign too? A sign that the union first mooted in that square back in my home town is not after all the one destined for me? That the life that was mapped out for me that day, a life I embraced without really thinking about it, is not the life I will lead after all?

I'm still trying to work out how I'll feel about all that when I see him. Pale, walking with difficulty, but very definitely alive and looking about as well as we could have expected given the time he's been away and the experiences he's endured.

Enrico.

His face breaks into the largest, widest, happiest smile imaginable on seeing the two of us waiting for him among all those dozens of others on that quayside.

I run to him. Everything else is forgotten: Michele, everything. I don't care about any of that, and in that moment I don't think of anything else, either. All I can think of, all I want to think of, is the man who's now standing just a few metres away. I run straight into his arms. I bury my head in his chest and he holds me as if I'm the one who needs succour and comfort, as if I'm the one who has been to hell and back, not him.

I do that because it feels right. Not because I'm feeling guilty at even the small indiscretion I've committed with his brother. I do it because at that moment, the moment I see him, all doubts vanish and all temptation is banished along with them.

Enrico is back where he belongs; and so am I.

Frankie

HALF AN HOUR later and the wheels on the bus are going round and round, as the old kids' song has it. Maybe it's a song you sang when you were a kid. I did, and I know Tyler and Vicky did too. Maybe it's one of those timeless songs that stretches back decades.

Doing it again, aren't I? Talking about anything and everything apart from the one matter of the moment, like what am I actually doing on a bus bound for a country hundreds of miles away, travelling in the clothes I put on that morning, no bag, virtually no money – apart from my ticket money fronted to me by Uncle Tone – and very definitely no sort of plan. I've only got my passport because I managed to get the bus driver to divert to Psaila's for me to pick it up.

Tony hasn't spoken for the whole of the last half hour. Partly that's because he knows there's no point. He's a wise old soul, but you don't exactly need to be Solomon to realise – from my body language alone – that this is very much a time for action not words. Anyway, I don't have any words, or reasons or explanations. It's like I'm acting on autopilot.

Unless I'm not acting at all. Unless this really isn't my decision. Unless that really was you whispering in my ear.

But in a way, that's even more crazy than me just acting on an instinct, isn't it? If that's what I'm doing right now – acting on an instinct – then like all instincts it could prove right or it could prove wrong, but it's got at least some small chance of working out.

But if I'm doing this because someone I never knew and who might have died years ago (if they even definitely existed) is whispering sweet nothings in my ear, then it really is time to call in the men from the funny farm.

By my side, Uncle Tony's tensing, always a sure sign he's about to say something and I tense too, knowing exactly what he's about to say.

'Have you really thought this through, Frankie?'

'No.'

And now he's hesitating again, really not too sure where to go next. But he tries.

'Frankie –'

I cut across.

'And for the next few days, I'm not going to think either.'

Then I ask it. The question I didn't even know was in my head before the words come out of my mouth.

'What's that song?'

Tony stares at me, totally wrong-footed by that one.

'What song?'

'The one you're always playing back in the café?'

'I play lots of songs in the café.'

'There's one on more than most, I'm sure there is.'

And then I sing it. I actually sing it, just a line or two – and in Italian as well – which really gets me a couple of Brownie points from some of the older passengers on that bus, even if I don't know what the hell I'm actually singing and they probably don't either.

Tony pauses a moment.

'It's from the thirties.'

'I'm not after a history lesson, Tone, just what it is'll do.'

He's still just looking at me.

'Why do you want to know?'

I don't reply.

Because I don't know, I truly don't.

Tony looks at me a moment longer, then shrugs.

'*Senti L'Eco.*'

'What's that mean?'

'*Senti l'eco, piano piano, da lontano torna ancor.*' 'Hear the echo –'

Tony pauses, musing.

'Though it could be *feel*, mind you, *senti* can mean both –'

Then he shrugs again, finishes it anyway.

'Hear the echo, very quiet, it returns again from far away.'

We're rolling over the bridge now – the bigger one, the newer of the two bridges, although I'd always preferred the old one – the grey waters of the estuary below us, a white building – some sort of nuclear power station, I think – shimmering in the distance on the far bank. And Tony looks at me again, not all that interested right now in ancient songs I've never had much time for anyway, something else much more on his mind. It's the same something that's more on my mind, in truth. Maybe that's why I'm talking about songs I don't really understand and ghosts I don't believe exist.

'So what about the kids?'

But I cut across again.

'I told you, for the next few days I'm not thinking about nothing, not even them.'

And that was that.

Chiara

AFTER HE ARRIVES home, Enrico doesn't talk about the time he's spent away. He doesn't talk about his recapture after the sinking of the *Arandora Star* or the subsequent journey he endured across to Australia, although he was at least spared an additional sea crossing to Canada. All he talks about is a shoe.

After being turned away by one of the lifeboats, Enrico was picked up by another that had managed to be launched, but it was in a parlous state. Overloaded and shipping water, it just made it to a nearby island called Mull, off Scotland, where it ran aground on rocks on the island's south-western coast.

Some crofters, who'd heard that a German U-boat had torpedoed a ship out in the Irish sea and who were desperate to help any survivors, ran out to haul the boat to safety.

The islanders were all haunted by another lifeboat from the same stricken ship that had been spotted out at sea the previous day and which had been towed to shore. On that lifeboat they'd found no survivors, only a handful of bullet holes in the side. Dark mutterings had spread the length and breadth of the small island, speculating on what might have happened. Some of the islanders had even gone so far as to suggest that guards from the ship must have shot at the lifeboat to stop the internees from escaping. Like so many stories at that time, it was impossible to know what was truth or fiction, but it made the sight of a whole complement of living, breathing human beings something of a miracle.

It was the young daughter of one of the crofters who'd found it. No-one in the boat, including Enrico, had noticed it before, but there it was in the bottom. A single, red, lady's shoe. It was impossible. There had been no women on board the *Arandora Star* on that voyage. Only men had been interned and only men had guarded the prisoners and crewed the ship.

'So where did it come from?'

Enrico seats himself on his usual high stool behind the counter, inviting suggestions and speculation from the regular customers who are all now crowding the café. Robin is the first to answer.

'Perhaps it was from one of the earlier voyages.'

Sergeant James, by Robin's side, nods.

'From the days when it was a luxury cruiser.'

Grace cuts in.

'So what was it doing in one of the lifeboats?'

I nod too, exactly the same thought in my mind.

'Any why one? Where was the other one?'

But Michele is looking at his brother.

'Perhaps it was a keepsake.'

Enrico smiles back. Clearly he'd had much the same thought.

'Something one of the internees had brought with him from home.'

Grace cuts in again as she realises, her eyes shining now.

'It's Cinderella!'

Enrico nods back. He'd come to exactly that same conclusion too. Then he nods down at the shoe, the only possession he'd returned with, one that wasn't even his own.

'You know what this means, don't you?'

All round the room, everyone looks at him, the same thought in everyone's minds right now.

Enrico eyes the single red shoe again.

'Now we've got to find the lady it fits.'

Enrico returned to a hero's welcome. Almost the whole town turned out to greet him. Well-wisher after well-wisher stopped him, clapping him on the back, pumping his hand. He was the town's very own living miracle. A much-loved son, for that's now what he truly was, as everyone kept telling him over and over, returned from the dead.

Once home, he began to recover, albeit slowly, from everything he'd gone through. It helped that within another few months the war was thankfully, mercifully, over. Unfortunately, Enrico was still a long way away from his former state of health. Inevitably he left the running of the café in other hands, meaning mine, Michele's and Grace's. We never stopped in those first few weeks, not from early morning to late at night. The fact that Enrico had come home made the café even busier, meaning we worked even harder.

Grace didn't mind. It meant she spent more and more time in Michele's company. The café could have opened twenty-four hours a day as far as she was concerned. She still harboured the fondest of hopes in his direction, even if progress had been derailed, hopefully temporarily in her eyes, by all that had happened to Enrico.

As we all worked together in those weeks after his return, Grace confided in me that she wasn't going press Michele too hard. She was going to give him the space he obviously needed at the moment to get over everything that had happened to his brother.

As far as Michele and I were concerned, we barely spoke aside from work matters. We certainly never referred to the conversation that had taken place on the way up to Liverpool or the words we'd exchanged on that dockside as we scanned the arriving survivors. Sometimes it was as if all that had happened had happened to different people in a different time. It was as if we'd each now placed ourselves in some sort of cocoon into which nothing could, or would, be permitted to intrude.

However, we both knew we had to talk about it eventually, and as the days and weeks went by, the silence grew heavier and heavier. Then, one day, the opportunity presented itself. Michele had to go down to Cardiff again to negotiate some more deals on our fast-dwindling supplies. He could have taken Grace but I offered to go instead. It was time to settle things once and for all, I told myself.

That is exactly what happened, though not at all in the way I expected.

It felt so right, running into Enrico's arms on that quayside. Life felt simple and everything seemed to be in its place again. I felt at that moment like I used to feel sitting in that old hand-carved seat at home in Italy: protected, cosseted, at peace.

I didn't stay in that hand-carved seat in my old home, though, did I? I looked beyond it, beyond those hills above me and started dreaming of something else, even if I didn't know what that was at the time. Does that mean it was always inevitable I'd do the same now too? Look beyond one man and see another?

The day trip to Cardiff passes in another blur. Once again we maintained the fiction, to Grace and to Enrico and to ourselves, that it is all totally innocent, that we are there on business. That's all we talk about on the way down there. Once again we talk about ice cream (or what still passes for it in these strange days) and stock and customers. Of course, once again, we are talking about anything but those things.

We go back to see the same supplier we'd seen before. We take tea in a different small café. We wander through an open air market, then we walk through a nearby park and past a bandstand, pausing to listen to some music played by a military band.

That's when Michele takes hold of my hand, and I don't stop him. He keeps hold of my hand as we walk on through the park and is still holding it as we walk back along the bustling city streets again to take the train home.

Once again neither of us says a single word. I don't know why. Perhaps we don't need to. Or perhaps, once again, we are afraid. All I know at this moment in time is that it felt right running into Enrico's arms on the quayside that day, but this feels right now too: holding hands with his brother as we walk among strangers on those city streets.

It is just as that thought is going through my head that I look across the street, still hand-in-hand with Michele, to see Enrico staring back at us.

To this day I still don't know what he was doing there. I knew he had had appointments with a local doctor who had referred him to a couple of other doctors down in the city. He was still having trouble sleeping because of flashbacks to the moment the *Arandora Star* was hit by that torpedo.

It hardly mattered why he was standing on that street looking across at us. All that mattered was that he was there. Of course, I had no idea how long he'd been watching us as we paused outside shop windows, as we looked at some display or other on our way back to catch our train.

Michele drops my hand guiltily and shoots a glance at me, colour rising high in his cheeks as from across the street, Enrico calls.

'Chiara?'

Any last, fond hope that perhaps he hasn't seen us is immediately extinguished as he now begins to make his way across the road.

I look at Michele, hissing at him as Enrico approaches.

'What do we do?'

Michele stares back at me, his tone as hushed and urgent.

'I don't know.'

Enrico is now almost upon us.

Oh God. It's all I can think as Enrico, looking more and more puzzled with each and every step, comes ever closer. Then there he is, standing before us. He looks at Michele first, but his younger brother keeps his eyes fixed on the pavement, a sure sign of guilt if Enrico needed it; but he doesn't need any sign at all, does he? It's all too obvious anyway.

Then Enrico looks at me, but his expression, as ever, and his tone when he finally speaks, is mild. Even there, standing on that street, looking at two people who really should not have been hand-in-hand like that, he still looks like some kindly old uncle.

Michele still hasn't said a word. He still hasn't looked up to meet his brother's eyes. What sort of picture did we present? Even now, looking back after all this time, it still makes me shudder.

Enrico looks at Michele, whose head is still bowed, for what seems like an age. Then he looks back once again at me. I haven't spoken, mainly because I can't think of anything to say.

'Can we talk, Chiara,' Enrico says to me, 'when you get home?'

Then, and with a last slight nod in his brother's direction, Enrico turns, crosses the street once again and is gone.

We ran into trouble on the way back. It seemed fitting somehow. There had been riots for the preceding few days again, though I can't remember what about. There always seemed to be riots around that time, about the usual sort of thing: money, or the lack of it. Men returning home from war to find the world hadn't changed as much as they wanted.

This latest outbreak of trouble delays the train while the police clear some of the rioters from the line, but I hardly see them and I don't even register their shouts and protests. The world could have ended there and then and I'd hardly have paid it any heed.

Michele is with me for the whole of that ride home. He wouldn't leave my side even if I yelled at him to do so, and I do feel like yelling at him despite the fact that we are in a train carriage with people crowded around on all sides.

It's already becoming clear that Michele doesn't see this as I see it: a disaster. He sees just the opposite, in fact. As far as he's concerned, this is the opportunity and the moment we've both been waiting for. Now the moment is upon us, in Michele's opinion, we should seize it with grateful hands.

'This is it, Chiara.'

'Stop it.'

'The end.'

'Please.'

Outside, some of the rioters are banging on the carriage windows. Most of the passengers inside are staring back at them. No-one seems to be taking any notice of the huddled couple talking in strained tones at the far end of the compartment.

'This is our chance to tell Enrico what's been going on since he went away.'

'Nothing has been going on.'

It has and I know it. I just haven't wanted to say it out loud, to make it real; but perhaps that was just cowardice, because it was happening anyway.

Michele pleads with me.

'It feels right.'

I all but explode at that.

'And when Enrico saw us? When you saw him looking at us across that street, when you looked into his eyes as he looked back at us, did that feel right too?'

'This is our chance to make it right.'

'Out of something that feels wrong?'

'What choice do we have? You saw him. You saw the look on his face. Whether it feels right or wrong doesn't really matter now, does it?'

Michele nods at me again.

'He knows, Chiara.'

I don't reply.

Michele repeats himself.

'He knows.'

I don't reply because on that count alone he's right and I know it. As I know that something has changed, something, now, that can't be altered.

I was right about that too; but what had changed, what couldn't be altered, wasn't quite what I thought.

I leave Michele at the train station. I walk around the town for half an hour, trying to compose myself before I go back to Enrico.

Those latest riots, whatever they might have been about, I still don't know, have spread up from the city to our small town by now. Once again pockets of men are roaming the streets looking for trouble, once again shop windows are being smashed and a couple of the larger factories are even being broken into by the growing mob. Sergeant James is dashing from premises to premises, trying to secure them and repel the rioters with his trademark combination of good humour and brute force. Everywhere I look, everything and everyone seems to be in turmoil.

Finally I take the deepest of deep breaths. I know I can't put this off any longer. Just walking around like this, even in the middle of that riot, is cowardice and I know that too.

I now have to decide what to tell Enrico about Michele and me and what's going on between us.

Do I do what Michele wants me to do, if he hasn't done it already? Do I finally tell Enrico that in our heart of hearts we're a young couple? And do I believe that myself? Am I actually sure of that, even now, after all this time, or is there still some small doubt?

I just can't think properly and I know I probably won't be able to until I stand before Enrico. Perhaps then everything will be clear.

I walk back into the café a few moments later in as much of a fog as before. Nothing is any clearer and Michele is nowhere to be seen. There's just Enrico behind the counter, but then the door to the whitewashed rear room opens and Grace stands there. That's when I really think my heart is going to break, because she's crying. Tears are rolling down her cheeks as she looks across at me. That's the moment I feel our betrayal, mine and Michele's, as never before.

We haven't really done anything. We've only kissed once,

and have just held hands, but Michele and I have still deceived her. For a moment I just stare back at her as she repeats my name in between great sobs that seem to be forcing themselves out of her.

'Oh, Chiara –'

Then she says something that makes absolutely no sense at all.

'I'm sorry. I'm so, so sorry.'

I keep staring at her but she doesn't say anything else. She can't. It's left to Enrico to come out from behind the counter and put the closed sign up on the door, which also makes no sense because there are hours to go before closing time.

Then he turns to face me, and tells me he has some news from home.

One hour later, I'm on the mountain top. Grace still hasn't stopped crying. Enrico also had tears in his eyes as he told me the news, but I haven't cried at all and I don't understand why. Perhaps it's the shock, or perhaps in some way I again feel that it's my fault in some way; that this really is some kind of strange retribution. All of this makes what happens next all the more inexplicable.

I turn to see Michele behind me. He's been sent out to check on train times by Enrico to see which ones I can catch in the morning. Grace and Enrico himself are already packing a trunk for me for that journey home to Mamma and to Luigi and to Peppo but not, now, to my beloved Papà.

For a moment Michele just stands there, looking at me. For the first time since Enrico told me the news he himself had received just an hour or so before, I feel a prickling behind my eyes as well.

'I'm sorry, Chiara.'

I don't reply. What can I say?

Michele tails off, then looks at me again and this time tears are rolling down his cheeks.

All the time I'm looking at him, and it's like someone else is looking at the young man before me and as if someone else is acting now because, and before I even know I'm going to do it, I reach out my hand.

Michele looks at me for a moment, puzzled, this clearly the last thing he expects. Then he moves towards me. For a moment he stands close, closer than he's ever stood before and I rest my head on his chest. For another moment he remains still, then he reaches his arm around me, enveloping me as I incline my head up towards his, and then we kiss for only the second time in our lives.

It feels so right, so natural. That's when it happens: up on that mountain with the lights of the town below, with Enrico and Grace finalising preparations for a journey I never expected or wanted to make, I fall into the arms of a man and, with my own father lying dead in my home town, I give myself to him.

It isn't someone else doing all of this. It's me. There isn't anyone else directing my movements or telling me what to do. I'm directing my movements. I'm telling my own body and my own mind what to do.

The next morning, Enrico takes me to the train station. He didn't say a word the previous night as I came in from what was supposed to be a walk on my own up on the mountain. If he was aware that Michele had been absent at exactly the same time, he never made reference to that either. In fact he didn't mention Michele or that sighting of the pair of us down in the city the previous day at all.

But before I leave, before I go away for what's going to be an extended time (or perhaps even permanently; I really don't know), I know I have to say something. I can't leave things like this. I'm a mass of unanswered questions at this moment but, and as with so much else where Enrico is concerned, matters are destined to take something of a surprising turn.

'You've everything you need? All your tickets, enough money?'

I nod.

'For the train and the boat?'

I hesitate. It really is now or never.

'Enrico –'

He just looks at me as if he knows what's coming.

'When you saw me, and Michele. Yesterday.'

Enrico keeps looking at me, his expression not altering for a moment. No hardness comes creeping into his eyes. He just speaks, his voice as soothing as ever.

'There's no need for this now.'

'But –'

Once again, there it is: that same soothing tone.

'No need.'

'I want to explain.'

'There'll be plenty of time for that.'

He won't be persuaded. That same slightly sad smile just plays on his lips, the same kindly light sparkles in his eyes.

'Just go, Chiara. Go home. Say goodbye to your father.'

'But Enrico –'

Once again, there it is, that same, reassuring, voice.

'Ssh.'

The train pulls out of the small station a few moments later. My valise is at my feet. I still haven't said anything to Enrico about Michele.

Perhaps he's right. Perhaps there really will be plenty of time for all of that, and perhaps that station platform really wasn't the right time or the place. If that's actually what he was saying, of course.

I look out of the window at all the sights and sounds that have become so familiar in the last few years; sights and sounds that were so strange to me when I first arrived. Then I look out at the smashed windows of the houses and shops that were caught up in the latest bout of rioting.

As I leave all of that behind, I keep returning to Enrico. To our parting on that station platform, to his gentle refusal to let me speak, and I wonder. I wonder all the way down to the docks and when I'm on board the ship that takes me across the Channel, and I also wonder when I board the train that will take me through different countries before I finally reach home. The same question keeps hammering away inside my mind, and I'm no closer to answering it when I arrive than when I left.

Was he frightened? Was that why Enrico wouldn't let me speak, why he refused to let me unburden myself? Was he frightened, or just very, very wise?

PART SEVEN

'The End of God's Correction'

(Job 5)

Frankie

I'M GUESSING THIS place has changed a bit since you were here. Tony's still a bit hazy on dates and stuff. Well, to be honest – and I know I've said this before – he's more than a bit hazy on everything so far as you're concerned. Where you went, what you did, why you disappeared in the way you seemed to – no-one seems to know. But he reckons he still knows enough about you to definitely put you here, in this hillside town, all those years ago.

The castle's still here and, by the look of it, it's going to be here long after just about every cottage, farm and tree in this whole valley has gone the way of all flesh. They certainly knew how to build things in those days.

Quite a few of the old houses look like they would have been around when you lived here. Some of the people do too – this is very definitely a bit of a wrinkly old town all the way round, but whisper that quietly. I made the mistake of saying it a bit too loudly on the first night we arrived, spurred on by just that little too much local *vino* – well, way too much if the truth be known – and it didn't exactly go down too well. Unlike the *vino*.

The bars look new. Whether any of them, in one form or another, were here in your day, Tony can't say, although there could well have been something on the same sites. These days the best of the bunch are Bar Grande and the Piccolo.

There's Bar Enzo too, sometimes known as the Communist Bar for reasons I still haven't worked out yet.

The smells would probably be the same though. Everywhere you go, you can almost taste the ripe tomatoes and the rosemary. Not to mention the parmesan that most of the visitors are having vacuum packed, all ready for taking home.

In most of the town's restaurants there's never a sign of a menu. Maybe it was the same in your day as well. Just a waitress who runs through the dishes they're cooking at the time. It's simple enough: if you want something on the list, you have it; if you don't, you go somewhere else – although I've never seen too many people leave. The aromas wafting out from the kitchens usually see to that. Maybe the favourites I'm choosing now are the ones you grew up with too. *Anolini* – pasta stuffed with veal, beef and Parmesan and served in a broth – or *pasta fritta* – deep-fried pasta with parma ham. Beats that Chinese takeaway back home any day of the week.

But my favourite restaurant in the town right now must have been the old butcher's shop in days gone by. You can still see the drain in the floor where the blood from the carcasses would have seeped away. Now it's in a courtyard with just four or five tables, run by a husband and wife.

Doing it again, aren't I? Talking too much, and about anything and everything. Restaurants and recipes and old shops. Anything and everything apart from Steve and the kids and what I'm doing here.

And something else too.

'Hey, just look who it is!' Tony suddenly cries, looking behind me on the second night after we arrive. I turn to see Zeno smiling back at me.

And I'm out of there. As in straight away. Do not go there, do not pass go, do not collect two hundred pounds. OK, maybe that last bit isn't going to make any sense to you either – or maybe it will, because to be honest I've absolutely no idea when Monopoly was first invented. But you probably get my drift anyway. I did not get on that sun-bound bus only to fall for the first wide smile I see and make my already way-too-complicated life even more complicated overnight.

So I go with Uncle Tony to your old house instead.

We walk from the town high up into the hills. But it doesn't matter how high we climb, we're still looked down on by that old castle. Whoever built that definitely didn't suffer from vertigo. The house itself is a bit of a ruin now – there's not even a front door any more, so anyone can just walk in – and there's an old estate agent's board outside. So far there's been no takers but a recent price reduction might change that. From the look on Tony's face he might even be tempted himself. Sell up the café – cut his losses, more like – and move out to the sunshine all the year round, do up your old place.

The inside is still pretty habitable even if the outside needs a fair amount of work. There's some small rooms on the ground floor including an old kitchen and a room at the front that, I guess, would have been saved for special occasions. But first we head upstairs to take a look at the view.

All the best views are from the back of the house, but the best of all is from a small room high on the right at the rear, a room with the remains of what looks like a carved wooden seat set into a curved wall. As we approach the window, the sunlight's sparkling, reflecting off a few whitewashed cottages in the wooded valley below. You can still see the outline of the old strips of land that must have belonged to them at one time and were probably their main means of making a living back then too, running down from almost all those cottages to a road – once a potholed lane, according to Uncle Tony – that feeds down in turn to the main, long, winding street.

Orchards are still dotted across the hillside, as well as vineyards, with mushrooms and chestnuts growing there too.

Uncle Tony looks out on the view beside me.

'Still can't be sure.'

He looks round the room as if searching for clues.

'Everything I've read points to this being the old family house – her house.'

Tony shakes his head.

'Difficult to know for certain though.'

But I shake my head in turn.

'This is it.'

Tony looks at me, puzzled, as if I've just spotted some all-important hidden clue he's missed somehow.

'No question about it.'

Tony keeps looking at me.

'And you know that because?'

I pause. It is, and I know it is. But I could no more explain that than open that small window in front of us and fly. I just know, without a shadow of a doubt, that not only is this your old house but this is your old room and that you used to sit here, at this very window, looking out much as we're looking out now, down onto your home valley and all your friends and neighbours. Maybe you sat here dreaming of a world and a life far away from the one you were living back then, unsure whether you'd ever have that life or see that world, and none too sure what would happen if you did. But I know one thing. This was yours and, in some weird way I was never even going to attempt to explain to Uncle Tony, you're here too.

As in right here.

Right now.

Tony keeps looking at me as I lapse into silence, growing amused now.

'Psychic, are we?'

I don't reply, just keep looking out of the window.

Looking out from your room at your view.

Is that when it started? Or was it back home, with Uncle Tony, standing by that bus, the bus that was about to bring him here and – even though I didn't know it until it was almost too late – about to bring me here too?

I thought at first it was just inside my head. I thought it was just like this diary or whatever you call it that I'm recording, just something I was saying to myself. And even though it didn't sound like my voice that day standing by that bus, that's not all that unusual these days either. Some mornings I'd play back everything I'd recorded the previous night and wouldn't recognise any of it.

It's all true, don't get me wrong. Everything I've said actually happened. But sometimes it's as if someone else is saying it all. So when I first hear a voice that doesn't really sound like my voice at all, I don't think too much about it. Until I'm sitting here, in this small room by this window looking out on that view and then I get that same feeling again. That there's someone else here with me and it's the same someone who's been with me for a long time now too. And it's not Tony and it's not Steve and it's not the kids. It's someone I've never met and never will but who's still as real somehow as they are.

Maybe I'm finally beginning to do it. Maybe I'm finally beginning to work out what this is really all about.

I'm definitely not psychic though. It's not like I can see

into the future. If I was and if I could, I'd never have gone to the festival that night and I'd never have sat in that open air restaurant watching a choir from home serenade the diners. I'd never have watched all the local boys taking part in those competitions, most of which seemed to involve greasy poles (the climbing of), pasta and pizza (the eating of) and local wine (the drinking of – and lots and lots of it too).

And I'd never have gone dancing in the town square under the stars either. And I'd never have ended up in Zeno's bed in the small hours of that same morning, and I'd never have stayed there till noon the next day, and then decided to stay there till noon the day after as well.

Frying pan to fire again. And I leap. Despite all my fine words and despite all my best intentions, I do it, even as I'm telling myself I'm not going to do any such thing.

Maybe you were different. Maybe you were wise beyond your years and never did a single thing wrong. Maybe that's why Uncle Tony couldn't ever really find out anything about you. Maybe you led a totally blameless life and so there's nothing to find out. But somehow – and I can't explain why – I think that somewhere there's a story here, a story about you, even if I still don't know what that is.

Chiara

NOTHING HAS CHANGED; and everything has changed, of course. The town square is still how I remember it. There's even a small crowd of people waiting for the incoming bus, a small band of excited, nervous travellers, each one much like the excited, nervous traveller I was myself at one time, waiting to head away to a new and hopefully better life in France, England, America or even (and whisper it quietly, because no-one really knew where it was and there were rumours that dragons lived there) in Wales.

Dragons don't live there; or at least if they do, I never met them. I encountered kindness for the most part instead, from friends and from strangers. Most were not like the Reverend Keller. Most were like the lovely Sergeant James, and the even lovelier Grace. Every time I think about them, tears prick my eyes.

I don't make any friends on my return journey like the friends I forged before. Seeing my black clothes, most people leave me alone as a mark of respect. News of our family misfortune soon circulates and it's true that my beloved and now absent father is weighing heavily on my mind, but it isn't just the future that's oppressing my thoughts. It's the past as well.

Michele and all that has happened. All that still might happen. All that is still left to resolve.

I get off the bus, tired and hot. From across the square,

I see Mamma and Luigi and Peppo, my two brothers now grown into young men. They are all huddled together, all dressed in black. That's when I see you too, the girl this diary is addressed to: the person I see now.

It's impossible, of course, that I should see with my own eyes the woman I'd conjured into existence from generations to come: a woman not yet born. Nevertheless, I see you. As Mamma runs to me, with Luigi and Peppo following just a short distance behind, I see a young woman cross the square behind them. No-one else seems to see her, perhaps because no-one else can. Perhaps only I have the eyes to do that.

Mamma embraces me. Luigi and Peppo hang around for a moment before they turn away, busying themselves with taking down my trunk from the bus. It's heartbreaking in a sense because they're already doing what Papà would have done. Taking over his role.

Behind my mother, I keep watching you: the girl that no-one else can see, who now seems to be looking back across the square at me, looking out across time. There seems no spark of recognition in your eyes as there is in mine. If there is to be a connection between us, it's not to happen now. Perhaps it never will. Perhaps, as with so much else at the moment, all of this is just stupid imaginings on my part and none of it is real.

Or perhaps I'm looking into some kind of mirror and seeing someone just like myself. Someone searching for something, something she can hold onto, something that will last. You look to me just like I must have looked when I first arrived in Wales. Someone whose life is in turmoil, searching for certainty in a land that's not her own.

Then Mamma folds me tight into her arms and presses her head against mine. We both close our eyes and when I open them again, you're gone.

One day later and everywhere I look, I see Papà's face. His image hangs from the walls of houses, from trees, on restaurant and café walls, on the door outside the Town Hall. It's something I've always found the most difficult about any funeral in my home town. Whenever someone dies, posters are displayed of the deceased to alert friends and neighbours to their passing, as well as telling everyone when the funeral's to take place.

It's as if those you love are there and not there. They're at their most visible in a sense, with their image displayed on every street, adorning almost every building; and yet they're lying somewhere, not smiling or laughing as they often would be on the poster, destined never to smile or laugh again. It was something I simply couldn't reconcile as a child, and I'm having even more difficulty now it's my own Papà who's smiling everywhere I look but who, I know, will not smile again.

We also have to choose Papà's most prized possessions to bury with him. Again, I've never really understood the age-old ritual, though Mamma tries to explain. It's something to do with allowing the deceased to depart the earth in peace, without hankering after some object they wish to take with them on their journey to whatever awaits them on the other side.

Some departed souls we knew had taken their favourite pipe or brand of cigarette, but with Papà there's never any question as to what he will take. It's what Mamma would have taken and what I would have taken too. A simple photograph of the family: of Papà himself, of Mamma and me, of Luigi and Peppo, all together in a way we never will be again.

At least one old ritual never takes place these days. I remember being told of mourners (so-called mourners, anyway) being paid to wail at local funerals. No-one will wail at Papà's, even if we might all feel like it. He'll go to his grave as he lived his life, with dignity.

He'll certainly travel to whatever now awaits him with his family well fed. That is one tradition that will never be dispensed with in my country, nor yours either, from the few funerals I've seen over there. From the moment that news of Papà's passing spread around the valley, Mamma has fielded a steady stream of callers all bearing gifts: bowls of fruit, desserts, casseroles, even wine. When I walk into our small kitchen on my first morning back, it's like entering one of those new department stores that have recently opened down in Cardiff.

There are so many flowers. Everywhere you look, on every surface, stacked on the floor: flowers, flowers and even more flowers; a riot of bloom and colour.

Papà's casket is open. That's the tradition too, but I've never found that distressing. I think I'd have found a closed casket more disturbing. It's almost as if the Lord is telling us they're still there in some way. Their soul may have departed but not all has been lost. The face we used to gaze on day by day is still the same, and somewhere, in a place the mourners themselves will journey to one day, everyone will be reunited once more.

We walk to the church in silence. What feels like the whole town walks behind us. Everyone's still dressed in black, of course, and the bells of the church toll as we approach and then fall silent. A couple of friends of Papà's from childhood, men who had been boyhood friends but who are now town elders, say a few words about him and recount a few of their past adventures.

There are no tears. Later they'll come, but for now there are none. Then we head into the cemetery where, one by

332

one, the whole town walks up to Papà's casket which has now, finally, been closed and sprinkles a handful of earth down onto it.

We're lucky in Bardi. In other towns, coffins are often stacked in mausoleums due to lack of space, but Papà has his own space, as he and we would wish. Then I look at Mamma, who looks back at me. Luigi and Peppo join us and we turn and walk back down the hillside.

I could tell you about the wake that followed. I could tell you about the dancing that broke out, unbidden and unexpected, in tribute to Papà and his youthful prowess on the dance floor, a talent that had first, literally, swept my mother off her feet.

I could tell you about the dozens, if not hundreds, of well-wishers who came up to me with their own memories of the man I simply knew as my father. I could fill pages and pages more with the sights and the sounds of that never-to-be forgotten day.

I should be telling you instead about a conversation that took place later that same night, a conversation between Mamma and myself which was nothing to do with Papà, for once that day. This was a conversation which had been waiting to happen ever since I got off that bus and saw you passing behind Mamma and Luigi and Peppo across the square. A conversation Mamma could see in my eyes that I had to have with her, but a conversation I didn't even begin to know how to start.

She does it for me, starting it herself. On the night we bury Papà, we finally talk about the life I've been living in Wales.

First, though, we talk about the law.

'What will happen now?'

It's a question I've hardly dared ask. We both know the hated old law that is still in force; the law that has split so many families in the past and, it seems, is about to do so again.

Mamma struggles to put on a brave smile.

'I can go to your aunt's.'

I ask the next question, even though I already know the answer.

'You can't stay in the house?'

Another brave smile is Mamma's only response.

I turn and look at the cottage on the hill, the only home my brothers have ever known. Mamma follows my stare, looks up at that same cottage with the same expression on her face too. She's known other homes in her time, but none happier.

'You know the way it works, Chiara. The estate has to be sold. There will be claims from the rest of the family.'

All of whom will receive a pittance from that eventual sale: money that will mean nothing, that will change nothing, that will be frittered away in weeks, perhaps days; while we lose everything. That's one of the reasons I was sent away, of course; why a new life had been sought for me. It's that life which is on Mamma's mind now.

'Before –'

She hesitates, still having difficulty saying it out loud, still not able to talk about Papà in the past, to accept the fact he really is gone.

'Your papà and I talked about Luigi and Peppo.'

I tense, knowing exactly what's to come. Mamma senses it and it only serves to confirm what she already seems to know.

'You know our hopes. You know what we wished.'

'Yes.'

The silence stretches between us. Clearly she expects me to say more, but I don't. How can I? What can I say?

Mamma struggles for a moment that feels like eternity.

'Has he been everything we said?'

I look at her, misery flooding my eyes.

'Has Enrico been all we promised? Has he been a good man, a kind man?'

I nod.

'Yes.'

Mamma hesitates again, making to speak once more, but I don't let her. I cut across instead.

'Let's walk.'

She looks at me.

'Now?'

I nod again.

'Now.'

Mamma hesitates a moment longer, then she nods back and I take her hand. We walk out of Papà's wake, leaving all the mourners, and walk across the town square and up to the castle, where we look out over the lights flickering in the blackness below.

'You don't need to tell me.'

I look at her. I've been trying for the last half hour to find a way to explain all that has happened, about Michele and Enrico and myself. All I've managed is silence. Finally, she's taking pity on me.

Mamma looks out over the valley, the sound of the wake still floating up from the main square. People will not stop saying goodbye to Papà for a good few hours yet. Of course some, his closest friends and all of his family, won't ever stop.

'I saw it in your eyes the moment you came home. I'm hearing it in every word you've not said since.'

Mamma looks at me, her clear eyes boring into mine.

'You've met someone else?'

I don't reply for a long, long moment. I don't need to. Then, hesitating all the while, I look back at her.

'Enrico is everything you said he was. He's good and he's kind and he's –'

I tail off. What else can I say?

I don't need to, because Mamma says it for me.

'But you've met someone else.'

It wasn't a question this time. It was a statement.

'Yes.'

'And this someone else: you've fallen in love with him?'

Again I don't reply. Not, this time, because I don't need to, but because that's still the question that's tormenting me. Some would say the fact I can't answer straight away is the only answer really needed. If I didn't love Michele, I would simply say so. The fact I can't means I am battling against the inevitable. In love with him, but not wanting to admit it.

Is that what's really happening here? Is it really as simple as that? Even now, after all this time, after that winding and tortuous journey home, after all the thinking I've been doing every step of that way, I still can't decide.

'Can you fall out of love with him?'

Again that same silence settles and again I can almost feel myself wrestling inside.

'I don't know.'

I feel I'm getting closer and closer all the time, though. Closer and closer to that fatal admission, an admission I don't want to make, an admission or maybe a decision I know I have to face, one way or another, to confront this, to

336

move on in one way or another, towards one man and away from the other.

Perhaps Mamma senses that too, because she now asks me a different question instead.

'Can you fall in love with Enrico?'

I just look at her and she looks back at me. Again, I don't answer, but she can see it in my eyes, and I can feel it deep inside now too.

No, I can't. What I didn't want to happen has happened. Somehow, a heart that should be someone else's has been taken. Standing on that hill looking out over my home, my valley, the life I left to find a better one, I really don't think things can get any worse.

In that, as in so much, it seems, I am wrong.

Luigi and Peppo have been told to leave me alone. Papà's death has hit us all, but they'd seen him fall ill, they'd watched the slow wasting away of a man who'd been so vibrant and so alive and so they'd been prepared for it in a way. I'd had no such preparation and so my shock was all the more acute. At least that's the story Mamma told them to explain my long absences from home and our extended walks in the hills in the days that followed.

It also explains a trip myself and Mamma next take to a town some kilometres away, a town where we're less likely to bump into people we know, any neighbours, friends or family, and where the doctor we see won't be likely to share what happens in his consulting room with those same neighbours, friends or family. For this, Mamma wants, in fact demands, the strictest confidence.

All of a sudden I have a new decision to make, and this one is even more complicated than the last, because all of a sudden there aren't just three lives involved here. All of a sudden it isn't just myself, Enrico and Michele.

'It's confirmed.'

I stare at the doctor with an expression on my face he must have seen a thousand times. A young girl looking back at him in disbelief, her eyes pleading with him to have made a mistake, to tell her he's got it wrong.

By my side, Mamma sags; only slightly, but I can feel his words hitting her every bit as hard as they are striking me.

'I can't be.'

The doctor just keeps eyeing me.

'Really. I can't.'

'It's not possible? That's what you're saying?'

I shake my head, slowly.

'It's possible.'

Of course it is. That last time we were together, up on that mountain, before I returned home; that made it all too possible. It's just... and then my thoughts melt into confusion.

'Does he know?'

I look back at the doctor.

'The father?'

By my side, I feel Mamma tense again and I can almost hear what she's thinking. Is this the moment? The moment she finds out who he is, the father of a grandchild her late husband is destined never to see?

'No.'

The silence stretches again.

'Would you like to bring him in?'

The doctor pauses.

'I could talk to him.'

To give Mamma credit, she doesn't ask me anything. At least, not directly. She simply leaves it up to me to decide whether to tell her any more or not. For now I stay silent. As I stay silent on everything.

There was no question as to what I'd do, of course. I don't know what it's like now, in your day, but in those days there was never any issue regarding a child. A child was a gift from God; even if, at that moment, it didn't feel all that much of a blessing.

Mamma leaves me alone, and she makes sure Luigi and Peppo continue to leave me alone as well. Alone to walk around the hills, to climb to the top of the castle, knowing that everything has changed.

I can try and forget Michele, of course I can. I can return to Enrico's café and to Grace and to my work and pretend he doesn't exist. I can walk straight past him in the street, never look at him and try not to think about him ever again. But what can I do about his child?

Frankie

I'M BACK HERE again. In your old home.

Tony's asked me more than once how I can be so certain, but what can I say? That, somehow, in some weird way, I've been talking to you for the last few weeks and months? That you've been talking back to me? That I heard your voice telling me to get on that bus? How crazy is that going to sound? He's very definitely going to start rationing my *vino* intake after that.

I haven't heard you since though. Maybe that's because I'm here, in the place you must have called home. Maybe your mission – whatever it is – is done now. Maybe you just had to get me over here and then the rest of whatever's going to happen is just going to play itself out somehow. Or maybe I really do need to ration that *vino* intake. Maybe I'm just spending too much time in an old ruin of a house talking to a ghost I can't see.

The last bus of the summer leaves tomorrow. I've been here almost three weeks. I've talked to the kids almost every day. Poor old Uncle Tony's mobile phone bill is going to be through the roof. The way they're going on, it's as if I'm on some kind of extended holiday, keeping Tony company while he meets old friends and family. Maybe they know it's more than that, but they don't ask and I don't say. They don't ask because they don't want to hear the answer, and I'm not saying because I don't know what that answer is.

Tony asked me just now what I'm going to be doing tomorrow. Am I going home? I don't answer and he doesn't press it. But he's going back, he has to. He can't leave his café in the hands of the small amount of help he's just about managed to drum up from God knows where for too much longer. And much as he'd love to – because he loves this place, he really does – he can't stay here forever either. In the end, he belongs somewhere else and so do I. The only problem is, I'm not sure exactly where that is right now.

I haven't talked to Steve. I've talked to the kids about him – asked them vague-sounding questions about the house, his search for work, all that. They gave vague-sounding reassurances back that everything's fine, that they're all eating OK, that they're keeping the house reasonably clean and tidy and looking after Vicky's now-not-so-little pup – but that's about it. For most of the time we could be strangers talking about other strangers.

Are you still the key to all this in some weird way? That's the question I still can't get out of my head. Is that what this is really all about? I don't believe in fate and stuff, but is there something in your story that's going to give me some kind of way out of mine?

The problem being that I still don't know what your story is, of course, or even if there is one. Which is maybe why I keep coming back here. Maybe I'm hoping these white walls and this white room will start talking to me or something. Or maybe I'm hoping that you'll appear, just like those women who pass outside this small cottage on their way to the local market, and we'll sit down and chat.

See what I mean about losing it?

Or maybe I'm doing something else. Maybe that voice I heard was just my voice, telling me what I wanted to do but didn't dare admit, even to myself. Maybe you're the kind of invisible friend kids sometimes make up because they don't have any other kind. But if you are real in some way, now's the time I really need to hear from you because that bus goes tomorrow. What do I do, do I get on it and go back to my old life and my family, or do I stay here? That really would be making a statement and a half, wouldn't it?

I'm sure Tony would have gone back sooner if it hadn't been for me. At least I think he would – he's been in a strange mood lately, too. He's been going off for long walks as well, hunting out some of the old places he used to visit when he came here as a kid, looking up some old acquaintances he made way back then too. Maybe it's happening to him too. Maybe he's hearing voices from the other side as well.

But finally I turn and leave. And there's no last-minute sighting of any apparition. Just the stars shining in a clear sky through what may have been a door in your day, but is now just an opening in a ruined wall.

But I've made my decision. And if you really are out there somewhere, if you really are keeping me company in some spooky-but-not-spooky kind of way, then I'm guessing you know what that is.

So now the only thing to do is go and see Uncle Tony and tell him too.

I knock on his bedroom door an hour or so later. He's rented this old cottage up in the hills. Two bedrooms, even though he only needs the one. Typical Tony. One for him, one for his free-loading, flat broke niece who isn't even a proper niece.

I knock again when I don't get a reply. Then a third time. He's there – his sandals are by the door, where he always leaves them for some reason. God knows why, because no-one's going to take them away and clean them are they? So unless he's decided to go in for a bit of sleepwalking, he's definitely home.

I push open the bedroom door and call out his name.

Which is when I realise that it doesn't matter what decision I've just made. Because I'm not going anywhere, at least not for a while.

Chiara

MAMMA HAS JUST come to see me. She asks if we can go for a walk. She's obviously been doing a lot of thinking. That much I expect. What she says to me, I don't.

We set off on our usual route, heading up to the castle, where it's always quiet. When we're on the ramparts with the whole of the valley spread out before us, and with what looks like that same ox trying and failing to plough up one of the steep hills opposite, Mamma looks at me and starts talking about Enrico.

'He's a good man.'

I nod, miserable. I know that, only too well.

'There isn't a single ounce of harm in him. That's why we agreed to your going to work for him: we knew he'd care for you, look after you.'

Every word is like a knife twisting in an open wound, every word a reproach.

'He will understand.'

I stop at that, and look at her again.

For a moment she doesn't speak. For that moment I can see the struggle that's going on inside, a struggle etched in eyes that have been troubled for so many days now, but which today, strangely, seem saddened still but troubled no longer.

'There is heart, Chiara, and there is head.'

She nods back at me.

'And you know the most important of all?'

Mamma nods at me again.

'Heart.'

I don't know what to say for a moment. If I was floundering before, I'm well and truly lost now.

'Enrico is everything your father and I promised you. A good man.'

'But Luigi, Peppo... everything we talked about –'

Mamma cuts across, firm.

'They must make their own lives as you've made yours. They can't expect you to make it for them.'

'But –'

Mamma cuts across again.

'Your father would have said the same. Between heart and head, choose heart, Chiara.'

She nods at me, the subject settled.

'Every time.'

Frankie

I THINK HE knew all along. I think it's what this last trip was all about. The letters I found in Tony's bedroom after he died – all those letters from the hospital – they all told the same story. Given the state of his heart, he really didn't have that long. And if his end was near, if his time really was nearly up, then he would have wanted to spend what little he had left in the country he'd come to love every bit as much as if he'd been born here.

He'd left specific instructions for his funeral too, a funeral that's also to take place here. And it's to be a traditional funeral too, harking back to the sort of funerals you must have seen in your day.

So now Tony's picture is everywhere, his image pasted on the walls of houses and trees, on restaurant and café walls, on the door outside the Town Hall. And there's flowers everywhere too, a kaleidoscope of bloom and colour. I have to choose a prized possession to bury with him, which is going to be – what else? – a photo of the café and as many of its customers as I can find.

On the day itself, I walk to the church in silence. What feels like the whole town walks behind us. Everyone's dressed in black and the bells of the church toll as we approach and then fall silent. A couple of friends of Tony's from his childhood visits say a few words about him, but it's all a blur. There's no tears though. From them or from me. Later they'll come, but for now there's none.

Then we head into the cemetery where, one by one, the whole town, or what seems like it, walks up to Tony's casket, which has now been closed, and sprinkles a handful of earth down onto it.

I could tell you about the wake that followed: the food, the music, the dancing, the special tribute to and celebration of my dear old Uncle Tony's life which was everything he – and I – could ever have wanted it to be.

I could tell you about the song I insisted was played – '*Senti L'Eco*', what else, again? The song I heard playing almost every day in his old café. The song I never really listened to then, but now can't get out of my head. Especially that first verse. It just seems to sum everything up, somehow.

But what I should really be telling you about is a conversation that took place later that same night when I turned round and saw Steve standing behind me.

I'd actually seen him just before the service started, shuffling along at the rear of a small group of mourners. I couldn't believe it at first. What was he doing here? He'd never exactly been close to Tony. Steve always saw him as something of a dinosaur. And were the kids with him? If they had been, I'd have gone straight over, of course, but it was pretty obvious straight away that he was alone.

And as he didn't approach me, I didn't go to him either. I just let him shuffle along behind while I got on with more immediately pressing matters like saying goodbye to the nearest thing I'd ever had in my life to a proper father. Definitely more of a dad to me than the bastard who'd walked out on us all just a couple of years after I was born.

A man who'd stepped into the breach as naturally as if

he'd been born to what was at times, I knew, not the easiest of tasks – particularly when I was an arsy teenager and called him far worse than a dinosaur. The sweetest, most good-natured, kindest man in the world.

But now the goodbyes are over. And now I've said mine too. And now it's time to deal with the here and the now in the shape of a husband mysteriously materialised from far away, standing before me for reasons that are about to become only too clear.

'Nice service.'

I don't reply, just stare at him for a long moment. He shuffles his feet.

'What are you doing here, Steve?'

'I liked him.'

Steve struggles.

'I thought one of us should make the effort at least – come over, to pay our respects.'

'So where are the kids?'

'Mum's looking after them.'

Steve's mum. Better known as the Wicked Witch of the West. But it isn't where they are that's really on my mind right now.

'How are they?'

Now it's Steve's turn to pause for a moment, and I can feel panic starting to rise in my stomach. Is there something more to this visit than a simple farewell to an old man he's never really had all that much to do with anyway?

'Steve?'

'Missing you.'

He looks back at me, holding my stare.

'We all are.'

And he keeps looking at me, as I relax.

'I still want you back, Frankie.'

'Take my advice, Steve: buy a punch bag, much more durable.'

He looks at my cheek – can't help himself – the mark where he hit me still just visible.

'I'm sorry.'

'You said.'

'I want a second chance.'

I stare at him.

'Did you say second?'

Steve takes a deep breath. To his credit, he is taking all this. Then again, he hasn't much choice.

'All right, seventy-second, ninety-second, I don't know – all I do know is I really, really want to try again.'

I shake my head.

'Too late, Steve. Way too little and way, way too late.'

Steve pauses.

'I'm getting off the drugs.'

I pause now too. It's the first time he's done it, ever even acknowledged he had any sort of problem, actually acknowledged those drugs I'd found in that shed of ours were actually his.

'Detox programme. I went to this clinic – the doctor put me onto it. They've done this schedule for me. They reckon in another month, if I stick to it, I'll be clean.'

I eye him, picking out what I was suppose you'd call the salient word in all that.

'If.'

'I will, Frankie. If you come back.'

I turn away.

'I can't go on without you, none of us can.'

'Piss off, Steve.'

But he just follows me.

'And I know what's happened to Tony's terrible, but I've been thinking, maybe this could be our chance.'

I stop at that, look back at him, that one coming from way out of left-field.

'What are you talking about?'

Steve hesitates.

'The café.'

'Oh, I see. That's what this is all about. All of a sudden Steve's sniffed some dosh.'

Steve just cuts across, impatient.

'What dosh? There's no money in that place, hasn't been for years – you know that.'

Then he pauses.

'But there could be.'

'You hate that café, you always have. You're always telling me how it should be knocked down.'

'I hate it as it is, yeah, how your Uncle Tony always ran it. But if someone else was in there, someone not so locked in the past, someone who'd change it round a bit, put some fruit machines in there maybe, change the menu a bit, put on a few party nights now and again, it could be a little goldmine.'

'So this is about money?'

'You'd run it. I could help. The kids could come in at weekends, maybe the odd evening, pick up some pocket money.'

Steve nods at me.

'It'd be what it should be, Frankie. Something for all of us. The whole family – our family.'

I look at him, not saying anything – I don't really know what to say, in truth. Maybe I'm already suspecting that, despite getting absolutely zero marks for timing – Tony hardly being cold in his coffin and all that – some bit of this is actually making some sort of sense.

And maybe Steve senses the mood change too because he just keeps looking at me.

'Please, Frankie.'

Later that night I'm walking high up in the hills again. Steve has left me to think things over and I'm thinking about lots of things now. And not just about Tony and his old café.

In a sense, Steve's right, of course. And if we do what he suggests, it would have been Tony's dream. Everyone connected to that café was family so far as Tony was concerned. He'd have been over the moon about us carrying it on.

And maybe, with a bit of updating – which Tony was always reluctant to do – the old place could begin to pay its way. And maybe it could be a family business again, a proper business – something Steve and myself could work at together, something the kids could get involved in, like he said. And maybe not just during high days and holidays either, maybe in other ways too. Maybe Tyler or Vicky could do catering courses or something.

And if all that did come to pass, Tony really would see it as a present from the dead to the living.

A gift from the gods, if you like.

And if he was here now, at my shoulder, I know exactly what he'd say. I'd stuck with Steve this long and maybe it was our situation – him being out of work, not having anything to do, the constant scraping for pennies here and there – that was causing all the problems. Maybe if we resolved that we could resolve our relationship too. No-one could know for sure, of course they couldn't, but with two kids in the frame it had to be worth at least considering, surely?

Only there aren't, are there?

Two kids involved.

Or, at least, not just two.

And that's what I'm really thinking about as I walk around that hillside town that night. Call me a stupid cow, blame it on the sun, the *vino* – none of that really matters now does it? The fact remains I've been careless and I've got caught.

So how does that fit into Steve's brave new vision of the newly-restored family all working together in some brand new family business?

What's going to happen to that cosy little dream when he finds out he and our kids are going to have to share it with an unexpected and – to him anyway – very much unwanted addition?

It's so weird. As in really weird. Because that night, half-drifting between sleeping and being awake and dreaming – that state you get in sometimes when you really don't know where you are or what you're doing – it's like I'm actually having a conversation with you. As in an actual, proper, exchange.

Not that I hear a real voice whispering in my ear. And I don't see you either. But I still feel like we're having this conversation and that you're there somehow. In a way I really can't explain – and I'm not going to try either – I feel you. I feel your presence beside me, hovering around me, listening.

Letting me work it all out.

What I should do.

Chiara

A WEEK OR so later, I'm travelling again. Once again, I take the bus from the main square down to the station. From there it's that same interminable train ride before the short ferry crossing and then another train ride, which seems even longer than the one before. Certainly longer than the one I remember taking when I first travelled from the city I thought would be my home to a town I never believed could be, at least when I first set eyes on it.

Perhaps that's because I was travelling in a state of high excitement before. I was nervous, yes, and I was afraid. I was already getting the first awful blast of homesickness, but I was still so excited as to what lay ahead.

Now I'm travelling in something like dread, because now I know what lies ahead. If I could have done anything to avoid what's going to happen, I would; but I can't. It's decision time and all those chickens (another of those phrases Enrico loves and which I've now learnt too) are well and truly about to come home to roost.

I walk up the steep hill from the station to Carini's. I haven't told anyone I'm coming back so there's no-one to meet me from the train, which is how I want it.

I walk past the chapel where we'd faced the challenge of Reverend Keller and defeated it.

I pass the police station, where I just catch a glimpse of a perspiring Sergeant James, who seems to be caught up in some dispute involving two old ladies and a small dog.

Then I turn the corner and catch my first glimpse of the café. It looks exactly the same. The same lettering on the front, the same handwritten notices on the window urging passers-by to come and sample the delights within. It looks the same, but it's totally different; like everything else.

What would you have done? It's strange, but on the way over, in quiet moments alone in train carriages, it's almost as if I'm talking to you. Rehearsing with you what I might do, or not do.

On the one hand there's Enrico. On the other, there's Michele.

Enrico is a home, a job, a life for myself and perhaps a life for Luigi and Peppo as well. Something that has been planned. Something that in some strange way, and perhaps even more so since Papà's death, almost seems ordained.

Michele is disgrace: a marriage that will please neither his family nor mine, despite all Mamma's brave words.

So? Which one?

It's Grace I see first. She's about to lock up for the evening. It doesn't strike me as strange at first, but it's always been Enrico who's done that in all the time I've been here. But Grace, as I am about to discover, has taken over quite a few of his duties in these last few weeks. Partly that's down to her employer's ongoing recovery from his experiences as an internee, and partly it's something else.

Something to do with his brother, even though perhaps Michele hasn't behaved in all that fraternal a way to him lately, and something to do to with the girl he'd always thought of as his future bride, although maybe that fond hope has dimmed more than a little in the last few weeks as well.

Grace doesn't know any of this. I can tell by the way she throws her excited arms around me as I approach, and hugs me so hard I feel as if my ribs might break. Then she tells me to stay just where I am while she goes and tells Enrico that I'm back.

And now I'm thinking my heart will break again, as well as my ribcage. She's so excited for him, so keen to be the one who delivers what she clearly believes will be some much-needed good news.

I move close to the door of the rear whitewashed room. Dimly I can hear their voices from inside.

'Enrico –'

First, Grace's voice, high on excitement.

'Not now, Grace.'

Then Enrico's, and he sounds different already: quieter, almost defeated.

'You've a visitor.'

'I told you.'

I can't stand it any longer as I listen to a man that imprisonment could not break, who did not break even when he was plunged into an icy sea by an enemy attack, but who sounds broken now.

'Hello, Enrico.'

Enrico's head whips round and he stares at me for a long, long moment as I stand in the doorway, perhaps searching for some sign in my eyes. Then he speaks; softly, as ever.

'Hello, Chiara.'

It's pitch black and raining outside, but we go out anyway. Enrico can't settle in the café and despite (or perhaps because of) all those days of travelling, I can't sleep either.

Michele doesn't know I'm back yet. His room's at the back and he's taken to spending most of his evenings in there, alone. The two brothers rarely mix at the moment, it seems. Grace doesn't know why, but I do.

'I didn't know whether you'd be coming back.'

I look at him as he looks, hesitantly, back at me.

'I didn't know whether –'

Enrico hesitates, still not wanting to put it into words.

I look out over the pinpricks of light that stud the valley below. Now it's time to put it all into words; to say what has been, up to this moment, the unsayable.

'I've been thinking, Enrico, while I've been away. About the business, about you.'

He just nods.

'Yes.'

And now I hesitate again.

'I tried talking to you about this before I went home.'

And now it's my turn to falter.

'I'd never thought about it before. It was just something that was there, that was part of my life, like getting up in the morning and looking after the customers, it was just something I knew that one day I had to do.'

'Getting married, you mean?'

'Yes.'

'To me?'

I nod and Enrico pauses.

'You're not bound to anything. Yes, I talked to your father and your mother before you came over here, and yes, we reached an understanding, but even then I knew –'

Enrico pauses, then smiles at me with eyes that look as if they've lived a thousand lifetimes.

'I know you understand the situation. I know your father spoke to you about the arrangement, but none of that matters – not now.'

Enrico nods at me.

356

'It's all right if you've changed your mind.'

I keep looking back at him.

He made it so, so easy for me, didn't he?

The next morning I walk out once more, but this time with Michele.

During the night it had happened. Halfway between sleeping and waking, this time there was a voice to go with the vision I first saw in the town square on the day I returned home for Papà's funeral. A voice I christened with your name, a voice I know can only exist inside my head, but it's still like some spirit has arrived somehow, summoned from the ether.

Once again we're high up on the hill, overlooking the town. This time we're looking down on the smoke as it belches from the factories and collieries. Not that either Michele or myself are taking much notice of the view. Michele is staring at me, the disbelief clear in his eyes.

'I'm not hearing this.'

'I'm sorry.'

'This isn't true.'

'It's true.'

I force myself to meet his stare, knowing I have to; that I have to keep strong or this moment will be lost, that I will be lost.

'You're going to marry Enrico?'

There's just a moment's hesitation, but only a moment. Perhaps he notices, perhaps he doesn't. Perhaps in that moment he grasps at some sort of hope; but if he does, it's a hope that's extinguished a moment later because I keep my gaze steady, my eyes fixed on his, my voice as calm and controlled as I can.

'Yes.'

'But you don't love him.'

I keep silent. I've said what I had to say. Nothing can be gained now by saying any more.

'You can't.'

Again, I remain silent.

Michele pauses and his tone becomes softer now, cajoling, more persuasive, more dangerous.

'Come on, Chiara.'

Still I don't reply.

'Plenty of girls come to this country believing they'll marry one person only to find themselves falling in love with another.'

I just look beyond him, down at the town.

'It causes trouble – of course it does. Trouble here, trouble back home too.'

Michele hunches closer.

'But everyone comes round in the end.'

Then he all but explodes, ever more unnerved by my silence.

'Chiara?'

I turn away, speaking just one last time as I do so.

'I'm marrying Enrico.'

Frankie

I'M BACK IN your old house again. Well, in the half-ruin that used to be your house. It's strange, but for some reason this tumble-down old place is where I can actually sit and think. Not that I'm doing too much thinking at the moment. Or sitting. At the moment I'm sorting through all Uncle Tony's stuff – things he'd brought out with him, family mementoes and the like.

I hadn't really thought too much about it before. But it's the same story all over again isn't it? For whatever reason – foreboding? – because he had a mini-Tardis tucked away in his suitcase too and could see into the future? – he just seemed to know he wouldn't be going back to Wales again. So he brought out all his most treasured possessions with him, maybe so when the end came they'd all be within reach.

Some of this stuff beggars belief. There's actually a medal I won for an egg and spoon race when I was six. And stuff from when Tyler and Vicky were little kids too. I've had to stop sorting it at least six times to try and stop sniffling.

But all the time I'm sorting through it I'm thinking, even if I'm not conscious of thinking at all. All the time, some sort of dialogue's going on in my head. And because – again – I really don't want to come across as some sort of saddo talking to herself, I seem to be conjuring up my invisible friend again.

Hello.

So what shall we talk about today?

As if I don't know, eh?

And then it happens again.

It's as if I actually hear your voice once more.

It could be simple.

I'm not showing, won't be for months.

And it's really early days, no-one need ever know.

I hurry on.

And I don't mean get rid of it, course I don't.

I hesitate.

What I mean is, Steve needn't know it's not his.

I look out of the window.

One little white lie, that's what it'd be. And what's that against the whole family being back together, the kids with a new little brother and sister, Steve with a new little son or daughter?

Then I pause as I come across something else in Uncle Tony's stash of forgotten goodies. Or at least I think it's from his old stash. I've just not seen it before and I don't recognise it either. It's some old book, but not the kind of book you find on shelves in a bookshop. This is like a kid's exercise book, only not from any school I've ever seen. This one is old and I mean really old, the pages yellowed with age, the paper curling at the corners. The covers are faced in what looks like old wrapping paper to try and preserve them, but that battle's fast being lost. Another few years and the spidery writing inside will be gone for good too.

And looking at it I get the strangest feeling again. As if I've seen it before, which I haven't. But I still feel as if I know exactly what I'm going to read even before I look at the first page.

I keep looking at the exercise book, which I can now see

is some sort of diary, but I'm holding it as if it's some sort of bomb – which, as I'm about to discover, isn't actually that far short of the mark.

Thirty minutes later, I suddenly stop reading. There's more, a lot more, but it's not the dim and very distant past that's in that diary/journal – call it what you will – that's before my eyes now.

It's something much more immediate. Much more recent.

And much more raw.

So is this the point?

Is this really what it's all about?

I look back at those suddenly incendiary few pages I'm holding. You're telling me everything that happened in your life but it's more than that, isn't it – a lot more?

You're trying to tell me about mine too.

Chiara

ENRICO HAD AS good as told me I was free, and as far as Mamma was concerned, she'd told me the same. I was not to sacrifice myself for Luigi and Peppo.

I had a mind of my own, though. I didn't need to listen to anyone. I could make decisions and all this has helped, it really has, writing everything down like this. It certainly gave me the strength to face Michele down every time I saw him in those weeks before the wedding.

Suddenly, there was just one week to go. Michele had kept his distance for the last few days and I was starting to think he'd accepted it. I thought it was all over, that he'd work out his time with his brother and then go home. Or maybe he'd travel to some other town somewhere and start his own business. I didn't know; but I thought he'd just forget about me, begin all over again.

Perhaps he would have done. If he'd come to see me just moments later. If I'd been there when he arrived. If he hadn't found what I'd been writing to you just a short time before.

I walk back into that white room at the rear of the café less than a minute after he arrived. There is some more trouble outside and I've been to see what's happening. It looks like another of those mini-riots has started up and I've come back to look for Enrico and get him to secure the doors and check the windows, just in case.

Then I walk in to see Michele reading what I've just

written, as well as all I wrote a few days ago, and a few days before that too.

He turns to look at me as I stand rooted in the doorway, staring back at him. Then his eyes flicker down, towards my stomach.

I don't have time to say a word. I can't speak anyway; my eyes just stare back at him. From outside, in the near distance, I can now hear the sound of smashing glass.

Then, suddenly, Michele strides towards me. For a moment I don't know what he's going to do. Then I realise he has my journal in his hand. I move to stop him, to snatch it back, but by now he's marched past me on his way into the café, shouting for his brother.

By the time I've caught up with him he's by the front door with a bewildered Enrico. Enrico had heard the sound of the approaching rioters himself and was in the process of lowering the blinds on the windows. But, like myself, he isn't even hearing the sounds outside right now. Now he's just staring at Michele, with my journal, my words, in his hand.

For a few moments it's obvious that Enrico can't understand a single word his brother is saying. For those same few moments, perhaps Michele doesn't know what he's saying either.

Even now, all this time later, I can't imagine how Michele must have felt, reading about himself in words written by the woman he loved, the woman he now discovered was carrying his child. The woman who was about to marry his brother.

I try to step in, try to stop Michele, to stop them both, but I don't think they even realise I'm there. Within moments, Enrico understands exactly what Michele is saying to him, understands the truth behind everything that's happening now, realises the lie our marriage will be based on.

I try to intervene again, but Michele is shouting louder

all the time, his yells and curses almost drowning out the sounds outside as the latest wave of rioters approach. By now Enrico is yelling back at him too, everything just spiralling more and more out of control all the time.

Looking back, I've still no idea who landed the first blow. I still can't even begin to recall the exact sequence of events. All I know is that within seconds they are on the floor, brother fighting brother, two grown men men rolling over and over, smashing into chairs, upending tables as all the time I stand by the entrance to that whitewashed room, yelling at them to stop until, suddenly, there is silence.

I look across at Michele, who's now slumped in a corner, bleeding from a huge wound to his head. I dash across to him and frantically begin trying to stop the blood with one of our napkins.

Then I see Enrico.

Enrico's just lying by the counter. There isn't a mark on him: no blood, nothing. He looks like he's asleep, but I know he isn't. I go to him, standing over him for a moment. Behind me, I can almost hear Michele holding his breath. Then I turn Enrico over, which is when I see the side of his head, which is now just skin and jagged bone.

Across the room, Michele begins to moan as he too now sees what he's done to his brother; but all I can do, all I can think is: he hasn't. I have. I've done this.

Outside, the sound of the rioters is getting louder. They are drawing closer all the time and I can hear screams now, too, from some other shopkeepers caught up in it all, traders desperately trying to save their stock as Enrico would have been trying to save his.

They made the arrests a few days later.

Some of the rioters admitted to being on the street that

364

night; some even owned up to being outside Enrico's café. A few also admitted they'd thrown missiles, bottles and sticks, and that one of them could have smashed through the café window and could have felled Enrico as he tried to move his stock into the storeroom at the back.

On one point all the suspects were adamant. Whatever happened to Enrico, if it had happened at their hands, was an accident. No-one would have wished him harm.

There had been just one person who did wish him harm. I knew that.

Two days later a different Michele returns to my room, no less anguished but different somehow: calmer, more controlled. Michele tells me that he wishes, more than anything else ever in his life, that he could turn back the clock, that what happened had not happened. Tragically, it has. We can't turn back the clock, can't undo all that has been done; but now, surely, we should try to make some good come out of it, at least?

I know what he's saying to me even as my ears try to block it out. He's telling me, much as he told me on that train ride home once before, that this is our chance; there's nothing standing in our way now and this could be it: the beginning of our future together.

He's still talking as I close the door on him. It seems like the next time I open it again, I'm back home in Bardi, which is where I remain.

So, now you know. I started all this with just one secret. One secret I'd vowed no living soul could ever know about; only you: a girl I'd never know, a girl I couldn't be sure would ever even be born.

Just the one secret, or so I thought. How could I have known there'd be a bigger one to come?

Frankie

ONE HOUR LATER and I'm down in the main square with Steve. He's taken to helping out at one of the bars. Hanging out, more like. But the sun's warm and the wine's cheap and the customers – the ones who speak English, anyway – are good company. It's almost as if he's been here forever.

So how long, exactly, has he been here?

That's the question on my mind, and it's a question he doesn't seem too keen to answer.

'I don't understand.'

'Seems simple enough to me.'

'You know when I got here.'

'I know when I first saw you. Skulking around at the back of Tony's funeral.'

Steve hesitates, growing nervous now.

'I wasn't skulking.'

But he was. I couldn't pin it down before. When I first caught sight of him he looked strange, hunted almost. As if he really shouldn't be there. At the time I put it down to the fact he was very much an unexpected visitor. Now? I don't know. Was it something else?

'So you hopped on a plane, got a taxi from the airport and arrived here just in time for the service?'

'Pretty well.'

'So that's a yes?'

Steve shifts on the balls of his feet, looking and sounding ever more uncomfortable.

'I might have got here a bit before, I can't really remember. Anyway what does it matter?'

Like a dog with a bone on this one, I repeat his own words back to him.

'A bit? As in – what? – an hour? – two hours? – a day?'

'Frankie, what is this?'

'OK, maybe you're not quite going to remember if it was an hour or so, but you'd remember a whole day, wouldn't you? You'd remember having to find somewhere to sleep the night before, for example – a little detail like that isn't exactly going to slip your mind?'

That tell-tale red flush is starting again at the base of his neck. The same tell-tale red flush I saw when I came back from our garden shed that day with what turned out to his secret stash in my hand. A tell-tale red flush that's already telling me Steve's been found out and he knows it.

'I got a late flight, I might have kipped at the airport for a couple of hours before coming over here, I really can't remember.'

'I called Psaila.'

And now that tell-tale flush is mottling, a dark stain seeming to spread across the whole of his face. We're sitting out at a table in the main Square and around us men are moving away. Even if they can't really understand what we're saying to each other, some age-old, battle-hardened instinct seems to be at work, telling them this really is no place for eavesdroppers right now.

'She couldn't work it out. According to her, you left two days before – she saw you getting on the bus down to the airport herself. But I only saw you outside the church just before the service, so what the hell were you doing for two whole days? A bit of sightseeing?'

Steve struggled a moment longer, then took a deep breath.

'I needed time, OK? To think. Work out what to say, how to approach you. For Christ's sake, we hadn't exactly parted on the best of terms, had we? How would you have felt if it had been you coming all this way, knowing all them bridges you'd burnt?'

And it all sounds plausible.

All too plausible in fact.

Apart from one tiny detail. That tell-tale blood-red stain that's now almost completely covering his face.

'You went to see him, didn't you?'

Steve just stares at me.

'You went to see Tony. Why, Steve? What for?'

And I can see it in his eyes.

How much should I tell her?

What can I get away with?

Steve takes another deep breath.

'OK, I got here a couple of days before. Like I said, I didn't want to come and see you straight away. You'd been gone weeks, and I didn't know what was happening with you – even if you were still here, not for sure. But I knew Tony was – he'd been in touch with the people looking after the café, making sure everything was OK.'

Steve hesitates and I nod at him again.

'Go on.'

Steve hesitates a moment longer, then takes another deep breath.

'So yeah, I called in on him. I found out where he was staying from the people back in the café – they had a number and an address for him in case of any emergencies. I went to the place where he was staying, that pretty little cottage up on the hill –'

'I don't care where he was staying. I don't care if you met him in the cottage or the castle or up on the moon. What happened?'

Steve hesitates again.

'He didn't seem that surprised to see me. It was almost as if he was expecting it, to tell you the truth. He asked about the kids, then wanted to know what I was doing there.'

Steve nods at me and now the blood-red stain has receded a little. Whatever other tale he's been spinning me here, this bit at least seems true.

'I asked him to have a word with you, to tell you how much we were missing you. All of us – me, Tyler, Vicky. Even that daft pup of hers hasn't been eating properly, as if it knows something's not right too.'

'What did you want him to say?'

'I wanted him to tell you to come home. Come back where you belong, with us – with your family.'

'And he said?'

And now it starts again. Now that stain begins to spread across his face once more, up from his neck, and he knows it. He's starting to perspire and that isn't because of the sun that's beating down on us both – Steve is burning up from the inside now, and all he's concentrating on, with all the resources he can muster, is making sure I don't find out why.

Steve pauses a moment longer, then – reluctant – he grimaces.

'He didn't think it was any of his business.'

I stare at him.

'And that was it? You asked for help, he said no and you said fair enough and walked away?'

'Yeah.'

I just keep staring at him, keeping silent. And now Steve starts to unravel.

'Look – it wasn't my fault, Frankie.'

I keep staring.

'Believe anything you want, but believe that, please. None of it was supposed to happen – I didn't even realise it was happening, for Christ's sake, not till it was too late.'

'You never realised what, exactly?'

'I was just so caught up in everything – trying to make him understand how much it meant, not just to me, but to the kids, to all of us. And all he kept saying was it was down to you, that he couldn't interfere – he wouldn't interfere. That that's what this trip was all about, so you could make your own mind up, work out what you wanted to do for yourself – but I could see it in his eyes, I could see what he was thinking, what he's always thought about me. He's never thought I was good enough for you – it was obvious, always has been.'

Sweat's pouring down Steve's face now.

'And who was he to look down on me, some bloke who runs a shitty little café, who was he to tell me I'm not good enough for my wife, that I'm not a decent dad to my kids?'

'Tony would never have said that.'

'He didn't need to. He didn't need to say a fucking word. I said it for him.'

Now Steve's anger stoking all the while, much as it would have been when he was shouting at Tony too.

'He told me to get out, get a grip – but he wasn't saying that, not really. He was telling me to get out of your life, to leave you alone. He was telling me it was over and I couldn't handle it, Frankie – just think of it, think of everything we've got. The kids are already telling everyone how much they miss you. I knew what'd happen – you'd call or visit and that'd be that, they'd go off with you or you'd stay and I'd be kicked out. And what would I do then? You're all I've got, you and them, and he was the only one you'd listen to, the only one who might actually make some sort of difference.'

I cut across.

'So what happened?'

Steve looks at me, his eyes pleading with me now.

'I never laid a finger on him. You've got to believe that. Yeah, there was a bit of shouting and that and I might have pushed him, I can't remember. He was trying to get me out, push me towards the door – I might have pushed him back, I can't remember.'

Steve pauses. But he remembers. He remembers everything. I can see it along with everything else now in his lying eyes.

'He fell. I thought for a minute he'd just slipped, but then he just lay there. And he started making these panting noises and when I leant down his eyes were closed and his face was covered in sweat. There was nothing I could do, Frankie – nothing anyone could do, I swear. I knew what everyone'd think if I called a doctor: that it was all down to me, that I'd done something to him. But it wasn't – I didn't. It was just a heart attack, pure and simple – it could have happened to him anytime.'

Steve looks at me again.

'There was no point me even trying to get help, anyway – he was already gone. Seconds, that's all it took. One minute he was just lying there, staring at me, sweat pouring off him, the next minute his eyes closed and that was it, it was all over.'

I cut across again, a dog with a bone once more.

'Next minute.'

'What?'

'That's what you just said: one minute he was lying there, staring at you, next minute he was gone.'

Steve nods, vigorous.

'That's right.'

'So it was more than seconds then?'

'What?'

'Because that's what you just said as well, that it was all over in seconds, that's all it took.'

Steve just stares at me, twisting himself ever tighter now into ever more tortured knots.

'I don't know exactly, how could I? It all happened so quick, I don't really know.'

I just nod at him.

'I do.'

Then I turn and walk away across the square, past the open-air bar and the men and women who are still drinking and will be drinking till the early hours, and head for the mountain and your old home.

Chiara

THE BABY WAS born a few months later. A boy. But before that, things had been sorted out for two other boys.

Luigi and Peppo left home and made the journey I'd made all that time before. They went to work in Carini's. Michele had taken it over after his brother's death.

I'd talked to him just once after that night. A subdued conversation on a railway platform as I waited for a train to begin another journey home. He agreed to take my brothers in return for my keeping quiet about what had happened on the night of the riot. I still don't know whether that was cowardice or plain common sense. We couldn't change what had happened, as Michele himself had pointed out, but at least this way some good might come out of it. At least this way, Luigi and Peppo would get the fresh starts they'd hoped for when they watched me leave that first time for a new life in a distant country.

I've come home and I've taken their place. Mamma's been allowed to keep our old home by the rest of the family. Common sense has prevailed there too, it seems.

We haven't attempted to hide my pregnancy. We couldn't, of course, and anyway it's not exactly an unknown story. A young girl goes away to foreign shores and falls in with the wrong sort of company. It happens to quite a few girls who stay at home too.

The baby, my baby, my boy, doesn't survive beyond the first

couple of days. He's born sickly and that's how he remains, despite all our attempts to save him and despite the blessing and prayers of our local priest. Which seems quite ironic really. All that trouble, all that upheaval, and just a short time later: nothing.

We bury him next to Papà. A tiny casket next to Papà's full-size coffin. I stand there for what seems like hours after the service. All these changes, in just one year. How many lives have altered irrevocably along the way?

There's one more change to come. News of it is brought by Luigi and Peppo when they come home for their first visit just one year later. Michele and Grace have announced their engagement. They're to marry next spring. I'm not surprised.

Frankie

SOMETIMES I REALLY do wonder if you can actually see me. Even though I've never seen you, of course – although I feel like I've heard you from time to time – I still sense you sometimes.

But if you can see me, or even if you can just sense me in the same way that I think I can sense you, then you'll know where I am right now. Even if you may not recognise the old place at first.

Quite a bit has changed in these last few months, and that's not just me growing a bit of a bump out front. Actually, make that one hell of a bump out front. The baby's due any day now and from the size of me I could be carrying twins, if not triplets. But I'm still up here, in your old house in the hills, painting, decorating, sorting out furniture, generally turning a tumble-down old ruin into a family home.

And it's going to be a proper home now too, because I'm not alone. Tyler and Vicky are out here with me, as well as Vicky's pup. I thought it might take a fair bit of persuasion to get them to up sticks and make the move, but if truth be told, it didn't take much at all. They could see the way things were going back home – and not just with Steve, although that was bad enough. He hadn't been that much of a dad to them when they were little, and with me away they were left to their own devices most of the time.

At the start, their time with him was like a holiday. As

time went on they came to hate it. So when I showed up, told them I'd sold Tony's café to the Chinese takeaway across the road, that I was using the money to do up your old house and that's where I was going to live from now on and did they want to join me, they jumped at it.

Tyler – typical boy – didn't ask about the bump. He pretended nothing was unusual about me waddling around like some kind of duck. Vicky was a bit more forthright. I just told her that me and Steve had tried to make a go of it but it hadn't worked out. But that didn't matter now, not really – all that did matter was they were going to have a little brother or sister and that was that. And after a minute or two of thinking about it, she and Tyler both just nodded and said, cool.

Steve has accepted everything too. He's had to. That's my price for keeping quiet about Tony. I don't for a minute think what happened was anything like your story. If I even suspected that what happened to Tony was anything more than a heart attack, that Steve in some way had had a hand in anything more sinister, then I'd have had him tarred, feathered and slung in the Tower or something.

Not that I told him that. I just spelt out the deal and he said yes. He can still see the kids when he wants. But I've got my suspicions that won't be too often, and I've got the same suspicion the feeling's pretty mutual so far as the kids are concerned too. They'll always be his kids and they will want to see him from time to time. Just not too often.

I've already decided what to call the baby – which, by the way, is a boy. The hospital asked if I wanted to know and I said yes. The name's pretty much a no-brainer anyway. His money made this fresh start possible, after all. So Tony it is.

I just had this really weird sensation. Along with the

strongest feeling yet that you're watching me, looking over my shoulder, maybe trying to tell me something again.

As if there's still one last piece of this story to put together – but I've come to the end of your diary now, so maybe I really am starting to hallucinate. Or maybe I've lived so long with a ghost that I don't want to let you go.

Chiara

I THOUGHT LONG and hard about this last entry. Should I write it down and complete the tale? In the end I decided not to, because it's not just my tale I'd be completing. I'd be stepping into someone else's tale too, and perhaps that's not fair.

Besides, I've already seen the cost of the wrong words getting into the wrong hands at the wrong time.

I don't know if you ever suspected the truth. Perhaps you just did what everyone else back home did at the time and accepted it at face value. We had a service, after all, and we buried a casket. Only the casket was empty. My baby didn't die.

Mamma and I talked about it for weeks, before the birth. We knew what life would be like in our home town for him. I'd carry my disgrace to the grave and so would he. He would always be referred to as the bastard offspring of a girl who went away to a land across the sea and returned a fallen woman. Forever tainted by association.

Mamma knew of a family where the wife was desperate for a baby. She knew of several in fact, but we couldn't entrust my precious boy to someone from the same town, or even the same country. That was to protect me as much as my son as he grew to adulthood. How could I bear it if he was in the next town, or even in a town a few miles away? How would I be able to resist travelling to see him, making sure he was being well-treated, continually checking on him? It would be as intolerable for his new parents as it would be for me. It was decided that my new-born baby would be entrusted into the care of a family from Italy who'd moved overseas. When a suitable family presented itself to us and when I learnt that they lived in the next town in Wales to the one in which I'd spent so much time over the last few years, it seemed fitting somehow. Before the awful events that had enmeshed us all, I'd been happy there. It seemed right somehow that my adopted country should now become a home for my child.

There was no possibility of Michele ever finding out about this arrangement, despite his proximity to the new arrival. It would never have crossed his mind, for one thing. Like everyone else, he'd accepted the fact of his son's death. It wasn't unusual in those days and maybe it suited him, anyway, to draw a line under all of that. He had a new wife to concentrate on, after all, and from the reports I received from Luigi and Peppo's letters, he soon had a growing family of his own as well.

Despite my firm intentions, I did keep track of my son from time to time, of course. Maybe it was in the genes, but he ended up going into the same sort of business as his mother. He had a couple of jobs working in some large hotels but he always seemed to be drawn back to his home part of the country in the end.

And then, when an opening came along, a chance to actually buy his own business, he took it with both hands. This was despite the fact that the business in question had very definitely seen better days. It was a business I knew well, very well, in fact, and from much better days, too.

He didn't marry, but he wasn't lonely. He had the good fortune to make many friends and even became part of an extended family of sorts.

Chief among his favourites was a little girl he seemed to have adopted as some kind of surrogate niece.

But I don't need to tell you that.

Do I?

Acknowledgements

I'm very much indebted to Giannina Moruzzi and to Carolyn Hodges for all their help and insightful suggestions. Many grateful thanks to them both.

Rob Gittins
May 2018

Also by the author:

£8.95
£17.95 (hb)

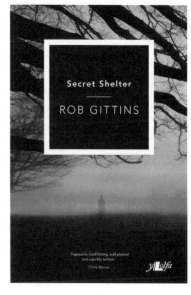

£8.95
£17.95 (hb)

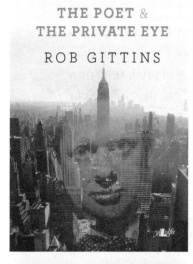

Dylan Thomas's last days – and someone's watching...

THE POET &
THE PRIVATE EYE

ROB GITTINS

£8.95
£14.95 (hb)

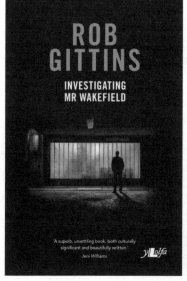

ROB GITTINS

INVESTIGATING
MR WAKEFIELD

'A superb, unsettling book, both culturally
significant and beautifully written.'
Jeni Williams

£8.99
£19.99 (hb)

Hear the Echo is just one of a whole range
of publications from Y Lolfa. For a full
list of books currently in print, send now
for your free copy of our new full-colour
catalogue. Or simply surf into our website

www.ylolfa.com

for secure on-line ordering.

TALYBONT CEREDIGION CYMRU SY24 5HE
e-mail ylolfa@ylolfa.com
website www.ylolfa.com
phone (01970) 832 304
fax 832 782

Printed by Y Lolfa
Ask for a quote